OBSCURA

Anthony Harwood

ISBN: 978-0-9567479-7-6

Obscura

By The Same Author:

Hippy

Cartoon Heroes

Amazing Things

About This Book...

Obscura is the unintentional sequel to
'Hippy'.

UNDERPANTS AND OLD LADIES

The novelty wears thin. Living in London. But every so often you find a day when you're walking past Trafalgar Square and it suddenly hits you - I'm in London! That's awesome.

Today wasn't one of those days.

Sitting in the tube can have that effect. It was hardly crowded, but it was still overly warm for a late October day. Strangely enough, the same could be said for the climate outside. With all the talk of Global Warming, everyone's mind goes off on that tangent and who can really blame them? I suspect it has something to do with it. Or maybe our sun is getting bigger, or the weather patterns are simply changing naturally.

Either way, the heating was too high in the carriage I was sitting in.

I had adopted one of the typical postures of a Tube Traveller. Legs sprawled in front of me as I lean back in the multicoloured, yet not altogether uncomfortable seat. My eyes were staring out at nothing. An awkward attempt to dissuade contact with any other traveller.

The train itself was moving too fast for me to focus on the individual lights let alone the bricks that made up the dark tunnels we were speeding through.

All the same, I was still very aware of the people around me. Okay, I was far from a tourist having moved to London over eighteen months ago, but the idea of a big city still had me wary.

A stick-thin elderly lady sat dressed like she was half her age. Her low-cut beige blouse revealed far more than a man of my age would want to imagine.

In the seat behind her was a young Anglo-African couple chatting loudly about the film they had just seen. Some sort of 'Gorno'. Not one of my favourite genres so I ignored it.

One person, hard to tell beyond the fact it was human behind the wretched, long, bird's nest of hair that had fallen across their face as they slept, was emitting a smell so strong the many other travellers had already swapped out for another carriage.

I looked at my watch. 11:00am. I still had half an hour. Easy.

The train started to slow as it approached the station and I stood up, pre-empting its arrival. I was lucky, having developed a good sense of balance. I was able to stand in the tube without holding a rail for support. Unless, of course, there was a sudden jump on the breaks.

As the doors opened, I jumped out, ignoring the four people on the outside of the train who had hogged the bright red doors in the hopes of grabbing a seat all to themselves. Little did they know of the olfactory assault that would have them wishing they had been less hasty.

I nearly landed on one of them, but kept moving, holding my satchel to my waist as a nervous tourist is want to do.

Due to the smell, the carriage was mostly empty so they had nothing to worry about in terms of finding a seat. It was simply psychological that you had to grab a seat quickly and make sure no one else sat next to you. Or at least hope they didn't. Sometimes it was simply unavoidable. And in the cases when I have had someone sit next to me, I can't say they have all been pleasant. The tube is so anti-social, despite the numerous times you can't help but see or smell the person next to you. You can tell what people have had for lunch but you can't say hello.

I walked down the tiled, white corridor that joined the other platforms together and took my wallet from my pocket. Flashing it over the sensor, my debit card completed its transaction and the display on the gate told me to exit.

Liverpool Street Concourse. A hive of activity. A melting pot of all the different walks of life. People travelling to Stansted Airport to go on holiday. Some to catch a train to some exotic - or not - destination in the United Kingdom. Or just the everyday commuter trying to get in and out of the tube station. I smiled to myself and kept walking. Why did I smile? I don't know. Maybe I thought that I was above all of them, that I was somehow wiser, all-knowing.

Well, it was partly true in some aspects, but by no means was I actually any better. I won't let my ego get that far ahead of me. Still, I smiled. People rarely did anyway. It makes a nice change. Besides, it might put people off and make them steer clear of me.

Before heading out of the station, I hurried into the WHSmith store and picked up a bottle of coke, a double Snickers and a packet of Starburst fruit chews.

Healthy, I know. But it never stops me.

Enjoy the moment, I say.

Picked up, paid for and I was out of there, noting the half-hearted service I got from the woman behind the counter. Nothing unusual from the service I had become accustomed to.

Up the escalators and onto the main road. I have no idea what it is called, but I know it becomes Shoreditch if I turn left and that is exactly where I was heading.

Strangely, this is the tallest part of London I have been to. Nearby is the Gherkin which gets such a mixed response from the locals and visitors alike. By that, I mean the great big glass building that looks like any number of things depending on your state of mind. A gherkin, a cigar or something considerably ruder if that's what you prefer. I'm not a fan. But I can't see it for the buildings around the station.

It isn't as though they are skyscrapers, but they are generally taller and closer together than in Central London.

I keep walking into a fresh gust of wind coming down from the direction I am heading. There's that cold autumn weather in England. I've already experienced one winter. I wasn't exactly sure if I was looking forward to the next one.

Pulling my thick jacket together in front of me, I continued forward.

I was probably overdressed, compared to some natives. However, I still only weighed around fifty-eight kilos and was five foot nine. That made me relatively skinny and lacking natural insulation. So I layered.

At least I wasn't wearing all that black I used to wear. Well, the jacket was black with a couple of Russian patches for decoration. Why Russian? I have no idea. I'd never been there. I'm Australian for goodness' sake, but to make it even more confusing, I bought the thing in France.

It was warm. That was the whole point. What it looked like; I wasn't too worried.

Ok. I reached the first major intersection and pulled out my 'AtoZ' from my satchel and tracked my path to my destination. Turn left, cross this road, then over the first intersection and turn right. Easy. Then hope to god the street number was on display.

That was one thing I noticed about London. Most of the buildings didn't have any numbering, which meant you were stuck with guesswork or tracking from the rare building that told you it had to be at least thirty buildings from your desired number, but in which direction?

In all, it took me less than ten more minutes to find the studio.

Yes, studio. I was heading to an audition, and thankfully the studio had been kind enough to be clearly labelled at knee height, as it was a basement room.

I hurried down the stairs and inside.

It was clean, sparse and white. Nice.

A single room with a row of desks on the right-hand wall, and a bookshelf that didn't quite touch the ceiling was being used to create a false wall about seven metres in. Before that was another desk with a large Apple screen on it. As in the brand, not the shape.

The tables on the right were largely vacant of people, but near the door was a woman looking slightly nervous talking to a man.

She was blonde, attractive and about thirty. He would be a couple of years younger, about my age, but had a shaved head to hide the fact he was receding in the hairline department.

He looked up and smiled before turning his attention back to the woman.

I was going to eavesdrop when this tall man well into his thirties with a thick black beard and the same hair problem as the younger man, though he had let it grow out, approached me with a large hand outstretched. I smiled and took hold of his offering, shaking it firmly.

"Hi, I guess you're here for the casting?"

I nodded, slightly dumbstruck as I usually am at auditions, "Yes."

We let go of hands, "What's your name?"

"Scott. Scott Crossman."

His smile got even wider before he turned to look at a clipboard on one of the tables to the right; ticked off my name and turned back to me.

"So, are you ready to get naked for us?"

I nearly gawped but my self-control managed to keep my surprise from showing outwardly. Maybe he was joking.

My agent hadn't told me a thing about the casting, just a short message with a time and location. I assumed I just had to turn up, do as I was told – preferably with clothes on – and leave.

Indicating a seat next to the Blonde, "Take a seat and Ryan here will sort you out."

I did so as he turned to the Blonde and invited her to do her casting. Now I had an idea why she might be nervous. The two of them vanished behind the bookcase where two other men were waiting.

I took off my jacket and sat down, placing the jacket over my knee.

Ryan, as the other guy must have been, smiled at me and handed me a clipboard with the usual application form and a pen under the clasp.

"Just fill that out."

I nodded and did what I was told. I could never remember my inner leg measurements nor my chest, but if this guy had been serious about undressing, I wouldn't need them. But the fact they were asking for them implied I should be safe.

And then he appeared again Mr Cheerful Beardy Big-Hands, "Ready to get your clothes off so we can oil you up?"

As quickly as he came, he vanished.

What is this? I was pretty certain I had not signed up for any pornographic work.

Ryan took the clipboard and then told me the idea: I was going to be in my bathers. I had to essentially be a nerdy sunbather who doesn't put on sunscreen except on my nose. I fall asleep on the beach and end up with a white nose but a beetroot-red body. Easy enough.

Then another man came along and asked me to come through. The Blonde had just finished up as I headed behind the bookcase. There was an impressive-looking camera there. The weird guy had gone somewhere and the second unknown man had moved out to work on the Apple.

"So you know what we need?"

This man, whom I assumed was the cameraman, seemed nice enough, though I hadn't caught his name.

"Sure."

"Great, take a seat there."

He indicated a chair in an alcove I couldn't have seen from the main part of the room. I did so and then Ole Beard Face appeared again.

"Aren't we going to have him strip off for us?"

The cameraman actually considered this for a moment. Then, "Okay. Just down to your underwear, thanks."

There wasn't even a thought to ask me.

Okay, it isn't as if I'm a prude. I've done enough theatre to be able to get undressed in front of people. But there was a level of decorum you should use in approaching the idea. It's like forgetting foreplay, or even asking the person if they want sex and heading straight to third base.

Fine. In all honesty, as an actor, you do what's required generally – within reason.

"I hope you didn't wear a thong," from the man with the beard. He wasn't being seedy or anything, he must have simply found it amusing to put people in this sort of situation. Again, not in a mean or hostile way; more like he was new to the concept.

So, there I was in my boxer briefs for five minutes while they took photos of me. Not exactly what I had been expecting, but if I got the job, it would be worth it.

Wouldn't it?

So much for dressing for an audition. I had my blue jeans and a grey t-shirt with an orange jumper that has a zip that runs from my left hip up over my shoulder to the neckline. Then my brown felt-like casual jacket with my thick black bomber-type jacket over the top. As I said, I layer up, probably too much. Thankfully I was wearing a pair of red Bonds boxer briefs for my modesty.

Beardy McBeardface, who I realised quickly was the director, then ran me through several different scenarios. Lathering my considerable nose with sun cream – pretend of course. I was sure the size of my nose helped get the casting. Then settling down to sunbathe. Waking up after said bathing and being unable to move for the sunburn. I added some quirkiness to the performance, trying to make the vague character endearing and amusing. This had the director chuckling behind his hand as he watched it all back on a monitor.

After the shoot, I dressed quickly, or as quickly as I could with all those clothes; said my goodbyes and left swiftly, slinging my khaki satchel over my shoulder. It had to be one of the more disconcerting castings I had been to.

"Thanks, Champ!" He shouted after me as I was leaving before saying to a fellow auditionee, "Ready to get naked, buddy?"

Back on the street, it didn't matter though. Out of sight, out of mind. Oh, that so wasn't true.

What was I doing? In London? In life? Had I become this? Am I someone willing to take his clothes off for a small advert? I had developed a career worth something back in Australia. Okay, I wasn't a household name, but I had been fulfilled.

Now, here I am in England scraping at any possible work I could get.

It was insane.

After everything I had done for this world? Maybe I had saved it, maybe I'm exaggerating. But that had only been a few years ago. A few measly years since Bob, Narelle, Tom and One.

I still saw Bob and Narelle from time to time, but they had a kingdom to run. I was bound to become an afterthought after a while. Sure, I had helped save them too, but celebrity is fleeting and so are friendships.

So much for gratitude though.

My life had returned to normal. No, not just normal. A struggle. I'd fought all my way back in Australia. Now here I am in England starting that same fight all over again.

And how damn selfish am I?

It isn't as if Bob and Narelle could help me in any way. And why should they? If I hadn't done what I had, who knows what would have happened? I would most likely be dead. And Sarah.

Sarah. She is married now. Not to Morrissey. They hadn't lasted too long after the whole cross-dimensional, cars flying through the air debacle.

No. He vanished shortly afterwards. Sarah was a little annoyed as it seemed he had dumped her by simply ceasing to return her calls. So, she stopped calling.

Now she was Mrs Sarah Duncombe. And she was happy. Lucky her. After the wedding, there had been so little time for us to get together. Especially as it caused her husband a little discomfort to have me around. I think the clinical word for it is Jealousy.

So there you had it. Me, in London. Alone and struggling.

Still, things could be worse.

And then they were.

Someone bumped into me from behind. Unlike a normal accident, however, this person had held onto me for a little too long.

I looked around to see who it was only to find I was looking at mid-air. Something tugged on my jeans and then vanished. That was when I realised my mistake. I was looking for an adult. The person that had hit me was a child. Probably eleven or twelve, a little scruffy looking, but his teeth were gleaming as he smiled back at me waving my wallet.

The little bugger had picked my pocket and he had done it quite clumsily.

What choice did I have but to take chase?

He was heading the way I had been going, so I bolted after him.

Now, although I had stopped my Tae Kwon Do classes a while before I left Australia, I had taken up a class of Ballet and one of Jazz a week over here in England. That had kept my fitness up a fair bit, so chasing him wasn't a problem when it came to endurance. The problem came with him being so small, he could dodge the people on the pavement with ease, whereas I was forced to navigate clumsily.

That was one of the drawbacks of London. In Perth, there had been a general understanding to walk on the left, the same as how they drove their cars. In London, however, due to the European Mainlanders driving on the right, there came a huge confusion as to which side of the pavement one should walk. So people chose whichever side they wanted to, often opting for right down the middle.

Apologising as I did so, I pushed a couple of people aside and bumped into others as I tried to keep up with the boy. My bag had been flailing behind me, banging angrily on my hip every third or fourth step when gravity took hold. I grabbed it with my right arm and continued running.

I could barely see his rusty brown mop of hair about eight metres in front of me as he was getting swallowed by the ever-thickening crowd. It was a losing battle. That wasn't going to stop me.

Making it back to Shoreditch Road, I stopped. And then I realised I had lost.

There was no sign of him. My eyes scanned the crowds on every side of the road, trying to see if I could spot him through cars as they drove by. Nothing.

I was about to give up hope when I saw him again. Curiously, he appeared where I had already looked across the road. He was standing there waving my wallet at me again.

What was his game? Was he trying to taunt me some more?

As if fortune had decided to take my side, the green man appeared on the pole beside me and I bolted across the road.

Still smiling, he took off once more. I was a little too out of breath to be calling out, "Stop him," but I tried nonetheless. It came out as a little wheezy whine. Maybe I wasn't as fit as I thought.

I hit the opposite sidewalk and charged after him. It was just as difficult going this way due to the number of people, at least for the moment. He was starting to move out of the crowds and into a quieter part of the area.

Although it wasn't far from Liverpool Street Station, the buildings were a little shorter and warehouse-like. And I still had a thing about warehouses.

The boy wasn't running as fast either. Maybe he was starting to tire.

I kept up the chase for another couple of blocks until I saw him disappear down an alley. And that is where I stopped.

An alley in London? I wasn't that stupid.

My wallet wasn't worth my life. But I wasn't going to give up, either.

I began walking, glad for the change of pace. I was on the opposite side of the road.

As I drew even, I stopped and looked.

The boy was standing there as if waiting for me.

The alley itself was clear. No large bins for someone to be hiding behind, no dark cars ready to run me over. The other end of the alley seemed to be blocked by the side of another building which sort of begs the question, what was the point of the alley itself?

There was nothing else.

Just the boy.

Cautiously, checking both directions as I did so; I crossed the road. I moved slowly, calmly.

When my foot stepped onto the sidewalk something else appeared in the alley.

Beside the boy, a door opened. A door I couldn't remember seeing earlier from across the road. It opened inward and an old lady stepped out.

She was very old. Her hair, although permed, was thin and wispy white. Her face was very wrinkled yet soft. Dark rings lay under her staring eyes as if she had been kept awake nights. Her body was hunched and slow.

The boy looked at her and then back at me. She noticed his movement and followed his gaze until she too was staring at me. It was rather disconcerting, especially when she smiled. The two had to be related to each other.

Without taking an eye off me, she put out her hand and the boy gave her my wallet.

"Excuse me," I began, but she cut me off.

"Come inside. I expect you'll be wanting this back. Have a cup of tea. It's the least I can do for your troubles." She waved my wallet much like the boy had, "You. Inside," the boy did as he was told and she patted him on the back of his head as he passed.

"Come along. I won't hurt you. Do I look like I could hurt you?"

Looks can be deceiving, I felt like saying. I had learnt that the hard way seven years ago in a room of mirrors. A shiver ran down my spine and across my knees as I remembered the pain that I had felt back then.

I still wasn't going to fall for it. She obviously realised this as she dropped the wallet in the middle of the alley, "There. I'll leave it there for you. Come, take it. Then if you will accept my hospitality, come inside."

She seemed genuine.

Still wary, I moved slowly into the alley as she vanished inside the door, leaving it open.

I was only a few steps from the wallet now and I started to bend down to pick it up.

The old lady's voice called from inside, "Please do come in and have some tea. Besides this little monster has to apologise for taking it in the first place. His mother would have my head if I didn't make him apologise."

She really did seem genuine and nice enough. Still, there was something odd.

As I bent down, I looked inside the building. A smell of sandalwood incense emanated from within. The light was poor, but I could see a little living room with a small dining table and chairs beyond.

"Just one cup," I said, trying to show my unease and anger with those three words.

"Yes, yes. Just one cup."

I stepped inside, pocketing my wallet as I did so.

No men were hiding behind the corner to jump me. No assault from in front or behind by the boy or old lady. Instead, there was what looked to be a little apartment, or flat as they were called over here, with a door draped by a wooden bead curtain leading toward the front of the building.

The boy was standing beside a worn leather recliner, wringing his hands. The smile was gone now, but he still watched me.

The old lady shuffled past me to shut the door and then back into the dining room, which was also her kitchen, "Sit down."

Looking around, I had several options for places to sit. Some were covered by myriad small trinkets which also occupied display cabinets and the walls. This lady seemed to be a hoarder of knick-knacks. Crystal candlesticks of various sizes covered the top of a chest of drawers while a literal zoo of ceramic animals infested a cabinet beside it. The burgundy curtains over her windows looked as if they were being held there by a pair of golden cherubs blowing their trumpets while their brothers sat on glistening clouds on a side table on the opposite side of the recliner to the boy.

Opting for a safer and less fragile seat, I moved into the kitchen and sat on one of the four chairs at the table. I made sure I could still see the boy and the old lady.

"My name is Kathleen Wainwright. But you may call me Kath," She started as she filled a kettle. It looked a little too heavy for her as she had to rest her elbow on the side of the sink.

I was about to stand to help when she shook her head at me.

"This is Luka. I'm not a fan of the name, but his mother thought it was… trendy," it was as if she had said the last word with inverted commas. Judging by the décor and her attitude, this woman was truly old school.

I nodded, "I'm-"

"I know who you are. You're Scott. You're the one we've been looking for."

I opened my mouth to speak then shut it again. I had nothing to say. This was just downright odd.

Struggling slightly, Kath managed to put the kettle on the hob.

"Luka, get the teacups ready and set the table, would you, Love?"

The boy, Luka, jumped into gear, doing as he had been asked. He was a bit like a puppy. As he passed me, I saw I'd made a mistake. He was older than he had originally appeared. Only by a handful of years. There was also something older in his eyes as he glanced at me.

Leaning against the counter Kath looked at me with bright green eyes. In the slight gloom of the room, the dark bags under her eyes and the way her skin seemed to hang from her bones gave her an eerily skull-like appearance. Her voice, however, remained sweet and undeniably English, "You have quite a journey ahead of you. Oh, the things you will see. Much like Luka has just experienced."

I could have approached it with "What do you mean?" but I opted to play it cool with, "I've seen a fair few sights in my life already."

"Oh, I know," she really did, somehow. She turned toward the now whistling kettle, "I know. And such adventures you've had. Other worlds. Fantastical creatures. Things of beauty," she finished pouring the water into a pot Luka had prepared and turned back to look at me. Her eyes were darker now, her voice deeper, "This time there will be no beauty."

As I had concealed my shock earlier at the audition when I heard the idea of auditioning naked, I wasn't quite able to do so this time. There was a depth to those last words. I let them sink in as she brought the tray loaded with the teapot, a jug of milk, a sugar bowl and three cups and saucers to the table.

Luka sat opposite me, staring intently at me as Kath poured the tea. I watched in silence as she scooped two sugars and a dash of milk into a cup and handed it to me. Exactly the way I liked it. I could smell it over the incense. Earl Grey. My favourite ever since seeing Patrick Stewart's character on Star Trek: The Next Generation drink it.

When everyone was catered for, she sat down with her own cup of tea and blew on it gently.

"A night without a day. A fear without relief. A world without peace," she muttered.

I couldn't bring myself to drink mine yet. She captivated me, "Where is this?"

"Not so far that you'll have to jump rainbows for it. Nor so far you'll have to go looking."

She was getting all riddley on me.

"Why me?"

So quickly, surprising for her old age and how slow she had moved previously, her cup was back in its saucer and her eyes glared at me, "Why you?"

She was angry. At me.

"Why you? Because you started it all. Because you're the one that brought it down on us. That is why you."

"Nan," Luka spoke for the first time and put his hand on hers.

His touch seemed to bring her back. She picked up her tea again and gazed into it. No one spoke for a time and then, "Because we need your help."

"How am I supposed to help? I don't even know what you're talking about."

"And I can't really tell you. I can say only one thing but now is not the time. You should finish your tea."

I took a sip and eyed the door. I could simply run. Neither of them could stop me. But I was intrigued. What had I done that had caused this problem, whatever that problem actually was? How could I possibly help?

The tea was delicious. The perfect balance of sugar, milk and the exact diffusion of Earl Grey. It had to be magic, or she was a superb tea maker.

"You keep saying 'we'. I take it you mean more than just the two of you?"

Kath nodded and looked over at her grandson who was twirling a spoon in his own drink, "We couldn't stay long in your world. It drains us too much."

"Does that mean you come from this other world too?" I had to ask but didn't need an answer, "So his stealing my wallet was all a ruse?"

Kath ruffled Luka's hair as I put my wallet away, "I'm afraid so. I don't like getting him to run my errands. Especially ones like that. But it was necessary. And I believe you have something to say, young man."

Luka looked up and looked a tad sheepish, "Sorry."

"That's okay," I shrugged, "It's not your fault. Apparently."

I downed the last of the warm tea and stood up, "Thank you for the tea, but I should be going."

Kath stood, her cup half empty, "I'm glad to see you're eager."

"Yes, eager to go home. If you know so much about me, you know what I went through last time I came across one of these stupid ideas. That is if you are serious or just some obsessive old lady who caught some whiff of what happened to me back in Australia. Either way, I'm not going for it. I have a life now and I don't plan on hopping dimensions all over again," I moved to the door. Neither of my hosts moved to stop me.

As my hand touched the door handle Kath began to speak, "Oh, I'm sorry."

I stepped outside into the moonlit alley and froze. It couldn't have passed one o'clock in the afternoon.

The air was icy on my skin and seemed to burn my lungs as I took a breath. What's more, the pavement beneath my feet was no longer the pavement it had been earlier, but a smooth and very regular cobblestone surface.

I felt a hand on my shoulder and Kath's warm breath on

the back of my neck as she continued talking, "You see, Scott, you don't have a choice. None of us do."

OUT OF THE FRYING PAN

INTO THE FREEZER

I turned on my heels so fast, if they had been steel, there would have been a spark on the cobbles. The look on my face must have shown the anger I was feeling because Kath backed up into her living room.

How dare they? I had gone through enough of this already. Cut to ribbons, nearly squashed by cars, eaten by giant magpies – the nasty Australian type, not the sweet English breed.

What more do these people want from me? I don't have what it takes. I don't even have what it takes to be even remotely successful in London let alone in my life.

"Where am I?"

Kath had retreated far enough into her living room so I couldn't grab her without having to travel. Not that I actually would have grabbed her. I'm not violent like that. Either way, Luka was now standing in front of her eyeing me defiantly. It was him that spoke, "This is our home. This is what you made it. If we have to live with it, then I think you should too."

"But I didn't do anything! I just want to be left alone."

"This all started because of you."

"No. This all started because I was sucked into some despot's idea of a joke. I had no say in that! I paid my dues over and over for that. Not just me, either. And who are you to kidnap me? What right do you have to do this?"

Kath laid her hand on Luka's head, signalling for him to be silent.

"We have no right. But we had no choice either. We're dying. We need help and you're the only one that can help us."

I wanted to scream. I could feel my anger seething inside me. But what was the point? It was useless. Just like my going for that stupid audition. It's all pointless. I don't seem to have any control of my own life anymore whether it is in my career or in staying in my home dimension.

"How?!"

"Your coming was prophesized."

"You what?"

Kath shook her head, "Your coming to help us. It was written down many years ago. I don't understand it all myself. It had only been whispers around our world for the last two years. When I looked deeper, the origin is a prophecy written over half a century ago."

"But what prophecy? What does it say?"

"A night without a day. A fear without relief. A world without peace. A one from away who crossed through the ether…" she waved her hand weakly in front of her face, "I forget the rest. I'm getting old. The crux of it is that someone who has travelled across the world and realms will find himself locked in One."

I didn't like the way she said that word. 'One'. It sent a shiver down my spine.

"A battle for realities. That's it. Yes. Realities. So if you wish to leave, who is to know yours will even be left standing for much longer? Like all prophecies, it is very vague. You do fit the bill quite nicely, though."

"But it might not even be me?"

"And how many other people do you know have travelled across realities?"

I had to shrug at that, "There could be others. It isn't like we have a social group. I wasn't the only one to take the trip last time."

Kath nodded sagely, "You are right. It is just that we are running out of time and we need a saviour. You've been one once, could it be you might be again?"

"Great. Suppose I am by a massive and, dare I say it, unfortunate turn of chance this prophesized saviour, I don't even know what your problem is."

"Our problem, Scott," I knew what she meant when she said the word 'our', "Our problem is him. He's come here. He has enslaved thousands. He has trapped millions. He has turned our day into night and he kills. Without reason, without mercy."

He? That sounded awfully like someone or something I came across seven years ago. Except he went by the name of One. Hence the little shiver when she mentioned him earlier. A little egomaniacal if you ask me, but a very dangerous monster all the same. I should never have let him walk. What I don't understand is why Bob and Narelle didn't keep an eye on him. They must have been able to stop him from leaving their dimension. He couldn't have left without them in the first place. Unless he had help from one of Bob's people. A traitor.

That didn't matter. If he was here, that meant trouble.

"Not only that, the cold. The cold is killing people as is the darkness and the creatures he has walking in that darkness."

"Where is he?"

"He's not as simple to find as just asking, Scott. No one knows. He doesn't sit on a throne basking in worship. If it were that simple, we could have taken him. But he is always on the move. Most people don't even believe he exists. They look for more explainable conspiracies. Of those that have seen him and lived to talk, they say he is searching for something."

"So he doesn't have a castle or anything like that?"

"No. Not a castle per se. The people he has taken are hidden away somewhere, doing what he has told them to do. No one knows what that is. No one has ever come out again."

"And this world's defences? The Army?"

Kath scoffed, "They must know of him, though they keep it secret. They don't know who he is for all their searching. This eternal night, this cold. They don't know how he has caused it. He has kept a low profile, maintaining power by being invisible, secret. Besides, against his magic? They would have no effect. So far, he hasn't left this island. He's left the other continents alone, but we don't know how much longer that's going to last. We are trapped. No one gets in and no one gets out of Great Britain."

Great Britain? We're still here? Maybe instead of being a completely different world, this was an alternate version of my own world.

"But you said he got rid of Day? Has he done that to the whole world?"

"We don't know. There is no communication with Europe or America anymore. It didn't just happen, either. It took months. And with it, the cold. Even the stars are getting darker now."

I had sat down on the edge of an overcrowded sideboard, knocking over several ceramic thimbles and finding myself not caring. What was more important was the fact I had no way to fight him. It was impossible. Did the same rules apply here this time? The ones that allowed me to alter the fabric of the reality in Bob's dimension with a huge dose of willpower? Or was I going to have to think of something else? Who was on my side?

"Who else knows about me?"

Kath, who had sat in the recliner Luka had stood beside earlier, looked thoughtful for a moment, "There is only a handful of us that know of you, of what you have done and of him. We've spent many months trying to find you. It had come down to a game of chance that put your arrival in my hands. Poker? Heads and tails? Oh, I can't remember. I lost quite successfully, though. Thankfully Luka volunteered to help out."

"And are you going to help me?"

"We can't. We have no power anymore. We're all old now. If he had come twenty years ago, maybe. But there is nothing we can do. There are others. The younger generation. But they don't know. They don't care. It was all hogwash to them when we tried to explain it. It wasn't long before they got too self-involved, using their powers to their own advantage. Some don't even understand their abilities. Most of those in his dungeons were like us. There are only a few dozen left who are free now and we can't find them. He can. He hunts them now."

At least they had some sort of power. But where did that leave me? With an army of geriatrics? Attack One with walking sticks and Zimmer frames? Not likely. There was only one question left that would get me on the path to getting home:

"So where do I start?"

A coincidence? Or just my luck? Coming from outside, there was a crash of some sort. It was faint, but I could hear it. All three of us paused and listened. I was about to ask my question again when what was unmistakably a scream, muffled by the walls, rang from outside.

Kath's eyes widened in panic. Luka grabbed her hand for his own reassurance.

Me? I was too busy running to the door to worry about getting scared. I was past that. I was scared the minute I opened the door the first time to find my world gone.

It was still night outside. Fresh, chilly air. It was more like winter now. A very cold one. Maybe this world was suffering from Global Warming affecting the weather extremes.

No. This was magic.

I hesitated and, holding onto the doorframe, turned back to the people inside, "Stay here. Stay safe."

I headed to the mouth of the alley and stopped. The echoes of a woman's screams were still drifting by. Either way, I didn't need them to tell me which way to go.

To the right was the way I had come. It was that way I could see a commotion.

I half ran, half jogged to get there. I couldn't do much more as I was still a little worn from the earlier chase.

I couldn't see any police yet, but I could just make out the bulk of a car at an odd angle with a wall. One side of its front crumpled against the stonework. But that wasn't what seemed to have grabbed everyone's attention. The crowd was gathered around something near the car.

What struck me first was what everyone was wearing. Greys, blacks and dark browns. It was as if the night had sucked any colour from their dress sense. Not only that, their skin was pale. More so than mine. I hadn't been blessed with skin for tanning, more for burning, so I kept covered up and pale. Thankfully for my black jacket, my own bright clothing was going to stay concealed.

When I arrived, I had to push my way through. The people were too stunned to put up much fight, plus I got the feeling that although the human instinct is to see the horrors of a crash, when they actually do, they don't particularly want to be reminded of their own mortality.

It wasn't until I saw what they were looking at that I realised it had nothing to do with the car crash. A man in his thirties. His face was bloodied and scratched, his body a lot worse. The gaping hole in his chest, for one, was obviously not caused by the car crash.

I had to concentrate to keep from gagging. Looking at the rest of his body, his legs were bent in two places, rather than the normal one and a bone was protruding through the trouser leg of one of them.

His blood, I knew, was red but in the limited light, it appeared a dark grey on the ground beneath the body, trickling through the cracks like water through a well-constructed sewer system.

I had to blink several times to let my eyes get used to the colour scheme. I mean I had seen the effects of the night before, obviously, but there was something almost misty about the quality of ambient light around this reality.

Not that being able to see more clearly would affect what I was looking at. It was quite obvious this man was dead. Not only that, someone had killed him intentionally.

It didn't take a forensic scientist to work that out.

"Help me," the voice was quiet, broken and barely heard over the whispered talk of the gathering crowd.

I looked around, as did some other people, but couldn't see the speaker through all the onlookers. So, once again I pushed through the crowd and away from the body toward the sound of the voice. Stepping past the last person, I found myself looking at the car.

The driver wasn't the one doing the talking. His head was twisted at the wrong angle on the bonnet of the car. It looked as though his seatbelt hadn't worked, or he hadn't been wearing one.

"Please."

The voice came from the side closest to me, the passenger side. I rushed over to the door and tried to open it. It all but fell off its hinges jolting my arms as it did so. I managed to scrape it aside, only to find no one bothered to help me.

I let it fall and clatter loudly to try and attract some attention. No one came.

Inside was a young girl. Her face was darkly stained by blood and her fringe was plastered to her forehead. She lay limply back in her chair, thankfully not looking at the body of the driver.

There were sirens now. Close by. They weren't like any I had heard before. More of a rolling call than the piercing screech of the English emergency services I knew. It was time I started getting used to the weird stuff again.

The worst part was the fact that the last world I went to was bright and wacky. This one seemed so dull, depressing. Everything seemed awash in grey. The stars were overhead, and although I could see them which was rare in central London, they didn't seem to sparkle as they should.

Street lights further down the road were orange. Nothing surprising there, but the light they gave off seemed to be swallowed by the very gloominess it was trying to eradicate.

Yes, my mind was wandering. It was all a bit much to take in at the moment. I wasn't a paramedic. I was no superhero. I was an out-of-work actor and already I had tried taking charge. Which was odd for two reasons. Firstly, why hadn't anybody else tried to help this little girl? Secondly, I'm not usually the person to do this sort of thing.

But I figure, needs must when the devil nips at your heels. Or throws you in the deep end. Or into an alternate reality. Take your pick. The sooner I got this sorted, the sooner I got home and found out whether or not I'd need to pose in my underwear for an advert for sunscreen. And who uses sunscreen in England anyway?

"I want my Daddy," that short sentence alone was enough to kick-start my mind.

Focus, I told myself.

There was no way I was going to move her without knowing if it was safe to do so or not. What I needed to do was keep her attention on me. She seemed very groggy, probably just woken up. At least I hoped so.

"What's your name, Gorgeous," it was worth a try.

Drowsily she seemed to see me for the first time, "Becca."

"Becca? Short for Rebecca, I guess?"

She tried to nod.

"Just sit still for the time being, Becca. Becca, what's your surname?"

"Turpin."

"How old are you?"

"Eight."

"Eight? You're almost a teenager."

A slight smile flicked at the side of her lips, but I got the impression the pain prevented it from going any further, "I'm just over halfway there. Are you an angel too?"

Sweet, but horribly sad at the same time. I was finding it hard to find words, let alone be able to say them, "No, honey. I'm not an angel. Just a friend."

What looked to be an ambulance and a police car pulled up on the other side of the car from me.

"I thought the other angel was going to take me away too. But he was scary."

"What other angel, Becca?"

She shook her head and began to cry, "I want my Daddy."

Without a word, I was pushed aside by two heavy-set men in black uniforms. Quickly and silently they huddled over the girl and started doing their job. I took them for this world's version of paramedics, which was good. I hoped she was ok.

Two police officers had cordoned off the body behind me. The crowd had backed off quite a distance. They seemed almost as scared of the police as they were of the body. More so, even.

Amongst them, I made out the faces of Luka and Kath. They were looking at me. A lot of people were.

On stage, I would have been used to that feeling, but here, it seemed completely wrong. I knew I wasn't being persecuted by them or anything, but there was this look of uncertainty, almost as if I was some sort of alien, having done something abnormal.

I moved away from the car watching as their eyes followed me. Not the police, not the paramedics. Me.

Kath had started to motion for me to join her. I didn't hesitate in doing so. Once I was safely amongst the crowd again, most of the eyes became preoccupied somewhere else, though the people around me now gave me a wide berth.

"We need to get home."

"Is this normal?" I indicated the activity behind me.

Pulling on my arm, Kath whispered harshly, "Yes, for us, it is. We don't make a fuss. We don't get involved."

I let myself be pulled along, keeping one eye on the girl, if I could see her, "No wonder he gets away with it then."

She stopped and turned on me, eyes flaring with a brief

rage, "If we don't, we're as good as dead. Like that man there," she calmed a little, "There is a story here. I will show you once we are inside."

Like a schoolboy, I followed her. Luka held onto one of her hands, offering support to the old woman as well as gaining comfort from her presence. When we were back inside her flat, Luka dead-bolted the door. We moved back into the kitchen where the teapot still seemed to be steaming. I poured another round of drinks and she dealt out the milk and sugar.

We sat in silence. I had nothing to say, really. This was becoming a habit. I'm rarely lost for words.

The tea was just as delicious as the first cup. I had no idea how that was possible, but I wasn't going to question it.

Kath took a sip of hers, placed the cup back in its saucer and took my hand in both of hers.

They were cold but gentle. The liver spots were so clear and plentiful on her pale withered skin.

"Will you let me show you something?"

I shrugged, "Sure."

I had no idea what she had meant, but I felt a wave of ice wash over me that seemed to emanate from the hand she was holding me with. It was followed by the prickly sensation of pins and needles that ran all the way up my spine into the base of my skull. And she, the room, the tea, all of it was gone. I was somewhere else.

Outside.

It was brighter than normal. I didn't know how I knew this. The moon seemed particularly high this evening, its near round glow reflected off the shiny surface of the cobbled street.

I began to notice there were thoughts in my head that didn't belong to me. Someone else's mixing with mine. Ideas, understandings. A knowledge of this world I didn't belong to.

A figure walked along the grey brick wall, head down,

hands in pocket. The safest way to walk these days. Any expression, be it joy or fear, was certain to attract attention. No one was around. People could be seen walking further down the road at the next crossroad. Every so often, the black bulk of a car would crawl past.

Something was wrong. The figure, a man, could feel it in his bones, his blood. He allowed his eyes to look up at the sky briefly. It was cloudless. Only the moon and the stars. Once it would have been beautiful if it wasn't always night.

He sniffed at the cold air. Nothing.

A shiver ran through him that he used to break him from his funk and depression.

Hugging the brick wall, he continued walking, lowering his eyes to the pavement.

A voice, a sense, he wasn't sure what it was. He never knew no matter how many times he had experienced it. Whatever it was, it was a blessing. Now it came with three words: 'It is coming!'

A swirl of images in his head; the flash of a car's headlights, a screech of tires, his body crushed between the vehicle and the very wall he was walking along.

And in a flash, he reacted. His legs subconsciously launched him into the air, just in time to avoid the car as it came racing at him. The world seemed to slow to a crawl as his body twisted as an Olympic diver mid-jump or gymnast mid-dismount, somersaulting, twisting high in the air to come down feet first in the street behind the car he had seen in his vision.

Breathing heavily, he looked up at the wall and the wreckage of the vehicle.

Only there wasn't any.

He was staring at an empty space.

There was no car. No accident. His sense had been off. That had never happened before.

A little dazed, he almost failed to notice his silhouette creep headfirst onto the base of the wall. By the time he had, it was too late. For the second time that evening, his body was launched into the air as the vehicle smashed into his legs, snapping both femurs and tearing numerous tendons as it did so. His hip smashed hard against the bonnet before he was sent crashing into the wall. His arms managed to make an impact first, lessening the blow to his head.

It was over in seconds as he collapsed back down onto the now crumpled bonnet of the car. His eyes staring hazily into the blank eyes of the driver, himself launched forward in his seat and through the windscreen.

He could barely feel the pain. In fact, he couldn't feel his legs at all. His arms were throbbing dully, but that was starting to intensify.

Somewhere in the dark, someone laughed. It was short, concise.

Then a hand touched his shoulder. Gently at first before he felt the fingers – no not fingers, claws – dig into his flesh.

He managed a garbled yelp of pain as the hand picked him up off the bonnet. All he could do was hang limply in the grasp of whoever it was that had him single-handed lifted off the floor.

A second hand lifted his chin with its index finger. He could feel the rough leathery skin, cold.

"You'll do," was all that was said, the voice gravely and echoing into the night. He tried to focus on who was speaking, but in his daze and the gloom of the night, all he could make out was the shape of an angel. It was strange that in this perpetual world of night, even the angels seemed grey. But the wings… what else could it be but an angel coming to take his pain away?

A moment later and the pain from the impact was nothing compared to the excruciating agony of the second hand plunging into his chest cavity. He was dead before the hand was removed, now holding the man's heart.

As if an afterthought, his body was dropped onto the cobbles.

The 'angel' spread its wings and disappeared into the night; the heart clutched to its own chest.

The image began to ripple and then shred itself as if it were made of fine crepe paper. It fell away from my mind to be replaced by Kath and her kitchen once more. I gasped violently for air as if I had just surfaced after a long dive. That was exactly how it felt. My heart pounded in my chest, and my lungs, in the same cage, felt like they had been constricted and finally released.

Kath's hand, which had been cold before, was freezing now. She shivered and quickly moved them back to her tea to warm them.

"When you said show me something, I thought you meant a book or one of your stupid little trinkets. Not some sort of mind rape."

"I'm sorry. I forget you wouldn't be used to this kind of thing."

"What was that? Was it what happened out there? How he died?" I recognised the man instantly in the vision. And the driver. Now, I also knew what Becca meant about the Angel.

"Yes. I picked it up from the energies around the accident."

"But what does it mean? Do you all have these powers?"

She shook her head, "No. Not many of us. But this is not the first time something like this has happened. We are dying. He's preying on us. Stealing our lives and our hearts and no one knows why."

"Is that him? The one you say has done all this?"

"Yes."

But it didn't look like One. Sure, from the blurry images floating in my head, this angel hadn't exactly looked human. But One was almost dog-like. He crawled on four legs for the most part, not only that, he was massive. This monster would have been seven-foot, maybe eight.

"It isn't him. Not the One I know," which meant, "You've made a mistake. I'm not responsible for this. I don't even know what it is you're dealing with."

"Be that as it may, does it make our plight any less worthy of your help?"

"I-," how do you answer that? Was she admitting liability? That she had been wrong and sucked an innocent man from the safety of his own dimension to this depressingly grey and horrific reality? And was she right, that I shouldn't simply turn my back on her now I am here?

I'd helped before. Where's the harm in trying to help again? It could mean my death, but it can't be worse than the existential pain I was enduring back in my London trying to build my career again.

"Well, no. Not when you put it like that."

She smiled hopefully, "So you will help us?"

I nodded. I had always felt I would be destined for greater things. Heck, I had saved two realities before. Though I was hoping it would be in the acting industry I'd be great in.

It was time for me to have another adventure anyway.

HOME IS WHERE THE HEARTS ARE

A street light, also fighting the darkness, shone down at the corner of two streets. Below it, a man, huddled, rubbing his hands along his arms and bouncing from one foot to another. He was cold, every so often blowing steaming breaths on his hands in a pointless attempt to keep them warm.

His eyes darted around, watching the darkness that enshrouded the small park on the same corner he stood. It was mostly grass, the odd tree and a park bench. How the plants survived without the sun was beyond this man's knowledge. Beside that were townhouses, their black and grey brickwork clean of grime, moss or any form of dirt. The roads too were spotless. It was as if rubbish didn't exist now He had control. Not the man under the street light. Him. The Angel of Death, he liked to think of him as.

No. Like was not the right word.

There was a faint sound of rocks tapping over and over again.

"Stop bouncing around. You'll draw attention."

The voice growled from above him and in the dark where two brick apartment blocks joined. Two blank walls, windowless, met in the shadows and, if one was to look closely, you could see something there.

No one looked closely enough.

"I will draw attention anyway standing here like this."

"I told you to keep an eye out. I felt something earlier when I collected this heart. Something wrong."

Under his breath the man muttered, "Wouldn't be guilt now, would it?"

There was a growl and a flash of red and amber light and the man couldn't help but look into the darkness. The tapping had stopped.

His shivering changed from that of cold to that of fear.

The face staring out at him was grotesque. Green eyes flaring with flames illuminated the grey-skinned monster. Its sharp teeth bared in an unmistakably hostile threat. Its flesh was scarred and torn.

No matter how many times he had seen that face, it still scared him half to death.

The flames ebbed and died and the shadows once more claimed the corner where the buildings met.

The tapping resumed.

The man stopped bouncing from foot to foot and quickly averted his eyes to the streets. He didn't understand why he needed to keep an eye out. The monster he worked for was far more powerful than anyone else around here. What had gotten him nervous? Whatever it was had also gotten his servant nervous too.

A faint feeling struck him. He couldn't quite explain it. Sniffing the air, like a dog, he thought maybe he could sense something coming. There was nothing there, yet, as his master had said, something was wrong.

Then it struck him. The tapping had stopped again.

Ever so carefully, he raised his eyes up to the darkness. Only to the edge so he wouldn't actually see what was hidden within.

It had stopped moving, once more, in the periphery of his vision, he could see the green eyes glowing faintly, moving slowly from side to side.

It let something drop. It appeared to be a small red gem of some kind. A soft thump when it hit the grass below.

"Not working?"

The monster let off another low growl, "No. I need another. And I think I have found one."

A whirl of its great wings and off it vanished like a shot in the night. Averting his eyes away and down so he wouldn't have to see it, the man let his gaze fall on the red gem.

He'd seen one before. Eight or nine times at least. Still, they captivated him and repulsed him at the same time.

The monster had gone and wouldn't be back for a bit so it was safe to leave his post for the time being.

Crossing the road to the small patch of grass between where the two buildings met, he bent down and picked up the stone.

Although it had been badly scratched and cracked in some parts, he could still make out the general shape. He brushed it on his clothes and regretted it straight away as it left a dark red stain.

Blood.

He looked at the gem in his hand and imagined what it had looked like before it had been plucked from someone's chest. Beating silently, giving life to something, someone. Now it was just a pretty stone.

He didn't want it anymore. Quickly releasing it from his grip, the heart fell to the grass with that same thud it had sounded out before. The blood was on his hand too.

Reaching into a deep pocket of his long overcoat, he pulled out a handkerchief and tried to wipe it clean.

It would not come off.

I'M IN LONDON STILL

We had decided the best place to start was to get as much information about this monster as we could. I couldn't refer to him as One because I was sure it wasn't him.

It was either that or scrying for him. When I suggested that, however, Kath had chuckled. She wasn't a witch and she didn't know of anyone who had that ability anyway.

It was worth a try.

Kath hadn't actually seen the angel except second-hand through her visions. But "It is always difficult to tell," she said, "It is as if my vision relies on the emotions of the person I am focussing on. If they are anxious, my visions get muffled, jerky. Like the one you saw, he was barely conscious. So my vision was blurry, hard to make out."

Made sense to me. We still needed to find out what we could. I thought the best place to start would be the witnesses.

Luka was replacing and relighting tea candles around the room. It seemed that Kath didn't rely on electricity. I hadn't noticed it earlier, but there wasn't one electric light. Only these little candles dotted around the rooms and the incense stick jutting out of a crack under a cupboard door in the kitchen. Luka replaced that too.

"How many attacks have there been so far?"

"That we know of, sixteen."

"And they all end the same way? With someone's heart being cut out."

She nodded and took a bite out of one of the biscuits she had placed on a plate for everyone to eat. They were every bit as delicious as the tea.

"Yes."

Ok. Enough questions. She was looking tired and I was getting anxious.

"Right. I'm heading to the nearest hospital. That should be where they've taken the girl in the car. I might be able to get something from her."

"You'll need to take Luka to show you."

I thought of something else. I didn't want to get the boy hurt. I pulled my 'AtoZ' out of my satchel and searched for the right page.

"Here's the closest hospital. The Royal London. Is that where it is in this world?"

Kath scrutinised the page for a moment then nodded, "Yes. The streets seem the same as well, though you might find a change in the buildings themselves."

"Great. Then I should get going."

I put the book back in my satchel and headed toward the door once more.

"Don't draw attention to yourself. You see how people are. Don't get involved unless you have to."

I laughed a little, "Bit late for that now."

The deadbolt latched itself again when I closed the door. I couldn't help wondering how much defence that would put up against the monster they were hiding from.

I made my way out of the alley and turned left this time, chancing a quick look in the other direction. The car was gone already as were the pedestrians. Quick work. Though the wall was clearly scarred from this evening's accident.

Putting my hands in my jacket pockets I slouched a little and walked toward the hospital.

It was bitterly cold. It was as if I was in the middle of winter already. I started singing random songs to myself to keep my head off the cold, but every time I took a breath, I found it hard not to feel it. Now I was wishing I had worn more layers.

The buildings were nothing like the ones from my home. They were all squat bricks. Most of them had boarded-up windows or none at all. No for sale signs, no for let. What's more, no rubbish.

Everywhere was clean as if someone had scrubbed up

recently. Not even cigarette butts or marks from dropped chewing gum.

But it was all grey. The bricks were grey, the cobblestones, the pavement. Just different shades. Even the wooden doors blocking off a vacant lot I was approaching were grey, with not one speck of graffiti.

I walked past the doors and was slightly impressed by the building next door.

What had once been a manor house of some kind was now burnt out and derelict. The walls, I could see there had been ornate brickwork and style, now crumbled and broken. An absolute shame as it was the first thing of beauty I had seen so far. It must have stood two or three stories, now it barely managed one and a half at the highest point.

As I walked past, I looked inside the first pane of shattered glass. It was hazy. It appeared to be some sort of stairwell that came down toward the window. Once it had reached the ground floor it banked to the left and became a corridor that disappeared into the dark. The walls were ashen with scraps of wallpaper hanging or at least trying to, their ends peeling and brittle. The bannister of the stairs was covered in dust and grime from years of disuse as well as never having been cleaned of the effects of the fire that must have consumed the upper levels.

The wooden floor – no carpets – was covered in twisted ornaments and useless knick-knacks, though in their prime would have been worth more than all those in Kath's house put together. Once silver candlesticks, a decorative tray, once silver also, both now tarnished and grey like everything else in this world.

At least I knew that not everything was spotless. Just the streets. I looked down at my feet stepping on the concrete. The blue trainers I had bought on my last trip to Perth. They were dirtier than the pavement was. It was amazing.

A few more steps and I noticed something odd. To my left, I felt a warmth, so rare in this cold weather, that I stopped and looked.

It was the same building. I was about halfway past it now. The exterior was still grey and weather-worn, but inside it was something else.

The warmth was coming from a large fire filling a fireplace at one end of a beautiful ballroom. Its light was swallowed by the wash of amber pouring down from three massive chandeliers that held what appeared to be a hundred or more candles each.

I had mistaken the glow for that coming from a street light. But it was too warm, too alive as it flickered here and there.

The opposite wall to the window I was gazing through was bedecked with mirrors at regular intervals or otherwise, a damask of what appeared to be lime green swans and peacocks floating in a forest of vines and leaves filled the rest of the walls.

Around the ceiling, white plaster decorations ran the length of the room. Angels and cherubs weeping as gods of music, love, war and beauty scorned, mocked or chastised them.

The parquet floor was a checkerboard of dark and light woods formed into diamonds. The natural hues of the polished boards radiated with the reflection of the light above. It was absolutely beautiful.

Yet it was empty.

No one was inside. Maybe it was being used for a function later. An odd choice of venue for a party, but if they had managed to resurrect the Ballroom's glory days after the rest of the house had been destroyed, well done to them.

There was a flash in one of the mirrors.

Something grey. Not the same as out here in the cold. It was a lighter grey. It was also moving. I tried squinting to see if it helped me make it out in the mirror or in the room itself but all it did was make my head hurt.

Then I saw it again, in a different mirror this time. A

graceful, fluid movement that lasted longer than the flash I had seen the first time, but by the time I had focussed properly, it was gone again.

I waited a few more seconds and it was long enough for the flash of light grey to reveal itself to me in the mirror closest to the large double doors that appeared to be the entrance to the ballroom at the end opposite the fire.

It was a person. Who or what they looked like, I couldn't say. But they were dancing. No, he was dancing. A man. He was spinning and leaping gracefully. He was there, but indistinct, like the double reflection in the rear-view mirror, or a poorly made mirror.

And in another moment, he was gone. He didn't return. I stood waiting but it was pointless. No one entered the room either.

It was time to get moving again. The chill was starting to bite through my jacket. I turned back to the pavement and continued walking past the next two windows.

When I passed the third, I noticed the glow had gone.

Once again, I stopped and looked inside.

Grime was crusted thick on the windows and it was hard to see inside this time. What I could make out was a large room. The same large room I had just been looking at was now without light. The fire had been extinguished and two of the three chandeliers lay shattered on the now pockmarked and buckled flooring.

Just to double-check my own sanity I backtracked to the previous windows only to find they offered me the same dilapidated vision I had seen in that last window.

Someone, or something, was screwing with my mind.

Or maybe it was just me. I couldn't tell. All I could say is that I had, for some stupid reason, been very quick to jump at this chance to save the world.

Oh, I could use the argument, what choice did I have? It wasn't as if I could get back home without Kath agreeing to it.

But why had I been so ready to help? Here's me, a

struggling actor in London; one of a million, and I'm helping little girls in vehicle accidents. Not to mention the fact I am hunting down a pan-dimensional being that had tried to kill me on numerous occasions several years ago.

Am I insane? Does this little hallucination I just had prove that?

No.

Was someone playing with my head?

Possibly.

I thought I was someone who had begun to accept his lot in life. Resign myself to the uphill struggle and not getting anywhere. So where did this whole burst of insightful energy come from?

And what was the point of showing me the ballroom in the first place? Was it portentous? Was it an omen? Or was it simply a freaky aspect of this new world? People had powers here, maybe buildings did too.

Now that sounded crazy.

Either way, I was cold and wanted to get to the hospital.

I resumed my walking and picked up the pace. I wanted to get to the hospital so I could get warm again more than anything else. But if I can learn something from little Becca, if she was indeed there and unhurt, then maybe I'll be one step closer to getting home.

It wasn't as if the strange image I had just witnessed, or hallucination, or whatever you wanted to call it, had completely left my mind. I just didn't want to dwell on it. Who knows, it might even be a side effect of dimension-hopping. I had seen a fair share of those in my time.

Not having seen the hospital before, I couldn't really have guessed if it had altered much from my reality. However, thanks to the odd spires and towers, I had a feeling it wasn't quite the sort of architecture the City of London circa my dimension would actually go for.

The building itself was larger than most of those around it, approximately four stories high. The towers went up an extra two or three while a central clock tower rose four more. That tower was directly over the main hospital entrance. I crossed the emergency drive that led to the quick unloading of ambulances and headed straight for the glowing doors at the front.

Thankfully, my mind was already wary about this place so I quickly picked up the fact that the doors wouldn't be automated. Of course, it took a very narrow miss to figure it out. They looked as though they could have been for the lack of handles. I pushed on one of the glass doors and went inside.

Oh, the warmth emanating from whatever heating system they had was a blessing. It permeated my hands, my face and eventually through the chilled fabric of my clothes.

The reception area was much like any other hospital I had seen. A slight amount of cheap decoration to try and make it almost welcoming and not too clinical. The main colours were navy blue and a sickly beige. On one side of the room was the waiting area where four people, all dressed in dark colours, sat reading magazines or newspapers. The opposite end was a small atrium-type area with a bright array of trees that looked too plastic to be real.

I let a final shudder of cold run through my body before I headed toward the reception.

The nurse behind the desk was busy talking to a security guard about some hospital problem or another.

I waited my turn. I don't like drawing too much attention to myself in the first place and after the funny looks I received from the car crash crowd, I thought it best to revert to my usual behaviours.

Besides, it gave me time to note the uniform she was wearing. As far as I was aware, in London hospitals scrubs are usually blue or pink and the admin workers were a little less formal. This woman was wearing a very dark blue uniform. It was also unlike the loose-fitting garments I had seen on Holby City and other television shows in England.

It was more angular; a flap of material ran from just under her right shoulder down to the centre of the bottom of her garment. Almost a military look from Star Trek or something. The sleeves fell short of her wrists by a couple of inches. The usual paraphernalia was present though. A watch, a name badge that read "Cora" and a few pens in a breast pocket.

She had noticed me already but continued her conversation a moment more before turning her attention back, "Yes?"

I was about to say, "Good evening," but I actually had no idea if that was the case or not, nor if anyone actually knew the difference. Play it cool and simple.

"Hi, I'm here to see a patient. She was brought in not long ago, I believe."

The nurse picked up a clipboard. No computer. Odd. "Name?"

"Rebecca. Rebecca Turpin."

I could see she was about to ask that universally known hospital question about my relationship with the patient, but I jumped the gun, "I'm her uncle."

She eyed me up and down for a moment, her gaze falling on my orange jumper and remaining there for an abnormally long time. Finally, allowing me to breathe easy again as I had been holding my breath while she watched me, she checked her clipboard.

"Room 2 oh 4. Paediatric wing. Head down that corridor," she indicated one of two that led from this room, "take the elevator to the second floor. Follow the green line on the floor until you reach the ward nursing station."

I thanked the nurse and headed toward the corridor. They at least had elevators. Transporting patients must have been difficult without them.

One thing I did notice was the absence of nice pictures or paintings. In hospitals where I am from – Perth, Australia – the hospitals were always amateur art galleries.

A sweeping vista here, a second-rate seascape there as well as the odd flower.

Here, the walls were bare. Maybe that was an altogether English thing. I had been lucky enough not to need a hospital so far, but I had heard some horror stories about their conditions from friends. My own doctor told me if I was to get sick, go back to Australia.

I did as I was instructed and made it to the nursing station on the second floor.

It was much like Liverpool Street station here with the clinical white walls, though the coloured stripe on the ground and the beech nursing counter helped break the starkness of it all.

The nurse behind the desk, a man, was in much the same uniform. He too seemed oddly distracted by my jumper.

Indicating the room I was to go into, his brow furrowed with a look of what could have been disdain or remorse.

I had expected a private room. To see little Becca propped up on a bed eating hospital food or watching television.

Instead, the room held five other beds, all of which were occupied. And no one was eating or watching television. I had to look carefully at the two girls in the room to see which one was Becca. I was dreading actually introducing myself. The chances were she would still be in shock or deeply upset by her father's death. The problem was all of the children looked rather mopey.

I had been hovering by the door for a few moments when I heard a man clear his throat behind me.

"Excuse me," a German accent but good English.

I stepped aside and made room. The man was dressed in plain clothes, but they were still unlike the usual dress I had seen in the general population. His top was a singlet. Green and brown horizontal stripes allowed for some colour. It was an interesting choice as he had a fair amount of dark chest hair poking over the neckline. Below that, however, he had the build of an athlete. Basically a body I would kill for instead of my skinny, though nicely toned shape.

His pants were black corduroy, however, they were an odd design. Two zips were on the front, one on either side of his groin. The legs flared slightly and they looked well worn. Under that he wore Mandals. Sandals for men.

The man would have been just over thirty. Handsome with a long face. He smiled at me, perfect teeth shining through the beginnings of a goatee and moustache combination. His eyes were brown but sat behind a pair of glasses.

"Thank you," he said as he passed.

With those two words, the atmosphere in the room changed completely.

Four of the children called out, "Andy!" and readjusted their beds so they were sitting up properly. Their faces were beaming with happiness to see the man and he was beaming right back at them saying hello to each one by name.

That made it easier to identify Becca. She was one of the two children not smiling. Instead, she looked confusedly at the man before looking over at me. Then a glint of recognition filled her eyes. Or were they tears?

I nodded hello and mouthed the words, but nothing came out of my mouth.

She smiled very tightly in response. She had recognised me.

Figuring the time was right to move, I approached her bed. It was at the far end of the room, nearest a window that had curtains drawn. The bed opposite had a young boy with a bandage around his head who was still confused by what was going on.

Andy was hugging the four other children one by one, being gentle with one or two of them.

When I reached Becca's bed, I had found my voice, "Hi, Becca. Do you remember me?"

She nodded, still not speaking.

"Are you feeling better?"

Her eyes dropped slightly.

Come on, I said to myself. Try and cheer her up a bit. I'm an actor, I should be able to do that, right? Besides, this other man, Andy, was doing a good job of it with the other children.

"Have you tried the food yet? Be wary of hospital food," I pulled a weird face, but she didn't respond.

"So we have two new arrivals, eh?"

I stopped and looked over to Andy who was holding centre stage. Even the boy opposite was looking at him in awe.

"And what might your names be?" He had such a way about him. A lightness that made you forget you were in a hospital, but maybe in a children's theatre performance instead.

"Lewis," came the boy's shaky voice.

"Lewis? Welcome, Lewis. Come on everyone, Crystal, Bradley. Give him a big welcome."

The four children chirped up with a uniform, "Welcome, Lewis," which brought an unsteady smile to the lad's face.

"And, if you don't mind me interrupting?"

I shook my head, "Not at all."

He winked at me before turning his attention to Becca, "And your name, young Princess?"

Becca didn't respond.

Andy took it in his stride and moved a little closer, "Come now, we're all friends here. How can we talk to you if we don't know your name?"

She looked up at him, still unsmiling, "Becca."

It was the first word I had heard her speak so far in the hospital.

"What do we say, everyone?"

The whole room, even Lewis, chimed in, "Welcome Becca!"

Did this man know what she had been through? He was obviously some sort of mascot or entertainment for the kids. Voluntarily or employed by the hospital, I don't know. He wouldn't be allowed in otherwise and the kids obviously knew him, which meant he was a regular. And no child was more important than the other.

I could understand that. I had nieces and nephews of my own and tried to treat them all equally. Of course, it was still hard not to have your favourites, except on those days they decided to be in a bad mood. But we all have those days.

I could tell Andy already assumed he had his work cut out for him when it came to the newcomers. Lewis, although he had smiled, had reverted to his quiet demeanour whereas Becca hadn't raised a smile.

"Well, I had heard we would have some new arrivals today so I brought along something special for you all."

He reached into a paper bag I hadn't actually noticed when he had come in and, like a sprinkler, launched small balls of fluff at each one of the children. Everyone caught theirs, even Becca. They were stuffed toys, just under a foot tall and of different animals. The kids in the room, regardless of what age they were, all beamed, apart from, of course, the young girl I needed to speak to.

While the other patients compared and played, Andy came over to me and regarded the young girl who stared mournfully at her present.

He leaned closer and whispered, his accent more than just a little obvious, "Forgive me for asking, but how do you know Becca?"

No point in lying. For one, the girl was right there to contradict me.

"I was at the scene of the crash. I spoke to her while she was still in the car," they say honesty is a virtue.

His gaze turned to me and I regarded him. He looked slightly impressed, "You did? That's something I haven't heard of for a long time."

I bobbed my head in a sort of shrug, "I wanted to see if she was ok. Plus I need to ask her some questions."

The expression changed, dropped, "Are you police?"

"Oh, no. But she said something a little strange. I was hoping if I could find out what she meant, then the doctors might be able to care for her a little better."

Ok, that was a lie. But in its own way, it was true. It was also enough for Andy to nod and say, "Sounds like a good idea. Would you like some help?"

"Love some."

I let Andy approach her first. He was on the side of the bed closest to the door, the side which she was tending to favour as she held the toy. I moved to the other side, watching as Andy leaned in closer and peaked over the top of the grey and white elephant whose trunk was being squashed into its face by her finger.

"Does he have a name, yet?"

Her eyes didn't move from the toy so he tried again, "Mind if I give him one?"

She shrugged.

"All right," he turned the elephant's head, "With a face like that, I think he looks like a Heimlich."

"That's not a name."

One of his thick eyebrows raised, "Really? My grandfather would disagree. So what do you suggest?"

"Edgar."

A look of consideration before he spoke, "Edgar? Are you sure?"

"Yes. Edgar. I'm calling him Edgar."

"Edgar it is. Well, hello Edgar, My name is Andy. And this is," he indicated to me.

"Scott. My name is Scott," I stammered, caught off guard. I never was good at improvisation. Then again, it was only my name he had asked for.

"Say hello to Edgar, Scott."

I felt like an idiot, but I knew it was for Becca.

When did I stop being human? If it were my own niece in that bed, I wouldn't have hesitated. Time to lose the chip on my shoulder and get into the swing of things.

"Hey there, Edgar. I think it's an excellent name, Becca.

Better than Heimlich," I smiled.

She looked over to me and then proudly at Andy.

"Okay, okay. You're right. Edgar is a much better name. So, Becca, Scott tells me you've met before."

Her expression threatened to return to the one she had been clutching to since I entered the room. I had to act quickly, "She was tremendously brave. A real champion. What did I say? Almost a teenager."

This got the smile, "Nuh-uh."

"Sure you are. You were so strong. And you're being so strong now too. Are you sure you're not a young-looking sixteen-year-old?"

She giggled but hid it behind Edgar.

Andy smiled at me encouragingly.

"Seems like you've got a good new friend here, Edgar. You've got nothing to worry about. Any of those other animals give you a hard time for having a big nose, she's going to wallop them on the head. Wish I had someone like her looking after me. My nose is almost as big."

So I was exaggerating about my nose, but only a little. She was loving it. I find self-deprecating is a huge laugh for children when adults do it.

"Now, Becca, I need you to be a bit stronger for me. Can you do that?"

I could tell by her eyes that she was a little unsure, but she nodded all the same. This was cruel, but I needed to find out everything I could before this demon attacked someone else.

"You told me of an angel you saw. Do you remember that?"

"Yes."

"Can you tell me anything about it?"

She thought for a while before answering, "I've seen it before."

This surprised me somewhat, "You have? Where?"

"I should have known he would come back for Daddy. He visited Daddy a few weeks ago. I didn't see much of him then, either. But I know it was the same angel. The wings. Big and grey, like a bat I saw in a school book. I thought angels were supposed to have feathers."

That last statement was more of a question and I didn't want to discourage her, "Angels come in many different shapes and sizes."

"He was the Angel of Death."

Andy spoke before me, "Why do you say that?"

"Because he took my Daddy away. And that other man, too. The one who got hit by our car."

"He took your Daddy?"

She nodded and was starting to retreat behind Edgar again. We would have to end this soon, "I saw him just before we crashed. He did something to my Daddy. I don't know what but before I saw the angel, Daddy was awake. Then he was asleep. And we crashed."

"We won't bother you much longer, Becca. But I have one more question for you. Is there anything more you can tell me about the Angel itself?"

She shook her head, "Only what I said before. He was big and grey with big wings."

There was a gasp from the other side of the room. I couldn't help but look.

The other new arrival, Lewis, was staring at Becca like she was some sort of monster. His eyes and mouth were all wide with horror.

I looked at Andy, unsure whether the boy was having a seizure or if something else was happening and the German looked just as unsure. With a quick head motion, he indicated I should go talk to him while he kept an eye on Becca who was unsettled by the way the boy was looking at her.

I hurried across the room to Lewis.

"What is it?"

The boy's big eyes turned to me, still wide but now welling with tears.

"I saw it, too. But it wasn't an angel."

LITTLE GIRL LOST

Amy Thompson was only twelve, but she was a genius. With numbers, anyway. That put her on the outside of the social groups at school. But that didn't bother her. She had made a good friend in Lewis.

He was scrawny, plain-looking and very bookish which also put him on the outside. The thing was that he kept her company and made her laugh. Neither child judged the other.

They were walking quickly, as his mother had told them to, to the off licence on the corner. Lewis had just given her an equation to solve. She knew he had just made it up on the top of his head and wouldn't know the answer, but she giggled at his efforts. That's what made him funny. He was always trying to challenge her despite his own inadequacies. Being bookish didn't mean he was particularly bright.

"Five million, seventy-five thousand and eighty-four," she told him the answer.

He looked at her almost suspiciously. He had gotten over the shock of her getting the answers long ago, even when he had a calculator to help him. It was more for show these days, "I'm not sure you're right."

She smiled at him, "Oh really?"

"Yes," his façade was beginning to break down into a smirk, "I think you forgot to carry the three."

"Lewis, there was no three to carry."

He laughed, "Fine. But I'm going to be buying my sweets first," with that he started to run toward the shop, now only a few metres away.

Now Amy could have beaten him if she had wanted, but she couldn't let him feel second best all the time. That wasn't what friends did for each other. So she kept her own speed down to let him win. His distinctive run, a side effect of his Spastic Diplegia, meant he knew all too well what she was doing, but he didn't care.

Lewis entered the shop first but held the door open for Amy – ever the gentleman. She thanked him and headed to the counter. Lewis stood slightly behind her eyeing the sweets in the glass cabinet.

"Can I help you?" The shopkeeper was Indian but with an English accent. He smiled down at the children. He didn't know their names, but they had been in often enough to know them by sight.

Amy stood back and tried to push Lewis forward. He stood his ground and shook his head.

"But you won. You should order first."

"Ladies first."

She gave a mock scoff, "You are so sexist, Lewis!"

That didn't stop her from ordering first, though.

She purchased a mix of sour worms, liquorice all-sorts and jelly fruits adding up to five pounds. They were going to last for a bit. She handed over her money and moved aside for Lewis.

"I'll wait for you outside," she called and looked into her bag. She liked this store because they still allowed you to pick and mix your own. So many stores now only had pre-packed bags of the same sweets. You needed more variety.

Amy wasn't sure if Lewis had heard, but she stepped outside anyway. He wouldn't be long.

Lewis took a bit longer than even he had expected. He had heard what Amy had ordered and didn't want to get exactly the same. So he had to rethink his choice after she had gone, "I'll have a few gummi bears, some chocolate butt-,"

Amy's scream burst through the air like a sports whistle.

Lewis straightened immediately and began rushing for the door. The shopkeeper, also concerned, navigated his way around his counter so he could see what was happening.

Lewis pulled the door open and his eyes widened even further in terror.

Amy was being held up by a demon. She was flailing and kicking at him, but having no impact at all as he calmly held her up with his left hand around her throat.

The monster was huge. It wore a mass of shredded black and red material. Its arms, wings and horrible head were the only part of it Lewis could see properly.

He didn't want to see it. But he didn't want Amy to be hurt either. Despite his disability and his diminutive size, Lewis launched himself at the creature and started punching and kicking as best he could, screaming for it to let Amy go.

The monster merely looked down at him and kicked him aside. Lewis went flying and cracked his head against the wall of the off licence.

His vision swam as he fought to stay awake. He was only barely conscious when he thought he saw the monster reach into Amy and take something from inside her.

As Amy fell, Lewis found his mind wandering, going sleepy. The colours of Amy's sweets, now spread over the pavement in front of him danced as his own slipped further away until he lost consciousness.

A LITTLE RAY OF LIGHT

I was horrified. How could anything be so evil? She had only been a little girl.

Lewis, who had broken down into a fresh bout of crying, had held up well while he retold the story.

Andy had come over to listen. Thankfully, in his nervousness and fear, kept his voice down so the other children couldn't hear. They were blissfully playing with their toys.

Andy was looking at me wide-eyed and amazed.

"Thank you for being so brave, Lewis."

"I tried to stop him."

I shook my head and laid what I hoped was a reassuring hand on his, "There was nothing you could have done. You can't blame yourself."

The boy didn't look altogether convinced.

"Just one last thing. Where did this take place?"

"On the corner of Roman and Globe Streets, near my school."

I didn't know where that was, but I'd have to check my 'AtoZ' to find out.

"Thank you, again, Lewis. You've been a tremendous help. And I mean it. He was a monster and, even if you couldn't help Amy, I know you were very brave for trying. I'm sure where she is now, she knows it too."

He put his hand on mine this time and looked at me, pleading with his eyes, "Are you going to stop it? The demon?"

I hesitated. Maybe a little too long, I don't know, but I still found myself saying, "I'll do my best."

I nodded my goodbye to Andy and headed back out to the Nurse's station.

Once out of the room I took a deep breath. It wasn't as if the air in the room was stale or anything, I just needed to get grounded after hearing Lewis' story. It was the lowest of the low.

I reached into my satchel and pulled out my map book and searched the index for the roads he had told me. It didn't take me long to find them on the map.

"Are you with the police or something?"

It was Andy.

I turned to face him and closed the book, leaving my finger inside to mark the page.

"No."

I could tell by the expression on his face he was doubting my ability to deal with the situation, "Then what do you plan to do?"

The simple answer to that was, "Anything I can. Someone has to stop him and no one seems to be doing anything about it."

Andy looked back into the room and then back at me, "I have heard other stories, much like Lewis'. Only from doctors and nurses here, but they sound a lot like this."

"I'd love to hear them. Well, not love to, but they might help."

"Coffee?"

Eww, "I don't drink it. Tea?"

"Either way. There is a canteen downstairs."

We walked to the lift, on the way I found out he was employed by the hospital on a part-time basis to entertain the children. It was a way of earning extra money while he followed his hobby. He had moved to England four years ago.

"How long has this," how do I put it, "days of nights been going on?"

"About three years," the doors to the lift closed when his brow furrowed, "You didn't know?"

"I've only recently arrived?"

A note of hope was tinged in his voice, "You mean you got through from outside?"

"In a manner of speaking, I guess you could say that."

"But how? No one has been able to get in or out for over a year now."

I held my hand up to calm him down, "It's not what you think. I came from England. Just not the one you know."

I'd lost him. Heck, if it had been me, I would have lost myself.

The doors opened and I followed him through the waiting room and into a fairly large canteen with several tables occupied by doctors, nurses or visitors.

We waited briefly in line at the counter to get a tea, which I knew would taste nothing like Kath's. Any more of that stuff and I was sure to be addicted.

I found a table as Andy greeted a colleague or two. I aimed for one apart from the occupied ones so we could talk openly. I put the AtoZ beside my cup and waited for Andy to take a seat.

"Andy? You sound German. Is Andy a common name in Germany?"

He smiled a toothy smile, "No. My name is Andreas," the accent highlighted the last two syllables sweetly, "It is shortened over here. I don't mind either way."

"So, three years? Did you try moving home?"

"I couldn't afford it. I had come over here to find some work. Then all of this happened and I found myself trapped. Many people left and with them, the jobs."

"Sorry to hear that. Do you know what caused it all?"

He shook his head, "No one does. It didn't happen straight away. It wasn't as if the sun went down one day and didn't come up again. It simply got weaker. Scientists were at first worried that the sun was dying, but they soon worked out there was nothing wrong with it. That didn't stop it from getting darker. Or colder. After a year, it was like it was just after sunset. I think you call it dusk. After another six months, it was night all the time. Even now, it is darker than it used to be. We used to be able to see the stars so clearly. I guess it was our only consolation. Now, even those are going," he stopped and I didn't know what to say. He spoke again, "Even the street lights are getting dimmer."

"Something has to be causing it."

"That is what everyone said. They fought against the scientists and the government. There was panic. Now, we are, what's the word, resigned to it, like we are simply waiting for this darkness to consume us. And you know what?"

"What?"

"I think it will," I didn't need to look at Andy to know he meant it.

I took a sip of my tea and nearly gagged. It was absolutely nothing like what Kath had made.

Managing to swallow, I felt it necessary to change tact, "So, you say you heard some stories?"

"Yes," he hadn't touched his drink, "Over the last five weeks, we have had eleven bodies brought in. Nothing unusual, except in the way they have died. Every one of them has had their heart ripped out. We have reported it to the police and they have taken notes, but nothing has been done. Not only that. We had a doctor transfer from a hospital near Brixton and he said they had similar murders a few months back that lasted for two months then stopped altogether."

He's been getting around then. Changing from one locale to another.

"And there is no suspect? No one the police have put a warning out for?"

Andy shook his head, looking down into his drink. He shrugged his shoulders as he spoke, "A lot of people have chosen to sit back and wait for the dark. We all see it coming."

I couldn't blame them. If the world looked like it was about to end, why wouldn't you? "But you don't. Why?"

He looked at me, his eyes defiant, strong, "I choose life. People may suffer. Die, even. But they will always need help, even if it is only to stay positive or happy. Yes, we may be nearing the end, but we can do with that time what we wish. Waste it or use it to the best of our abilities," He paused for a moment and although, when he spoke again, it lacked the force he had started with, it had not lost its meaning or its intensity.

"I choose life."

Life indeed. I wish I had this man's outlook. I used to, I think. Back when I first crossed between worlds. At least by the end of it, I had. Or had I? I had willingly tried to sacrifice myself if it meant one egomaniacal being would lose its grip on my own world.

But I had still chosen life. If not for myself, then for all the people back home. I would die so they could live; not that anyone ever thanked me for it, or knew about it for that matter.

I guess that was what Andy was doing too. Sacrificing himself in a less literal way so that the children upstairs could have moments of happiness before the end.

"I think I do too."

Andy smiled, it was slightly crooked but somehow suited his face, which in itself was a little skewered as if an artist had decided to experiment on a model made of clay. What if the nose looked slightly broken, or the mouth a little out of line? Nothing major, just that touch so it doesn't quite fit right.

It fit just fine from where I was sitting.

I wasn't going to finish the drink, so I pushed it further aside and leaned back in the chair, "Have you any idea where to start looking?"

He shook his head, "No. Whoever it is is close, but too distant in himself to get hold of," a thought occurred to him, "You mean to look for him?"

"Someone has to. I'm probably not the most qualified," nor the most enthusiastic, I could have added, "If I don't, who will? There has to be a way to stop him before all of this goes too far."

"I like your passion. It is encouraging. Though I think

what you search for may be more than you can handle. Grey angels. Demons with wings. None of it sounds real, or if it is, certainly not something a man alone can face."

"I have faced much worse," hadn't I?

He seemed impressed, "I wish you luck then. I wish it to all of us."

Amen to that, I thought, and I wasn't even religious, "I had better go. See if I can find any more leads, hopefully no more victims."

Andy put out his hand and I shook it, "It was nice meeting you. I really do hope you succeed in your," he struggled for the word, "mission."

"Thanks," I stood up, "and thanks for the chat. Hope to see you in brighter times."

Picking up my 'AtoZ' I left the cafeteria and made my way back toward the reception area. Deciding to take a quick glance over my shoulder, Andy was still watching me, that crooked smile on his face, kind of hopeful, not quite doubting. I wouldn't have blamed him if he took me for a lunatic, but something in his expression helped me believe he had more faith in me. Someone had to.

ON THE ROAD AND IN THE SH…

Outside, nothing had changed. It was as if this world was one gigantic cliché. A doomed and dimming world full of monsters. Metaphorical as well as physical perhaps?

Or was I just being stupid?

Probably.

I think the main point I am being stupid on is thinking I had a chance. I pulled my jacket tight around me and thought about what had just happened.

I don't mean the conversation I had just had. Well, it had something to do with that, but the complete change of my attitude as I stepped outside. Inside I felt like I had someone believing in me, outside, that thought was instantaneously gone.

I need a Coke. I should have checked to see if the cafeteria sold them. Certainly would have been better than their tea.

Then I remembered, I had one in my satchel. I flipped open the flap and removed a partially drunk bottle and took a swig, using it to wash away the taste of the tea. Thankfully, in this weather, the Coke would stay cold. There was one good thing about moving to England – either my own or this gloomy one. It was like a perpetual refrigerator outside. The fact I'd been running earlier and the time I'd let it settle meant it was completely flat.

I started toward my new destination, the corner store.

My main problem was I really had no idea how to tackle this. I had done journalism as a minor at university. Well, it had actually been part of my creative writing, but it should have given me the investigative skills to go on with this. Unfortunately, that was all nearly a decade ago. And what with the way my life had been playing out, it may as well have been a lifetime.

Oh for a muddy pond filled with talking frogs that jumped out of paintings. Illogical I can deal with. This? Frankly, it just scared me.

I was never a fan of the dark. Now monsters ripping out people's hearts? Every kid's worst nightmare.

Maybe not quite, but almost. I dreamt of people turning into skeletons when I was a kid. They would be perfectly normal people walking out of a supermarket that was actually my house but we know how dreams can be weird. Anyway, these people would walk behind a bush and emerge as skeletons on the other side. As a child, it scared me awake. This was a bit more realistic than that. And far more gruesome.

Or is it?

The streets were still empty. Rubbish and people both vanished.

It didn't take me long to get to the deli. It was cordoned off by police tape. A mishmash of yellow paint marks were on the floor around a discoloured portion of the pavement. That had to be where the girl had fallen.

Here, not even a car went by. I stopped at the corner by the tape and felt a shiver down my spine. See what I mean about clichés? I felt like I was being watched. And I was. Several curtains quickly dropped into position and drifted back and forth, as only the curtains of curious neighbours are likely to, as I looked up at the surrounding buildings.

Once I was sure I had scared off the peeping toms, I ducked under the tape and headed toward the deli door feeling unnervingly like an old Private Investigator from some American cheese flick. All I needed was an accented voice-over and some cheap piano or saxophone music.

I knocked on the door only to find it was off the latch. It squealed open an inch or two under the light pressure of my knocks.

"Hello?"

There was a little light inside.

What I would give for a gun and a police badge at this moment.

I pushed the door open further, cautiously, "Hello? Open for business?"

I knew they weren't but maybe they would treat me nicely if they thought I was a customer.

There was a noise from down the back of the deli, or off-licence as they are known over here. With the light as it was, I could see exactly what had been described to me. The counter with sweets inside, shop shelves. Well, you would find shop shelves in any store, wouldn't you?

"Excuse me?"

A voice came out of the gloom at the back of the room, "Sorry, we're closed."

A woman. Maybe the man from the boy's description was too upset by the whole situation and was hidden away. I wouldn't blame him. I don't know if I could handle seeing what he did.

"I thought so. I'm here about what happened earlier. I want to help."

In the dim light, I could see a lady's face peer around one of the rows of shelving. She looked extremely pale. She would have been no older than forty, but her face lacked the lines of age. It was the look in her eyes that helped me guess her age. Then again, maybe those were the eyes of a shopkeeper.

"The police have already been. We told them we don't need a psychiatrist."

For post-traumatic stress counselling, I guess.

"I'm not a psychiatrist," I held up my hands, showing they were empty and hoping it might help keep her placated, "When I say I want to help, I mean I want to get to the bottom of this. Put a stop to it once and for all."

Her brow furrowed as she considered me and what I had just said, "You? What do you think you can do?"

"Just what I was thinking," I muttered under my breath.

Shrugging, I spoke up, "I don't rightly know. But it seems that someone has to start sometime or this is just going to keep going. And I figured here is as good a place to start."

Once more she seemed to consider what I had said. Then, very slowly, she came out from behind the shelves. In her hands, which I could not see where she had been standing, she held a rather sturdy-looking broom. A good weapon of defence if she had needed it. Perhaps locking the door would have been better, though.

"What's your name?"

I told her.

"My husband's the best one to talk to. But he really isn't up to it right now."

Nodding, I said, "I can understand that. Maybe if I could ask you a few questions and perhaps come by and see him another time when he is feeling better."

"Yes. That sounds like a good idea."

She didn't come any closer. Nor did she offer her name. I didn't need it and I didn't want to ask.

"Did you see any of what happened?"

A shake of her head, her eyes closed momentarily as if she were wiping an image from her mind, "No. But my husband won't stop talking about it. I see it in my own mind well enough," she looked back at me, "The police taped off the road. They came in here to question us. I still haven't looked outside."

"Is that why the door is unlocked?"

"Yes," her voice trembled a little, "I couldn't bring myself to look out there. We knew her. She came in regularly with her friend. She was always so sweet. Such a rare thing these days. A nice child customer. Normally it's swearing this and swearing that. But she always said please and thank you. And would let that poor disabled boy hang around with her. How must he feel? Why would anything want to do that to such a child?"

I felt my eyebrow cock involuntarily, "That's what evil

does. Have you heard of any other incidents?"

Another shake of her head, "Not around here. I know there were some attacks very similar to this elsewhere in London. They moved around. I just thought it was some sort of gang war. Or perhaps some unrest because of the sky. But you can't think like that. Not anymore. We aren't invincible. We used to think we were. Before the war, I'm sure that's how everyone felt. Even the soldiers going off to fight. My mother told me of how she survived the bombings of London in shelters, and how that changed how everyone felt. No longer safe, but part of a greater evil.

"That's what is happening here. Oh, it is nothing like the War. But it is evil and no one is immune to it. Not the innocent, not the apathetic. Not you. Not me."

Wow. She had either been thinking about this a lot or she had a knack for hitting the nail on the head. I couldn't argue with her. One, because she would probably kick me out if I did, and, two, because she was right. I thought a change of tact might be better.

"Do you know what caused the problem with the sky?"

These sorts of questions were to find out how much the general population knew. It was all well and good to say that a small faction of people were willing to stand up and fight against this evil being, but how much do the people know?

She didn't even raise an eyelid that I didn't know myself. She was in the flow of things.

"It was gradual. Around the time the killings began, I think. At first, it was reported as a knife crime. A serial killer or something. Then a group like the Mafia with a particular way of killing people. Are they connected?"

She looked at me with wide questioning eyes.

They don't know. And I don't know. Why they are connected? Why is the sun dimming? What has it got to do with the murders? Surely if One is taking people's hearts it is to feed. To get energy. But if he is somehow sucking the energy and heat from the Earth as well, why did he need to do both?

Or is one a means to the other? Does killing and consuming the hearts of these people heighten his powers, allowing him to kill this Earth by starving it of light and life?

Maybe in this world, this Earth and its people are somehow connected. The universe gives life in my world, but maybe it takes from life in this one. If life is dimming, then so too is the universe.

Where am I pulling this stuff from? I was never a philosophical student for goodness' sake. I'm a lot more mature than I was the first time I crossed dimensions. Back then all I could do was whine and moan. Though it was a lot more of being chased by giant magpies, frogs and other creatures. Here, at least, I was able to investigate without too much interference.

Then again, I had a lot more help from Narelle and Bob back then.

The shop lady was still staring at me. Oops. She had asked me a question and I'd just gone off daydreaming. How much time had passed?

"I don't know. I really don't. But it certainly seems like there is a connection of some sort. It's still getting worse?"

"Oh yes. My friend Joe, she's into stargazing. She only said the other day that she couldn't see a couple more. They had simply gone out, she said. She uses a telescope and all," the lady looked at me again, "You're not from around here, are you?"

It was the accent, obviously, or maybe she had picked up on the fact I hadn't a clue what was going on.

"Australian. Moved here a while back and can't shake the accent."

"Before everything was closed off, you mean?"

I think that's what I mean. I must do. I don't know.

"Yes," I blundered, "Before it was closed off."

I didn't risk asking any more about that, because as an

immigrant I was bound to have checked into that the first instance it happened. I would have to find someone else. Maybe Andy if I saw him again.

"I really want to thank you for your help."

She shrugged, "What can I say? If you think you can help us, it would be nice to think I played a part in it somehow. If you have any more questions, please feel free to come back. I will keep an ear out and see if I can remember anything more."

I nodded gravely, not intentionally, but I know that that was how it would have appeared, "I appreciate that..."

"Sylvia."

I smiled, "Sylvia, thanks," I raised my hand in a still wave as I left the shop. She followed, still at a distance behind me and I could feel her eyes on me as I continued walking away. Then there was a click followed by the snap of a lock as she shut shop.

Well, it wasn't the most informative, but it was something to try and go on. It had me thinking anyway. Was the whole world freezing? Was someone on the outside trying to help and did they have the faintest idea that it was a creature from another world?

Surely in a world with people with weird abilities, someone must be able to do something. Or had One become that powerful?

As I walked, I felt the tingle of being watched and spotted a few curtains falling, having been let go by a timid voyeur. But it felt more than that. Something a little off.

It wasn't until I heard what could have been footsteps that I began to worry. I turned casually as I walked back toward the road the Hospital was on to see if I could see who was behind me.

The footpath was empty, the ghostly light from the dim streetlamps barely touching the grey pavement. It seemed that the whole world had gone to sleep. Admittedly, I prefer London like this. The normal hustle and bustle was, at times, ridiculous. Trying to get from one end of a street to the other was always a struggle, sometimes a battle. Pushing past, avoiding people who simply walk out of shops in front of you without looking or even caring if they end up in your way. Even worse, they simply stop once they have left the shop and you almost end up walking straight into them.

This quiet, mysterious London was, in a morbid fantasy sort of way, a nice change. You could hear the night, the world as it was. No rumbles of cars, no shouting or being rude. Only those damn footsteps.

I snuck another look as I was about to round the corner and turn away from the Hospital and toward Kath's house. As I did, I saw the fading remnants of a bright green glow. Whether it had been a flash or a neon light going out, it was still brighter than any other light I had seen on the street since arriving in this dreary world.

The footsteps stopped.

I hesitated at the corner. Do I go back and investigate or go to safety?

In my last reality jump, I would have gone headfirst into the fray, but this time was different. The illogical world Bob and Narelle came from was almost cartoon-like, death was a distant thought. In this film-noir-style world, things were very different. Death could be lurking behind any corner.

I shivered at the thought, and the cold. Hoisting my bag over my shoulder, I moved around the corner and kept moving. I would leave it for tonight.

Or would I?

Damn it!

I stopped and turned back. It was a possible lead, or it was nothing at all. Why be so stupid about it? Chances were it was nothing.

I felt my teeth grinding at my indecision. I was wasting time. I wanted to go home, didn't I? So the sooner it was sorted, the better.

My feet made the choice for me. I found myself back

around the corner heading toward where I had seen the glow. It was still there, but fainter than before, pulsing as if it symbolised the heartbeat of some giant glow worm. Not that I had ever seen a glow-worm.

Almost at the next corner, just around from the strange ebbing glow, I hesitated. I couldn't hear anything. No footsteps, no talking. All was silent. I stood with my back against the wall and took a deep breath and took my step.

The instant I was in view of the source of the light, it vanished. The cold darkness took hold once more. But this was more complete than what I had started to get used to. The street was enshrouded in a pitch-black shadow.

It reached from one side of the narrow street to the other and almost reached above the double-story townhouses that surrounded it. I couldn't see how far it stretched back, but it was approximately ten metres from where I stood.

Not what I had been expecting. I tried to see if it was just my eyes playing tricks by blinking a few times, but that had no effect. What I did notice, however, was something moving inside the shadow. I don't quite know how I figured this, considering how impossibly dark it was. It was as if someone had taken a massive piece of clean slate and stuck it in the middle of London. Yet, I was certain something was inside.

I took a step forward and the mass seemed to heave and swirl. I blinked again and as my eyes were shutting, I could make out a tall figure turning sharply within. It wasn't human and it was very tall. And it had seen me. I stopped moving, but I had a feeling it was too late for that.

Wrong move, I figured. I should have kept walking.

As I was about to move obackwards and follow my first instinct, two men stepped out of the shadow. It was as if they had simply stepped through some sort of doorway.

They didn't say anything. They didn't have to. They were glaring at me as if I were some sort of rodent that had to be squashed. Not swept outside with a broom, not to lay poisonous bait to get rid of quietly and peacefully but to step on and crush into a horrible bloody pulp. And these two looked the sort of men to do just that.

Dressed in black, one with a beanie, the other had a close-shaven head and both looked like they had been in several fights. Healed scars on their faces, a broken nose, they were enough to tell me that despite my years-old Tae Kwon Do training, I was no match for these fellows.

I thought back to when I had only just made it through a scrape with a robed Amazonian. Luck had been a major drawcard then and again, I wasn't alone. Here and now, my feet would have to be my defence.

They twisted over each other as I bound around the corner and back toward Kath's place. Sounds like a bar now that I think of it, that or a coffee shop.

They were after me. I could hear them. All I could hope was that I was faster. I made it back to the road leading to Kath's and charged as fast as I could. Each intake of breath was like a knife as the freezing air surged into my lungs. I'd always had a problem with breathing through my nose, preferring to be a fish gaper instead, but when running, it was made even worse.

There was someone on the sidewalk ahead. I certainly didn't want to put them in any danger. The best thing to do was keep running and get my pursuers to pass this pedestrian. Then they could either be out of harm's way or, preferably, run and call for help.

I hugged the curb as I overtook them, not bothering to look back or apologise as my satchel accidentally bounced out and hit them. I had more important things to worry about.

I could see I was approaching the big mansion-like building where I had had the weird hallucination. Perhaps I could use it as cover. Or would I just be trapping myself? I would have to make that choice soon.

Though my mind was racing as much as my feet, it was probably a smarter option to take cover in the mansion than lead them back to Kath and Luka.

I heard a loud crack and a chunk of brickwork in front of me erupted from the wall. Guns? Were they shooting at me? At least they hadn't shot the person I had passed. At least I hope they had left them alone.

I tucked my head down and tried to force as much out of my legs as I could. There was no chance I was going to be able to keep this pace up and I had too far to go before reaching Kath's anyway. Taking my chances in the burnt-out old building jumped to the top of my list.

Another shot rang out and the last window in the Manor House shattered, which was very fortunate for me. I reached it seconds later and saw that there were no little jagged glass edges left in the frame.

To be on the safe side I hiked the sleeve of my jacket over my right hand and used it to lever myself inside.

This must have been some sort of entrance hall before the building's demise. It was right next to a big set of double doors leading out onto the street again. Thankfully I hadn't tried them as a large piece of roofing was blocking it from this side. In front of me were two options. The first was the stairway leading up. From what I could tell, I would be hard-pressed to find anything up there.

In front of me was a wide corridor that led to three doors that I could see. I thought that was the better way to go, give them a choice. Though there were two of them and one of me, giving them much better odds of finding me. All I knew, for now, was that I needed to find somewhere and it couldn't be that big ballroom or they would be able to see me through the windows.

My feet carried me down the hall before my legs could start to tell me how tired they were and my lungs began to agree with them.

The first door, I figured, led to the ballroom, or whatever it was. The door on the back wall seemed a tad obvious, so I took the middle one that was on the same wall as the Ballroom entrance.

I grabbed its dirty, twisted handle and turned. Thankfully the door didn't fall on me as I thought it might. It swung a quarter of the way open before jamming in the hinges. It was enough space for me to squeeze through and I didn't have time to waste.

Pulling everything in, I forced myself through and pulled the door to as quickly and quietly as I could. I then turned to face whatever room it was I'd found myself in, striking a distinct note of déjà vu. Big house, mysterious doors.

"No magpies, please no magpies," I found myself whispering under my breath.

Instead, there was a dark hallway. It was quite wide, having been lined with runner tables for displaying now destroyed ornaments and clocks. Above these were those clichéd rectangular patches of light wallpaper where picture frames had once hung, the surrounding edges were darkened and dirty. I thought they were myths, images set designers used to intimate an old abandoned building, and yet here I was seeing it in the flesh, so to speak.

Between the runner tables, some now lying broken on the frayed and holed carpet that ran the length of the corridor, were four doorways on the right and a large set of double doors halfway down on the left. That would be the ballroom again. The others? Who knows? I would skip the first couple in case they led to wherever door number three in the entrance hall led.

As I reached the third door, I heard a loud crash from the entry. I suspected the men had decided to smash the door instead of climb through the window.

The handle to the door was crusty and rattled precariously in its socket. I was slightly worried that I would turn it and it would come off in my hands. Didn't happen though. Instead, the door creaked loudly open, giving away any chance of confusing the two men as to where I had absconded.

I darted inside and pushed the door closed as I heard them talking.

What I had been expecting was a bedroom, perhaps a living area. What I didn't expect was to find myself standing at the base of several piles of rubble. The section of the house that used to be here was now all underfoot.

In the darkness, I could see sections of wall standing here and there. To my left, the actual structure continued on back a few metres. I could see vague dusty outlines of old furniture and walls.

It was just as well I had skipped the second door as it was completely barred by a large piece of flooring that was still connected to the floor above. Ragged pieces of old carpet were tearing away from the floorboards beneath. It lay at a steep angle to the rubble I was standing on.

In all, it appeared to me like some post-apocalyptic world long since ravaged by age and fire.

But where do I go? The back of the property was lined with brick walls from adjoining buildings and I knew both ends leading out to the street were blocked by big wooden fences. And I most certainly couldn't go back.

One direction they might not even consider was up and that's what I decided to try. I moved back along the piles of ash, bricks and debris giving myself a run-up.

I took a deep breath and charged at the awkwardly shaped makeshift ramp. My shoes found purchase and a decent grip for the first few steps, but I could already tell after that I was in trouble. The grimy carpet was tearing underfoot, dust erupting from each beating it took as I scrambled with my hands at the ragged material.

The height of the ceiling in older building was taller than I was used to. They were normally around seven-foot high in Australia. English architecture seemed to find its origins in the lands of giants. Ironic considering historically, the English were supposedly a lot shorter than they are today.

My left hand clawed at one of the flaps of carpet that had already come away from the floor. It gave a few centimetres before jagging to a halt. My feet didn't stop moving, scrabbling for purchase as I tried to find a higher handhold.

I had never been abseiling or rock climbing before and this was nothing like it, however, I was starting to wish I had a bit more knowledge about it all.

Managing to struggle halfway up, I thought I had a decent chance of making it when I felt the ramp beneath me jar suddenly. Something had hit it.

"Here!" I heard a voice call. They had found me but were using the door blocked by the collapsed flooring.

Using the fear that rose to my throat as an impetus, I launched with both my hands and my toes that were planted on the carpet and scrambled, in the manner of a squirrel, the rest of the way up. I was breathing haggardly when my arms slammed hard against the intact floor above.

I also yelped as a number of sharp, jagged boards from both edges of the crack in the flooring pierced my upper arms.

The men below were still trying to bang open the door, one using brute force, the other had taken to shooting at it. I wasn't particularly convinced either method would work. They must have thought I had barricaded the door with a cupboard or something. Surely it would not open far enough to show them what lay beyond.

Either way, I couldn't hang around. Ignoring the stabs and pain, I levered myself up until I was perched directly above the door the men were trying to break through, unsure whether I should trust the floorboards in front of me.

I had never been a fan of jetties. This comes back to my old fear of heights. I would prefer walking over the solid support beams that you can see running below the jetty, supporting those horribly thin slivers of wood you were meant to be walking on. Anyone with a fear of heights or water might know what I mean. Often it is just a case of following the bolts in the jetty with your feet and that pretty much ensures you're walking on the safer, more solid part of the jetty.

It must work, I've not fallen through one yet.

Thankfully, during my last encounter with One, I had had to deal with my fear of heights on several occasions. It was still there, but I was much better at handling it. Still, falling through the floor at this point in time would find me in the arms of the bad guys.

I had no idea where it would be safe to tread as the carpet, albeit rotten and putrid here, covered everything. Besides, anywhere could be a death trap waiting to spring or collapse.

There was a wall opposite me; this must be the upper half of the Ballroom. Above me was the odd patch of ceiling or roof. From the looks of it, it had been quite a nicely decorated house in its heyday. To my right and left, there was the odd section of a ruined wall of varying heights.

Kath's place was now to my right and that's where I needed to get to, so I had to make a choice. Slow and steady, holding onto the walls, hoping by displacing some of my weight, I would make it safely through this potential death trap. Or bolt for it. It wasn't as if I weighed much. 58 kilograms or just over nine stone in this Old-World Country.

Below me, a loud crack accompanied the bang of the obstructed door. Two more followed.

Gunshots. They'd used five. If they each had a gun, there could be at least 7 more shots left.

The detached piece of flooring, or my makeshift ramp, however you wish to know it, creaked threateningly for a moment before giving up the ghost. With the quiet snap of already brittle bits of wood, it collapsed, jamming hard against the door and sending a considerable cloud of foul-smelling dirt into the air. I covered my face with my sleeve as I began to cough, the dryness assaulting the back of my throat.

After the running, my heavy breathing as I tried to climb

up, I was already fairly parched. With my allergies, I was surprised I wasn't sneezing as well.

As it turned out, I didn't need to. Another gunshot, but this time the carpet just in front of me erupted upward as the bullet fired into the sky. I'd given myself away. I choked back another cough, the shock helping to silence me.

There wasn't time to stuff around anymore. I had to make a choice.

Right...

Right!

I sniffed carefully, taking some air in as best I could, and slowly turned myself toward my right.

Another gunshot and a small portion of the carpet, around the size of a dinner plate, disappeared a few inches from my feet. If it weren't so dark below, I would have been able to see the men now. As it was, I could hear them swearing as they dodged more falling pieces as a result of their attack.

Time to move.

I launched myself forward once more, hearing the ground beneath my feet groan, creak and thud as I pounded down what wasn't exactly a corridor. In old castles, you would find that rooms were joined by a series of doors that seemed to be one long hallway when viewed from one end. You would go through the waiting rooms, then the Queen's chamber and finally to the King's. I had found this out from my numerous visits to the landmarks around London. It had been completely unlike what I had imagined.

This mansion seems to have had a similar design as I ran through two doorways, the doors thankfully missing from their hinges apart from the one at the very end.

I had almost made it to that particular door when my left foot inconveniently found a weakened section of flooring to make contact with.

As my heel came down, there was a snap and everything

else simply crumbled around it. The lower half of my leg slid through, cracking hard against the other side of the hole and my right knee buckled as I collapsed to the ground in a very unattractive jazz split position. I was definitely going to feel that tomorrow, provided I lived so long.

I couldn't contain the squeal of pain as the strain in my groin and thigh jarred through me.

'Sitting duck' were two words that came to mind now I found myself in this extremely awkward position.

It wasn't going to be a simple case of rolling to the side to dodge a bullet. My leg would snap off. And I wasn't so young and spry that I could gracefully swing my leg around and jump up. Maybe if I had continued with martial arts and focussed more during the dance classes, keeping my flexibility wouldn't have been a problem.

Something tapped my foot from below.

They were trying to grab me. But those same high ceilings were proving to be an obstacle.

Why weren't they shooting, though? And why wasn't One coming after me instead of sending his goons?

Then again, that hadn't been his style. I remembered that I had had to dodge several of his minions before actually meeting him face to face. He was certainly scraping the bottom of the barrel using men with guns with all the creatures he had power over back in Bob's world.

Well, as they say, never look a gift horse in the mouth.

Using my hands to lift my body, I managed to get my right leg under me and lift myself up, pulling my left leg from the hole as swiftly and carefully as I could. Saying that, it wasn't very swift and definitely not very elegant.

There was more swearing from below followed by another gunshot through the hole I had left. The bullet pierced the mouldy plaster above my head and showered me with more dust.

A little more hesitantly, I moved onward, each step causing a sharp stab in my thigh.

I reached the door and grabbed the handle, only to find this one did snap off in my hand.

"Damn," I muttered to myself and turned around.

I remember there being a set of stairs at this end of the house from my first inspection through the old windows. The men below would be able to use those to get at me. I had to find another way, yet most options were closed to me.

There was only one choice.

Hugging the wall, I started to run gingerly back toward the other end of the corridor.

I figured staying close to the wall would mean the floor would likely have more strength through lack of use as well as proximity to the supporting wall beneath. Apart from my earlier stumble, it seemed to be holding true.

The door at the other end was missing, but the roof was still intact. I charged through and found myself on the landing above the stairs I had seen when I first entered the building.

A quick look over my shoulder, no one was following me. I couldn't hear anyone down below either, so I had to chance it. I took the stairs two at a time and bolted for the doors.

There was a grunt as someone smacked my arm but failed to find purchase.

Too close and I couldn't risk looking behind to see them.

I was out the door like a shot and heading on my original course. There was no way I could run as fast as I had been earlier. Apart from being exhausted, my groin strain was really starting to hinder my running capability.

At this rate, I should be at Kath's in ten to fifteen minutes.

They were likely to catch me before then.

The footpath curved around to the left and I followed it.

There was another gunshot and a brick just ahead of me shattered, launching fragments of grit into my face.

Caught by surprise, I cringed and lost my footing, bouncing into the wall. I tried to blink, making my eyes water and sting as my body and instinct tried to flush them clean.

I couldn't see.

There was no point running blind. I leaned against the wall and turned to face my pursuers.

Despite having been so close as I left the house, I could just make out the two hazy figures in the distance. One was barely a few metres away, the second a few steps behind.

That close, they were definitely trying to shoot me or my brains would be all over the brickwork.

I held my hands up in a defensive stance, knowing it was futile.

The first man was so close now, even with my eyes tearful, I could see he wasn't slowing down. He meant to hurt me.

Cowering back, turning my left shoulder toward him and keeping my hands up, I closed my eyes and braced myself for impact. My mind wishing I could erect a forcefield to keep me from hurting.

There was a grunt of surprise tinged with pain and something hit the floor. I half expected it to be me.

Something was up. I opened my eyes, for all the good it would do me, though I found that I had mostly recovered my sight, and noticed the first man lying on the pavement, his head rolling side to side as he clutched his face.

The second guy had stopped and drawn his gun.

"Oh. Wait! No!" I shouted uselessly.

His response was to pull the trigger. For the second time in as many minutes, I cowered and prayed for protection.

And again, there was no pain.

"What the?"

I looked again and the man was exchanging glances from his gun to me to a little dark patch that had appeared on his shirt by his shoulder.

One last look at me and he crumpled over dead.

A voice called out from the gloom, a familiar one at that, "Oh my god! Are you alright?"

Someone was running toward me, I could see again, but the low light meant that even though he was only a few metres away, I couldn't quite see who it was.

"Scott?"

Obviously, he could see me. I hadn't moved, I was still torn between running, checking out the corpse and the prone man and finding out who was talking to me. But I recognised the voice now.

The accent helped.

"Andy?"

By now he had reached the body of the man that had just died in front of me, he stepped around the body, careful not to step over. I understood that, superstition and all.

"Are you okay," he asked, extending his hand out to me. I hadn't realised before but I was shaking. It had been a while since I'd been faced with death, but never with such certainty, and yet something had happened. Had the gun backfired? What?

"Scott?"

His hand touched me and I found myself calming slightly, feeling somewhat safer. I found my voice again, "I'm fine. I'm fine. I'm fine," that last one was for myself.

Andy pulled me away from the wall and turned me away from the fallen men, leading me away.

Half guiding me and almost carrying me, Andy led me onward with his arm around my shoulders.

"I need to see Kath," I informed him.

"Where?"

I pointed and he ushered me on, quite quickly in fact. We left the old ruined mansion and the men behind. A few moments later I was better able to walk on my own and, though I found his arm around me very comforting, I started to lead and he followed. Was it a smart idea to get him involved further, to take him to Kath? I don't know, but I don't think I had a choice in the matter either.

He noticed I was steadier and, much to my unexpected disappointment, took back his arm. But he also found it a cue to start asking questions.

"So… Would you mind explaining?"

Where did I start? Some things I couldn't explain. Like what had happened to that guy. Besides, I really didn't know much more than when I last spoke to him. I owed him something though, "I think I know who is doing this."

"This grey demon?"

I shook my head, keeping my now-seeing eyes on the lookout for further attacks, "Yes. I'm pretty positive I have met him before. Or so I've been told. But he's worse, more dangerous, more powerful it seems. Where I met him, I could understand the things he could do, but here, in this world…"

I was at a loss. One had been able to control things with his consciousness in his own world. So had I for that matter. But we were no longer in his world. How was he exerting such forces against nature itself, to draw the light from the sky?

Andy had obviously been listening closely, "This world? What do you mean?"

A little smile crept onto the edges of my mouth, "I'm not from around here. And I don't just mean because of my accent. Australia is a lot closer than where I am from."

He scoffed a little at this and muttered something in German under his breath. Did he think I was mental?

"An alien then?" He asked.

"Yes and no. I'm from Earth, just not this one. This Kath I need to see, she can probably explain it better, but it's because of her I am here in the first place. She thinks I can help you, help the Earth. Stop One who is doing this."

"One?"

"That's what everyone calls him. It. The demon monster angel."

We walked in silence for a bit while he either processed

what I said or was wondering how he got messed up with an asylum escapee and how to get away without getting hurt.

We were nearly at the alleyway before he spoke again, "I want to help."

It wasn't what I was expecting, but it wasn't unwelcome either.

"I don't think that's a good idea. He's dangerous and-"

"Exactly," he cut me off, "and look what happened to you tonight. You were lucky not to have been killed."

"And what makes you think I won't be in the future, and that you won't be because you tried to help?"

He stopped and pulled me to a standstill by grabbing my wrist. I looked at him. So earnest, so determined, "And if I don't, I will die anyway," he indicated the night around him with his hands, letting go of me in the process, "We can't go on like this much longer. Soon it will be pitch black and we will not be living anymore. If this is my one chance to help, I will take it. If I die in the process, it is better than living like this."

And I thought I was the righteous one. I was impressed if not a little worried. He was right, but so was I and if he died, that would be on my head. That was something I didn't particularly want to contemplate.

The brave and steadfast expression on his face, his eyes boring into me forced me to look away. We were only a couple of steps from the mouth of the alley now. He had come this far. I had come further and something about him being here felt right. I had felt it the minute he had grabbed me back at the ruined mansion.

"Okay."

It was all I could say.

THE WORLD FALLS DOWN

Kath's aged face peered around the door as it creaked open. She looked relieved to see me, but I could see the sparkle of suspicion as she caught sight of Andy.

"It's okay, he's with me. Andy, this is Kath."

Kath pulled the door open further and made room for us to enter. Andy took one step inside and extended his hand to her. Still a little wary, she responded by extending her own frail arm which he took warmly. His large fingers dwarfed her bony white digits but he was gentle with her as if she would snap with the slightest effort.

Something passed behind her eyes or had I simply imagined it, but she smiled and withdrew her hand, "Come in, take a seat if you can find anywhere to park yourself. I'd get Luka to make you a fresh tea but he's out on an errand. The pot is still warm if you don't mind a milder one."

We both declined politely, though I could remember the tea from earlier and found it difficult to do so.

Saving the recliner for Kath, I chose a dusty, felt-covered ottoman to perch upon, letting Andy take a smaller armchair that had to be freed from a pile of old tabloid magazines which he put on the floor beside him. This took less time for him to do than for Kath to shut and lock the door before making her slow, almost painful to watch amble to her seat. She began to speak before she sat down.

"An exciting night?"

I scoffed a little, "You might say that."

I was looking at the rip in my coat. I took it off and saw it had continued through my jacket and my jumper. The orange of the latter had turned a dark brown from my blood. I'd stopped bleeding, but I could do without an infection.

She lowered herself with a groan from the old worn leather recliner and her own worn lungs.

"Would you have some antiseptic or something?"

She waved her arm toward the kitchen, "Beneath the sink. There's a first aid kit."

"Handy."

I went in search as Kath turned her attention to Andy.

"And where do you fit into this, young man?"

He smiled at her, but not in the patronising way one would expect from a young stranger interacting and trying to placate an elderly citizen, "This, as you call it, is affecting us all. I have seen first-hand what this monster has been doing and," he looked at me as I returned with the kit. He was still smiling, "Scott can't do this on his own, whatever it is you expect of him. He nearly didn't make it back here."

"I think I saw him," I spoke only because her inquisitive eye had turned to me, "but I can't be sure," I located the ointment as I spoke, "There's something different about him. And he sent two men after me. Ordinary men armed with guns. A strange thing to do, especially considering all the power and people One had following him before."

Kath's head shook ever so slightly as she thought about this, "These men are from this world. They do his bidding perhaps for payment, maybe promises. They've turned their backs on us for their own fortunes."

"Don't they see what they are doing? What is going on around them?" Andy was disgusted.

A sad smile rose on her lips, "Of course they do. And I am sure some of them enjoy it, like kicking puppies or drowning ants. Others simply don't care or see it as a means of survival. If you can't beat them, join them."

Strangely that thought had never even crossed my mind. And after hearing her say it, it might have been a good ploy if One didn't know what I looked like. There was complete logic to what she was saying and it also put the idea of the henchmen in the movies into perspective. Why else would these people turn bad? Influenced by threats, dreams of good fortunes or simply enjoying dishing out pain. Scary how humans could be like that despite the evidence being on the news every day. That thought made me realise something.

"The problem is he knows I'm here. He saw me. I don't know for sure if he recognised me, but why else would he send people after me?"

"And what happened to these people?" She looked at Andy for this answer.

I could feel my eyes widen as I tried to find an answer to this. I didn't actually know what had happened.

"Something. I don't know. Luck?" on this last word I looked to Andy for help.

He nodded, "Luck. It had to be. I saw it with my own eyes."

"One is dead," I continued, "the other knocked out."

"So he knows you're still alive. And resourceful. He will be concerned, perhaps double his efforts. It is not the most helpful that he found out about you so quickly."

"I couldn't exactly help it. I was trying to find out as much as I could. Now at least we're more likely to get things rolling. He's bound to come looking for me," which also made me think, "Which means I should get going. I can't lead him here."

The expression on her face confirmed what I had thought; she would be a sitting duck if he found her. That meant I had to lead him away, but at the same time, get closer to him.

I'd managed to apply some antiseptic gingerly to the cut in my arm without taking off my jumper. I threw the ointment back in the kit and left it on the ottoman beside me.

As I stood, I accepted the fact I still didn't have the means to deal with him. His sending men with guns after me was bad enough, but when it comes to cross-dimensional, reality-warping monsters, I was completely out of my element.

Actually, I had sort of dealt with them before. Guns, not

so much.

Andy stood as well and followed me to the door.

"I really can't ask you to come along."

There was a humour in his expression that wasn't completely suitable for the occasion, "You don't really have to. This isn't your choice."

I looked back at Kath. She had her left arm outstretched. In her hand, she held something small, her palm facing down. I put my hand under hers and she let the item fall.

"Take this. I most likely won't be seeing you for a while, but this should make things easier to communicate."

I looked at what she had given me. It was a trinket, like one of her porcelain pieces of tat she had lying around. A small Turtle with a tiny Frog on its back. It was bone white and looked extremely fragile. It actually looked to be made of ivory.

"Wouldn't a mobile be easier?"

She looked at me strangely. Did they even have mobiles in this world?

Andy spoke up, "They don't work. Whatever is happening here has affected most radio communications. Hard wired telephones still work, though."

"And how does this work?"

"Speak to the turtle and I will know to listen."

That would have to be the most cryptic and bizarre thing I've been told to do in my life, but I would go along with it, "Right, we should get going."

She nodded, "Good luck. We're counting on you."

I smiled, hopefully reassuringly, "I'll be in touch."

Andy followed me out. Kath remained in her chair. It was too much effort for her to be jumping up and down every five minutes so I locked as many of the locks as I could that would allow the door to pull closed securely.

As for where to go, I really didn't know.

"We could head to a café, talk about it. We'd be in public, but should be able to blend in. Or we could return to mine," Andy suggested as if reading my mind.

"Well, I could certainly use a drink."

He smiled, "Café it is, then," and he walked to the mouth of the alley. I hesitated briefly. Not for the first time, the question of 'what the heck am I doing' popped into my mind. Surely there was someone better able to deal with all of this, to confront One and his lackeys.

What about Bob or Narelle? Now, she had gumption enough to take on any reality that might look sideways at what she was wearing. Then again, Bob was a bit of a pacifist.

Ahh, stuff it. What else would I be doing now? Riding the tube home to watch some television or call my agent about any possible auditions that might pop up, usually unpaid and for badly written short films.

That wasn't, strictly speaking, true. Some of the short films I'd done had been very well written and probably deserved a bit more exposure than a screening in the director's film school class. Others were not so well written, but skilled new directors had made something of them. I remember watching an old tv series in Australia called 'Eat Carpet' on SBS, better known as the foreign language and culture channel. This show would air short films from across the world and some were absolutely fantastic. What, ideally, should happen is that the BBC recognised the short film industry and started airing them regularly in some time slot or other. 'Eat Carpet' was on around midnight on a Saturday; a time when families were in bed or party-goers were slowly getting oblivious to the world. An ideal time, really, to not interrupt normal television viewing but allow those that wished to see the wonderful world of the Short Film to work its magic.

By the time I reached the alley mouth, Andy was checking both ways as he crossed the road. I had to keep a swift pace to keep up, which was rare for me. I figured he thought the faster we got into a public and populated area, the better. My groin strain wasn't agreeing with him.

"You keep some interesting company," he said when I

had picked up his stride and walked beside him.

"You don't know the half of it."

"This the sort of thing you do then? Chase after monsters, get shot at," he paused briefly, "Hop dimensions as casually as you would catch a bus?"

"Only for the last few years. But believe me, it wasn't intentional. The first time, I was kidnapped. So was a friend of mine. But that reality was nothing like this one. Nothing like Earth at all. It was One then too. This same creature is terrorising everyone."

"How did you defeat him?"

I hadn't really, not if he was back for more, "I confronted him with what he feared most. That's what he was doing to us. I figured turning the tables would have some effect. I was lucky. I was stupid."

He looked at me, slightly concerned, "Stupid? Why?"

I scoffed a little, "I let him go. I gave him a second chance."

Andy grabbed my arm, we didn't stop but we slowed a little, "That is not stupid. That is admirable. These days, in my world at least, we are too quick to kill. You gave him a chance. He blew it."

"But who is suffering for it now?"

He smiled, it was infectious, "You beat him once. You will do it again and I will help you."

We had reached the main intersection I had chased Luka over earlier. It was identical to my own world apart from the hazy darkness that was the air.

To the left, toward Liverpool Street Station, I could see there were more people. We had passed a couple as we walked, but nowhere near the numbers that would crowd my London.

Where had everyone gone? Was it just that this world was less populated? Had so many people left the country? It didn't make much sense and it brought a lot of questions to mind, hopefully questions Andy could answer.

We continued down toward the station, mingling into

the somewhat crowded sidewalks.

"Where is everyone?"

"They left. When the darkness first started, people could still travel. It was on the news but no one listened at first. It wasn't half as dark as this when people started to realise something was very wrong. Especially considering Spain, France and everywhere else seemed to be as bright as before. It started slowly. Then there was a rush. And then the wall came down."

"The wall?"

"There is a kebab shop there, we could eat and drink."

It took me a moment to register his change of topic. I looked where he pointed. It was actually a familiar kebab cum falafel shop. I'd seen it in my reality.

"Sure. I just hope my currency is valid here."

"We will sort that out later."

It was much like a Subway. Order the type of kebab or wrap you want, move down the counter as you watch it get made and then collect and pay at the end. Thankfully, they had an identical Queen on the throne and whoever designed the money in my reality also seemed to have existed here as my currency was good. I just wondered if my bank card would work too.

There was a thought. Was there another me around? Was I in England or still in Australia? Too much to think about and too much else to worry about.

The eatery was practically empty and we opted to sit inside at a small, round, metal table with matching chairs. I felt a little exposed sitting by the window, but I felt a lot more at ease with Andy there.

"So what is this wall?" I asked before I bit into my garlic lamb kebab.

Andy had to chew a bit more and swallow before he could answer, "Not a physical wall. But it somehow encased us. As I said, mobiles stopped working, radios. We no longer received communication from anywhere. We had no way of knowing what was going on in the world.

Planes no longer landed and those that took off had to return. For some reason, their instruments kept directing them back home. We became prisoners."

"And what about the government? The Police?"

"The Prime Minister was on holiday, they say. He is gone now. The government then acted like a headless monster, unsure of what to do with itself despite having an acting Prime Minister. They operate still, but they have not been able to coordinate any action as there is too much in-fighting and a lack of resources. We keep getting told they are investigating options, much like the Police are investigating these incidents. That is all they seem to do. Investigate."

He was getting a little riled up. It was understandable, it all seemed futile. No one was doing anything; no help was known to be coming to help and things were only getting worse.

"What about the food? If you have no access outside?"

"It still grows. With a lot fewer mouths to feed, we are managing to live off what the United Kingdom offers. I was quite impressed. The major supermarkets and the farmers all have worked together. It is all locally sourced, though the prices have gone up a bit."

That surprised me. Not just the news about the supermarkets, but the fact it was still growing.

"How does it grow? There is no sunlight."

Andy nodded, having to swallow another bite of kebab, they were actually rather tasty, "Yes. We don't know why, but the trees, the animals, the grass; it all survives. We don't get a sunburn, but everything somehow continues to live."

"Then he needs us alive."

Andy looked at me quizzically.

"He's not trying to kill you. At least not yet. If he wanted to do that, he'd have allowed the plants to die, you to starve. He needs you alive for some reason. What is also odd is that he hasn't taken control. He hasn't usurped the

Queen. That's what he did last time. Here, no one knows about him. Why?"

"Maybe he can get what he wants faster if he is secret. Without being in the open, we have nothing to fight against."

"That makes sense. Not having to run a country, no responsibility apart from finding what he wants. But what is that?"

We ate in silence for a few moments. I was weighing up what exactly he would be looking for in my head. Maybe Andy was doing the same thing. Maybe he was just enjoying the food. It was very tasty.

He'd been going after people. Particular people. The little girl, the man hit by the car. Something else. I couldn't quite put my fingers on it, but there was something in my memory. Then, like a switch being flicked, I had it.

"Abilities."

I was worried I'd said it a little too loud, but no one seemed to have noticed apart from Andy.

"Abilities?"

"Abilities," His stare was blank. Not quite lost, just blank, "Kath has them. The man that was hit by the car. He had them. Kath showed me using her own. He had some sort of precognition or prediction thingy."

Again, Andy was just staring at me.

"He could see the future."

"I know what it means, but not what you're talking about.

"The man had this ability but something played with it this time and it didn't work for him. Then One came and ripped out his heart."

It dawned in Andy's eyes, "Lewis' friend had her heart removed as well. She had an extraordinary mental capability."

That was a horrible thought. She was only a little girl.

"He's collecting their hearts? The hearts of people with abilities. They must have some sort of power," Andy suggested.

"Or he is just an evil sicko," I supplied, though I knew that was not the case. He wouldn't do all this simply to get his kicks. There had to be more to it.

So now we were getting somewhere. Or were we? We knew what he was doing. We didn't exactly know why and we sure as heck didn't know how to stop him. I didn't have any abilities, so what could I do?

"So we have that. What do we do with it?"

Andy scrunched up the foil that had held the kebab he had just finished, "We could set a trap."

"A trap? How? With what?"

"With someone with abilities," he said it so matter-of-factly.

"Kath said there aren't many such people left."

He shook his head, "No. They are not so open. There have been rumours about them, but nothing concrete. So they are rare."

"So we'd have to find someone with abilities willing to sacrifice themselves, or at least put their neck on the line. Then when we have One's attention, we…" and there I was stuck again.

We what? Tie him up?

"He has abilities of his own. Teleportation seemed to be one, or at least teleporting his underlings like I saw him do. Then there were those very underlings we would need to deal with. We'd need a practical army."

"Or someone with the right ability," Andy said.

I realised I had said my last few thoughts out loud.

"Right, I'll contact the classifieds, you organise the posters, I'm sure we'll get volunteers jumping at the chance."

"No need to be sarcastic," Andy was a little annoyed. He was right to be; my attitude was not helping.

"Sorry," he shrugged. Just shrugged like this was all nothing, "You really shouldn't be here."

He looked at me, possibly a little hurt and then a big

toothy smile crept onto his face, "Where else should I be?"

I shook my head, "You know what I mean. You don't need to be involved in this. You have your own life to live."

"We have a saying in Germany. Roughly translated into English it goes something like 'I am a colourful dog.'"

"Okay then."

"No. Let me explain. Like when I applied to come here, I came with a scholarship; to dance."

"Dance?"

"I'll come to that if we have time. I had to sit in a meeting with the people who hand out these scholarships. They ask, 'why do you want this?' I said to them, 'I am a colourful dog with blood beating in my heart.'"

"Passionate," I offered.

His smile broadened, "Yes. Passionate. It means I am someone different, someone with a drive."

"And here you are."

"Yes," he nodded, "Here I am. And, you know, I would not change it for the world."

Was this guy mental? We were talking about the possibility of dying and he sits there smiling at me saying he is content with that.

As if he read my mind, he responded, "I am still that colourful dog. I still have that fire in my heart. If I can make a difference in this dark world, I will do my best. Look around you. It isn't just this darkness. It is the people. They are suffering."

"That's the same in my world," I said. I thought I was on the same wavelength, "Living their lives, but not actually happy to be doing so."

Andy slapped the table with his hand and almost leapt out of his seat, "Yes! Exactly. There is so much life to be lived and yet these people are allowing themselves to be consumed by an inner darkness. This one, this darkness in my world we see; it is just a copy of what they already have inside."

I was surprised. This had taken a far more profound turn than I had expected, but I knew what he was talking about. I couldn't say I wasn't guilty of allowing myself to be consumed by that same inner bleakness, but I had my moments.

"So you work with the children."

"I do now, yes. I did not before."

"Dance?"

"Yes," he nodded, the smile was gone from his face, "I danced. Ballet. It was my life in Germany but I wanted to help others too, so I thought I would explore how dancers could train safer and better. I studied briefly here until this came," he indicated the darkness outside, "People started closing themselves off from the world. The arts died. No theatre, no music. It became simply go to work then go back home. Day in, day out. Again, look around. No people are eating out or having fun. They are locked up indoors. Life is practical enough to get by, that is all. So I was forced to give up."

"That was what you had a passion for? The blood in your heart?"

"Exactly. Now I try to bring that to the children in the hospital. I don't know if it truly works, but I can hope."

That reminded me of something. The old building, or, rather, what I thought I had seen in the building. A man dancing in the ballroom. Had it been Andy? Or a vision of him? I never saw a face, but I knew it was a man and it was a dancer. Coincidence, maybe?

I finished off my kebab and wiped my mouth with the standard paper napkin provided. As you do, I checked to see how much oil and food had gathered around my mouth by examining the napkin and was fairly embarrassed to think I must have looked like I'd been wearing some mal-applied lipstick. It had tasted good though, so that was okay.

I screwed up the napkin and put it down on the table.

Although this world was so much more like my own,

there was that same awkward twist of coincidence and weirdness that I had found in Bob and Narelle's. Or maybe that was something One had brought with him.

"I just wish I had half the passion for life you seem to have."

As I spoke, my napkin had started to unravel. I saw it in the corner of my eye, but it wasn't until it actually slipped off the side of the table that I reacted. I practically dove clumsily to grab it, missed the slowly falling paper and had to bend down to collect it. At the same time, a loud click came from the window, as if someone had rapped a coin against it. I sat up startled and was about to look at where the noise came from when Andy grabbed my shoulder and hauled me back down off my chair.

"Down!"

He was stronger than me by far so there was no chance I could have resisted. I hit the floor quite hard on my left arm. The one that I'd sliced open earlier. Hopefully, it wouldn't reopen the wound.

Andy was already moving.

With one arm he swept the metal table over so the top was facing the window, his other hand guided it down and prevented it from moving anywhere.

"Get behind it!"

"What the hell?"

"Sniper."

My mouth opened to respond, but what did you say to something like that? Sniper. Instead, I did as I was told and huddled in next to him, though it was a tight squeeze. He kept one hand on the stem of the table and wrapped his right arm around my back, keeping me down.

That was when the noise really kicked in. There were a series of similar cracking sounds followed very quickly by loud clangs as bullets connected with the tabletop. I could see the impacts on the underside as little centimetre wide mounds began to poke out a few inches from my face.

I had to be grateful they weren't using armour-piercing

bullets. Not that I knew anything about bullets, but I had heard of certain rounds that could pierce tank armour or something like that. Then again, I wasn't sure how much the table could stand.

The window didn't last long before completely shattering, showering us with glass.

"We need to move," I shouted over the noise.

Screams from outside had joined the din as well as loud shouts from the kebab shop workers as they vanished behind their counter.

Why guns? I guess if One's minions had powers, he'd have ripped out their hearts too.

"Wait," Andy whispered at me after the latest burst of gunfire died out, "They're reloading now. It's an eight-round mag."

"You know this, how?"

"National service in Germany. I spent a year in the army. Besides, I've been counting each burst."

"Great, so how does that help us?"

He indicated the exit door. It too was made of glass, but it opened onto a side street, whereas the window looked over toward the entry of the Liverpool Street Station.

"We'll roll the table over there."

"Okay, then we're outside. They still have guns!"

"Stop being so pessimistic! We will no longer be trapped once outside. They know we are sitting ducks here and they are getting closer. It won't be long until we are completely cornered."

And the closer they got, the more dead we'd be. Got it. I nodded and as the next burst of gunfire came, he pushed me toward the door but still held me back enough so the table would provide the two of us cover as it rolled.

Somehow, maybe it was his military training, maybe luck, he managed to get us to the door just as the last bullet was fired.

"Run," he hissed as he pushed me.

I charged out the door, slightly unsure which direction to

go. Andy didn't give me any time to decide as he grabbed the scruff of my neck and yanked me to the right, away from the station down a narrow road that ran perpendicular to the station. A quick glance up and I saw a sign declaring it as New Street. Though the bland old buildings on either side of the street did nothing to support the name.

We didn't have much time to find cover before they reloaded, I figured. I was actually surprised we had as much time as we did. In movies you see people reloading guns in seconds. There was at least a half a minute delay before each volley of shots came from our attackers.

At my reckoning, we had another 23 seconds or so.

There were people around, not as many as would be normal in my world, but they were still panicking. Some were running the same way as we were down New Street. I didn't think One's minions would be too discerning as to who they shot as long as the final target was hit. We couldn't put these people in danger.

The fact that, as far as I can remember, every burst of eight bullets had made contact implied no one had actually been hit so far. Or so I had to hope. They could have passed through someone...

No, I didn't want to think about that. They hadn't been trying to kill me last time. That doesn't mean they hadn't changed their mind or that they wouldn't kill Andy.

I followed Andy as he ran in a low hunched position. I probably looked like a complete knob, arms flailing, but he did it with such style. I could imagine him in a Bourne or Mission Impossible movie or something. What I wasn't so sure of was his mingling with the people running away. I didn't want to make them targets, was he thinking of using them as a shield?

There was no way to argue with most of my breath being forced out of my lungs as I ran. The pain in my groin from when I fell through the floor in the old house wasn't helping much, either.

Soon finding myself surrounded by terrified pedestrians, I resolved to stick with Andy's plan.

Suddenly, after maybe another ten seconds of running, he disappeared. Faltering slightly, I was barged from behind by a reasonably heavy-set bloke I was consciously surprised could run so fast.

"Here!"

I looked to my left and found Andy had found a small hiding spot. It was an archway with a black wrought iron gate across it. Wide enough for a van, though manoeuvring anything larger into the opening would be nigh on impossible in the narrow street.

The gate was about three feet back from the facing wall of the building. I lunged past a few people, hoping not to trip up or do the same to them, and threw myself at the gate.

My menial weight didn't even make it rattle, though the bars were very solid and dug into my chest when I made contact.

This would definitely provide us with some cover, but for how long?

Would they give up?

No. They hadn't in the old house. Why would they here?

Pushing my body up as tight as I could to the gate and then as comfortably as I could up to Andy without being too awkward, I asked, "Are we not sitting ducks if we stay here?"

He simply smiled and raised his right forefinger to his lips.

I guess he meant 'wait and see'.

My mental clock was on a countdown from five to the next round of shots.

Four.

Three.

Two.

One.

None came. I hadn't exactly expected my counting to be

accurate, nor my knowledge to be worth anything so I continued to wait with Andy. A mental timer was still ticking away in my head.

Still no gunfire. Admittedly they had used a silencer because we heard no loud bangs when they fired. The screams had already died down, there was no evidence of bullet impact anywhere nearby or sounds of such.

It was actually growing very quiet and I found it a little disconcerting, to say the least. We were being hunted and that brought back some rather horrid memories. Namely, one in a mirror maze wherein I couldn't keep my mouth shut. I had learned a little from that, but already I could feel myself wanting to talk or sing, to do something.

Fight or Flight. Not Fight; Flight or Wait.

I could feel my heart beating fast in my chest and that wasn't from the running.

I was about to say something when I felt Andy go tense beside me.

He had sensed something, heard it, seen it, whatever, but there was definitely something.

He crouched down a little in anticipation, making very little noise as he did so. I was tempted to follow suit, but what would I do? It had been years since I'd done my Tae Kwon Do and though it had come in handy in Bob and Narelle's world, I doubted my flexibility would be up to standard. Still, maybe I could be of some help.

I saw them first. I was further along the gate from the wall near which Andy was hidden. There were two that I could see.

The dark barrels of their weapons gleamed. One had a rifle of sorts. The Sniper, I gathered. The other held what looked to be a small machine gun. Not quite an uzi, though.

When I started to see the hands of the furthest person, the one carrying the rifle, I knew I was about to be seen. That didn't matter though because Andy sprang into action.

Much like a curveball, he swung himself around the corner of the wall and launched himself headfirst at the person carrying the machine gun. The rifle carrier was surprised as they jumped away yelling, almost dropping the weapon. Almost but not quite.

He started to bring his weapon down to bear on Andy who, from what little I could see, was caught in a bit of a wrestling match on the ground with the machine gun minion.

The energy in my speeding heart suddenly wrapped itself around my stomach and I felt myself charging. My brain was asking my legs why they weren't listening and running the other way, but my legs were still ignoring it as I pelted toward the still-standing assailant.

It wasn't much of a surprise attack and therefore, he was quick to start angling his rifle toward me. It wasn't until I saw the barrel pointed directly at me that I realised my mistake.

Everything seemed to slow, I felt my eyes widening, straining even as my feet started stumbling over the road surface. My stomach was no longer seized by the fire that had taken control seconds before, instead, it had returned to my heart which felt like it was about to explode with fright.

This was it.

I was a goner, finally.

Point blank, Bang.

I'm dead.

RELIEF ISN'T ALWAYS A GOOD THING

Despite my mental resolution to the fact of my demise, my body still reacted. I twisted my body to the right so my left side was now in his view, a slightly narrower target, and ducked down as far as I could, wrapping my arms over my head.

In that same slow-motion sensation, I heard the click of the trigger before I heard the muted eruption of the bullet. A scream escaped my lips despite how tightly I had clenched my jaw in anticipation, ready for the pain as the shot pierced my skin somewhere and mutilated my inner organs before breaking through my puny frame and out the other side. I just had seconds to hope that it would be quick.

There was a metallic ping beside my left ear that left a ringing followed by the horrid squelch as the bullet finally penetrated flesh.

It took me a moment to realise that it hadn't been my flesh being assaulted.

"Get up!"

I opened my eyes and looked up from where I was cowering, surprised, but definitely thankful I was alive.

How?

He grabbed my left wrist and hauled me up. Unconscious at his feet was the second minion, now bereft of his machine gun as Andy had it in his own right hand.

What about my guy?

In the brief time I had before Andy yanked me forward again, I saw that my minion was lying on the floor, rifle useless beside him. Even as I watched, blood was oozing from a hole in his chest. Not the sort of thing I ever wanted to get used to seeing, I gladly looked away as Andy moved me on.

We ran a few paces before I noticed we were heading back toward the Station.

"Why this way? What if there are more of them?"

"Optimism, Scott! We took those two. We can take the rest."

I could hear the smile in his voice. He seemed to be enjoying this somehow. Not the killing. With his job and what little I knew of him, that wasn't in his nature so much. And so far he had only killed the guy who was shooting at me.

Hadn't he?

What about the bullet that should have hit me?

The guy had been shot. I hadn't heard the machine gun go off as well. Andy couldn't have shot him.

What else could it have been?

There was too much else going on to dwell on it right now as we made it to the main road.

It was all but deserted now, thanks to the shooting. Pedestrians were gone, though in the distance were sirens. With Andy holding a machine gun, I figured we were better not to hang around.

The station was opposite us. It looked the same as mine – the one from my world, I mean. An arched, white metal framework filled with glass sheets covered a set of escalators heading down. The rest of the station was hidden below and under the large, triangle topped building behind the entrance which was enforced by tall towers on either side made of the same brown brick.

Right now it seemed to be the best option for finding cover too. I mean, there were several businesses around we could go inside, but they would have us trapped. Though the station was large and, for the most part, open, it would provide us with some escape routes as well as hiding opportunities. It seemed that was what Andy was thinking as he indicated for me to follow him across the road once he thought the area was secure.

We ran up a couple of concrete steps before jumping onto the escalators. They were still working. I never like standing on them if I can help it, so I ran down as fast as I could. Strangely, it wasn't that fast. I wasn't sure why, but I was always wary of going down escalators and this subconsciously slowed my legs. I'd seen people charge down them so swiftly it didn't even look like their legs were moving much at all. Andy was one of these.

He reached the bottom before me to a renewed scream of welcome from people that had taken refuge in the station.

The gun was not a good idea and Andy knew it. He sighed resignedly and fiddled with it quickly until he had removed the magazine. He then dumped the gun in a nearby plastic garbage bag that hung from a ring designed for normal trash. The bag lost its grip on the ring and the bag, rubbish and gun fell to the floor with a loud bang. I froze on the escalator, still a few steps from the bottom.

He turned to me and smiled meekly, realising his mistake. I shrugged and jumped the remaining distance. Tucking the magazine into his belt, Andy ran to the left toward a WHSmith store.

It was strange how despite the massive difference in my reality and this one, so many things were the same. If you compared mine to Bob and Narelle's, there were very few similarities. Theirs was full of monsters and magic whereas mine was just a plain old boring home.

This one was just like a plain old boring home for the most part, though I had definitely seen my share of odd occurrences, not to mention people having special abilities.

I guess it was comforting to know I wasn't that far from home after all. Well partially so, I couldn't help thinking when faced with a wall of Haribo jelly sweets as I ran into the store after Andy and down one of the aisles. The English just didn't know how to do confectionery right. All this chewy jelly stuff of the same consistency and flavour.

They definitely lacked the variety of Australian sweets.

That was one thing I had missed since I had flown the eighteen hours, not including a stopover, to the United Kingdom. Lollies. Black Cats, Raspberries, Strawberries and Cream, Snakes Alive, Kool Mints, Minties; the list goes on.

Okay, so I had a bit of a sweet tooth, but at least it relied on varied tastes. I can see why I would be ostracised for liking lollies in England, they had no flavour!

"Head in the game," Andy whispered to me. He had somehow noticed I wasn't completely focussed, which could potentially be fatal. Yet, he wasn't angry. He actually had a slight smile on his face.

"Sorry," I responded quietly and noticed we had stopped in an aisle that allowed a view out a second exit onto the main concourse of the station.

The station itself was large. Though we had come downstairs, the roof still towered above street level creating a vast cavernous room. On the other side of the shops were the gates to the various overground train platforms with large blue and white numbers over them.

To the right, back under the escalators, the ceiling became low and led to a few more platforms and shops. The way to the left led to cafes, fast food joints, stairs down to the toilets and up to the upper shopping concourse on street level inside the station as well as the underground station about fifty or sixty metres away that I had exited goodness knows how long ago.

The upper concourse could be a problem if any more armed people turned up. There was a walkway that ran the whole way around. It would make a perfect shooting gallery.

A large digital display in the centre of the station hall that showed departing train information provided some cover from either end of the hall, but that was very limited in the grander scale of things.

I had to ask, "Did you see any others?

Andy shook his head, his eyes hawklike as they examined our options, "No. You said you had two chasing you before. Another two now. It is possible that is all."

"I hope so. Thanks for saving me back there, by the way."

"Saving you? I just told you to get down."

"I meant when the guy was going to shoot me."

His brow furrowed. His eyebrows were actually a fair bit darker than his actual hair colour. I would have said his head hair was sun-bleached, but that would be ludicrous in the current situation. No sun, just darkness. Then again, the plants were still growing.

Besides the point.

"I did nothing," He was back to keeping guard.

"But he was shot. I saw him."

"It must have backfired. It happens," He said matter-of-factly, "You were very lucky. I would not have liked to see you die."

Me either. That would explain it, though. That strange noise I heard after he'd pulled the trigger could have been something going wrong. But another coincidence if that was what had killed that earlier attacker by the mansion.

"Well, thanks for everything else. I'd still be dead without you."

"You are not out of the woods yet, as they say."

The sirens were outside the station now. They were still muffled but sounded close enough.

There were shouts, but not scared ones, more like someone barking orders. So the cavalry was here, we'd be safe for sure.

Though if they found the machine gun, I wasn't sure if they could test them for fingerprints. They do it on television. If they could it would lead them back to Andy if he had a criminal record, which I doubted, really. Besides, he would not have any gunshot residue on his hands. Or didn't you get that from machine guns, only handguns?

It didn't matter. There were two people outside. One

dead, the other, hopefully still unconscious. Easiest day for the police, the work is already done for them.

Clumping came from the escalators. Heavy boots, it sounded like. So they were coming to sweep the area, make sure it was all clear and check for injured civilians, I guess.

We could easily sweep into the crowd and make our exits.

Sure enough, at least eight black-clad policemen with helmets, body armour and carrying machine guns of their own entered the main hall off the escalators and spread out.

Eight down here, potentially a lot more upstairs. Then there were the other exits I had no way of seeing.

If One wanted to come at us now, at least we'd have more firepower on our side, though I doubted he'd try something this public.

These officers were heavily armed. Along with their machine guns, they had pistols in holsters, what looked like stun batons and probably a taser in their utility belts too.

I couldn't see where all the men had disappeared as they ran a sweep of the area. One officer remained at the bottom of the escalators keeping their exit guarded, also with a fairly decent view of the main hall. From the sounds of it, there were still a fair number of people down here that hadn't known where to run once the shooting started. They were calling out to the police who barked orders at them to stay down.

Someone entered the store we were hiding in and I glanced at Andy who spread out both hands in a 'wait' sort of gesture. He was smiling. I just wasn't sure if he was smiling that we were safe or at the whole adventure.

I did as he suggested and it wasn't long before I saw the barrel of the Policeman's machine gun come round the end of one of the fixtures. Neither of us moved. He clocked us and held out his hand in a similar fashion to how Andy had just done. Same message.

Wait.

That was easy for him to say. Or not say. My heart was pounding in my chest. The natural instinct of fight or flight was still tearing through my veins. Normally I'd be up for a good flight, but that would potentially get us arrested or shot.

Then again, if we waited, there would surely be a round-up of us all, questioning and then checking security cameras.

And if there was one pointed at the escalators, they'd see the two of us running down, one carrying the machine gun which-

"Here!"

-they'd just found.

The call had come from the bin bag in which Andy had deposited his weapon. An easy bit of police work for them, I guess. Though it was still missing its magazine. A quick search of Andy, he'd be locked up for who knows how long.

The policeman in front of me turned and ran back to his colleague, as did a couple of others.

There was some muffled talking then one of them said loudly, "Tag it and bag it."

"Someone's already bagged it, sir," another joked.

I felt a breath against the back of my neck which made me shiver. Snapping my head around, I thought I'd find Andy peering over my shoulder.

He wasn't.

He was squatting half a metre away, no longer smiling, but rather looking quizzical. His eyes were staring at the top shelf of a nearby magazine stand.

I followed his gaze and didn't notice anything.

"What is it," I whispered.

"Shh," he didn't move.

Again, my body shivered, though this time the hairs on my arms stood on end.

They didn't go down.

There was something in the air. I sniffed, I don't know

why, but I did. An odour that hadn't been there before had crept in from somewhere. It was light but sharp. Like catching a whiff of cleaning fluid as someone shuts a freshly cleaned bathroom door nearby. But it lingered.

It was then that I noticed what Andy had. The magazines were moving, being blown by a gentle wind. Only the front covers of the thinner GSM pages appeared to be affected, vibrating quickly in the breeze.

The police were still talking as other things started to move. The bags of sweets opposite me began to rustle against one another as the thicker covers on the magazines began to respond. Pages of the smaller ones began to flip open as if some invisible reader was flicking quickly through.

This wasn't natural. I wouldn't have thought any wind could affect inside the store let alone have any effect in the station proper. Granted, there were open entries to the station, but there was no way a wind from outside would be having this effect. Not unless it was a tornado.

A cracking sound, very much like what I thought a bullwhip might be like, burst out from somewhere in the main hall which had the policemen swearing in shock.

"What the hell was that?" One asked.

From what I could see, they had all turned away from the escalators and toward the main concourse; the more alert officers raised their own weapons, aiming them at something in front of them.

Someone cleared their throat.

No, that wasn't right. Someone made a short sharp noise from the back of their throat. Almost scoffing.

"Find him," came a vaguely familiar voice, but it wasn't the voice I had been expecting.

Footsteps from the concourse.

"Freeze!"

Multiple police officers had shouted that and not just from the group I could see. Their loud voices echoed around the main hall, but I could tell there were others situated at the other end, perhaps on the upper level.

The footsteps continued, and then someone fired. I didn't know who. It sounded like the rifle that Andy had taken off the thug earlier, but it could have been one of the police.

One shot begot another; soon the hall became a cacophony of weapons' fire. The reverberating echoes made it worse and I had to put my hands over my ears despite the shelves providing some insulation.

The police vanished out of sight, taking cover, perhaps falling under enemy fire. I withdrew back to Andy. He was the ex-Army dude.

"Stay down and follow me," he veritably yelled in my ear simply to be heard.

No arguing from me. Already the gunfire was being interspersed with screams and shouts. Orders, some of them, others too pained to be intentional; all unintelligible.

Andy moved to the other end of the aisle we were squatting in, closest to the service counter, furthest from the store entry.

Checking the path was clear, he led me to the left, away from the main hall and toward one of the store's exits that would in turn lead to another way out from the station itself.

There were a couple of loud popping sounds which made Andy hesitate momentarily.

"Gas," was all he said and I remembered seeing shows on television when people would fire those little canisters that would quickly begin to hiss out smoke or gas of some kind. I couldn't hear the hissing because of all the noise.

We passed a couple of terrified-looking individuals huddled by the exit who simply gawped at us open-eyed. I felt sorry for them, as this was actually my fault. If we hadn't come down here in the first place, they wouldn't have even known anything was happening.

Andy checked the corridor that the exit led onto and bolted across to the next store. I was about to join him when something caught my eye to my left.

One of the policemen was crawling away from the main hall. Half his body length had made it into the corridor, the other half concealed behind the wall. What was clear, however, was the agony he was in. His face was contorted in pain; blood was trickling from the side of his mouth, mingled with tears. He seemed to be propelling himself only with his arms. I didn't particularly want to know why his legs were out of action, but I also couldn't leave him to struggle in the open.

Instead of following Andy, I stayed low and hurried to the corner. He was within arm's reach and I was thankful to see he still had his legs attached. I had been harbouring some horrid images of a man cut in half by a barrage of bullets. Something more out of a horror film, though I imagine it wasn't unheard of during a war.

"Give me your hands," I didn't whisper. He wouldn't have heard me otherwise. He heard me, nonetheless.

Gripping palm to wrist in a sort of monkey grip, He let himself flop and I dragged him into the corridor and a bit more safety.

I didn't want to move him any more than that. I had no idea what had happened to him and I would simply risk more damage by trying to get him to sit up. Lowering him down back onto his elbows, he managed a grimacing smile before reaching for the radio just below his shoulder.

Calling for backup? Surely every officer had been doing that.

He didn't get very far.

Just as he opened his mouth to speak, the ground in front of him ruptured in a wash of red and he collapsed, dead.

What the hell? Who does that? Who shoots a crippled, unarmed man?

I looked up, unable to do much else.

I could feel my mouth and eyes wide in the deep surprise and horror I was feeling. It simply wasn't humane.

And what had done it was not human.

It stood on two legs, approximately seven feet tall. It was dressed in a rambling makeshift outfit that appeared to come from the middle ages, but its face and skin were like nothing I'd seen before, and that was saying a lot.

Its arms, what wasn't covered by the ragged beige material that clothed it, were a dark pink, ridged down the length of them, like a series of mountain-lined valleys. It could have been reptilian, but rather than being the supple texture I had seen on a baby crocodile I'd had the chance to pet on a holiday to Florida a couple of years earlier, this skin looked like it was metallic, inflexible and impenetrable.

The face was a different matter altogether. The same pinkish skin, with the same striated ridges that ran from every edge of its face and converged on what would have been its nose. It gave the monster a cone-like face with two very small and nearly imperceptible eye slits directly on either side of the cone.

There was no way of reading how it was feeling, there was no indication of an expression. It might have had changes of expression readable to its own kind, perhaps subtle, but it was a complete blank to me. I, however, was not the same to it. This thing, and the hefty-looking weapon it held with both hands, was terrifying and there was no doubt my face was showing it.

I acted out of fear more than anything. I lunged at the officer's belt, scrabbling for the holstered pistol. The pistol guard unsnapped and just as I was lifting it to point at the creature, someone else fired. I didn't see them do it, but I saw the result.

The bullet simply ricocheted off the side of its head and lodged into the wall beside it.

They were impervious to bullets!

It didn't raise its weapon at me. It simply stood there.

Did it not perceive me as a threat? Was I a threat? Even with the pistol?

No.

I wasn't going to stand around to find out what its next move was. I felt bad for the policeman, I had tried to help him, but I couldn't hang around mourning him.

I lurched sideways, toward the second shop Andy had run into.

As I moved, hoping I wouldn't run smack bang into a wall, I noticed that all it did was watch me. Those small eye holes followed me with a slight twist of the head but nothing more.

A hand grabbed me and pulled me backwards slightly and behind a display stand loaded with folded t-shirts and jumpers. They looked, at a quick glance, to be female attire and of fairly poor quality.

"It's just standing there."

He nodded. It was strange, he was different somehow. The ends of his mouth were slightly raised in a form of smirk, but his eyes were telling a different story. If they truly were a window to the soul, his was bolting somewhere very quickly and in much less of a calm manner than his exterior was implying.

He was scared, but he wasn't letting it show. I was very grateful for that as I was feeling the shock of what I had just witnessed start to well inside my gut.

I couldn't look down. I was worried I would be covered in parts of the policeman, even his blood. It sent another shiver through me.

I'd never really seen someone killed before. Dead people, yes, I had seen at funerals, but not actually killed.

Uh-oh. I'd let my mind wander. I closed my eyes trying to shake my brain free, another big mistake. Instead, I saw the contents of that poor Policeman's head spray the floor all over again, this time with a lot more detail than my slightly amped brain had been noticing the first time around.

The feeling in my gut twisted and I managed to duck my head behind a pile of woollen jumpers before the contents of my stomach made themselves known to the outside world once more.

Andy put his hand on my shoulder and handed me another pullover with his free hand. I used it quickly to wipe my mouth. He took the pistol from me as I did so and tucked it in the back of his jeans.

"We must keep moving."

I shrugged in agreement and we both moved off once more. There was no sign of the weird monster. No way to hear him over the noise, though all of that was starting to diminish.

Another horrid realisation came to mind. There was less gunfire as there were fewer humans left to fire the guns. Was he taunting us? It had to be him. It certainly seemed like his methodology.

What got me, however, was the fact he was killing all of these people. Or, at least, allowing them to be killed. Did he want control of this world or not? Surely with this amount of power behind him, he could have taken it by now. So why all this hiding and mystery?

That hadn't been his way back in Bob and Narelle's world. He just took what he wanted. He was brutal, upfront; not conniving and devious.

Physically he had changed a lot but had that changed his mental state as well? Surely, he'd simply become more powerful, more brutal.

Andy stopped in front of me. We had been keeping low, trying to stay out of sight so we hadn't built up speed and I was able to stop before barging into him.

Another corridor? A dead-end?

I looked around him and realised both were correct.

Another of those pink monsters stood in our way. I could tell it wasn't the same by the clothes it wore. Similar style, just different. Other than that there was no way of knowing how to differentiate the two.

It too held one of those big guns. It wasn't pointing it at us, but it didn't need to be for us to understand what was being implied.

We were its prisoners.

It didn't indicate for us to do anything. Didn't speak. I figured that meant we sit tight for the time being.

"Are these things from this world?"

I kept my voice as quiet as possible so that I could still be heard over the dying din, but not be too conspicuous to the creature.

"No. I thought you may have seen them before," Andy replied, never taking his eyes off our captor.

"Surprisingly, despite what everyone seems to think or say, this is all very new to me."

A genuine smirk slid onto Andy's lips.

"What?"

"No offence, but that does seem a little obvious."

Finally! Someone who didn't take me for some sort of cosmic hero.

"None taken. I honestly have no idea what the heck Kath thinks I can do here. I have no weapons, no powers. To be honest, I barely survived the last hostile reality I encountered. Come to think of it, I barely survive in my own."

Andy risked a moment to look at me. Study me. Not long, but when he finished, he looked directly into my eyes, "You have something, don't you worry about that. You may not know what it is, but you will. When the time comes, you will."

I felt a small shiver run down my neck.

That had to have been one of the nicest things someone has said to me in a while. Not nice as in platitudes or compliments, but nice as in honest and reassuring.

I opened my mouth to say, 'thank you,' but shut it again. It didn't seem the right thing to say. He smiled and looked back toward the pink guard.

I said it anyway and he just nodded slightly.

It was only a few more minutes before the firefight ceased altogether. There had been a few stragglers still clinging on, it seemed, but I didn't want to think about that. I didn't have much left in my stomach to lose. I still felt awful about it. These people were essentially dying for me.

No, that wasn't true.

I had been an element in bringing this situation to a point, but they were dying for this reality. If there was a remote chance these policemen could have defeated One, then surely that was worth it? Wasn't it? It isn't all about me all of the time. Someone had to fight. It was about time someone did.

It seemed, however, that there hadn't been that remote chance of them winning. Or if there had been, it was missed altogether.

We were led silently back toward the main hall. All it had taken was a slight flick of the gun barrel and we knew what to do. The first pink creature I had seen walked behind us.

I say walked but it was more of a glide. Their torsos and head didn't seem to move or sway as they stepped; a little disconcerting, I must say.

There were bodies clad in police uniforms strewn around the hall. More than the few that had come down the escalator. At a rough guess, from what I could see on this floor, at least thirty. Then there was the upstairs walkway.

Arms and bodies were draped over the railings. The glass was covered in splashes of blood and who knows what else.

Were reinforcements coming or had this body count included them?

I tried to avoid looking too closely at the corpses, instead eyeing the ground around me as I walked. It too was strewn with splashes of blood, spent weapon magazines and the strangely snub-nosed remains of the bullets that had simply bounced off their targets. The glass from shop fronts, the walkways above and even the ceiling made a delicate, glittery carpet over the rest of the floor.

Taking a few deep breaths to try and calm myself, I looked up at the overhead display. Normally it would show the various arrivals and departure trains along with their multitudes of stops and destinations. Now it lay dark apart from a few sections that had caught fire and crackled away.

The large hanging overhead lights were still on. Some bulbs were blown, shot out or flickered. The night sky was directly overhead, no longer shut out by the arched ceiling. With the loss of light and the exposure to the natural elements, darkness had crept in. That same swallowing gloom that sucked the glow from street lamps and the stars now curled its way inside, hovering a few metres above the floor.

And in that gloom, hard to look at in so many ways; the fear in my gut, the gloom and something else, like an aura that made it difficult to actually focus on it, was One.

He looked much like he had in the vision I had seen earlier. Bat-like, something like a Dracula reject, but all the more fearsome because of it. His grey skin was hard and leathery, but, unlike the pink creatures, his expression was easily read. There was a gloating to his expression that was even more evident in his eyes.

If I could, I'd have hit him with Thor's hammer, which, of course, I didn't even have, but oh it would have felt so good to use such a weapon to wipe the smile off his face. Mind you, the way his nose seemed to curl at the end into a tip that pointed almost directly up, a kind of snout, it looked as though someone had already tried.

We were walking directly toward him.

Obviously, he wanted to transfer some of that gloating into words.

He hovered over the ground, wings extended, but from their lack of movement, I had to figure it wasn't those that were keeping him afloat but some other 'power'.

"Show off," I muttered under my breath.

When we were about a dozen metres from him, I felt a tap against my right shoulder which I took to mean 'stop'. Andy had obviously received the same indication as we both halted.

Struggling through the gloom and whatever else it was that was trying to prevent me from seeing him properly, I tried to look into his eyes.

They were glowing, much the same as they had the last time we met. And that same green, too. But there was something different. Before, they had been primal, animalistic, much like his body had always been, but now. I don't know, they seemed to hold more, show more. There was a deeper intelligence there than there had been, almost like he had undergone some transformation that had altered not only his physicality but his mind as well.

I knew these eyes.

"Strange how we keep running into each other like this, don't you think?"

His voice was different too, yet familiar in an odd way. It was deep still, but breathier with a very noticeable sibilant 's'.

"Not exactly the word I would use, but I'll just pretend it means something else," I mumbled.

"Yet, petulant as ever."

"And you seem to be as ego-maniacal as ever. I guess there are just some things about ourselves we can't change. Though it certainly looks like you've been trying."

"You like?"

He folded his wings individually, twisting each respective shoulder as he did so, almost like a woman showing off a new dress.

"What's to like?"

He ignored this, instead, turning his attention to Andy, "You have a new friend. You can't seem to keep them out of trouble, can you?"

That wasn't strictly true. I hadn't been responsible for anyone being involved in our last encounter. In fact, it had been all him, sucking me and my friend, Sarah into another reality.

"Him? No idea. Tag along, groupie, whatever you want to call him, but he has nothing to do with this."

It was worth a shot trying to get him set free, though it could also work the opposite way and get Andy killed for being redundant.

One cocked his head to the left, a smirk etching its way across his rough features.

"Just as stupid and naive as ever, too."

"Now you're just being rude," what he had to say about me didn't bother me. I had learned a lot about him the last time we met. He was all about intimidation, making people scared of him. Obviously, with a face like that, it wouldn't be too difficult to achieve, however, that was also his weakness. Without fear, he had been powerless.

"What will you do now? This world's army is defeated and I don't see any stray vehicles coming to save you from me this time."

"What?" I couldn't stop my surprise from voicing itself. The word was out before I had a chance to close my mouth.

He nodded, admiring himself again, "You still haven't realised, have you? Pity. Maybe I will get to see that exquisite look in your eyes when you understand how wrong you are. Hopefully, as I watch you die."

"What is he talking about," Andy asked.

"Oh. No. There it is."

He was right. There it was. My realisation that I had got it all wrong.

How could I have been so stupid?

Granted, there had been little evidence to the contrary, but if I had really thought about it, it would have been blindingly obvious.

I already knew how to defeat One. He had been a giant bully, nothing more. His power came from fear which was easily turned back on him.

As much as this horrid monster in front of me was controlling the world with fear, he wasn't using it like the demonic despot that One had been. That wasn't his aim. If it had been One, the world would know his name and he wouldn't be skulking in the shadows as he had been.

This creature was worse in his own way. He was more than simply fearsome. He was sadistic, brutal and very, very scary.

I really should have known I hadn't seen the last of him, even after my unpatriotic speech that I had given him, after which he had simply turned and vanished. Unpatriotic in that I was telling the truth about my world; the wars, the horrid nature of mankind. I had been far too idealistic in hoping that he had listened and turned for good.

And here he was. Very different from the last time I saw him, but, even then, he had been very different from the first time I had seen him. Something about crossing realities, maybe, had an effect on his physiology. This last visage seemed to be more revealing of his true nature than the last.

"Grekon."

"Who?" Andy asked again.

"Aaahh," like a sigh of relief coming from his ghastly, monstrous throat, "I'm glad that you will now truly know who it is that will be killing you."

I was in a lot deeper crap than I had first thought.

"Now," I whispered to Andy, "now we are screwed."

STUCK BETWEEN

The question that now rang clearly in my head was, 'Do I die fighting, take it like a man and go with it or do I flounder like the skinny, bullied lad in the boys' locker room?'

The answer was pretty obvious. It was what I always did in these situations.

The instant I grabbed Andy's arm, I shouted, "Run!"

Grekon had already raised his arm in a threateningly magical manner.

Thankfully, due to his good reflexes and physical state, Andy virtually lifted me off the ground as he charged with me to my left.

I felt a wave of heat wash over us from behind as Grekon loosed a fireball or something at the ground where we had just been standing.

I assumed fireball as that used to be his preferred method of attack.

Andy overtook me, being a fitter and faster runner, but managed to grab onto my shoulder and haul me along. We weren't going to have much time before we were in the monster's sights again.

As luck would have it, we wouldn't need much time at all.

The entrance steps to the underground section of the station were directly in front of us. If we could make those, we'd have a little protection, for a while at least.

Grekon roared behind us and when I say 'roared', the whole building shook. I thought my eardrums would burst even as the sound echoed around the great hall. It had been something like a cross between a lion and a hawk screech. Piercing but low and throaty at the same time.

We were only a few metres from the steps down, giving me only a few seconds to contemplate the fact that I was still rubbish at descending stairs, just like escalators, possibly worse. I was one of those uncoordinated idiots who had to take them one at a time and at a sensible pace as my legs didn't seem to cope with the speed of running down them and my mind faltered when it came to aiming for the next step if I took them two at a time at any pace. Now going up was a different story. Two at a time in a hurry was not an issue.

Down was always a challenge.

Andy yanked me to the right-hand side of the entrance.

I nearly asked him what the hell he was doing when the ground behind me once more erupted with heat. This time I felt chunks of debris shoot up at my legs.

Thankfully the denim was thick enough to prevent any burns or cuts.

I hoisted my satchel in front of me with my right hand and continued running. I'd grown pretty adept at that; running with my bag. Not simply due to tonight's practice, but I was a fast mover anyway and being able to manoeuvre through crowds without hitting people with my bag and cutting down the risk of being pickpocketed, I had learned to control the movement of the bag with one hand. I knew I must look like an absolute knob, but I always figured, time saved is better than caring what people are thinking. Yes, it sometimes got heavy or bounced painfully against my leg, often the edges of books threatening to carve a permanent cleft into my thigh, but I endured.

Before we made it to the entry, Andy hauled me back the other way ever so slightly and we managed to reach the far-right side of the stairs heading down.

From behind, I could hear footsteps, heavy and fast. Most likely the pink creatures coming for us as Grekon was flying the last time I saw him.

Andy let go of me and charged down the first set of

stairs. I grabbed the railing and used it as leverage and guidance as I went as fast as my pathetic legs would carry me down the treacherous steps.

I managed it in short order, but there was a second, longer set to go. I charged across to them as quickly as I could and once again found myself slowing down slightly to cater for the awkwardness of my step usage.

The next thing I knew, my left shoulder erupted in pain and heat. My breath was knocked out of me too, giving me no chance to yell.

I was knocked forward and sent tumbling down the remaining four steps coming to land painfully in a heap at the bottom. There was still heat from my shoulder and it was starting to sear my cheek. I opened my eyes, which had closed for a second after I came to a stop; perhaps expecting to be dead.

My arm was on fire!

I yelped and started struggling with my jacket, trying to get it off.

Managing to free my right arm by rolling awkwardly on the ground, I pulled the rest of the jacket from around my back and over my left arm.

The strap of my satchel got in the way, but the desired effect was still there - smothering the flames.

Something 'whooshed' over me.

I was torn between looking up and deciding whether the jacket was salvageable. It was already starting to smell bad. One thing though, the thick insulation had done wonders in keeping me from being burnt. Then again, so had my jumper and felt jacket, which hadn't survived completely unscathed either.

To be honest, I didn't really need to look up to know what was flying over me.

"Can't you just leave me alone! Seriously!"

"This is just too much fun," came Grekon's response, but it didn't sound completely genuine.

Allowing myself to fall onto my back; unwise as my bag

has been pulled behind me in my struggle to undress and the Coke bottle inside now dug into the small of my back.

Meh, it was nothing compared to the grazes I was now starting to feel on my hands, the twisted ring finger on my right hand, the clobbering my right shin made against the edge of one of the steps, the wound in my arm that, from the growing stain on my jumper had clearly reopened and numerous other bumps and bruises that were all beginning to make their presence felt.

What was it with this guy and pain?

This reminded me of when I first encountered him in the mirror maze. I had ended up cut to shreds then.

"You can have this world. Take it. I won't stop you," I hope Andy hadn't heard that.

He moved toward me. Glided toward me. Glided? Is that even a word? Shouldn't it be 'glid'? It wasn't 'hovered' as that implies staying in one place above the ground.

So, anyway, he was still above the ground, but he approached me while doing it until he chose to swoop in like a bird of prey until he was looming over me; that bat face of his scrunched into a horrible grimace of pleasure.

"You even thought you could stop me?" He had a point, "I don't want this world. Much like I didn't want yours. Everything you told me, you were right about your world."

"Then what's it all about, Alfie?"

He didn't get the reference, merely regarded me for a moment, then, "I want all of them. Yours, this one, the next. I've been to scores of worlds, some so similar to this one, others like mine. I've crushed them all. I want to make one that I do want to live in, to control. To own."

He's done this before? He'd destroyed worlds?

"You crushed them?"

"I've been scouring these worlds for the one thing that will give me the power to control them all. Not just one at a time. But each one has only provided me with a doorway to the next world to be devoured. I was beginning to lose hope with this one until you arrived. Your presence here means something. And I think I know exactly what that is."

"Well, I might have a problem with that!"

Grekon was about to turn to see who had spoken when he was catapulted forward and into one of the pillars on the mezzanine level between the two sets of stairs. It exploded with blue and white shards of tile and concrete as he connected, hard. The underground station entrance echoed with the rattling of gunfire.

I enjoyed watching that but knew I wasn't going to have much time to do so.

Rolling onto my feet which were still a little shaky from my tumble, Andy stepped up beside me. In his hands was one of those nasty-looking weapons the pink creatures had been carrying, the end of the barrel was smoking slightly.

As for how he got it, I would save that question for later.

"You alright?" he asked.

"Feeling better now that you're here. Thanks for coming back for me."

Grekon was prying himself off the column. A little trail of green mucus, which I supposed could be his blood, trickled from his snout.

Andy hoisted the gun again, ready to fire.

"Back up," he instructed and started to do the same.

"Your friend has more bite than you do," Grekon spat, "I'm surprised you managed to survive this long on your own."

"I remember kicking your arse a few times."

Grekon had turned around to face us both. His eyebrows raised in surprise, "Do you? That's not how I recall it."

I knew he was right. But that didn't matter! So it had been Morrissey's fortunate arrival in his car that saved me last time. And the time before that, I hadn't won. Nor the time after, really.

I hadn't beaten Grekon before at all.

"You're nothing. I don't even know your name, just that

you are an annoying gnat who keeps getting between my toes. It's about time I simply stood on you. Crushed you, too."

"So shut up and get on with it!"

Grekon released another of his roars and five pink creatures appeared at the top of the stairs.

Andy fired a spray of bullets, swinging the weapon back and forth to cover all our assailants.

Whereas the Policemen's weapons seemed to ricochet right off their pink hides, their own weapons were a lot more powerful.

Each time one of their bullets connected with their leathery skin it dented, like a large pockmark and it was obviously hurting them as they all covered their faces and fell back, cowering.

Grekon, on the other hand, merely raised his left hand in front of him and I watched as the bullets connected with an invisible barrier he had obviously erected to protect himself.

Resourceful twat!

Andy kept firing as we continued to retreat. We had sped up somewhat the instant the assault began and I felt the ticket barrier against my back in a few short steps.

"Andy?"

"Go, I'll be right behind you."

London Underground barriers were rather hard, heavy and awkward to simply climb over. There also wasn't much space to crawl under, either.

Unless you were a pram.

The access barrier for pram pushers, luggage carriers and disabled access was set higher off the ground for some reason, it was also wider and a lot flimsier.

I bolted to the only pram barrier and pushed with all my strength against one of the swing doors and managed to open it. As I made it through, I continued to push against it, holding it open for Andy who followed me through.

As I let the barrier door go, I heard a hefty click come

from Andy's gun and the bullets stopped flying.

Out of ammo, it seemed. Without a word, he dropped the weapon and we both turned and ran.

To make ourselves less of a target, we turned the first corner we could which was to the left and ran across to the first entry point on our right which led to the Eastbound platform for the Metropolitan, Circle and District lines.

It was empty of people.

To be honest, I'd have thought there would have been some stragglers, but it seemed they had all managed to escape, whether that was through fire or service access or the train services themselves, there was no one around which, to be honest, could only be a good thing. No more random deaths.

As for the trains as a means for our escape, I thoroughly doubted it. News of the assault would have travelled and the lines would have been stopped.

A quick glance up at the small displays for the trains said the next three trains were delayed.

Nothing new there then.

"Come on!"

Andy kept his voice low. He had moved to the edge of the platform and looked to be about to jump down.

"You're kidding me?"

He cocked his head as if to say, 'what the hell do you expect?'

And he was right. Where else could we go?

I hurried across to him as he jumped down, avoiding the legendary third rail. Quickly following him, I avoided all three rails as I had absolutely no idea which one of them was actually deadly.

Keeping low, he headed Westbound on the Eastbound line.

Was he trying to confuse the bad guys? I doubt it, but I wasn't going to argue.

As I said before, moving at pace is fine for me, even good for me, as long as we're not going down steps. We managed to move quickly, but we hadn't cleared the end of the platform before the first of the pink men stepped onto it.

I think the next most horrid thing about these creatures, after their weird skin texture and the fact they are pink, was the issue with them not talking at all. There didn't even seem to be a hole through which to talk, but, then, how did they communicate?

Was it a hive mind thing? Were they telepathic? I doubted that as they would be able to read our every thought and so far, they hadn't been that clued up.

It took them a few moments longer to spot us, by then we were halfway to the main tunnel.

I should explain. On the Westbound platform there is a short section of the station that opens partly to the outside world and is as spacious as the rest of the platform section. On a normal day, it is fairly well-lit thanks to the sun. In this reality, however, we were provided with a modicum of cover from the dimness. It was, however, the darkness of the tunnel itself we wanted. This started a good fifteen or so metres from the edge of the platform.

We weren't there yet.

With the uneven surface and the danger from the rails as well, we were making good progress considering.

Not good enough.

I heard a familiar click which I recalled hearing sporadically through the gunfight between the police and the pink people. The loading of a magazine? Switching off of a safety? Either way, I had a strong feeling we were about to become cannon fodder.

And then Andy stopped.

He was in front of me and I almost charged into him.

Instead, he stepped over the rail to stand between the two sets of tracks and looked back toward the platform.

"What are you doing?"

I had slowed but not stopped. Still floundering, see.

"Keep going. I'll catch you up."

I hesitated. Was he lying to me? Was he sacrificing himself for me? That would be insane!

"You can't do this."

"Don't worry, Scott. I'll be-"

Before he could finish, the shooting began.

I squealed like a baby and tucked my head under my arms as if that would do any good.

But it did.

Or at least I wasn't being hit by bullets.

I waited a few seconds and dared to peek out.

Andy was standing in a similar position to the one Grekon had been hovering in a couple of minutes before. Hand out in front of him; bullets hitting an invisible wall and all.

On the platform were the five pink creatures. Every one of them was firing at us. The visual effect on the wall Andy was creating, exuding or whatever you wanted to call it was like watching rain fall on a pond. Around his feet, the bullets, squashed and mangled were gathering. Some were bouncing off the invisible shield and back at the attackers.

"Andy?"

He was shaking with effort, "Ok, so I didn't tell you everything."

Andy had a power!

I repeated that thought in my head. He had a power.

He'd used it a couple of times that night already.

Of course! What an idiot I am.

I was going to be shot point-blank on two occasions and on both of them the bullets missed or backfired or even ricocheted off an invisible barrier.

That had been Andy! He'd already saved my life I don't know how many times tonight and there he was, doing it again.

A very nifty power, that's for sure.

"Now, if you don't mind. Move your arse! This is not easy," the strain was telling in his voice.

I didn't say anything, simply nodded wide-eyed to myself

and continued as quickly as I could toward the tunnel. He was following but at a very slow pace.

How lucky was I to have come across this guy? Not only his powers, though. His selflessness, his compassion. His military knowledge. An all-rounder, you might say. The sort of person who normally makes me sick with jealousy, but, right now, I owe him my life several times over.

Once I made the tunnel, I hugged the wall on the right, not really caring what effect that would have on my already ruined felt jacket. Heck, call it character building.

I was still in the line of sight, but looking further into the tunnel, I wouldn't be able to see the rails at all and the best way to stay alive would be to hug the walls.

At this rate, however, we wouldn't get anywhere.

As if on cue, the first of the pink men's guns clicked empty and the others shortly followed.

Despite being built for battle, they weren't that good at ensuring the onslaught continued undisturbed. Then again, they probably weren't used to encountering indestructible walls, instead charging over the masses they wiped out with ease.

Andy took advantage of the ceasefire by turning and bolting toward me.

It was ungainly and awkward and, despite the dark, I could make out heavy beads of sweat rolling down his face. That had taken a lot out of him.

As soon as he reached me, he collapsed a fair bit of his body weight onto me for support. He was hot, not just warm, but I could imagine a few seconds more of whatever it was he was doing and that sweat would boil right off his body.

All fifty-eight kilograms of me did their best to keep Andy upright while the poor man's legs endeavoured to keep him moving.

By the time the pink men had reloaded, we were deep in the dark tunnel and out of sight.

That wouldn't be the end of it, though. I knew Grekon

well enough to be certain he would keep coming.

For now, we'd have to get as far away as we could.

Keeping my voice low, I asked, "Are you ok?"

"I don't know. I've never done that before."

There was a trace of humour to his voice. I couldn't tell if he was smiling or not as it was too dark and all I could make out were outlines of shapes.

"Thank you."

"It wasn't just for you, you know."

"I mean for every time you've done that for me, not just that one."

"Ahh," the way he said it was knowing. He'd realised I'd found him out. Sure he had lied to me earlier, but I had no right to be angry with him.

"I should have said," he started.

"It wouldn't have made any difference if you had. Except instead of believing I was bloody lucky; I'd have believed I had a guardian angel."

Not that I really believe in angels.

Hang on. Why not? After everything I've seen, why shouldn't angels exist?

"You are sweet."

Sweet? Really? Is that a compliment or an insult? Coming from him, I would take it as a compliment. Heck, English was his second language.

But 'sweet' is so banal, useless. Condescending.

'Second language,' I reminded myself.

Not 'brave'? 'Daring'? Ok, not relevant to the conversation as it stood now. How about 'considerate' or 'poetic'? Not really appropriate, either.

Sweet it was then. Plain old Sweet Scott.

There was a silence in the air, apart from the sound of our footsteps and the clinking of the large stones underfoot. Not exactly great for hiding. Yet, there was something else in that silence. Was I supposed to say something? A thank you or something else?

I was never very good with people. Too complicated, I

think.

"He's going to keep coming," I thought a change of topic would be best and it broke the silence which was starting to ring in my ears, much like Andy's sweat was starting to soak through his sleeve and onto my neck.

As if on cue, a rumble filled the tunnel.

Not only that, but the darkness was no longer that dark at all.

That certainly made things easier to see, but, on the other hand, did not bode well for our well-being.

It was at least polite of Grekon to announce his arrival, not that there was much we could do to welcome him other than wet ourselves in fear.

Andy was not in any condition to fight back anymore. Why should he, anyway? He'd done most of the work so far. All I had done was run around like a headless chicken nearly screaming like a little girl every time things got tough.

Maybe I should give myself up. Then Andy could get away and continue our quest for whatever it was we were questing for.

Considering that thought seriously, it did seem like the most logical thing to do; most likely a selfless act of suicide. Then again, that was exactly what Andy had been doing a few moments before.

I pulled away from Andy as best I could, feeling his cold, damp sweat wipe against the nape of my neck. The bottom of my hairline was drenched with the stuff.

"Right, time for you to go," I had to be quick. Grekon would be with us soon.

Andy hobbled to a stop not that far from me. I hadn't waited to watch him go, instead turning to look back down the tunnel and toward a very bright orange light. It was steady, unflickering, so I knew it wasn't one of Grekon's trademark fireballs. Most likely him posturing for dramatic effect. That was one thing both he and One had in common.

"I'm not leaving you!"

"Then we both die and so does this world. Get out of here!"

"He said he wanted you! You can't give him what he wants."

"Maybe by me surrendering to him, you get a chance to save this world. That's what my role in this mess could be."

"It could be you living to fight another day too!"

I couldn't argue with him. If he wasn't going to go, I had to make some distance between us so I headed back down the way we had come.

Grekon was clearly visible now, as we probably were to him. There were no more pink men with him. I could now see the source of the light was his right hand. It was clenched in a fist but hanging by his side as he hovered slowly along.

It was plain that he didn't expect to give much of a pursuit. We hadn't been travelling very quickly and neither was he, though sufficiently to have gained on us.

There was a tumble of gravel behind me. I couldn't tell if Andy had heeded my instructions or not. To be honest, I sort of predicted he wouldn't. Why would he? It wasn't as if I was some sort of Alpha Male type that people actually listened to.

The stupid thing was, I wasn't even getting emotional about all of this anymore. I had done it too many times before, preparing myself to die.

I'd done it the last time I'd truly faced Grekon down. When I confronted One. A few other times here or there in between. On those occasions, I remembered my heart beating wildly inside my chest as if it was the only part of me not wanting to die and trying to find the easiest and quickest route out – through my rib cage.

Not this time.

I reached into my bag and pulled out my bottle of Coke, still walking toward the winged megalomaniac. I was a huge fan of the stuff. You could say I was practically addicted. I gave it up as a New Year's resolution for a year and a half and I just found myself with no energy and very moody. When I finally gave in to my cravings again, I was right back to being my old self. Not sure if that was particularly a good thing or not.

"I have to be honest with you," Grekon began, "You do perplex me sometimes."

"How dull things would be if I didn't."

"Don't be so arrogant. I didn't mean you. People in general. From your world, or the ones like yours."

"Oh, how so?"

He stopped now, still a fair way down the tracks, "Despite your technology, your claim to intelligence; you are so very much like the vermin that crawl these tunnels. Mostly insignificant but annoying all the same."

"Nice," not quite a compliment, I guess. How could I expect anything else from this guy, though?

"Not only that. Your actions are as manic. One moment running, the next creeping back. Still, predictable."

"Predictable AND perplexing?"

"AND annoying. You didn't let me finish."

"Please, be my guest," I was still creeping toward him, much as he had just described. I hadn't opened the bottle in my hands yet.

"It is your superiority complex that I find puzzling," he was watching me with those horrid glowing eyes, "in that you seem to think that, simply because you walk on two feet, that you have these wondrous machines, that you aren't as decipherable as the rats."

He spat the final word, I felt his saliva hit my face, he had done it with such force. I was a good three metres from him now and that was as far as I was going to get.

The hand that wasn't glowing shot up and out toward me and the instance it did so, I felt a vice-like grip around my throat.

I tried to make a sound, but nothing came out.

His claws weren't even touching me, but the way he had

posed his hand, it was as if it was placed around my neck, much like I was feeling something was.

It was tight, not yet painful, but it started to ache very quickly.

"You are not clever. You are not superior. And yes, boy, now I am talking about you. Creeping back to me like the vermin you are."

The pressure on my throat increased. I tried to grab at the invisible hand with my left and felt nothing but my own skin. What was horrifying, though, was that I could feel the grooves in my neck from these invisible fingers. Not only on my neck but as my own fingers ran across the surface of my neck, there were horizontal ridges that could only be from another hand, albeit an intangible one. Well, semi-intangible because I could feel it getting tighter.

I tried to talk, but still nothing, not even air was escaping and, what was worse, no air was entering either.

The pressure in my lungs was starting to increase with the need to breathe.

"You come waltzing back to me and I am meant to think what? A rat returns for food, it needs something. You? You don't need something, but you think you can DO something. Now, see what I can do!"

If he squeezed any tighter on my neck, I was worried it would snap. Not that he would care and I guess I had walked into this, literally.

All I could think now was that he was speaking so calmly. Like he was lecturing to an attentive class of year 7's. My own calm, the one I had felt when I had decided to sacrifice myself, was now long gone. It was strange how being suffocated did that.

My feet were probably the best indicator of my panic as they were scratching along the gravel trying to find purchase to push off and away, but the grip on my neck was holding me firmly in place.

The pressure in my chest had also risen to my face with a horrid heat. My eyes were watering and everything was starting to blur in my tears. I couldn't make a single sound. I wasn't going to be conscious for much longer, I could tell. My limbs were getting weak; tired and even his voice was starting to get distant.

So I did the only thing I could think of.

I could still feel the Coke bottle in my right hand. Still closed, still half full. Strange how I was thinking of it that way with death staring me in the face. I always figured myself as a half-empty kind of guy.

I pitched my arm back and threw with all my remaining might, which wasn't much, I had to admit.

It was enough, though.

The bottle didn't have time to arc, nor complete a vertical rotation before it hit Grekon on the side of the face.

Three metres wasn't far, but any further and I was sure I'd have missed.

He snarled as the lumpy base of the plastic bottle struck just below his eye. With that, his concentration lapsed and the light went out.

We were plunged into darkness once more and the hand around my neck was gone.

There was no way I was going to be able to run because I collapsed to the ground gasping for breath. My throat was sore and the intake of the dirty air in the tunnel seemed to burn my trachea. The ensuing coughing didn't help much to alleviate that pain.

It wasn't completely dark, however, as Grekon's two glowing eyes hovered in the gloom.

"You know something?"

The German accent was unmistakable.

"You like the sound of your own voice too much."

I couldn't tell where he was; that was until the gunshots started.

There was a succession of flashes and loud bangs that reverberated through the tunnel. At such close quarters, my ears continued to ring for a while after.

Six shots in total. I couldn't tell if all of them hit, but some had to have as Grekon let out another all-mighty roar, louder than the gunfire.

A hand grabbed me and I nearly shied away from it. It wasn't firm, not like Andy's grip had been in the past.

He was still weak and I wasn't much better. Using him as a guide, rather than for support, I hauled myself up and pushed him on.

We were moving blindly once more and Grekon would be off with his fireballs again in no time.

Not that there was much point, I glanced over my shoulder to see if he was using any of his powers and was surprised by what I saw. Or rather, what I didn't see.

The eyes were gone.

No, there they were.

Well, there was one.

It disappeared again and when that single green glow reappeared, it was somewhere else in the shadows, moving this way and that, flickering on and off like a drunken glow-worm who couldn't keep its butt lit.

What had happened to the other one?

Had Andy been lucky enough to score such a critical hit as to take out one of Grekon's eyes?

Where did he get the gun from?

Then I remembered the pistol I had taken from the policeman. Andy had then taken it from me. I guess we were completely out of ammo now.

We were hugging the wall to use as a guide again and being unable to see didn't help at all. All the tunnel lights that sat at intervals down the walls were off. Power cut or switched off, I didn't know.

Andy stopped in front of me.

His left hand reached out for me and pulled me along slowly.

I felt my foot kick into something and attempted to step over it, thinking that was what Andy was warning me about, yet, when my foot began to descend, it came down early on a hard surface.

Not an obstacle, but a step. I'd skipped one and landed on the next one up.

Managing to haul myself up, I found another one and then the ground seemed to even out. Gone were the awkward large pebbles underfoot and back was firm flat concrete. Well mostly flat. I could feel a few cables and stones beneath my shoe.

We were off the main track, but we hadn't actually left the tunnel. The air was the same and the sounds were still that same resonant echo you expect from caverns and caves. The question was, where was it taking us, if anywhere at all?

Grekon still hadn't recovered. He was somewhere back in the dark, but there was no sign of his glowing green eye. Had he retreated? Hopefully, but not likely. This man kept coming.

The first time I had faced him, I managed to escape back to my home reality. He found me.

I managed to escape thanks to the timely arrival of a reasonably bad driver. He found me. In fact, he found me and used the very vehicle that had saved me as the signal for his return.

That was when I finally managed to talk him out of taking over my reality.

Well, from the sounds of it, what I managed to do was convince him to take over EVERY reality. I'd undersold mine so well that he wanted more.

I guess I should be grateful he hadn't decimated mine like he said he had done others. Yet, there were all of those helpless victims he had destroyed. And this reality wasn't far off following in their footsteps.

There was a noise behind us.

We both froze instinctively.

It had been the soft clunking of pebbles knocking together after one is disturbed and sent tumbling. Almost like the sound of rolling a handful of dice.

It was close; maybe ten metres behind.

Then there was silence. I was about to move on, but Andy's hand against my chest stayed me. He held it there just in case, palm flat against my sternum.

I tried holding my breath, hoping that would help us hide a little better in the pitch black. Thankfully I had recovered sufficiently to be able to manage that for a few reasonable lengths of time.

There was another slight tumble of stones, a lot closer, almost parallel to us on the lines this time.

With any luck, they will simply move past us.

Then again, luck rarely fell on my side when I most wanted it to.

A few seconds later and I slowly released my, once again, held breath. I wasn't going to say anything and Andy still hadn't moved his hand from my chest which was now creating a very warm patch where he touched me.

Surely, they were well and truly past us now. As for what? I figured it was those damn pink monsters again.

How long would be long enough to wait? Were we going to have to stay here for the next hour or so, just in case? I wasn't stupid enough to ask. Having seen enough horror films, there is always one idiot who speaks or makes a noise leading the bad guy to their position.

As it turned out, no one needed to.

Something ran by the side of my foot.

Ran, slithered, I couldn't tell. It moved. The next breath I was about to hold caught in my throat and my right hand acted on its own, swiping up and grabbing hold of the one Andy had planted on me; squeezing what would hopefully be perceived as a warning into the fingers to be sent to the hand's owner.

That grip managed to give me a few extra seconds of consciousness as I felt whatever it was that had moved by me wrap around my ankles, ever so gently. It was that that helped it catch me off guard.

The soft caress of this thing as it wound around me gave

me the impression it may have confused me for a part of the furniture. The sudden jerking motion that followed corrected my mistake.

My feet were pulled so swiftly from beneath me. The actual sensation of the rest of my body falling was brief as whatever had a hold of me kept pulling and my solid grip on Andy kept my head from smacking against the floor.

The man had to have been strong, there was no way I'd have been able to keep my hand up like that with a nine-stone weakling dangling from it.

"Andy!"

There was no point keeping quiet now. It had me.

I felt his fingers twist around mine, trying to get a hold of my hand but, with what felt like an ankle snapping yank, my attacker pulled me free and those last few seconds of consciousness I had managed to save for myself ended as my head did, in fact, connect with the concrete ground.

Anthony Harwood

WHY CAN'T WE LOOK AWAY?

Being unconscious is what I figured being dead would be like. No dreams, no nightmares. No actual sensation of existing at all. If you've never been unconscious, remember those times when you've been asleep and not dreamt? There is a lot of it.

We sleep for eight hours a night if we're lucky. We supposedly dream for only a few minutes of those and yet what do we do for the rest of that time?

I didn't feel or sense anything until a few moments before I managed to come round. Then I felt all the pain come crashing back down on me and I wanted to be unconscious again.

My shoulder still throbbed from the fireball, my hands were stinging where they had been grazed, along with my twisted finger, which had been aggravated by grabbing hold of Andy and my throat was raw from being strangled. Both my knees felt like someone had been kicking them for the last half an hour and my left ankle was numb, though there was definitely an inkling of pain calling to me from a long way off in that general direction. I had a feeling standing on it would be pretty impossible.

To top it all off, my head was ringing and I just knew I was going to have a massive bump just above my right eye. To be honest, I was lucky I hadn't smashed my nose on the ground, as big as it was.

There was a strange crawling sensation running over the entirety of my skin like little black beetles were marching around aimlessly across every millimetre of my body. That sensation alone made me want to keep my eyes shut just in case that was exactly what was happening.

What was peculiarly comforting, however, was the grass beneath me. It was slightly damp but was suitably giving and soft to provide an agreeable place to rest.

I had been moved.

There was no concrete beneath me. The air was cold, still. Colder now I no longer wore my big jacket. The fact it was dark through my eyelids didn't mean anything due to the fact night and day didn't really exist separately anymore.

The one thing I couldn't tell that bothered me the most, was where Andy was. I'd have to open my eyes for that and I wasn't sure I was quite ready for that.

There was muffled talking. It could have been coming from a fair way away or perhaps people talking secretively. Other than that, very little sound to give much of a hint as to what was going on.

Risking a slight peak, I did my best to ease one of my eyelids open ever so slightly, hoping that the movement wouldn't be seen.

I'd obviously been out for a while, though, as my eyes seemed to be slightly crusty. Everything was blurry due to a combination of my eyelashes and my unfocussed vision which would soon correct itself.

Sure enough, a few moments later and I could see the blurry outlines of my eyelashes perfectly. However, not much else was in view apart from the grass and a brick wall.

From that, I could at least confirm I was outside as I could make out some small shrubbery at the base of the wall which, if we were underground, would not survive. Then again, as I discussed with Andy earlier, with the darkness, not even these plants should be surviving.

I needed a better view and the only way to achieve that was to roll over. Did unconscious people roll over? I highly doubt it. Then again, maybe unconscious people can come back to consciousness but remain in a sleeping state. I could pretend that this was the case and try to turn over.

That would most likely earn me a kick somewhere unpleasant to ensure I was fully awake again.

The good thing, perhaps the only good thing, was that I

was still alive. Though, with all the pain and what I suspect is coming next, I don't know if that was entirely a good thing at all.

One other option was to simply own up to the fact I'm awake. From there I could see what was going on.

Ah, what the heck? Other than my life, which I had been willing to give up earlier, what have I got to lose?

There was one thing I wanted to do first.

Ever so slowly, I dug my good hand into my pocket. I wrapped my fingers around the cool ivory pair of animals and withdrew my hand again.

Still moving as slowly as I could, I raised the turtle to my mouth and whispered to it.

Sure I felt like an idiot, but what harm was there in trying?

"Kath? I don't know if you can hear this. We've lost. I was wrong. We were wrong. Keep listening if you can. You might learn something useful.

As quickly as I could I pocketed the turtle into my felt jacket and I moved my arms around in an attempt to use them to lever myself up and then, hopefully, manage to stand.

What I hadn't realised, however, was part of the ache in my shoulder was from lying on it too much. It had gone to sleep, along with the rest of my arm. I could still feel the grazes and bruises throbbing, but when I tried to use it to sit up, I nearly ended up collapsing back on my face again. My good arm instinctively reacted and countered my balance so I was at least able to sit up.

Almost in relief, the blood started to flow back into my arm. I would have it operating again soon enough, but not before that awful pins and needles sensation and horrible crampy feeling that makes you dread even the thought of moving it took over.

More importantly, I looked around.

There was grass, which I already knew. A park, albeit a small one, perhaps one of those decorative features on plots too small to build a house on so the council allocates it to landscaping instead. A couple of trees, a park bench.

Over the road was another small patch of grass that marked the point where two townhouses met at an odd angle.

It was there that the voices came from.

I could make out the shape of a man, a normal man. He was just visible from the light of a nearby streetlamp. There was another shape, taller, but a lot harder to make out. I didn't need to see any more clearly, though. I knew who it was.

The conversation stopped as soon as I had sat up.

Blood was pumping viciously through the veins in my arm now and it was starting to herald the arrival of that tender, excruciating period of reawakening in the limb. There was no way I could simply jump up and run away. Neither this damned arm nor my almost as useless ankle would allow it.

Doing my best to ignore this, I managed to see a third person in the shadow of the townhouses.

This one was lying on the ground and I only needed one guess as to who it was.

He wasn't moving from what I could tell.

Some more muttered words and the man turned and came toward me.

I thought he was bald, initially. He actually had blonde hair but trimmed to a very close shave, the kind of look you had an urge to run your hand over to feel the little soft bristles against your skin. His face was broad, brutish, but not aggressive, oddly enough. What I might have expected was a skinhead bruiser like you see in some British movies. Not this guy. Jeans, yes. Leather jacket, yes. He probably even had the stereotyped red bracers on underneath.

There was no malicious smile on his face, no inherent threat. He simply walked toward me, hands dug deep in his jacket pockets, showing he was feeling the cold as much as I was.

"Right," he spoke with a gravelly tone, perhaps a smoker, "Up."

I didn't think that was going to be possible just yet, but who was I to argue?

Still favouring my now electrically charged arm – well it felt like that – I managed to hobble to my feet, or foot, rather. There was no putting weight on my left foot without a stabbing sensation shooting up my leg.

He stopped a couple of feet away and flicked his head toward where Grekon was hiding in the shadows.

I shrugged and said, "It'll take me some time, but I'll try."

I limped very awkwardly forward in that overly dramatic waddle that required me to almost throw my shoulders into the air to keep me moving.

The guy rolled his eyes and let out a deep sigh before pulling his right hand from his pocket and grabbing my still very tender right elbow.

Very nearly howling with the sensation of his fingers closing on the extremely sensitive, pins and needles ridden limb, I gritted my teeth and let my mind get lost in thoughts about his hand.

It looked to have been covered in blood, still shiny as if he had only recently dipped it in a bucket of the stuff so I expected a nice handprint on my felt jacket afterwards. Heck, it already had tears, scorch marks and stains, what was a dash of someone else's blood?

A little rough, he was, but he was actually very helpful in coping with the stuffed ankle, allowing me to put a fair bit of weight on him to compensate and not a word was said.

It took almost two minutes for me to cross the small section of the park and the street beyond. I was hoping that would have been enough time for Andy to wake up.

No such luck.

When the guy deemed that we had moved far enough, he simply let go of my arm, now much more under my control, and stepped back against one of the townhouses' walls.

Grekon turned to face me, though he seemed almost transparent in the shadow of these buildings. Only one of his eyes glowed now. I must have been right about Andy scoring a good hit. One, however, was enough.

It still burned with a deep fire, flames seemingly dancing just underneath the surface. It was captivating, mesmeric but not enough to keep me from asking, "Why am I still alive?"

His manner was a little less showy now, almost petulant, "I told you. There must be a reason for you to show up here."

"So I'm what you've been looking for?"

A flash of white teeth. Fangs.

"Hardly," he scoffed, "No. What I have been looking for, I believe, is right here."

There was a faint movement in the gloom below and I could only read it as Grekon indicating Andy's prone body.

"I told you, he's nobody."

"To you, maybe. I have a talent for sniffing out the people I need. I missed him earlier because he is not like the others I have been hunting. He smells… foreign. A little like you, but you are empty. Useless. This one has power and that is why I am sure he is exactly what I need."

Of course. His abilities. We'd been talking about using someone as bait to draw Grekon out. Well, we had thought it was One at the time, but still. And Grekon hadn't even registered Andy as having an ability earlier, almost believing he was nothing. But the smelling foreign? Racist much? Is that all it is though? That he is from Germany? I don't think so.

Some more movement in the darkness and I had to hop backwards as Andy's body began to levitate off the ground. His body remained rigid as if he were still lying on the ground.

"I have been able to manipulate others' abilities before. Trick them almost, because I could sense them, understand them."

That made sense. Having seen that vision earlier at Kath's, it sort of explained what the man had been doing before he died. He had jumped as if trying to dodge the car, but there had been nothing there. Well, there was, but he had been early. His gift must have been to see into the future, but Grekon managed to skewer it, twist it to fool him.

"This one, he's different. Like you are. He isn't from around here."

"He's German!"

Grekon snarled, "You idiot! He doesn't smell of this world."

Now, Andy had not mentioned that at all. Could he have been a dimension-hopping person too? He kept his powers from me. Maybe he left that out as well.

Then again, he had been grabbing onto me all afternoon and had hung out in Kath and Luka's house. Maybe it was like when I visited my grandmother. She had an obsession with mothballs and Naphthalene. So much so, that if you visited her for an hour or two, you were bound to be warding off moths and silverfish for hours to come.

"Consider yourself lucky," Grekon said as Andy started to rotate in mid-air so that he was upright. To look at him, you'd have thought he was standing casually, with no hanging limbs or droopy head, "I know his purpose. Yours, I'm yet to find out."

And with no more ceremony than that, I watched in horror as Grekon's claw snatched out and punched through Andy's ribs burying itself deep inside.

I felt like he had just done it to me as any thought of breathing left my mind and a massive lump rose in my throat. The numbness I had felt in my arm earlier was nothing to the wave that poured through me now.

My legs buckled and I fell to the ground.

There had been no blood as Grekon's hand violated Andy's chest. Andy hadn't even reacted, no scream;

nothing. The only thing I noticed was his body somehow managed to go limp and the colour seemed to drain from his skin.

When the claw came out again with that same swift motion, I felt flecks of warm wetness splash my face and I didn't dare think about what it was.

Grekon turned his hand to show me what he held. Between his horrid grey fingers was Andy's heart. No longer beating, but blood continued to pour from the various veins and arteries that now dangled uselessly off the organ.

If not for the lump in my throat, I was sure I would have vomited. I could only stare in horror as he squeezed the rest of the crimson fluid out and shook it as one might do a sponge.

Andy's body collapsed to the ground, another piece of garbage to simply be disposed of, at least in Grekon's eyes.

As it hit the floor, his body appeared to swim out of focus, becoming that same semi-transparent state that Grekon had taken on, like he wasn't altogether there.

How true that was now. How easily his life had been taken from him after all the fight he had put up.

I wanted to do the ignoble thing of beating my hands uselessly against Grekon, much like a terrified child might do, but I couldn't. I couldn't let myself become that, not for Andy's sake.

Grekon turned the organ over in his hand, bringing his other up to cradle it and as he did so, though it may have been a hallucination on my part, I saw light gleam off the heart as one would expect from a mirror. Its surface looked to have transformed from something wholly organic and life-giving into a metallic stone of sorts. Then I realised the light wasn't only coming from the streetlamp's reflection. There was something inside Andy's heart giving off another light. This one was a warm pinkish colour, so faint, but unmistakably there.

When Grekon saw it with that horrid one eye of his, he

smiled once more.

"Yes. This is it," he looked over at his underling who was still huddled against the wall looking decidedly as if he wished to be somewhere else.

"What will it do?"

I had to ask. Grekon liked to talk. I wanted to know if I was about to share Andy's fate. The words were barely audible even to my own ears.

"This is the key to all realities, the missing link that will connect all of them together, allowing me to walk from one to the other. And to control them all."

Brilliant.

He was looking at me now; that solitary eye trying to bore its way into my head.

I recalled he used to be able to read minds back when he visited my world. He didn't seem to actually be able to do that here.

Not being funny, though, but even if he could, he wouldn't have found much. I mean, what was I supposed to do now?

Andy was dead. Grekon had what he wanted. I had no plan. I hadn't from the very beginning, really. I had said I wasn't the right man for the job. I was a nobody who just kept landing in the wrong place at the wrong time, and here we were again.

He'd won.

What could I do? Really! I was wracking my brain and I couldn't think of a single thing.

There was nothing to say, nothing to do.

Yet, there was something in that eye. The way it was boring into me, like it was trying to read my mind.

Grekon was worried.

Was it that he knew something I didn't, or that he thought I knew something he didn't?

He had kept on saying there was a reason I was here. A purpose.

It was rather strange that it was me here. Me specifically

and, I guess, not Narelle or Bob. Two people who actually had powers far greater than Andy's or Kath's.

The fact fate had put me in charge of saving the whole of all realities did seem a little odd. If you believe in fate, and it seemed that Grekon just might.

So what was his plan for me? He had killed Andy but said he was yet to find out what I was here for.

If Andy's heart was the key, what was I?

Well, it seemed neither of us knew.

On that very thought, at that precise moment, he pulled away back into the shadows, though the glow from Andy's heart was enough to illuminate his face. It was hard to read such a bestial expression, but if I had to guess, he seemed satisfied. Not solely with the fact he had the heart/key.

Had he read my mind? Had he realised I was clueless?

If he had, that was probably a good thing. Maybe he'd let me live, though to live with him as ruler of all realities, I'm not sure it was worth it.

"Don't you worry," he sounded almost nice, "You'll be looked after."

And with that, at extraordinary speed, he disappeared upward, further into darkness.

A few moments later, there was a loud 'chink' of a sound, the kind a blacksmith's hammer might make against the anvil.

A flash of light. No particular colour, but all colours at once. I didn't even bother questioning this. Having travelled between realities before, I remembered colour, for some reason, had a very big thing to do with the boundaries between realities. All colours, actually, rolling together like a liquid kaleidoscope.

Another chink and flash, this time followed by a cracking sound; loud and ominous.

How odd that the demise of all worlds was happening here, somewhere unimportant in the middle of London with only myself and this other guy as witnesses.

A shower of glittering sparks fell to the grass like

glowing embers from a fire. I expected them to die out, smoulder away and vanish to the winds, but they didn't. Instead, they continued to sparkle, imbuing each blade of grass they touched with a little bit of their light.

And again – chink, flash, rumble, shower.

Grekon was now groaning with each strike. Clearly, it was a massive effort for him.

I could see the glowing heart as he smashed it against a particular point where the two townhouse walls met. Its light was getting more brilliant, also fluid. All across Grekon's semi-transparent skin was the ripple effect one sees when light is reflected off a body of water. Once again, no longer grey, but a mix of colours.

The showers of sparks were getting thicker, richer and they were starting to carpet the ground until it seemed I was kneeling in the middle of some outdoor hippy disco. The area was soon awash with colour.

Andy was partially buried under some of these sparks and they seemed to return some of the qualities of life that had once been there, a brightness to his skin as if the blood was coursing through his veins after a long bout of exercise.

I couldn't look at him for too long, tears were already battling to come out.

I raised my hands to catch some of the sparks, only to realise they were already dotted with them, like a light fall of snow, how it sticks to your clothes and skin, though, this time, it did not melt away.

There was no particular sensation where it touched me. I had been completely unaware that it had been making any contact at all. No heat, no tingle. They were, however, having a similar effect on my own body; like someone had rubbed a mystical moisturiser or revitaliser all over me. Tiny golden, rippling waves dispersed from each tiny speck as it came into contact with my pasty skin much like shockwaves from falling meteors.

What was strange was that I didn't feel the specks of

light, but when those tiny ripples that ran across my skin intersected with other ripples, I felt a slight stabbing sensation. Ever so slight that, if I hadn't been watching them, I would never have noticed.

Chink, flash, rumble, chink…

With every strike, the flash was getting brighter, the rumble louder. Within nine or ten hits, the grass was completely covered by the sparks.

I tried wiping them from my clothes and my skin, but they wouldn't budge. I simply couldn't seem to make contact with them, as if they weren't there. In short order, I, too, was completely covered. I stood to examine myself, with some difficulty.

Turning to look at Grekon's underling, I got a fairly good idea of what I must look like. He was completely encased from head to toe in shimmering light, even his eyeballs had been covered. I could still make out the details of his clothing and the features of his face, but it was as if he was made of this ethereal light.

He stood, dumbstruck, watching his master's work, oblivious to what else was happening.

Those rumbles had transgressed across the sound barrier and now vibrated through the very earth. My bones also seemed to react to each swing of Andy's heart, lurching inside my body, almost sending me off balance. I could feel myself starting to sway like some sort of drunkard standing on the deck of a ship in very choppy waters.

There was no point trying to run. There was no way I could have climbed up to stop Grekon.

Another three strikes and a jolt of pain lanced through my body, up my spine and dispersing out along my nerves. I screamed in response and was startled to hear a second voice in chorus with mine. Grekon's servant.

The next strike and the pain had become agony, ripping through every muscle, nerve and fibre of my body. My brain felt as though it had gone thirty seconds in a blender. I had to fight to keep my thoughts from becoming mush.

This time, however, the screams came from elsewhere, too. The people of this reality must have felt their world starting to come apart, maybe feeling the same jolts I was experiencing.

My knees gave way once more and I collapsed to the luminescent ground on the next clang. I screwed my eyes shut, stupidly hoping this would alleviate some of the dreadful effects of Grekon's assault on this reality.

No such luck as, with the next strike, I felt as though someone had tied every molecule of my being to the back of a horse and then set them on a hard gallop, essentially trying to tear me apart. It was excruciating and I was really starting to wish he had simply killed me too. It had to have been a better option than this.

Something vibrated against my body. Localised so I knew it was unrelated to the onslaught of Grekon's actions.

A voice, strained and barely audible, "It isn't finished."
It was Kath.
"His prize is but the wooden spoon."
She was losing her mind. If she was experiencing the pain I was, I wasn't surprised.

I wasn't sweating, the sparks had somehow sealed my pores. I wasn't able to move anymore, I was somehow frozen in a semi-foetal position, eyes closed, arms practically wrapped around my body trying to hold it all together. The pain I had felt around my body earlier was infinitesimally small in comparison to the wracking and slicing sensations that were coursing through my entire being.

I didn't hear the next blow, but I felt it.

It was as if those imaginary horses had won the struggle to pull me apart from my very atoms. One second, I felt whole, complete, albeit in agony. The next, there was a gentle popping sound followed by a whooshing of air as though someone had opened up a vacuum and allowed oxygen in. With that rush went my pain and my mind somehow separated from my self.

Now that sensation was not unknown to me.

Like with the colours, every time I had traversed realities, I had become disembodied, astral if you like. There was my Self, but no physical me.

That was what it felt like this time.

I was present, but gone were the colours. Without eyelids, or eyes for that matter, I wasn't really sure if I should be able to see or not. As it was, there was only darkness.

No sensation of flying or falling.

I just was.

Me.

Alone in a black void.

Reality was gone and there was nothing I could do.

It felt like an eternity, but I really didn't know how long had passed. The fact I was able to register anything at all was far beyond my comprehension.

How was I existing if nothing else was?

Was this a prison Grekon had created for me? If it was, it was effective. I couldn't move for there was nothing to move. I couldn't speak as I had nothing to speak with.

I had a sense of my physical being, but it simply wasn't there.

There was an itch to scratch, but it wasn't a physical one. It was my thoughts running through my non-existent brain trying to comprehend what was happening to me. How was it even possible for me to think? Yet I was!

Was this my soul? Had I, as an avid Atheist, well, Agnostic, been naïve in assuming the human soul was a fable, that our beings were only the product of billions of electrical impulses coursing through our brains?

Without a brain to have those impulses, it shouldn't have been possible to exist, to have these thoughts. So, were our thoughts more than biological?

Yet, if religions had been right, where was I? Purgatory?

Or was this heaven? Was heaven simply a construct from

our own minds that we are destined to live in and this is all my soul could dream up for me to spend the rest of eternity in? A void?

Maybe it was hell. No fire or brimstone, but an eternity trapped with only my thoughts for company would surely have been someone's idea of hell. I am sure some of my acquaintances believed so.

I wanted to try singing out loud, to see if I could make noise, or if I could somehow project my thoughts but I couldn't even think of a song to sing.

A few jumbled notes came to mind but couldn't form anything coherent.

So, why try singing when I could try talking?

I very nearly couldn't think of anything to try saying when one word came to mind.

'Hello.'

Right. I tried saying it, but nothing actually came out. I didn't hear anything except in my head. Or what I assumed was my head, though I knew it didn't exist.

Or did it?

Maybe this wasn't heaven or hell but I was trapped inside my head without access to my body.

Was this what Locked-In Syndrome was like?

No, as they were meant to be able to hear and see things.

A coma? Had I succumbed to the pain? Had it all been too much and this was some medically induced dream?

I felt something.

A tugging. It felt as though something was tugging gently on what should have been my big toe. Though I didn't have a big toe, it must simply have been tugging on one of the extremities of my mind.

The tugging turned to a yank. A single, hard, yank but my mind felt stuck in place, unwillingly fighting against the pull.

No third chances, it seemed, as the yank escalated even further and my mind/soul was wrenched from wherever it was and the darkness vanished from around me, disappearing upward like water down a plug hole.

It swirled and gurgled upward and, in its place, came a greyscale wall or shades that also went the way of the blackness.

Next came the more familiar colours. First, the pastel colours of the rainbow quickly mingled and mutated into a vast array of hues. These too rushed past me, appearing to speed up as they went. My 'soul' eyes were unable to keep up with the wash of colour that sped past me and I knew that if I had a stomach, it would have lost its contents by now. I was starting to feel so ill and dizzy.

Soon the colours were accompanied by a sound. It started small, low like a gentle hum, but, like the colours, quickly altered, rising in pitch, gaining a vibrato of sorts as it increased in volume. From its bass notes, it quickly skewered through the middle range and up into the piercing screech one associated with nails running across a blackboard.

This screech didn't go any higher but wailed on as I was continually dragged 'downward' by this unseen force until I felt my non-existent self squashed and mangled through what felt like some sort of funnel.

All I wanted to do was scream.

My thoughts lost cohesion, much like my body had, and in contrast to the colours, I feel darkness clawing into, through and over me until there is nothing left. Even the god-awful sounds disperse in a matter of seconds that could easily have been years.

Then there is nothing.

Anthony Harwood

THE FIVE STAGES OF GRIEF

I feel something before I see or hear.

Weight on my shoulders, pulling them backwards and down. Heat. Coming from within, from above me, all around me.

A bright light comes into being against my eyelids that are closed giving me a pinkish wash of existence to replace the horrors that had come before.

I don't mind the brightness, or the pink now that I have eyelids again.

There is something on my head and a sweet dry smell in the air that is vaguely familiar.

I don't know how long I stood there basking in the glory of being again, but it wasn't long before sound rushed into my ears like water pouring down a plughole, swirling and mixing, it was a garbled mess.

The only thing I could vaguely make out was someone yelling something that sounded vaguely like a New Zealander saying 'shin'.

There was a loud cracking sound which was also very familiar. A gunshot.

My eyes snapped open and the brightness revealed itself as a burning hot sun that seemed to hover only metres above my head.

There was smoke in the air and movement all around me. Unaccustomed to the light, I could only see great hulking silhouettes charging backwards and forward as more and more guns went off.

I sensed people beside me, I had no idea who, but they weren't hitting me so they had to have been friends.

"Get down!" I scream at the top of my lungs and through some weird instinctual impulse, I blindly dove forward onto softly packed sand. Strangely, there was a sort of giving to the ground beneath me, an almost sponginess that meant I didn't hurt myself.

In fact, there was no pain at all. Not in my ankle, my shoulder, my hands. All I could really complain about was a large mass that seemed to fall down on top of me as I land. It pressed me hard to the ground.

Somewhere to my right a loud clap followed by a wave of heat and light as something explodes.

People scream behind me and something falls over my legs.

I look up trying to make heads or tails of whatever was going on and all I can see are rocks, sand, fallen branches and smoke. The sun is too bright still and I am very close to losing it.

I try to crawl forward but whatever is on my legs is holding me in place. I turn to see what it is with some difficulty as whatever is on my back is restricting my movement.

There is a man dressed in army greens lying awkwardly over me. He is also wearing some kind of backpack which added to his weight and I realised that this was exactly what was holding me down too.

Was I in the army?

Am I in a war?

Who am I fighting for?

I'm not built for this! I know for a fact there is no way I'd survive a war! I just want to go home!

I can feel the scream that was trapped inside through my incorporeal journey start to swell inside me.

It's about to escape my lips when someone shouts, "Cut!"

The gunshots cease and the man on my legs starts to vibrate and then lifts himself up onto hands and knees and I see he is actually laughing.

"What the hell?"

The words come out with the energy and volume that was meant for the scream and the man freezes and looks at me in terror.

"I'm so sorry, Mr Crossman. I didn't mean to laugh."

My head started to shake slightly from side to side like it had a mind of its own. I couldn't control it. Then I realise my hands are going as well.

The man hasn't moved, nor has the look of fear in his eyes, almost as if he were waiting for something.

"Get him out of here," someone whispered from somewhere and a woman dressed in jeans and a very tight red t-shirt appears, helps the man up and leads him away.

A hand appears next to my face positioned in what appears to be an offer of assistance. I stare at it for a few seconds before accepting the gunfire and death has actually stopped. With the mysterious hand's help, I manage to get back on my feet, heavy backpack and all and try to see through the sunlight.

Only, it isn't sunlight.

It is hot, but it's white and it is actually only standing a few metres from the ground. There are several others positioned around me too of varying brightness.

"I'm sure he didn't mean anything by it, Scott."

"What?" I don't snap this time; I am genuinely confused.

"It was his fifth time landing on you like that. It can't be comfortable."

"Ok," why bother arguing in a conversation you have no clue about? Not that that has really stopped me before, but better to play it safe right now.

"I'm happy," someone calls from behind one of the suns, "Check the gate."

There is movement and all I can do is stand bewildered.

All around me is a landscape of scorched earth and rockery. It looked like a war zone, but it only stretched six metres in each direction. Where I stood, however, was what appeared to be a natural bunker of sorts, providing enough cover for three or four people at a push. Two if they were wearing the massive packs I seemed to be lugging.

"Gate's clear!"

"That's a wrap for today! Thanks, everyone. Check your call times with Mandy. There have been a few changes in the shooting order for tomorrow. Great day!"

There was an explosion of movement all around the battlefield, though not on it.

I spun around to look at the guy who had helped me up and spoken to me. He's tall, about six-four and built like a swimmer. Dressed all in black. Jeans, long sleeve t-shirt. Clean-shaven, close-cropped hair, a good-looking lad in his mid-twenties.

"Want me to take your pack?"

I just nod.

He moves behind me and the relief as he lifts the backpack off me is enormous; as if I had been wearing it for hours. My back is absolutely soaked in sweat and I can smell it wafting off both me and the pack.

The man moves around to my front again and I am almost gobsmacked when I see he is lifting the damn thing with one arm and no signs of strain.

"Shall we?"

I nod and he moves off into the glare of one of the 'suns'.

As I follow, another man in a black jacket and jeans, this one in his forties with salt and peppered hair and a long, thin scar across the left side of his forehead approaches with a big smile on his face. He runs the back of a hand across the scar and places a cap on his head.

"Brilliant, Scott. Loved it. You pulled that out of the bag. That look on your face. Not what I was going for, but even better. Sort of like terror crossed with absolute bewilderment. Pure genius."

I nearly stumble over a boulder as I splutter out, "Umm, thanks."

"So you have tomorrow off, but I've had some notes and changes sent to your trailer, sorry about that."

"Not a problem," I managed as the battlefield became a step down to cold flat concrete.

"Right," a hint of uncertainty in the man's voice but there isn't much I can do about that, "Well, see you Friday."

"Yes, I'll see you then," what else can I say? The man falls behind as I keep walking.

I don't want to lose sight of the man with the backpack. He knows where I am meant to be going and that is a safer course to follow than standing by completely lost.

I do manage to catch a few glimpses around. I'm in a big warehouse with various constructions around. They're set pieces, some fully assembled, others waiting to be either removed or erected.

It isn't a warehouse but a soundstage. They're filming a movie here.

I'm filming a movie here.

People are moving around adjusting things, packing stuff away, however, my guide is leading me away from all of that toward a small door. He opens it and holds it until I walk through into the bright sunlight.

With whatever it is I am wearing, the added heat of the sun is slightly uncomfortable, but compared to the cold I'd been feeling only minutes before, it was a joy to feel the natural light on my face.

The sun, the real one and not one of the bright lights they had used inside, was low on the horizon and since the day's shooting was over, I figured it was summer. The temperature suggested that too.

We were on some sort of production lot. A couple of other warehouse buildings stood nearby as well as quite a few large trucks.

"This way," my guide calls, having let the door close and moved off to my right. I follow.

We pass techies and other crew as we walk as well as many oddly dressed people who were either actors or extras.

The crew seemed to ignore me, which I was absolutely fine with, but some of the extras and costumed individuals faltered in their step when they saw me and mumbled something to their colleagues excitedly.

I smiled at them and they beamed back; their eyes alight with something I couldn't quite place. Very strange.

"Janine's sent through a couple more scripts for you to have a look at and she's still waiting for your answer on the

Hooperman project. You had three calls from PTZ regarding the campaign and getting some extra clearances. Janine okayed it with them to call directly. Also, I've RSVP'd for tomorrow night's party for the President."

"Great," was all I could muster and I could hear the hollowness in my voice.

The man stopped. He'd disposed of the backpack before we exited the sound stage, but I hadn't noticed. He was now looking at me with a slightly worried look. It didn't quite have a concern, but there was the feeling that something wasn't right.

Was he sensing it too? Could he tell this was all wrong? Or was he just some sort of illusion? Maybe this whole thing was, like in Star Trek with the holodeck.

No. I've experienced too much to know that to be true.

"Are you alright, Scott?"

He clearly sensed there being something off about me.

There really was, too. I felt it, almost like my insides were striving to get out. With that thought, I felt my stomach lurch and barely managed to keep myself from throwing up.

The man noticed, though, and instantly reached for his mobile, "Should I call a doctor?"

I waved him off, not ready to open my mouth to speak in case something else came out instead.

He kept hold of his phone but put his arm under mine to offer support. The fact he was a good half a foot taller than me meant he had to lean down to do so and I was hoisted almost off my feet. There was no doubt this guy could carry me without slowing his pace.

Again, there was no actual concern in his expression, though. You know that feeling when someone is looking at you while you're talking but there is a slightly glazed look that indicates they're probably considering their options for dinner or perhaps worrying about having paid too much for a new pair of shoes instead of actually finding interest in you or the conversation.

I couldn't worry about that now. I literally couldn't. My mind had become awash with a jumble of images and memories, some of which I couldn't actually recall experiencing the first time.

People's faces I'd never met and names inherently attached to them, half-remembered conversations and vivid situations I swear I'd never lived through were starting to rinse themselves through my brain and it was starting to hurt as my own memories fought to maintain their own place.

Andy!

It was one image that still stood out amongst the old and the foreign that were both clashing and speeding around in my skull. The queasiness came flooding back and I felt the bile rise at the back of my throat, though only through a sheer force of will did I prevent myself from losing whatever lunch I don't even remember eating – though an image of a plate full of roast chicken with greens and gravy came to mind the instant I even considered it – all over this man – Edward, though he prefers Eddie. I'd somehow managed to snag that out of the quagmire my mind had become.

Andy lying lifeless on the cold ground, the air around him aglow with ethereal, dancing spark lights. But they were falling lights. The image was wrong. They should have been rising, carrying his spirit away to the skies.

I'm certainly not a religious man, but it was an image from so many films and Andy deserved such a Hollywood ending; one that came a lot later than it actually had done.

All the other memories, false or otherwise, were butting hard against this one, trying to swallow it up, bury it, perhaps even eradicate it, however, it was far too fresh, too vivid to simply be wiped away. It was as if it were attached not only to my brain but somehow tied to my very heart and being too and that was somehow proving to be an unbreakable connection.

It had to be due to the fact it was the very last I could recall of that life. Even so, it had been twisted, distorted. I was sure it had been cold, near to freezing, yet there was a warmth to this memory that, even now, I found settling and calming.

I latched onto that warmth, that sensation and everything else seemed to settle down.

"Scott?"

He didn't like me. This Eddie. That was what was in his

eyes. I could see it now. I was looking straight into them, coming back to Earth, to now. This reality, wherever that was and whatever it entailed.

It wasn't outright hostility, but there was a definite dislike lurking just behind the pupils, unfortunately not well hidden by the slight tightening of muscles around his eyes as he looked at me.

Nothing I couldn't handle. Nor something I had not experienced before. He was my Personal Assistant. I know that now. He was paid to look after me. With me gone, he was unemployed and thus came the concern, as maligned as it was.

But why didn't he like me?

Yes, I'd experienced dislike before. Heck, I'd had fireballs hurled at me out of anger. That didn't mean I understood it or liked it. Was I high maintenance? I couldn't imagine so. I kept myself to myself when I was at home. My humour could rub people the wrong way at times. Or should I say grate them the wrong way?

No. The man back on the set, the one who had fallen on me, had been terrified of me.

Oh, no.

This was one of those clichéd waking up in another version of you situations where you find out your whole life has been led horribly and you're actually a nasty person. Jennifer Garner's 'Suddenly 30' movie springs to mind.

"13 going on 30," I corrected myself. That's what it was called in the UK, if indeed that was where I was, though the accents and temperature seemed to be right.

"I beg your pardon?"

Eddie's expression changed. I realised two things. One, that I had just said that out loud and, two, I had been staring at him for a while now.

That had to be it, though. For some reason, Grekon had turned my life into a cliché. Wouldn't be the first time it had been in that condition.

"Nothing," I told Eddie, managing to find my own two feet and plant my weight firmly on them and taking the load from him, "Just one of those awkward moments of..."

What?

"Spontaneous Amnesia. Nausea, too. Too much to remember," I tapped the side of my head to illustrate and realised that was Beginners Acting 101 like using your fingers to highlight quotation marks in a monologue, "Lines and all. And those lamps didn't help with all that heat. And that pack!"

With that, Eddie's eyes returned to his, from what I had seen so far, normal apathetic glare. I was whining and he was obviously used to that.

Maybe it wasn't so much of a cliché, then. I do tend to whine a lot.

I shut my mouth and allowed him to lead me back to my trailer. I had a trailer! How cool was that? Actors mainly only dream about having a trailer.

As exciting as that thought was, my mind managed to push it aside and focus back on my anchoring memory.

The invading images had started to subside as we spoke. I'd have said conversed, but it wasn't. I got the strong impression we didn't converse. We spoke at each other. They were foggy, unclear but still lingering in there somewhere like a ghoul or goblin lurking in the shadows ready to pounce. My own true memories had won out, held their ground, except that last memory. It was all wrong but I knew that knowing that it was wrong was what was helping keep those alien thoughts at bay.

It would be good to be able to sit down on my own and go over everything. See if I could make something out of these new memories, dig through them to see if Grekon is in there somewhere.

A couple of hundred metres more and Eddie produced a key from his pocket and unlocked my trailer door. It was a nice white one. I'd seen the like before, usually in the form of makeup or costume trailers on location. Maybe forty feet long. I wasn't sure if that was a good length or not, but I didn't really care right now.

I stepped inside and Eddie followed me.

It was very clean and decked out like a small one bed house. A kitchenette, dining table and a lounge-like section took up the majority of the space while a small door led to the left-hand end of the trailer from the entry.

Keeping calm, which I must say was very difficult, I turned to the right instead and moved to the lounge section where there was a couch on one side and a small but comfy-looking armchair on the other with a small white coffee table in between. On that lay a couple of scripts. One looked a little worse for wear and covered with pencilled notes, the other was clean and freshly printed. Besides these, politely placed so it was exactly in line with the edge of the table, was a call sheet with a few different coloured pieces of paper clipped to the back.

Well, at least I knew where I was going to be getting my lines from for the next day of shooting. Which wasn't for a few days according to the man on the sound stage. The Director. Carlos.

So what did I do next? What could I do?

Was I supposed to sit back and enjoy this new reality? I could already see it had perks. I was a jobbing actor, for one. Not just jobbing, but a successful one, it seemed.

How could I be happy with that, though? Andy had died so I could live the life of my dreams? By putting it that way, it could sound heroic, but it wasn't a selfless sacrifice. He was murdered.

Either way, I couldn't just accept this if that was the price to pay. I think I know a few people who just might, but that wasn't me.

Grekon had taken control of reality, of all realities it sounded like.

Then why did I exist at all?

Now that one stumped me.

"Scott?"

I realised I was screwing my face up unconsciously as I was thinking it through. I had jutted my jaw to the left and stuck my lower lip out while squinting my eyes and gazing into the distance. I hadn't even seen Eddie move to stand by the armchair. I blinked and saw him and quickly realigned my features to what might be deemed normal, though, with my face, that might not be said by everyone.

"Are you sure you're okay?"

I nodded vaguely and muttered a quiet, "Uh-huh," that nearly caught in the back of my throat.

He looked different now. Again, in the eyes.

"Did you want me to call your agent? If you're not happy with the trailer, I'm sure they'll change it."

"What?" Was he kidding? "No! I like the trailer. I love it! I just have a lot on my mind at present."

Eddie opened his mouth to say something but let it go.

He was actually concerned, now. That was what it was. He was starting to worry about me and who could blame him?

"Look, Eddie, it's nothing, really. Just a few personal things I've got to go over."

"No you don't," He crossed his arms.

Now I was a bit lost for words. How the hell would he know?

I asked him that, too.

"That's what you employed me for! To deal with all your personal 'things'."

Bugger.

Was I really that busy that I needed someone to deal with my personal life? Surely not. Though I certainly could have used someone like that back in Kath's dark world.

Kath! Where was she? Was she around here? What about the boy?

The kids in the hospital? Had Grekon simply transferred them here? Given them wonderful and happy lives?

Had he done the complete opposite? Made their lives a living hell? Or snuffed them out completely.

I had no way of knowing! I didn't even know where I was. Studio and film lot names were dancing in the back of my head but I couldn't quite find the right one. Was I even in London still? Or England?

"Seriously, man!"

Once again, Eddie's voice broke me out of my reverie and, once again, I had to let my face relax.

"Seriously? Why do you care?" I snapped back. It's all I could think of. There was no way I could tell him the truth. Besides, he hadn't really cared earlier. Why now?

There was a flash of a memory. He was sitting in front of

me laughing, relaxed. Not at all like he was now.

"Because you pay me to."

That was honest, in a way.

I had nothing to say to that. I mean, it was me he was talking to, but it wasn't the Me me. It was this other reality's version of me that I had been slotted into. For all I know, Eddie was the only person in the world I actually talked to. Until I could straighten out these new memories and isolate them from the real ones, I had no idea who this person actually was.

Right now, I was all alone with a paid Personal Assistant who didn't actually like me very much as my only sounding board and I had no idea what to do next.

I collapsed onto the couch and felt my head start to shake from side to side ever so slightly like I was merely hinting at the world, 'no', too scared to actually say it. Who would listen anyway?

"Oh, Merde," crept over my tongue and out of my mouth, "I'm screwed."

COMFORT IN A PROBLEM

I found myself lost in my head again. I don't know for how long, but the next thing I knew of the outside world, a steaming teacup was clattered against the coffee table.

Must have been a while if he had time to make tea.

Unconsciously, the words, "Thank you," fell out of my mouth and I looked up in time to see him sink into the armchair opposite me. The concern still playing in his eyes.

Why the eyes? I was always scrutinising his eyes.

He leaned forward, elbows on knees, hands clasped in between the latter, "What is it? What's going on?"

My mouth dangled open in its haste to explain what had happened only to find words weren't exactly forthcoming in the act. That was a good thing, I suppose.

One thing I needed was to find out if I was alone here.

"I need you to find someone for me."

Eddie sighed and shook his head, "I thought we were past that."

"What?"

What the heck did he mean by that? A few possible explanations came to mind but I didn't have the time nor the desire to go into those.

"No. Umm. Not like that. However 'that' is. I need you to find an old lady for me. Kathleen Wainwright. Maybe seventies. White. Grey hair. I don't know if she's around here. I don't even know her address. Or her actual age. Or anything about her," this was starting to sound hopeless even to me. Then I remembered, "She might have a grandson called Luka living with her."

Eddie sat staring at me.

"Does that help at all?"

I could tell from his expression it didn't. But it was his job and he responded, "You've given me a name. I guess it is something. May I ask why you need this woman you don't know anything about?"

"No," was the best answer I could think of, "Eddie, this is very important. It's just an address or a phone number I need. Then you can forget all about it."

Maybe I could too. Maybe Kath will be the key.

There was a knock on the door.

"Come in," I called, standing up.

A bespectacled young lady, I say young, but she was probably my age, came in. Her strawberry blonde hair was wrapped around and locked in place on top of her head with a pencil. She wore a tank top, or vest as they are known in the UK, with a faded black shadow print of Pink's screaming face from Pink Floyd's The Wall on the front.

"Scott! We need your costume, please. Did you want Claire to help with the make-up?"

I'd forgotten I was still in Army gear. I wasn't even sure from what period it was, though it did look like something potentially from World War Two.

"No, I'll have a shower, that'll be fine."

Thankfully I'm not a complete novice in this business.

"Great. Do you want me to wait outside?"

"What for?"

She hesitated, looking a little uncomfortable, "You're costume."

Still an idiot, though.

I smiled at her, trying to make it look like I was joking, "No, I'll get changed now."

A look at Eddie and there was no doubting he knew something was absolutely not right. I tried to mentally ask him what I should do. Did I just strip? Not likely. Did I have a bathrobe to get into? More my cup of tea.

My quizzical look was answered with one of as much bewilderment.

I could sense the ticking of the proverbial clock and made up my mind.

Unbuttoning the shirt, I headed toward the other end of the trailer and the little door I had opted not to go through earlier.

Behind it, I found a small bedroom setup. A single bed ran the width of the room against the back wall. A small toilet and shower room were to my right with a cupboard to my left.

A quick look around I found there was no bathrobe. So this other me wasn't like me in that regard. Mind you, I'd done the same thing earlier for the audition.

Was that earlier? How much earlier? Was it yesterday or still today? Funny how not having a sun can skew your sense of time. Then again, this whole new reality business could mean it is in the future, past or whenever. In all honesty, whenever it was, it was worlds away and I seemed to be someone else completely different now, so why should it matter anyway?

To keep the girl from waiting, I quickly undressed down to my underwear and handed the costume to her through the door, using it to protect my modesty.

Which was strange. Especially after the audition. I'd been sitting in my underwear in front of complete strangers and here I was cowering behind a door from people who clearly knew me.

Strangely, it felt that if I was to have undressed in front of them, I'd have been betraying the other me, in case he was a prude. It was his body, not mine to show off. Yet, seeing myself in a quick glimpse of the mirror on the cupboard, it was…

Not my body. Not in the slightest.

I was ripped! I had muscles where I had previously been either bone or flab.

My vague two-pack and underlying keg had turned into a veritable eight pack and, for the first time in my life, I had pectorals and biceps and not the type you get from doing push-ups every day; these were guns.

I had been so lost in my mental awkwardness, I hadn't noticed the physical one. I grabbed my pecs to see if they were real and felt the muscles spasm slightly under my touch. They were!

The change wasn't absolutely miraculous. I wasn't Arnold Schwarzenegger or anything like that, but my once skinny body had become lithe, streamlined, proportioned and, well, attractive.

"Oh my God!"

"Are you alright in there?"

Eddie. He was outside the door. I had heard the girl leave with the closing of the trailer door.

"Umm, yeah, I just," what? I had to think of something, "realised what time it was."

It was the first thing that came to mind.

"Yeah, okay."

He didn't buy it. This man knew the other me well. I heard him swear under his breath on the other side of the door and muttered something else containing the words, 'talk to me'. I couldn't make out the rest.

How could I? What could I say? He'd have me committed even in the best-case scenario.

I had to stop looking at myself. It was pervy and wrong in so many ways.

Looking around the room, I saw a pair of jeans, a white t-shirt and a red hoodie lying on the bed next to two or three magazines.

I had clothes, thank goodness.

"Eddie? Just give me a minute."

He moved away from the door, no more muttering involved; at least that I could hear.

I got the jeans and shirt on in quick order, liking the choice of shirt. It was white but it had a picture of Ernie from Sesame Street on it. Refreshing to think the Muppets exist in this reality too.

Reaching for the hoodie, I actually looked at the cover of the magazines and froze

The man on the cover.

It was Grekon.

He was a man, though. Gone were the wings, the monstrous features. This was the man I had encountered all those years ago in the mirror maze. Even the scars he had back then were gone.

Dressed in a deep blue business suit and smiling, arms crossed with the headline 'Man of the Year - Again' in bold underneath.

What the hell? Man of the year he is not!

My hand diverted from the hoodie to the magazine instead.

I read the smaller print title out loud, trying to get them to make sense, "World President Grekon tops list for third time running."

"World President," I repeated. What was that supposed to mean? He'd recreated reality to place himself as leader of the planet? Not surprising, but why had he kept it like my reality and not one he hails from?

Dark caverns, burning torches, weird monsters? That was the type of place I'd first encountered him.

The question was, what type of world leader was he? This magazine was painting him in a very nice light. Had he reformed and become the benevolent man portrayed on the cover or was he as conniving and heartless as I knew him to be?

President Grekon.

Hang on, Eddie had mentioned the President when he was spouting all that nonsense as I'd left the sound stage. What was it?

Grabbing the hoodie, I opened the door and stepped back into the lounge, "Eddie?"

He wasn't there. I'd probably annoyed him enough to make him leave. Or maybe he had gone to get a psych ambulance to take me away.

The problem was that I had nowhere to go. I was probably in the safest place I could be for the time being. I wouldn't even know how to get off the film lot. Do I drive? Do I have a driver? Taxi?

The tea Eddie had bought me was cold, but I wasn't in the mood for tea. I opened a few of the kitchenette cupboards until I found the fridge. I was surprisingly thirsty. Mind you, lugging the backpack under those hot lights all day probably hadn't helped this other me.

And, where was he? I had usurped his body. Where had he gone? Or had he existed at all? Those memories that had tried to bulldoze their way into my consciousness must have been his, or was it just part of the effect of Grekon screwing with reality?

Thankfully, this other me also liked Coke, so I grabbed a can and snapped it open. Grateful for the sugar, I tried to neck half of the can and followed it through with a rather loud burp.

If he had changed reality so much, who were all these other people? Had they existed in the other world which wasn't mine either? Or even in mine?

Surely if he had such immense power as to either completely alter these people; or create them from scratch; I shouldn't be able to remember a thing about my previous life.

Yet something was holding my own memories, my own life securely in place.

I took the can with me and sat in the armchair. At least I had some reading material while I waited for some idea of what to do next to pop into my head.

The article was clearly a biassed puff piece on Grekon, gushing about his strength of character and forceful command that quashes any uprisings or problems around the world.

Despite knowing all of this to be completely skewed, I had to admit that it all sounded pretty good. Yet that wasn't the Grekon I knew. He was a malicious, sadist of a man. Someone had to be suffering somewhere.

Didn't they?

I mean this alternate me was living the dream. So, what was wrong? He couldn't be a softy at heart.

I wasn't going to get the answers from this drivel, though. There might be a less butt-kissing publication and, then again, there might not. If he is so swift at crushing a rebellion, he must be pretty hard on the negative publicity.

Still, no inspiration was coming so I flicked through the rest of the two magazines.

They were tabloids. Stars and celebrities enjoying various public aspects of their lives. Eerily, there was a picture of this other me with a beautiful brunette lady on his arm at a gala event of some kind. They both looked happy. The blurb underneath described the 'possible lovebirds gracing the red carpets of the LFTCA - London Film and Television Charities Awards in brackets. Absolutely nothing of use.

There was a knock on the trailer door.

I stood up and went to open it. Eddie was standing outside, his expression one I couldn't read anymore. He looked at me as if I were some stranger he had never met, which was pretty accurate.

He didn't wait for an invite, instead nearly barging past me to get in.

"I found her, sort of. I don't know why you're looking."

"Kath?"

He'd stopped in the middle of the lounge and was looking directly at me.

"If I'd known this would end up where it did, I would have told you to shove it all, regardless of… everything."

Everything? What everything?

"Where has it ended up? Please? I need to talk to her."

He shook his head and fell back onto the couch, "No chance."

That didn't sound good. Had she died? Had Grekon wiped her from this reality? No. She obviously existed or Eddie wouldn't have found her.

I sat down next to him on the couch and a flash of memory told me the other me had done this a number of times before. Obviously, personal assistants and all that, of course they'd sit and chat.

Shaking that from my mind, "Why? What's happened to her?"

"She's gone."

"Gone?"

He nodded as if I knew what that meant, "I'm sorry."

"Sorry? Eddie. Please, tell me what happened to her?"

His eyes narrowed, suspicious, "Scott, we talked about this two days ago. Argued, more like."

I strained my brain to see if I could find a sliver of a memory in there to help me out and found something I had not expected.

Eddie and the other me were kissing.

It was a short flash of memory but it was so vivid it made me start. Definitely something to file away for now as there were more important things at hand, but it left me a little jarred. Still, nothing to help me along in this conversation.

I struggled to find words. The memory had thrown me, but so had the fact he had caught me out.

Eddie wasn't going to give me a chance to get out of it, though.

"Who are you?"

I looked at him and I knew I must have appeared like a cat in headlights, "What?"

"Who are you or what has happened to you? Something has happened to you and I'm not leaving until you tell me. Do you need a doctor? Or Phyllis. You've not seen your shrink in months."

"I don't know what you're talking about," I tried to argue.

He bounced back in his seat and pointed at me, having caught me out somehow, "There! The Scott I know would never do that. He would have an answer whether it was a lie or not. Usually was a lie. That's how I know you're not Scott! That and Scott was never that good of an actor."

"I am Scott," it came out half-formed. Clearing my throat, I tried again with a bit more energy. Heck, it was the truth, "I am Scott!"

"When's my birthday?"

Oh. Damn.

"See! Scott is callous but he'd never forget that. Where was our first date?"

I was floundering and I knew it. My brain wasn't talking to my mouth or body anymore.

"Our last?"

He asked this last one a lot harder than the previous ones. Obviously, things hadn't gone so smoothly between the other me and Eddie.

"Fine!" I blurted, "You got me! But whatever you think, I am Scott. I may not be your Scott, but I am still me. Scott."

Eddie looked as though he was about to speak but then thought the better of it.

"I am me!"

That last one was more for my benefit than his.

Something appeared to dawn on Eddie as his eyes widened with realisation, "You've been processed?"

He sounded almost horrified.

"What? No! I've not been processed; I don't even know what that means. I mean I read about it a bit in those magazines there, but I don't know what it all involves. I was hoping you could tell me."

He was incredulous, "But we talked about it all a couple of days ago! How can you be Scott and not remember that?"

"Why did we talk about it a couple of days ago?"

He was about to answer but clearly changed tack, "No. I'm not giving you that until you tell me what the hell is going on."

How was I meant to do that? That would be the end of me for sure. He'll just think I'd lost it and have me committed or arrested. Processed even, whatever that means.

"Tell me! I deserve to know," he was almost pleading. He clearly had cared for the other me regardless of what had happened between them.

"Honestly? I don't know what to tell you."

"The truth is always a good place to start."

"You wouldn't believe it. Seriously."

He shuffled a little closer, "Try me. I may surprise you."

"I highly doubt it."

He was losing patience, "Just tell me!"

"Right! I am Scott. I know I keep saying that, but I am. I'm just Scott from another reality."

He stared at me briefly, eyebrows raised in anticipation. Then they furrowed as what I had said sank in.

"I'm actually two realities removed. I come from a world much like this one. I'm an actor, but not like this," I indicated the trailer, "Though I'd kill for this. I'm more of a retail specialist in my career. I also have managed a bit of reality hopping in the past."

He drew away from me a little, but still didn't say anything. His brow still creased in concentration, perhaps computing what I was saying, or a means to escape.

"Anyway, I was minding my own business this morning - or yesterday morning - whatever. I was pickpocketed. Next thing I knew I was in a completely different reality. England was under the control of," I wasn't sure where Eddie's allegiances lay so I thought it best to keep some details to a minimum, "a despotic monster," so still true.

I ran through a very brief version of what had happened up

until Grekon took control. I was about to describe what happened when the two contradictory thoughts about Andy's death clashed.

Sparkling lights falling all around me or rising from his body. They fought against one another, juxtaposing with one another. Oddly, it took a bit of effort to shake them from the front of my thoughts.

"Andy was killed. He took control and I woke up back on the sound stage just before 'cut' was called," I blurted. He didn't need any more than that except, "I have to find a way to fix it all."

Eddie was looking down at his clasped hands, thinking.

"Do you want tea?" I asked after a silence I couldn't handle.

He raised his head to regard me, considered the offer and shook his head, "No, thanks."

I wasn't going to push him for a response. My life was more in his hands than before.

"If that's all true, which I'm having a hard time accepting, where is my Scott?"

I shrugged, "I honestly have no idea. I'd like to find that out too. He can't simply have vanished. I have a few of his memories, I have to admit. Not many. Your name, a few glimpses of, um, things. That's it. Not all of him. I like to think that he is somewhere else, somewhere we can get him back if we can just sort out this mess. Not that I have any idea how and that is why I needed to talk to Kath."

"I told you, she's gone."

He said the last word as if it meant something to both of us again.

"I don't know what that means."

"Disappeared. She was taken to detention a couple of months ago. She never reappeared."

My look of confusion made him roll his eyes. Standing up, he lifted a couple of the couch seat cushions. Under one of them was a less glamorous magazine. A lot thinner than the other two, there was more writing on the cover and the photography was patchwork, much like one of those conspiracy trash mags talking of Sasquatch being spotted in

Venice.

Eddie flipped through it until he found a particular page. Folding the excess pages over so the article he wanted me to read was now the cover, he handed it to me.

Much of the same propaganda you would expect from living in a dictatorship. There was an initial glowing commendation of our glorious President.

That did not, however, mean there wasn't the odd side note which seemed to hint at something as you read on.

Some journalists want to put the truth in their work and when they can't do it blatantly, they sneak the odd titbit in. There were a couple of such writers and editors at work at this magazine house.

'Detention Centres', 'Reaffirmation Processes' and one mention of 'the disappeared' popped up throughout the article. Although there was a positive spin put around the story, there was a clear hint that not everything was as hunky-dory as they were trying to make us think. Or perhaps they were trying to make us think that things weren't as hunky-dory as President Grekon wants us to think.

Further down the article was a list of historic rebellions that had taken place in parts of America, China, Russia and dotted throughout Europe, including the United Kingdom.

These rebellions ranged from the speaking out by three individuals in Dresden, Germany about the tyrannical rule of the President to full-scale militant riots in Atlanta, Georgia in America.

Regardless of how severe the transgression, the initial stage was to be forcibly removed from the streets or even your home and taken to one of these Detention Centres where the 'transgressors' are assessed - I take that as meaning judged - and sentenced accordingly. According to the article, not one of the detained was released.

Instead, they were forwarded onto the 'Reaffirmation Process'. This had less coverage as it seemed no one actually knew what took place here. It was from here that 'the disappeared' emerged. Or rather, didn't.

A couple of paragraphs delved into how a family had appealed against the Process being used for their daughter which was inevitably denied. Their daughter never re-emerged and the family were forced to get on with their lives having lost a loved one to no one knew where.

Now, I'm putting my spin on the article and, of course, I'm completely biased against this man-monster. I just can't believe any of these systems he has put in place is without persecution, punishment and pain.

"Kath didn't come through the process?"

He simply shook his head.

I couldn't speak. There was nothing to say really. She had been such a lovely lady and so frail. Why would anyone do anything to harm her? Even a monster like Grekon.

"No family to appeal on her behalf either, not that that ever matters."

This struck me, "What about her grandson, Luka?"

"She didn't have any family. She had a daughter but she died young."

Could it have been the same Kath? Without Luka? It figures that some people would have been wiped from existence when reality changes. He had been such a good kid, pick-pocketing aside. He was just another reason I needed to sort this out.

"Where is this monster now?"

"I'm sorry?" I asked. I'd heard him, it was just one of those stupid human reactions to being caught off guard.

"This monster you told me about. Where is he now? If he took control of all realities, why haven't we heard about him?"

I felt certain I could actually trust this man. It was clear the other me and him were more than a little aware that the utopia they seemingly lived in was not as pristine as they were being led to believe. I like to think that no matter what reality I was in, I would still be against evil.

"You have," I held up the magazine with Grekon on the cover.

Eddie scoffed when he realised what I was showing him, "You've got to be kidding me."

"Well, he had wings. Scars. All sorts."

"President Grekon? What would be the point?"

"I don't get you."

He grabbed the magazine from my hand and showed it back to me, "This? All of what you're saying he went through just so he could be president?"

"Of the world," I pointed out.

"So? From what you were telling me, he could have done that easily back in your other reality. Or the one you were in that wasn't yours," He shook his head trying to sort his own mind out.

"I know it's a bit confusing," I offered, but he had a point.

Had Grekon gone through all of that simply to be president? And have me still alive. Not only alive but living my dream.

"It doesn't seem right, is all. He could have been whatever he wanted and he chose the President?"

Eddie was right. I'd thought it before that it was all a bit odd, yet Eddie saying it made it actually seem all a little wrong.

Throwing the magazine on the small table and falling back on the couch Eddie said, "If you ask me, something went wrong. That is if you aren't putting on this whole act to be even more of a bastard than you have been."

You're telling me something went wrong, I thought. In more ways than one it appeared.

"Was he really that good of an actor?"

Eddie laughed, "Not really, no. Good point," but on realising the consequence of what he was admitting to, a cloud of worry and apprehension fell over his features.

"I don't know what you've seen in that head of yours, but I loved him. Love him," he corrected himself, "I still do. I want him back."

"I'm sorry, but I don't know how to make that happen."

Eddie looked at me, a glimmer of light breaking through, "I might."

"I'm all ears."

A NIGHT ON THE TOWN

I slept in the trailer. In this world, it was the only place I actually knew and I was never any good at sleeping in strange places. It also cut down the need for interacting with people who might already know me but I would be at a complete loss to talk to. It would only lead to me revealing I was not who I claimed to be or making me stand out like a sore thumb when I encountered people I was supposed to know.

Eddie had taken the couch.

It wasn't a particularly difficult plan, however, I was going to need to reasonably pass for the other me for some amount of time, not to mention know my way around a bit.

There was a lot this other me knew that I had never been privy to.

Thankfully I had today off from filming. Sure, I could have tried to learn the sides for the next day of filming, but I wasn't entirely sure I'd be able to pull it off the way the other me would. Not only that, I wasn't sure if I'd still be alive.

It was funny how the thought I may be dead soon no longer shocked me like it used to. With everything I've been through, fighting Amazon ninjas, being shot at, all sorts, it had become a bit of an inevitability. That wasn't to say I wouldn't mind if I died. I'd most certainly prefer to live. But I'd also prefer the world were put to rights and that I might die in my own reality.

If I were to die at all. Hopefully, it just wouldn't come to that.

Anyway, I need to be able to pass for the other me. Both Eddie and I had agreed the best way for me to do that was to simply keep my mouth shut as best I could. Eddie would accompany me as my attache. He informed me that was what generally happened.

"What about when you two were seeing each other?"

"That's the life you live," he'd explained, "I knew full well what I was buying into and had no expectations. He couldn't outwardly have a boyfriend or the work would dry up. Sad, but that is still the world we live in. I was okay with it as long as he came home to me. Then, one night, he didn't."

I hadn't wanted to push, but he was in a world of reverie, perhaps mourning for the now missing Scott.

"I knew that would likely happen too, that he'd find someone else, or he'd get tired of seeing me all day and night. I mean, I was on set, or if I wasn't, I'd be running tasks for him. I just figured with me doing all the leg work and making all the sacrifices, it'd be me who got bored first."

"For what it's worth, I'm sorry. I know I can be a selfish git, but it sounds like he was a right idiot for throwing all that away."

He smiled, "Thanks. Odd to hear those words coming from him. Well, you know what I mean. I guess that's how I know you aren't him."

"So you know I'm not him and you're willing to believe the alternate reality story?"

"I'm not one hundred percent with you on that, Scott. It is all so implausible. I'd say unbelievable, but that isn't right. I believe you. It's just difficult, that's all."

I guess I understood what he had meant.

Eddie had gone out a couple of times during the day. Each time I had been nervous about him returning with the police or whatever passed for authorities in this reality. I had grown to trust him, but you never know people. I guess that was a character trait of mine that has made me a bit of a loner my whole life. I hadn't ended up getting a flatmate when I lived in Perth, despite having a whole spare room. I realised I needed my own space, not that I used it for anything. It was just an empty room. Apt, really when I think about my own life. Hardly empty of experiences, but everyone I meet, it is only fleetingly. Sarah settled down and I rarely heard from her. Bob and Narelle... well they visited sporadically but they had their own kingdom to run.

The more I thought about it, the more I realised that with everything this other me had, he was an idiot to have thrown away the one thing so hard to find - someone who actually cared enough about you to stay.

Still, Eddie stayed, though, so maybe he had the best of

both worlds and that's just a little nasty in my view. Eddie deserved better.

When he came back last, he brought with him a suit pack, a pair of shoes and a small carry bag.

"Normally Scott would go the whole hog. Hairdresser, manicurist, make-up, the works. Thankfully, being that he is filming, it gives us a reason not to call in Natalie and crew on this occasion."

My blank look led him to answer my unspoken question, "His stylist. Besides, I've helped him enough times, I should be able to do a passable job of it."

"You'll be a damn sight better than me. I rarely even comb my hair."

"Yup, you're not him," Eddie laughed. Then back to business, "Right, hair first."

I had never been so pampered in my whole life and Eddie kept apologising the whole way through the process for doing such a poor job. It was hilarious how different our two worlds were despite being so similar.

Despite the shorter length of my hair, he spent a good forty minutes shaping and styling it before pulling a small kit out of the carry bag. Opening its lid, he revealed a range of make-up and tools which he seemed to be a dab hand at.

It wasn't much that he applied, but how he applied it. By the end of the process, I didn't look all that different, but I still managed to look a million dollars due to all his meticulous touches.

"Sorry, it's such a slapdash job."

"Are you kidding me? You're a miracle worker! If I could do what you do, I'd be doing just that. If that makes sense."

He shrugged slightly and started to pack away, "It'll do. Now you need to get dressed. The car will be here in an hour.

I looked at my watch, still amazed that it was worth a couple of thousand pounds according to Eddie. It was only four-thirty.

He noticed and helped. I was clearly not up to date with all this business, "Pre-dinner drinks. You're booked in for the whole night. It'll take us an hour to get into the city, at least. Start with the drinks, move to a seated meal and the actual event starts at eight. It's at the same venue as the dinner, so they'll simply remove some of the chairs and tables."

"Like a wedding reception?"

"Yeah a bit like that, just with more money thrown at it."

"So you're talking a couple of hours beforehand that I'm going to be fencing off people? Aren't we trying to limit my exposure?"

"We'll get you a booth at the bar, but you still need to be there. You don't show and that would be completely out of character. If you had been filming today, then you would have had an excuse but a couple of your co-stars will be there and we can't risk you looking out of character."

I was not looking forward to this at all.

"I did mention, I don't drink?"

Eddie froze for a moment.

This was clearly big news, "You may have wanted to mention that earlier because you drink like a fish at these sorts of events. So much so I am pretty used to covering your exit from the paparazzi and your colleagues. You're not a pretty drunk."

"I'm not normally a pretty anything."

"You are far too self-deprecating."

"You already know me so well."

"I mean it. I think you're cute."

I laughed, "No, you think THIS is cute," I indicated the whole charade I was packaged in, "If you saw the real me, you'd be barking up a completely different tree."

"Well, you're a lot more considerate than my Scott. And that's cute. It's not all about that," he indicated my body, as I had.

"So they say. I still say you put my brain in my body and you'd be hard-pressed to pick me out of a crowd. And even if you did, you'd want to put me back in short order. I'm an acquired taste."

"You're high maintenance, I can see that. So was my Scott. If you stopped stressing over the unimportant things, maybe you'd find there is more in there than you give yourself credit for. Just a thought."

"Well, I can only hope I get a chance to find out."

A couple of hours later and we were both sitting in the back of a limousine. It wasn't a massive stretched affair, just a Rolls Royce Phantom five-seater with a partition between the driver and us.

I'd been in taxis, but this was a very different affair. The seats were beyond comfortable. The vehicle itself was immaculate and exquisite. This was wealth beyond anything I had ever really dreamed of. Eddie reassured me it was a hire, though other me wasn't short on a vehicle collection. He also had to reassure me that the driver couldn't hear a word we said.

Who knows, there could be a hidden intercom.

The suit I was wearing was probably worth a year of my wages. It fit so well having been made by some name independent fashion designer. The shoes were the most comfortable I had ever worn. They weren't completely new, having a couple of polished over scuffs, but clearly, they were the other me's favourite pair of shoes.

I felt very reassured Eddie was coming with me. He'd told me that he normally tagged along at the events in some form or other, though he never got to sit at the same table as the other me. Nor did he make the formal entrances with him. That was saved for -

"Krisztina Văduva."

Eddie looked impressed, "I never told you about her."

"I saw her in one of those magazines."

"She's lovely. Understanding too. She co-starred with Scott in a film two years ago. She was huge in Romania and Scott had seen her in a small independent, her first English-speaking role. He requested her specifically and neither has looked back since."

"So she knew about you two?"

"Completely. The three of us went out one night and Scott let it slip after he'd had five too many. She didn't mind one bit, not only that, she actually offered to run distraction. So every time she is in town, they make a night of it on the town, giving the media something to nibble on. I'm not sure, but I think she may be a lesbian."

That all made sense.

"Anyway, we're almost there."

That didn't help, I felt a run of nerves rattle throughout my body.

"This first stop will be fine. It should be quiet to start. We'll go in together, I'll sort a booth. That way we'll have some privacy. I'll also be able to forewarn you on anyone who decides to pop their head in."

"You're going to be working hard tonight," I was so grateful. He was putting so much faith in me over this whole business. I still can't believe he is actually going along with it all.

"No different to most nights out, then. I'll set a tab for the table, that way no one will be buying you a round. I'll also sort the barman so we have a non-alcoholic drink at hand for you at all times, that way no one will be tempted to get you anything. You'll have to fob it off as Vodka and Coke or something, I don't know. Otherwise, Scott's closer acquaintances will know something is up. He has drunk most of them under the table more than once."

"Couldn't we say I have filming tomorrow?"

"That has never stopped you before."

"I'm in rehab? Going dry?"

"They'll laugh at that for a good half hour before plying you with drinks to get you back on track."

"Great friends," I whispered.

"I never said they were friends. Scott can be a right sod when he is out in public. I think he was always on guard, paranoid of everyone around him."

"I can relate to that."

"So can most actors, I think. A lot of them have one deep-seated problem or another. Confidence, substance abuse, abandonment issues. It goes on. Right, are you ready?"

The Phantom pulled up outside a building I had actually walked past several times during my stay in my own London. So there were similarities. It had a white facade and a short blue carpet leading to the front door. The tall arched windows were blocked by flowing white curtains which probably hadn't been curtains to start with, instead, being draped stylishly to add class and privacy.

The door on Eddie's side opened and gave me a reassuring look before stepping out. I edged across the seat toward the open door. By the time I reached it, my own door was opened behind me.

I turned and saw the valet stick his head in the door.

I smiled and said as confidently as I could, "This looked more fun," and stepped onto the pavement.

It was still light out and there were scores of people filling the sidewalk over the road. This side was kept clear somehow. I looked and saw some movable bollards connected by a blue rope running from the sides of the building to the street.

That didn't seem entirely legal, but no people were complaining about it as there were also two heavy-set security guards standing on either side of the enclosed pavement to keep things quiet.

I looked back over the Phantom and got my first real glimpse of this version of London.

It was more like my own reality than Kath and Luka's. People going about their business, nothing I would have found too out of the ordinary. For all the implied bad publicity, Grekon didn't seem to be too bad. However, that could be down to the fact he didn't have as complete control as he desired. And if that were the case, what was he planning so he could attain that?

That was why we were acting now. He was not the kind of despot to give in until he had exactly what he wanted.

"Scott!"

Someone in the crowd had called my name. A woman. Did I know her? She was waving at me. She looked to be about forty, blonde with faint red highlights, dressed in a nondescript pantsuit having just left work.

"Hi?" I offered.

She squealed and her hand covered her mouth. Several other people looked toward her and then at me to see what she was reacting to which led to several more squeals.

Someone grabbed my shoulder and Eddie whispered in my ear, "You are definitely not him. We need to get inside."

I wasn't going to argue and allowed him to drag me into the club.

Inside it was dimly lit by concealed halogens. They were hidden behind statues, plants and in little alcoves. If you were asked to point out a light bulb, you wouldn't be able to.

The design was simple. Deep red wooden panels were used to divide the entry from the rest of the club. Inside, that burgundy colour became the highlight colour. The small, round standing tables were topped with the same type of wood. The booths that were all set back in alcoves had benches upholstered in the same colour. Everything else was a mid-level grey or silver.

The lighting was subdued inside the club, but mobile. A few coloured spots rotated unevenly around the main room at a leisurely pace accompanied by a slow version of Alison Moyet's 'Is This Love'.

Oddly, this was exactly my type of club. No raucous dance music, blinding lights and screaming to be heard.

There were already quite a number of people in the club milling around, talking.

I figured as the night wore on, the whole system would change and liven up as people got more uninhibited due to alcohol intake. For right now, I felt a lot more like I would be able to handle the situation.

I merely had to flash a smile at the Bouncer to be let in. Another burly man who, on any other occasion, would have had me cowering in the corner. What saved me this time was the swiftness with which Eddie was directing me along.

"Keep your head down and go sit in that booth over there," he pointed at the third alcove along from the bar. It sat empty, "I'll have a word with the barman and join you in a moment."

Who was I to argue? Thankfully there was no need to push past people. The venue probably could hold three or four hundred people at a crush. Right now there were about fifty spotted or grouped around the place. Half of the booths had people inside.

I got to mine without a hitch and sat down on one end of the semi-circular bench that ran behind one of those red-wood tables. Once there I examined the back wall of the alcove. There was absolutely nothing on it. It was a grey painted brick. If I wanted to I could have tried to make out animals and faces in the brickwork much as one does with clouds, but I was not in the mood to do that at all. My heart was racing and I wanted for all my life not to be recognised again.

That woman outside had been a complete shock. I thought it had been someone I knew from my own life. It wouldn't have been the first time I'd walked through London and run into someone I'd known from Australia completely by chance.

This wasn't like that at all. She had been a fan. It's quite intimidating being recognised by someone you don't know. If that were a normal, everyday occurrence, I would go insane. No wonder celebrities go off the deep end.

The wall managed to keep my attention for a short while. Not long enough, however.

"Scott?"

I was so engrossed in the wall I had forgotten I didn't want to look, so I did.

Her teeth were perfect. Odd that I noticed that first, but they were practically glowing as she smiled. A leggy blonde in a long royal blue evening gown with a split running up to just below her left hip was stalking toward me, a huge smile on her extraordinarily beautiful face. Yup and her teeth were perfect.

"Hey," was all I could manage. I couldn't say I hadn't been spoken to by such a good-looking lady before. If I did, Narelle would probably hunt me down through all the realities and kill me.

She reached the booth and stood over me, "Budge up, let a lady sit."

What else could I do? So I did.

Her smile faltered a little and she didn't move to sit for a moment, then considered it and took the place I had just vacated.

She scanned the empty table in front of me, "Late start tonight?"

I had to man up. I couldn't be a total washout here. Besides, even in my own reality, I wanted to be an actor. So be an actor!

"Eddie's sorting me out. What else is a PA for?"

She glanced back at the bar, "Ah, of course. He better get a move on so you can get him to buy me a drink."

She leaned toward me, one elbow on the table, her chin lightly resting on her cupped palm. Her nails perfectly manicured ran the smooth, perfect lines of her cheek, "Where've you been soldier?"

"On set. Doing my duty for my country," that was what I had been doing. I'd been a soldier in the film the other me was filming. I think she was flirting, but it was just a coincidence that it tied so nicely with the truth.

"Oh, you're so brave. Maybe one day you could show me what weapon you're packing," I nearly jumped out of my skin when I felt the hand that wasn't supporting her face make contact with my knee.

"Maddi! How great to see you," Eddie was a lifesaver.

She turned to regard him, but her hand didn't move.

"Hi, Eddie. Scott was just saying he wanted you to run along and get me a-"

"Martini?"

Eddie slid the tray he was carrying onto the table. On it was a pint glass of coke, a pint of some amber liquid, I was guessing cider from the smell and lack of frothy head and a martini. He'd obviously seen or heard her approach and done what a good PA does.

Making a show of things he handed her her glass which she took begrudgingly, removing her hand from my lap at the same time.

"And one vodka coke for you, sir."

He smiled at me as he passed the pint glass to me.

"Cheers," I said, saluting the air and taking a precautionary sip. It was straight Coke. Good man.

He lifted his own glass and responded with a 'cheers' of his own.

As he sat down on the other end of the booth and scooted around next to me, he asked, "So, Maddi, how's the series going? What was it? Kept Family?"

She almost sneered at him. I could see he was going to have

a harder night of this than I was, "Keep it in the Family. You should try watching it, Eddie, we received BAFTAS."

That impressed me, but Eddie took another small sip of his drink and nonchalantly answered, "Weren't they for the writing?"

If Maddi were a cat, I'd have been backing away for fear of my life. Daggers were shot at Eddie before she decided he wasn't worth the effort and turned her attention back to me.

"You're quiet tonight, Scott. Want me to help loosen you up?"

With that, she eased both hands under my suit jacket and onto my shoulders.

No one had ever been so physically forward like that with me and it was most certainly not what I had been expecting of the night.

"Maddi," I pushed her arms aside, "Krisztina and I…" What? I had no idea what to say. Improvise damn it! So I tried, "We're trying to be exclusive for a change."

It was like I had slapped her, softly. She leaned away from me.

"Seriously? Exclusive? You?"

I tried to look slightly offended, "What are you saying, Maddi?"

"Come on, Scott, you used to have a different woman on your arm every week. You don't do exclusive," with that last comment, she started in on me again.

"Time to grow up sometime. It's my time," I pulled out the big guns and felt a certain satisfaction from her reaction, "I want kids."

The look on her face said it all. I'd turned into some sort of putrid excrement she had accidentally stepped on and couldn't be rid of fast enough.

"How… nice, Scott. You'll make a sweet little family, I'm sure."

"That's what Krisztina thinks. She's the one that actually talked me into it. I don't think I've been happier."

"Mmm," Maddi hummed, taking a large drink from her martini, her eyes scanning the rest of the room, "Well, I hope your film does well, Scott. I've just seen… Darryl. I really should go say hello."

And with that, she was off.

Eddie kept his own reaction down, but I could sense he was bottling his laughter, "Brilliant. Absolutely brilliant. Stick with that all night."

"Is she into me or what?"

Eddie shook his head, "She's like that with any man with a bit of power. It certainly isn't personal, more financial."

Maddi was by far the worst of the encounters in the bar. Twenty minutes later and the booth was full of an assortment of people from character actors, TV personalities and the beautiful. Most of them were actually very nice people and they became even nicer when I kept the conversation focused on them. They clearly liked the opportunity to talk about themselves rather than listen to what I had to say. Eddie informed me that his Scott was a little self-aggrandising at these events. He also kept my drink filled and I was sure I'd gone through at least six pints by the time he signalled that it was time to leave.

It was actually quite fun talking with these people. In this world they were celebrities but they were still normal people and you tend to forget that. One had told me about his search for a look-a-like kitten to replace Tinks, his daughter's, which had been hit by a car this morning. He hadn't wanted her to find out so had searched far and wide through all the pet shops in London. He was a very expressive speaker, arms and face working together to recreate a rather horrific story with an endearing twist at the end when he 'reunited' the feline with his four-year-old. Kids being kids, however, she knew there was something wrong but still said, "He's just as beautiful as Tinks was. Thanks, Dad."

Others in the booth had listened intently to the story and awarded him with the inherent "Awww" associated with the tale which was justly deserved.

I received a few odd looks when I made out-of-character comments, usually nice ones but they were quickly forgotten as the others chatted on.

Eddie was always there to whisper a newcomer's name in my ear and a very succinct background, "You filmed a TV episode with them." or "Your co-star five years ago in 'Winter's March.'"

The way he did it, I actually got the impression he used to have to do it for his own Scott who, to me, seemed a bit of a selfish git. Mind you, my memory isn't the best, either, so I'd be thankful for someone to do that for me too.

It honestly wasn't as bad as I had been expecting. All I had to do was keep my comments short and listen. No one was out to get me so I didn't have to fend off any personal attacks and any inquiries into my personal life, I simply waved them off as too tedious to talk about or Eddie jumped in about a mutually shared experience between me and the other person that led us in a whole new direction.

"We need to be going," was all he whispered to me when the time came.

"Right, Ladies and Gentlemen, and the rest of you," the usual perfunctory chuckles, "I must be making my apologies and departing your most glorious company."

No chuckles, some interesting looks and I'm sure I heard someone ask their neighbour, "Is he being sarcastic?"

"Seriously, it was great to see you and I'm sure I'll be seeing some of you again very shortly."

"A bit much," Eddie told me as we walked away from the booth, "but suitably flamboyant, I guess."

A fair number of others were leaving with us, most likely going to the same party we were. That meant a bit of hanging around while drivers arrived to pick up their passengers.

Ten minutes still waiting and trying to make small talk with some of the others, I asked Eddie if it would be better to walk.

"You do remember what happened outside, earlier, right?"

"I could keep my head down," I offered.

"In a suit like that, you'll be drawing looks anyway, besides, that's us now."

There were a few rows of onlookers now standing at either side of the closed-off pavement, squealing when they saw someone they knew come out of the club, which generally meant it was a consistent rattle that filled the early evening air.

It didn't get any quieter when I stepped out onto the blue

carpet and hurried toward the open rear door of the Phantom.

I dove across the back seat, gently, mind, to avoid damaging the suit. Eddie shortly followed and the car moved off before I'd had a chance to fasten my belt.

"That was fun," I exclaimed. Normally a homebody, myself, that had been something fairly new to me. And to think they were all famous people.

Eddie smiled, something was missing from his eyes.

"Don't worry, I'm not losing perspective."

"It's not that. I've been thinking about all of this."

"And?"

"If you're right, if President Grekon has created all of this, what happens if you do fix everything?"

"What do you mean?"

"Do I still exist? Does my Scott? Does any of this? Am I helping you to wipe out everything I know?"

Oh. This could be difficult. I certainly couldn't argue the fact that he had already destroyed several other realities. After everything, I couldn't lie either.

"I honestly don't know. I'm hoping that this reality will simply revert to what it was, or simply continue as it was before I got here. I think there are infinite realities out there and, if we're right, Grekon and I just got stuck here, if he is even my Grekon. This man might not know what the heck I am talking about and may simply be an alternate version of the monster I know."

"I guess we'll find that out tonight," Eddie said quietly. He wasn't saying he wasn't going along with it, but his earlier enthusiasm was waning, "I miss him."

I wasn't sure if I should be offended, being him and all, but I knew we were two sides to a many-faceted coin, "I'm sorry. It can't be easy looking at someone you know so well and having someone completely different staring back at you."

He smiled at me, "You really are doing well. You're better at this than you think. Some of those people, I think they like you even more than they did my Scott. I can see why."

I was flattered, all I could say was, "Thanks."

It wasn't a long drive to the venue and we travelled it

mainly in silence, Eddie ruminating on what the future meant for him and his world and me simply stressing that I would screw this completely even though so many realities and the lives of those within counted on me.

Should I even fix this? Maybe I should just let it all lie. I could try and fill this Scott's shoes and if I fail, I'm sure he has enough of a nest egg to retire on.

But what about Kath? And Luka? Eddie and Scott? What about my family and friends back in my reality? I couldn't let this lie, I had to do my best to fix this and if I failed, then... I guess I fail. If Eddie is right, Grekon hasn't won either so no one does.

It was getting harder to concentrate properly though as the six pints were starting to make themselves known again. I began to wish the luxury Phantom came with a toilet as standard.

The sound of the door opening next to me brought me back to the present. I looked at Eddie who smiled reassuringly at me once more.

Stepping out of the car onto a plush red carpet and into a veritable roar of audio cacophony. It was hugely disconcerting and my eyes were drawn all over the place by a hail of flashes from cameras big and small.

There were hundreds of people all around the road which was lined with long metal fencing. There were more on the other side of the road. The whole area must have been shut down to normal traffic as I saw a long line of limousines behind mine.

Eddie had gotten out on his side and I must have looked absolutely panicked as he gave me one look and practically ran around to me.

"Just breathe," he told me.

Taking his advice, I took several deep breaths and turned to face the venue.

My heart burst into my throat and I nearly tripped over the several hundred-pound shoes as my first step forward failed.

It was that building. The mansion house I had walked past in Kath's reality. Well, it was, but it wasn't.

The first-floor facade was identical, the large arched

windows, no longer grimy, but afire with the hundreds of electric candles burning in the chandeliers inside.

It was much grander, however. Taller, wider. Another four floors above whereas the ones in the other reality had been burnt down and destroyed. The building itself also stood a lot further back from the road, a large arched gazebo acting as the welcoming approach to two sets of open double doors on the right-hand side of the building.

Two large spotlights were angled at the sky and were idly revolving creating a bright spectacle below, but a range of eerie shapes and shadows on the clouds above.

There was already a long, though well-spaced procession of extremely well-dressed people making their way inside. Well-spaced to allow for reporters to interview and photographers to snap them as they waltzed by.

"I'm going to have to leave you for this. You're the star and the one they want to see, I'll be taking another way in."

I was still shaken by the fact that this building, where I was shot at yesterday amid all of the rotting and ruined decor, now stood in amazing glory directly in front of me. I didn't really want to make this trip on my own, but I understood.

He led me forward, "Just do your best to avoid answering questions. Worst case, if you can, just smile and deflect them."

"Deflect them?"

"Gabble about something else or pretend you can't hear them. There is enough noise here for that excuse to work and god knows Scott's used it enough when they've asked something too personal."

"Deflect. I can do that," He patted me on my shoulder and disappeared while I joined the procession making their way past the vultures.

If I was being honest, I wasn't so worried about the journalist as the building. I didn't have good memories of this place. Come to think of it, I didn't have many good memories of anywhere.

Right. I'm not me, I'm him and he is a confident, self-assured, outspoken man. I can do that.

Watching the people in front of me, they were waving at

the crowds and smiling for their cameras. Very little was being said by anyone as Eddie was right. It was almost what I'd expect standing on a runway would be like as a jumbo took off.

Time to fit in. Well as best as I could while my bladder was starting to pressure me to hurry for a toilet. I looked out to my right and the hordes that lined the fences and waved, a big grin on my face.

I couldn't tell if that had any effect or not, but I kept it up, swapping sides, trying to appear cool, calm and appreciative of their misdirected adoration.

It seemed to last longer than it really would have taken, my approach to the media. When I got to the stretch that was clearly allocated to them, I heard people start shouting my name. I turned wherever I thought the voice came from and wherever I looked was a camera or three. So I smiled and tried to look suave, which basically consisted of me putting my hands in my pockets and angling slightly away from the camera. Again, it was all a little fun and I wished I could really have gotten into it, but there was always that niggling at the back of my mind that tonight might very well be my last on this planet or every planet.

And then came the microphones and further nerves which were not helpful to my urinary problem. I strained down below while the fluffy black bulbs weren't quite shoved in my face, but they were certainly made to feel very friendly with me.

"Scott, where is that lovely Krisztina?"

"Abandoned me, this evening, I'm afraid. Better things to do than babysitting me, I guess."

"Scott, over here! Scott, What are you working on currently?"

I flashed a big grin and tried to be as cheeky as I could, "A film."

I really couldn't say anything about it as all I knew was I was a soldier.

Of course, that wasn't enough and I'm sure the publicity team on the film would be horrified, "What film, give us an exclusive!"

"I'll tell you this, It is physically draining, I've never been pushed so hard in my career," I tried. I wasn't lying, even if other me would be, "Explosions, excitement. You'll love it!"

I couldn't even tell who was asking me the questions.

"Who are you wearing?"

I actually laughed out loud at this one. I was literally wearing another Scott's body. Thankfully, Eddie had prepared me for this one, "Augustus Bertorelli. I wouldn't go to anyone else!"

And I was through. Well, I hurried past as fast as I could and made it to the stairs up to the entrance. Taking those two at a time, I was practically joining the couple in front of me, playing the third wheel.

I hesitated briefly before stepping over the threshold into the building itself.

I had an extremely bad feeling about this.

ONE FOR THE ROAD

I had an invite certificate in my jacket's inner pocket, but the guards at the door didn't even request it. I had to walk through a metal detector archway. I received a quick pat-down while the ladies had their purses searched. Once all of that was complete, they ushered me through, saying, "Welcome Mr Crossman."

The entrance hall was nothing like the entry into the alternate building. It was the size of a high-end hotel lobby. There were couches, coffee tables and armchairs dotted around the sides of the room, much like a hotel lobby. These were full of this world's elite and famous socialising or simply perusing the other guests as they arrived. I was doing the same, mainly to see if I could spot Eddie.

There were a couple of people who had briefly been at the bar with me earlier. They were meandering through the crowd or standing by the long bar that stood at the back right-hand corner of the room.

On the left was a regal, coiling marble staircase. It was at least 3 metres wide and ran up the side of the wall, curving around the back wall and above the bar before disappearing on the second floor. A couple of metres from the base of the stairs was a huge set of double doors which I assumed led into the Ballroom. Also under the stairs and beside the bar was a corridor that was signposted to lead to the toilets.

There was a cloudy golden hue to everything as if someone had taken a glamour photograph and brought it to life. The gilt mirrors that sat high on the walls reflecting the light from the smaller crystal chandeliers in this room certainly helped spread the effect.

Who needed the ballroom with a lobby this big?

The question was what sort of building was this? I was sure the alternate building had been some sort of manor house. This was clearly more a Function building for hire. Maybe it was all just a coincidence. God knows I've encountered plenty of those.

"Scott," a familiar voice. I turned and it was Eddie. He reached my side quickly, having approached from the bar, another pint of coke in hand and his own flute of, I was guessing, Champagne.

"Oh, thank God!"

"Are you okay, you seem to be a little distracted?"

I realised I was holding my breath while straining to keep my bladder from bursting.

"I am desperate for the toilet."

Eddie chuckled, "Ah, they're just-"

"No, it's fine. I got it," I cut him off as I moved very swiftly toward the smaller corridor.

It was fairly well populated due to the number of women who were patiently queuing for the ladies', as is always the case at big events. Thankfully, the men's door was line free. Hurrying inside, I noticed it was fairly empty inside too. A couple of guys at the urinal, one of the seven stalls was closed. I chose the stall furthest from the door and hurried to relieve myself.

And what a relief.

I chose a stall as I am extremely toilet shy. It would have been made worse by the fact these were big wigs. Stage fright at the urinal is the worst as you start to wonder if the other men are assuming you're there for nefarious business. On the other hand, the noises from the stalls can be downright embarrassing. Generally, I do my best to avoid public toilets. Especially in America. Each toilet bowl is a veritable lake you can sail a yacht on, the amount of water they fill it with. They clearly don't worry about water conservation.

Anyway, I completed my business, washed up and headed back to the party.

It was only slightly more populated. I did wonder how many more people would be arriving as it looked as though they might be struggling to fit everyone at a table.

It seemed I wouldn't have long to wait to find out. As I reached Eddie the double doors opened. Four ushers stepped into the lobby dressed in tails.

No one said anything, but people automatically started

heading toward the doors.

"I've checked the seating plan, I'll be two tables away, but able to keep an eye on you."

"There's a seating plan?"

Eddie pointed toward two large whiteboards on golden easels. that were on either side of the double doors. I hadn't seen them earlier as people had been surrounding them trying to sort themselves out.

"I'll take you to yours and leave you to it. The good thing is you shouldn't actually know anyone on the table. That will make it easier, not having to remember anecdotes, however, I'm hoping you remember your back catalogue of films because they're bound to pop up."

Eddie had spent the time with me earlier today going through the film and TV work other Scott had worked on. I remembered a lot of it, but some of the synopsis had woven themselves into each other. Mind you, with his wealth of experience, it was likely he wouldn't be able to remember half the stuff he'd done and Eddie would surely be needed to remind him who was who, why else have a PA?

We joined the slow-moving crowd entering the ballroom and once again, I had a sense of foreboding.

This was it. There was no turning back.

The worst thing was that our plan had only really taken us up to this point. There had been no way of predicting what would happen once we got inside. Chances were I wouldn't even be able to get close to the megalomaniac so it was all going to be me winging it from henceforth. I guess I should be used to that by now.

It was the exact same ballroom I had seen in the vision through the alternate building's window. I had thought what little I had seen through the grimy windows was beautiful.

I was wrong.

It was exquisite. The floor was polished to within an inch of its life. Or perhaps within an inch of the polisher's life as it was immaculate. If I had been a ruder man, I would have been not merely noticing that the surface was so reflective; one could practically use it to see up the gowns and dresses of the fashionable ladies strolling across it.

Long intertwined vines appeared to grow from the base of the walls and up toward the ceiling. Perched sporadically on short branches were lime green Peacocks in such detail that they looked ready to jump off the wall and stroll regally around the gathering.

Swans of the same colouring alternated branches, each one in a different pose. Preening, calling, sleeping, about to take flight. Every single one was hand-painted to perfection like the rest of the wall coverings.

The vines encircled and accentuated the Wall to almost ceiling mirrors that were spaced evenly along the massive wall opposite the windows.

Above these, again, were the pristine, white ceiling decorations. In the middle of each side, there were beautifully moulded scenes depicting the seasons using old Greek Gods for inspiration. For example, Hera in full regalia was strolling through the sunlit fields with cherubs and half-naked people enjoying the weather around him. Aphrodite, modestly covering herself, yet smiling at the harvesters and servants of spring while children danced gaily around her and birds fluttered around her head.

Along the rest of the ceiling's edges were laurels and ribbons being held in place by cherubs flying high and treating it all like a game.

Of course, there were the chandeliers. Four of them were the size of a small car. I really hoped I wouldn't be sitting below one in case the ceiling decided it had had enough supporting such massive structures and let go.

As luck would have it, I was sitting almost in the middle of the room. That wasn't to say that if one of the chandeliers fell, I wouldn't be showered with sharp shards of shattering crystal. Anyway, in all there looked to be maybe twenty tables, each holding sixteen people.

I had expected a sort of head table at one end where Grekon would sit, but that was not the case. Perhaps he was slumming it with the rest of us.

Eddie led me to my seat and left me to it, disappearing to the table one row closer to the door and the mirrored wall. I didn't even bother checking the name cards on the very well-laid table, instead, I admired the crockery and cutlery.

I had five forks. As well as three knives and two spoons. All gold. Five forks? Three were on the left of my plate, one above and one on the very right, next to what I knew to be the soup spoon which sat beside two of my knives.

Personally, one knife, one fork and two spoons would have been sufficient.

"It's a beautiful mess, isn't it," a lady who I actually recognised said as she sat down next to me. She was a politician from my own reality. A Labour member from what I recalled, though only in her mid-thirties.

It would be beautifully ironic if she were a Tory in this world, not that I affiliated myself to either party.

"It most certainly is," I replied, "I don't know where to begin."

"I'd wait for the food before you did that," she joked, "Then just go from the outside to in using your own judgement as to whether you can wield such weapons," She had picked up a unique little knife about with a broad, flat-ended blade about an inch and a half long and eyed it warily, "I'll try and help you if you promise to do the same for me."

I smiled, gratefully, "Deal."

She extended her hand, "Mary-Beth. Embeth for short."

I shook it lightly, "Scott."

"Like I didn't know," she laughed.

"I could say the same."

She looked a little surprised, "Could you?"

"Sure! You're on television more than I am."

"For all the right reasons, I hope."

"I'm sure," I smiled my best charm smile; which I don't think I've ever really smiled before; and hoped it didn't come across as creepy.

The other seats at the table were filling quickly. I didn't recognise any of the others. Embeth, on the other hand, knew a couple of them. It appeared I was on a bit of a political table. I was hoping they would feel sorry for the stupid actor, perhaps even leave me alone.

I nursed my coke while waiters came around and filled wine glasses. Not wanting a repeat of the bar, I was going to space my drinks.

I managed a vague chit-chat about the weather, the crowd outside and other rather banal topics from the guy on the other side of me while Embeth was speaking to her friends and then she turned to me.

"So are you working on anything right now?"

"At this very moment, I'm working on keeping my wits about me," I found myself saying and thankfully she laughed.

"Oh it can be a lot worse, surely you know that."

"Doesn't make it any easier."

She nodded, "Good point. I find it a lot easier just being myself. If they judge, that's their problem. So relax. And tell me what you're working on, work-wise."

Eddie hadn't known much about the film, hence why I hadn't been able to answer Maddi at the bar. I gave her pretty much the same answer before steering the conversation back to her. She made it easy to talk, being very down to earth and simply being nice.

We were shortly interrupted by the arrival of a tiny bowl of soup I couldn't name but was absolutely delicious. I finished it with three and a half scoops of the soup spoon in time for it to be removed and replaced with a small crab cake and a minuscule side salad.

This too was a pleasure, melting in the mouth and the crab was fresh and succulent. It was a good sign the rest of the night's food was going to be more than I could have ever hoped for.

And the courses kept coming, every so often interrupted by a sorbet or palette cleanser to better enjoy the next concoction of flavours.

Thankfully the courses, even the main, were of such small serving sizes I didn't actually reach a level of being stuffed. Contented would have been the right word.

Throughout the evening, a small 8-piece band was playing in the back right corner of the hall.

A grand piano surrounded by men and women on violins, violas, cellos and what I think is a double bass.

I couldn't name the music pieces they played delightfully through the meal, though I figured it to be Bach, Handel or

Mozart. Some you would expect to hear at a wedding, though it most certainly wasn't the Wedding March.

Finally the last of the dessert plates - an extremely light chocolate mousse layer over a delicate cheesecake with a hint of lime and a curl of gold leaf on top - were removed.

I must admit I wasn't actually intending to eat the gold. It made no sense to simply shove something so expensive in your mouth. Then considering how much the rest of the food would cost, I swallowed it in one go.

And immediately felt guilty. How many people in the world were starving? Then again, in this reality under Grekon's rule, were any starving or had he eradicated poverty?

No! If I start thinking like that, he becomes a good guy, even if he had done that, which I had no proof of, he still killed Andy and wiped out those realities.

What I hadn't noticed throughout the meal, was a lectern and a pair of auto-cue displays had been put in place on a small raised platform beside the band.

The one thing that was conspicuously missing was the media. No cameras, reporters with microphones or anything at all to record the moment when, a few moments later, the band erupted in an elaborate swell of music which I took to be the string version of a fanfare.

To accompany this, He stepped out of a small hidden panel on the peacock wall.

Grekon.

Suited and looking so professional and human. Even as a human, you could see the snake within. His bone structure was as I remembered when I first encountered him. They appeared to be protruding from his skin, creating eerie lines that were reminiscent of a reptile.

There was a round of applause which echoed tremendously in this hall. It was almost as deafening as the fans had been outside.

Some real brown-nosers even vacated their seats to give him a welcoming standing ovation. Only one person on my table did that and thankfully he was mostly hidden from me by the centrepiece floral decorations which were approximately a metre tall.

When he reached his lectern, Grekon bathed in the applause, his wicked smile of appreciation beaming forth and making me wish for the opportunity to ram my fist down his throat, shattering those horridly perfect teeth in the meantime.

"Ladies and Gentlemen," he began when the applause had dimmed to a suitable level, "Thank you and welcome! I don't get the chance to visit the British Isles as much as I would like. It is always a pleasure to meet warm and wonderful people such as yourselves."

I noted the lack of the United Kingdom and the reference to the entirety of the islands. Did that mean under his control, there was no Queen or King? They hadn't come up in conversation, which wasn't unusual really. Then again, an event with the World President would surely draw members of the royal family.

"Since you accepted me into your lives, allowing me to lead you toward the future this wondrous planet deserves. A future that, together, we will nurture and guide to reach its fullest potential. And you, all of you are integral to what plans I have in store."

I wasn't sure what the evening's event was about. All Eddie knew was what the invitation had said; tonight was a celebration of the President among the elite of London.

Looking around as he continued to speak, keeping one ear on his speech which became more flowery than concise as he continued, I could see that, for the most part, everyone was engrossed in what political jargon he was spinning. Enthralled, even.

However, apart from Eddie and myself, several others seemed less than comfortable with being present. One man seemed to be going through the alcohol as quickly as the waiters could bring him a fresh glass. All of the other detractors were picking at invisible lint on their clothing, refolding their napkins or finding some excuse not to actually look at the man speaking at them.

After a good ten minutes of glorification of himself and pandering to the crowd, he hadn't outlined any of his actual plans for reaching this better future together.

This was a political puff piece for himself. Make himself look normal, the everyman. He didn't even have security around, apart from those at the main entrance and outside.

He was one of us.

He was lying through his teeth.

Another five minutes later and the audience was doing one of two things.

The disinterested lot had been joined by a small proportion of the previously enamoured, including Embeth and were fidgeting where they sat, either bored, tired of pretending or put off by his self-aggrandising.

The devoted were almost in rapture, practically hovering over their seats in anticipation for the second standing ovation he would receive this evening.

Yet another five minutes later and the room erupted in that predicted applause. More people were standing than before the speech and they were making enough noise to cover those who were less enthusiastic this time around.

My attention was back on Grekon. I had stood up to be able to see him through the crowd between us, clapping evenly but avoiding any outward display of adoration.

Embeth remained seated, looking at me strangely, possibly wondering why my demeanour clashed so much with the fact I had stood up. It wouldn't be my first time half-heartedly giving a standing ovation. I'd seen a couple of West End shows in my own reality that had definitely been sub-par, still eliciting this overused and under-deserved method of showing approval from a large enough portion of the crowd that the rest of the venue succumbs to peer pressure if only to be able to see the actors give their curtain call.

"Now, let the evening begin!"

Another cheer and a crowd of waiters and men and women in black t-shirts and jeans swept in removing the lectern, some chairs, side tables and decorations to make way for a dance floor.

Most people were already standing, so that didn't bother many people. Unfortunately with the additional staff and the milling and moving of people and pieces of furniture, I lost sight of Grekon.

A mobile bar was wheeled in through the double doors we had all entered from, along with large refrigeration units that were then set up quickly by the windows to allow for further drinking and frivolity.

The band struck up once more and people tended to mill around watching the display of hard-working servants.

"Thank you for a lovely conversation. I hope we can chat again later," I told Embeth.

"Pleasure was all mine. I'm sure we'll bump into each other through the evening. Take care."

With that, I hurried toward where I had last seen Eddie.

His table was still there, but he wasn't.

I spun, looking for him in every face I could spot, but with approximately two-hundred and forty guests and who knew how many staff, he was invisible to me.

I had been hoping he would be my backup, but I needed to find Grekon as fast as possible with or without him.

The crowd was generally unsure of what was expected of them in terms of where to go so as I made my way toward where the lectern had been placed, I was faced with obstacle upon obstacle, dodging stumbling people and haphazardly abandoned chairs. I was sure I even stepped on a few feet in my haste.

By the time I reached the end of the remaining tables in the middle of the room, I hit a wall of people's backs.

They weren't moving. I understood why when I saw a flash of grey.

Where the tables had once been, a performance was taking place.

From the ceiling, long red ribbons had been unfurled between the last two chandeliers and a very flexible woman was in the midst of an acrobatic display rolling up and down the ribbons in a graceful series of twirls and rotations.

Below her, seven people, three men and four women were dressed in grey unitards and were taking part in an elaborate choreography of contemporary dance.

They moved in time with the slow tempo of the violins, using each other's bodies for support or leverage. The men often acting as anchors or lifts for the women to bound off and cling to.

This was so like my vision. The ballroom, a dancer clad in grey. There must have been a reason for it. A meaning.

I could feel myself shake. My skin had gone cold and clammy.

I scanned the men's faces and was disappointed. I was stupid to get my hopes up.

There was no getting through the dance space or the people watching, so I opted to circumnavigate the performance.

I still couldn't see Eddie or Grekon anywhere.

Moving along the line of bodies, I headed away from the windowed side of the hall toward the mirrors. The room magically transformed into a throng of thousands in the reflection and I couldn't make out a familiar face among them, excluding my own which was somewhat gaunt and pale. I actually looked as though I were on the verge of a panic attack.

A little odd, but it made me remember to breathe. I took several long inhalations as I moved, feeling a little better as I reached the wall.

From here, I moved along another row of onlookers' backs which was slightly harder as I'd need to squeeze between the wall and their bodies.

Well, normally I would find that more difficult, yet with my added physique, it really wasn't. I found my way was made clear a lot swifter than had I been my old self. Maybe people recognised me, maybe richer people were nicer.

I nearly laughed out loud at that thought. There was probably no actual correlation, though, from my own personal experience of how I was perceived as well as what I had encountered, it was slightly more likely not to be true.

I'd practically reached the band and I was still no closer to finding Grekon. Had he joined the gathered audience? Had he been swept off and away from the party having said his piece?

To test the first theory, I opted to try and get among the people.

This time, I'd actually need to be a little rude. Who likes people pushing in front of them to get a better view of a performance?

The first line of people wasn't too difficult to break through. These seem to be the least interested, more likely milling for something to occupy their time so they didn't have to socialise with the myriad of strangers invited to this posturing soiree.

As I made my way through the third level of people I observed that, once they saw who I was, they appeared to melt aside in deference with a few exceptions giving me dismissive looks and standing their ground. I simply moved around these people. They were well within their rights to not be impressed.

The music ended swiftly followed by a round of applause as the dancers took their bows. Shortly after, another melody was taken up by the band. I was close enough now to watch as the dancers separated and took up positions toward the back of the stage area leaving a gap in the middle.

This space was quickly filled by two people - one male and one female - who entered and paused briefly in the gap. They were dressed in the same grey unitards with various attachments of gold mesh material including a light sash that ran from the woman's left shoulder to her opposite waist and down around her right leg. This same mesh acted as hoods over their heads and faces.

The dancers then separated and adopted isolated positions and poses on the stage, ready to begin their performance.

The melody changed, slowed and became a gentle mewling chant. The dancers remained still for a few counts before she allowed her body to pulsate and gradually contort from a standing pose into a grotesque mass of ever-moving limbs.

Three sharp chords from the violin and she spontaneously burst upward into a split leap, landing closer to the man in a ball, rolling on the floor before launching herself once more like a rocket toward him.

In that instant he was alert and moving, managing a triple tour en l'air before landing and catching her on her descent.

From then on, they were in contact constantly - a hand, a leg, a foot. Something was always connecting the two as they manoeuvred through the space. It was mesmerising and the whole audience was captivated. Even I had stopped my advance. The way they covered the dance floor, using their bodies in captivating formations, was almost acrobatic at times. One moment she is balanced on his hip while he leans away in counterbalance, the next, she is carrying him on her back as she stammers forward, arms outstretched like some oppressed slave straining for freedom. Was it being blatantly symbolic to speak out against Grekon's regime?

Regime?

It was odd. There was no propaganda anywhere. Like with the Nazis who flaunted the swastika, there were no idols of Grekon, no posters, banners or blatant reminders of who was in power.

And where were the repressed? Was this Scott just fortunate enough to be part of the elite and kept away from the prison camps? Were there prison camps?

I knew there were realignment centres, but how many people were processed through them per day? Millions? Thousands? Tens?

By no means am I saying Grekon was a benevolent leader, but he didn't appear to be ruthless, not how history in my reality would deem, anyway. Here, he was a politician, a leader – albeit a corrupt one. He wasn't a despot like Hitler had been. No black-uniformed Stormtroopers were ranging the streets to apprehend the undesirables. This leader was mainly all talk.

And that was what worried me the most because it was so unlike the Grekon I knew. Oh, he liked to talk, but he was sadistic. He liked to make people suffer, eking out the pain.

Had power made him complacent? Or had the power he thought he had been wielding failed him somehow?

A misplaced arm of hers as she was raised into the air saw his veil lifted from his face briefly and my heart skipped a beat.

It was Andy.

I was right, I knew I would be. There had to be some constants in realities like these. There had to be meanings behind visions.

Then again, where had the vision come from? Why had I seen Andy dancing in this ballroom as I passed the derelict, scaled-down version of this place? I wasn't psychic. Not that I knew of.

I wanted to say something, call out, but there would be no point. He was dancing and he wouldn't know me.

The fact he was here, however, made me understand how something had gone wrong. This wasn't Grekon's plan, his world vision.

If my Andy's heart had been the key, there would have had to have been something unique about it. It would have to have been the only copy available. If this Andy had existed before I arrived, then that just wasn't the case.

Grekon had found a powerful heart, clearly, but not one that was so powerful he could control all of reality with it.

Of course, this was all conjecture. I simply hoped I was right and if I was, then whose heart was the key in this reality?

One reassuring thought was that clearly, I wasn't unique in all of these realities so it wouldn't be me. I had just stolen the body of another version of me.

My Andy was still dead, though. Actually, he wasn't mine. That hadn't been my reality. I didn't even know if there was an Andy in my actual home reality. The one I knew was dead while this reality's Andy was dancing his heart out right in front of me.

It was starting to give me the shivers. There was something oddly ghoulish about all of this.

I had to remind myself again that I didn't know this man, I had more important things to do.

Besides, Andy would have had the last laugh, Grekon had failed. Not entirely, but he wasn't all-powerful. Not yet.

That would mean he was still on the hunt for the right heart, the right victim. One way or another, I was going to have to stop him; or hinder him at least.

Lowering my eyes from the spectacle, I continued my expedition through the spellbound forest of onlookers. Infuriatingly, by the time I reached the edge of the crowd, stepping against a red rope barrier that separated the audience from the band and the raised platform on which Grekon had made his speech, the dancing stopped.

The room was once more filled with a howl of applause,

possibly even louder than all those Grekon had received put together. Instead of joining in, I strained to see through the twenty or so people who stood behind the lectern at the back of the room hoping to pick out my target.

He wasn't there. He would have stood out like a sore thumb. As it was these appeared to be his underlings, government lackeys and such. So either he had joined the rest of the crowd; which didn't sound like him at all, or he had made use of that secret doorway in the peacock wall. That would mean I'd have to trespass. I'd done worse. The problem was that I also figured there would be armed guards or worse protecting the route.

Was it worth the risk? When would I be this close to him again? Then again, was this a ploy? My name was on the invite list - would he have known that or had his secretary worked all of that out for him?

I hated feeling so lost.

Stuff it!

As quickly, but as surreptitiously as I could, I moved through the rest of the crowd toward the peacock wall. My eyes darted back and forth while I tried to exude as much normality and calmness as I could otherwise.

I was just a guest admiring the décor.

Secret doors were very rarely so well hidden that they were hard to detect. This one was no exception. The gap around the jam was fairly obvious despite the clever wallpapering and sculpting that gave the impression there was nothing out of place. What wasn't obvious was the handle or means to open the door in the first place.

One theory came quickly and that was simply to push on it, not hoping it swings inward, but with the hope it might have a pop latch of some kind, like some kitchen cupboards. Push it in once and it is pushed out slightly on release.

So as to not appear too obvious, I stood beside the door; one shoulder just over the door seam and leant back.

No one seemed any the wiser as to what I was up to. There were no security guards that I could see. No clear plastic swirls of cable hanging from beefy guys' ears to indicate they were part of any sort of secret service detachment.

A little more pressure with my shoulder against the door and I felt it slide into the wall about a centimetre before coming to a stop. I released the pressure and, sure enough, I was proved correct. The door snapped quietly out again, two centimetres now protruding from the wall.

Running my fingers along the side of the door, I found a small groove that was clearly the handle, allowing small fingers to slide inside and pull.

I had to be quick. One last glance around and in several swift movements, I'd opened the door enough to slide inside – not quite wide enough having expected my scrawny body to fit and forgetting my new pectorals were adding a fair amount of bulk to my front. I jarred momentarily before opening the door slightly wider and stepping into the secret room beyond.

On this side, there was a ring handle to pull the door to, which I did as quickly as possible.

It was a short corridor, well-lit with cream-coloured walls. About five metres in length, it turned to the right at the end. A pair of plain wooden doors stood opposite each other about halfway down the hallway.

I was about to start moving when I heard a tap on the door behind me.

I say tap, but considering how thick the door had been and how the music from the orchestra beyond was severely muffled, it must have been more of a hard knock than a tap.

To open or not to open?

Open seemed most logical. If they had been security or staff, they'd have known how the door worked, surely.

I took hold of the ring and pushed. There was a little resistance to start as the door moved away from the latch, but once I had it open about an inch, I was relieved to see Eddie's face staring anxiously back at me.

He glanced quickly over his shoulder then squeezed through the narrow gap I allowed before I pulled it to again.

"You'd be safer out there," I thought stating the obvious might be useful.

He flashed me a grin, "But it'd be nowhere near as much fun."

I shook my head seriously, "This isn't a joke. I've seen what

Grekon can do," a flash of memory came to the forefront of my thoughts – my knees cut to ribbons and covered in blood as I crawled through shards of broken mirrors, Grekon laughing down at me – "I've felt it."

His expression caught for a moment as he clearly spotted something in my own face. Then he resolved himself, "You're not getting rid of me."

I had to smile at that. It was reassuring. It was also nice not to be doing this on my own. That reassurance was short-lived, however, knowing that either one of us – or even both of us – could end up dead by the end of the evening.

Clearly, this wasn't the corridor the food was brought down. There was no close access to the kitchens or a dumb waiter. The doors were also standard handles, not on swinging hinges so this was more a utility access or perhaps an old access way from living quarters from the building's original purpose. Having said that, I don't actually know how old the building is. The one from Andy's world was smaller, burnt out and appeared to be from a much earlier time – maybe the 1700s. It certainly wouldn't have looked out of place in a Jane Austen film.

Apart from the ground and first floor, this one seemed a lot more modern. They'd done some renovations over the years so this corridor could be less than twenty years old. Or it could still be three hundred.

Either way, Eddie and I started to make our way down it. He started creeping slowly beside me, trying not to make a noise. I figured it would be safer to move as if we belonged. Eddie caught on after a few steps.

Ignoring the side doors, we made it to the corner and rounded it into a much wider corridor. No doors on the left. About seven metres down, there were some more doors on the right, similar to the ones we passed. At the end, a set of double doors that had those small rectangular windows and silver rectangles that implied these were swinging doors.

As we neared, I could see the room beyond was much larger. We reached the doors and stopped, looking through to the other side. The walls were black, though the room was well lit. It looked as though it was a loading dock as there were large roller doors on the left, the outside of the building, clearly. The room looked to be about half the size of the ballroom in most dimensions. Odd they'd need a loading dock this size.

In terms of people and vehicles, three small luxury sedans, a dark van, four motorcycles and what looked to be an armoured truck, like those used to pick up money boxes from banks and such, were parked inside. I couldn't see any people, though, which was very odd. No security, no workpeople.

The fact we hadn't encountered anybody so far was disconcerting. A high-powered function like this one, celebrities, politicians. Surely they'd keep all entrances and exits guarded.

This was not right.

I had to keep going, but there was no way I was letting Eddie take the risk.

"I'm going through. I need you to keep an eye this way," I pointed at one of the doors down the corridor, "Hide in one of those and listen for anyone coming."

"And what if they do?"

Yeah, I hadn't thought of that. They wouldn't know who he is so I quickly figured, "Play stupid. You got lost. Someone told you the bathroom was this way. No, that's too cliché. Use it anyway. But make a bit of noise about it so I can hear."

He regarded me with what could be construed as a suspicious eyeing down so I just shrugged.

Rolling his eyes, he headed back down the corridor. I waited a few moments before turning back to the doors to the dock. Still no one in sight.

Pushing gently against the door, I tested it for any squeaky hinges. When I found they'd been oiled recently, I inched my way inside.

My eyes felt like they were about to pop out of their sockets; they were so wide, trying to spot any danger.

Once again squeezing through a gap in a door, I let it fall shut behind me.

It was considerably cooler here. I could hear the big fans of an air conditioning system whirring away high above me adding to a loud hum that seems ever-present in loading docks. Perhaps it's just the silence of a large space echoes so much that it becomes audible. Who knows?

I found myself on a platform that, to my right, ran toward the back of the dock where it met a series of raised bays for trucks to reverse up to for easy unloading. To my left, it continued for a couple of feet before sloping down toward the street level.

Opting to play it cool, I strolled toward the loading bays, my eyes still slightly buggy, but I gave myself a slight swagger as I moved, all the while chanting in my head, 'I'm meant to be here,' over and over. Hopefully, if I thought it enough, anyone who sees me will believe it.

The second I stepped onto the loading bay platform, I heard a click and deep whirring noise which I recognised right away as the sliding door of a van opening.

Having not seen anyone enter the room and with the van now conveniently blocked by the armoured truck, I could only figure someone was getting out.

I froze, trying to hear anything over the buzzing silence. I didn't have to wait long for the sound of several footfalls to practically shout out their arrival. Nor much longer after that to see three men dressed entirely in black – jeans, t-shirts and each with a different styled overcoat – and carrying nasty-looking submachine guns step casually from behind their cover.

It had been a trap after all.

SURPISE, NOT SURPISE

"I had a feeling you'd latched on somehow," the voice came from the back of the loading platform. I didn't even need to turn to see who it was.

Grekon stepped out from what had appeared to simply be a shadow. Whether there was a secret door hidden within it or not, I couldn't tell. Truthfully, it would seem he had simply appeared and why not? He was a magical demon fiend after all.

The three men were casually swaggering toward me, their guns weren't trained on me, merely hanging loosely in their hands. I took that as an indication I was no apparent threat.

"You're the parasite, you'd think you'd be used to that idea," I responded.

There was no point moving. I was no match for any of these fellows and I wasn't about to enter my second firefight in as many days.

Grekon kept his distance as he walked in front of me and stopped, "You just can't keep your disproportionate nose out of things."

"I didn't do this. This was all you. The fact I'm here. You. The fact you were wrong about Andy and now find yourself in another world not completely of your making. You. The fact you're dressed like a third-rate politician from Gosnells. I'm guessing that's all you. No PR or stylist person is going to put you in that."

He actually looked down at his suit. Prideful, arrogant sod that he is, of course he did. It looked to be an expensive suit and a massive improvement on the winged demon look. For me, at least, as I could now talk to him without wondering if he would literally bite my head off.

Then again, how could I really know he couldn't do that now?

Grekon straightened his tie, "Clever. What gave it away?"

"Simple. You don't rule everything. If you'd been right, I'm pretty sure the world would be in flames."

"And not just this one."

"So, what now? Are you just going to keep ripping people's hearts out until you find the right one?

He considered the question for a moment, "Pretty much. Why stop now? At least now I won't have to worry about you getting in my way."

"I suppose you're going to kill me now."

A nasty laugh rippled around the large dock, "Why would I do that? This world has provided me with the perfect facilities to keep you out of my sight whilst making sure you suffer deeply and horribly every second for the rest of your life."

"Nice. Maybe I could get an upgr-"

"Enough of your nonsense. Take him."

The world suddenly went dark as someone behind me covered my head with a black cloth. This was swiftly followed by a kick to the back of my legs forcing me down to my knees. Someone grabbed both of my hands and yanked them together behind my back as another pair of hands wrapped them with a cable tie and tightened it to beyond what was comfortable.

They used my hands as a lever to lift me up again as if I didn't comply, my arms wrenched against the muscles in my shoulders.

It took two of them to move me. I'm guessing it was along the walkway I had used earlier as I shortly felt myself moving down a ramp. Not long after that and my calves bumped into the hard metal step that led into the back of the van. I was only assuming. Maybe it was the armoured truck, though I didn't hear any more car doors open until I was lying in the back of the van joined by one of the men in black, the door shut behind me and the remaining two getting into the front seats.

I can't say I wasn't scared, but I wasn't as fearful as I thought I would be. Maybe it was because I had expected this all along. Not the manner I was captured, but what else could have happened in following Grekon? This whole show had been a suicide mission, but it wasn't as if I had anything to lose. This wasn't my world, my life. I was already way out of my depth and carrying on the charade of being this world-famous actor would have more than likely ended with someone putting me in a mental hospital or rehab thinking I'd lost my mind or done one substance too many.

Really, I just wanted to go home. My home. Back to Perth, even, where my old friends and my family were. Or were they anymore? Had they been wiped out of existence after this debacle? If that were the case, I really did have nothing to lose.

The van had already taken a couple of sharp turns – the first after leaving the loading dock – both had me rolling all over the place until the man beside me planted his foot hard on my back, keeping me anchored.

Probably not meant as a friendly gesture, but I was grateful nonetheless.

Normally I'd be cocky and talk too much; making innocuous, unwitty or callous comments to fill the silence with the added benefit of allowing my over-active brain to calm down a bit. Not that I am saying I'm smart, just that my brain won't shut up sometimes. I was even surprising myself now with how quiet I was being.

It felt like half the evening we drove for, though I'm sure it was only an hour or so by the time we made our final stop. My fingers were tingly numb from the tightness of the cable tie around my wrists and the fact I had been subconsciously straining against the plastic.

I knew we had arrived as the man beside me began to move. Sure enough, the engine stopped, doors opened and I was once again manoeuvred by lifting my bound wrists. I stood up, bumping my head on the van's roof. A hand, surprisingly gentle, grasped the top of my head and used it to guide me.

Testing each step with my toes before I made it, I found the step of the van and the final one to the ground.

"It'd be a lot easier without the hood," The first few words were faint and crackled as I'd been lying silently in an awkward position.

There was a moment of silence before the hood was pulled away by the hand that was holding me.

It wasn't bright, still being night and a lack of lighting, so my eyes had no need to adjust massively.

We were in a large car park, the furthest edges of which disappeared into the evening darkness.

Oddly, we had parked several rows away from what appeared to be our final destination: a large silver building, multileveled and quite modern, stood up front and centre with wings extending to both sides. Looking like a cross between Frank Lloyd Wright's Fallingwater and the Guggenheim Museum in New York, someone had paid a lot of money for the architect. The attached wing buildings looked a lot less glamorous being starker and box-like. There was a severe lack of windows overall.

The external lights were pointed toward the buildings in what was clearly not an attempt to beautify, rather than make it harder for people to leave without being seen. Light was also shining upward from the rooves revealing a central building rising another three floors. These looked like a set of well-balanced fallen dominoes with quaintly curved edges.

Surrounding the buildings, sitting approximately ten metres away from the walls, was a very high W section palisade fence, the sort with the horribly hooked three-pronged vertical slivers of metal. The lights were perched on considerably sized technological machine boxes which were placed on the ends of the main fence posts a few metres higher than the fence itself. To get through to the buildings, there was a driveway that led from the car park to a gate. Beside this was a small outhouse-like building that would have been large enough to pass as a demountable classroom in a primary school.

It certainly had a feel of a prison, but from what I remember from prison films, usually, the prisoner is driven inside the compound, massive gates shut behind them. Why had we stopped out here?

Or was this site of my execution?

I looked at the men around me. One was holding me by my left elbow. None of them seemed to be paying me any mind as we simply stood there.

Two people appeared from behind the cabin by the gate, one tall and very heavily built, the other smaller in stature and frame. I couldn't see anything besides their silhouettes due to the light behind them, but I couldn't help feeling there was something peculiarly familiar about how the larger of the two moved.

From how far we had parked from the compound, it took these two over a minute to reach us. It was half that time when I could finally make out their faces and knew I was going to be in serious trouble.

Coming toward me was a face from my past that I had hoped never to see again. A face wearing a self-satisfied grin and a look in his eyes saying he was hungry for some payback.

It was Oafy.

He'd been the man to bring me into all of this alternate reality business in the first place a few years ago, kidnapping me and tying me up in some abandoned abattoir.

I should say, that isn't his real name but it's as good as any to describe the oversized Neanderthal.

I opened my mouth to speak but Oafy raised his hand before I had the chance, "No. Zip it. No way," to the men beside me he ordered, "I don't care what you do but you keep his mouth closed."

"Rude," I whispered as I heard the van door open and someone rifling through the glove box. Oafy tilted his head and squinted threateningly in my direction. I chose the silent option for fear of receiving his more physical response.

Shortly after the door shut again, I heard that tell-tale sound of tape being leased from its roll, that ripping sticky sound.

One of the men stretched a length of grey masking tape over my mouth and I thanked goodness I'd shaved before coming out this evening otherwise its removal would have been painful. Well, more painful anyway.

One thing I did notice was the fact I wasn't nearly so small compared to this brawny beast anymore. This reality's version of me really pumped it at the gym.

As if he read my thoughts and wished to contradict me, Oafy grabbed me with one hand and, with casual ease, threw me over his shoulder in a fireman's lift, winding me in the process.

I was completely useless. My hands were tied, my mouth gagged and I'm sure that if I kicked him, I'd end up worse off than him.

My head was dangling a foot above his buttocks so as he turned and headed back to the compound, I lifted my head to watch the men who had grabbed me load back into the van and drive off into the darkness. The red glow of their rear lights seemed to glare gleefully back at me before they vanished behind some trees.

Being that Oafy wasn't much of a conversationalist, the walk back was silent between my two new captors.

I had expected we would walk through the gate and to the main building so I was surprised when we entered the cabin instead. I could only see the floor and the door frame as we did so due to my terrific vantage point, though I did note that the ground inside was actually a metal grille which allowed me to see that this cabin sat above another floor. The width of the holes in the grille didn't allow me to see much more than that.

Oafy was currently bending his knees and stooping a little to fit inside the cabin, otherwise, his head would be through the roof. As would I, most likely.

He trundled across to the opposite end of the room and I heard a ding. Stooping even further and we entered an elevator.

I had to wonder how they fit an elevator inside the building as the mechanics of a lift would be above the shaft, yet there had been no apparent mechanism housed above the cabin from what I had seen earlier. I could have been wrong. Then again, maybe technology in this world was different.

The second guy squeezed in beside us just before the doors closed behind and we started to descend.

If I had thought of it earlier, I'd have started counting seconds as it would have been interesting to know how far we went down. It certainly wasn't a case of one or two floors.

This whole compound was large enough from a ground-level perspective, yet they had even more hidden below.

Why were they bringing me this way, anyway? Was this an after-hours entry? Not likely. Considering the size of the buildings, they must be used to a hefty number of being admitted, but this entrance was not really suitable for that task.

It wasn't an extraordinarily long time before the lift jolted to a stop, but I'd guess maybe five or six storeys deep.

The door behind Oafy – thus in front of me if I looked up – opened and he stepped back off the lift after the little guy had alighted.

He had more room now as he no longer stooped. I couldn't see the ceiling but I could tell the walls were also further apart.

White linoleum seemed to be the designer's choice for ground cover. This went nicely with the white painted walls that ably reflected the lights above back into the room making it almost uncomfortable to try and see.

We continued this way for a while before Oafy turned left and stopped.

Some beeping and a loud resounding clack and we were off again, Oafy pushing through a set of doors.

Another slightly narrower corridor, a turn right at what I could see to be a cross junction and we stopped once more. A door opened and we moved through it to the left.

One step through was all he took so when the door began to close, it swung against my shoulder. Not particularly hard, but it caught and stayed.

"This the one?" the little guy asked.

"Yup. Must be."

"Better put him down then."

Oafy grabbed the back of my shirt and hefted me up off his shoulder. A bit of manhandling and he dropped me heavily onto a chair, my arms screaming with pain as they were squashed at an awkward angle between my own body and the hard metal back.

"Think they'll mind if I knock him about a bit?"

The little man smiled as Oafy cracked his knuckles simply by tightening his hands into fists. He was looming over me and really wanting to take some frustration out on me.

The little guy put his hand on Oafy's considerable bicep – a symbolic gesture as there was no way he could have prevented Oafy from doing anything if he so chose, "Leave him be. He'll get what's coming to him soon enough."

And, with a final snarl, they both left me alone with my thoughts. Never a good idea, more so for me than for them.

They'd also left the tape on my mouth which was slightly frustrating as I'd most likely spend my time singing some inane tune or another and humming it through the tape just wouldn't be as satisfying.

The room was probably about six metres square. It appeared to be empty apart from the chair which had been placed in the centre of the space, though I couldn't really see if there was anything behind me while sitting down.

Blank walls, the same reflective white as the corridors. The lights looked to be neon bars set into the ceiling and covered with semi-transparent plastic strips used to disperse them.

The door was on a swing, hence why it had closed on my shoulder and although it had not hurt, it had appeared to be quite substantial. A single lever handle adorned it. This and the four black domes also set in the ceiling which I assumed were cameras were the only non-white items that made the room less Spartan.

Being that my feet weren't tied and I had little else to do, I decided to stand up and wander around.

There hadn't been anything behind me. Just another wall.

Amazing that they had a room of this size when space was in shortage in England. Well, in my England anyway. I felt worthy having been allocated this room, though I'd have felt less so had I been in Australia where this could be considered a decent-sized bedroom.

There were no sharp edges on the chair to cut my bonds, so I made a few circuits of the room feeling like a Policeman with his hands clasped behind his back and, despite the tape, found myself humming 'Agadoo' to fill up the space.

It is amazing how such a stark space can make you feel so isolated, almost claustrophobic but not quite.

By my twelfth perimeter sweep, I'd had enough and sat back down in the chair. I couldn't say I was bored. My heart was still beating at above-average speed and I was sweating despite it being relatively cool. I've faced death before, willing to sacrifice myself for the greater good.

This was different.

There was no greater good, no purpose to dying here. I certainly didn't relish the idea of being held captive for the rest of my life, either.

I'd achieved absolutely nothing in this reality, though I was limited by what I could conceivably hope to have achieved. This world was no different from the one I had first found myself transported to all those years ago. Where The One ruled with fear. No one was willing to stand up and fight. Well, that wasn't entirely true. Bob and Narelle had helped a lot, though they hadn't been able to play a major role in the usurping of a despot.

Now we have another despot, from that same alternate reality as it happens, and everyone seems to be getting on with their lives.

And why not?

There wasn't an endless night in this world as there had been in Andy's. People were still able to get on with their lives in a fairly pleasant manner – as long as you abided by Grekon's rule of course.

Yet, there was a facility like this one. Either a prison or one of those processing facilities. That implied some people weren't happy with the way he was running things. Or were they people he was testing to see if they had the key to controlling all realities which was his ultimate goal?

He'd missed a trick with Andy. Or made a massive error of judgement.

If I read what Kath told me correctly, there would be one key per reality. Grekon had gone the literal route of using people's physical hearts and this has had some effect. Yet, how was anyone supposed to know if they have found the right key?

Grekon had been trying a few times by the time I made it to Andy's reality but hadn't actually managed to change reality then. So what had made Andy's heart have this effect? Had he been the key but Grekon had used it incorrectly? Or was there something different altogether about Andy's heart?

This was all making my head hurt. I was starting to become nostalgic for talking paintings that came to life and mirror mazes.

I recalled seeing people manage to get their hands from behind their backs to their fronts by slipping their legs back through them and thought maybe that's what I should try.

Standing up again, I tried to loop my foot back over my hands and succeeded in scraping my wrists with my shoe and the cable tie.

Then I remembered that most of the time, they were sat down.

I squatted on the floor and fell back onto my bottom. It's quite difficult to do some things comfortably without the use of hands and arms. At least in this position, I rolled onto my back, again hurting my arms and hands until I managed to get most of my weight between my shoulders. This freed up my lower arms to try and squeeze my backside through the loop they made in order to get my hands below my thighs.

In my old life, this would have been nigh on impossible as I wasn't the most flexible, but I was a lot more exercised and nimble in this one. However, my butt was also bigger, as were the muscles on my arms.

I felt the cords begin to cut into my wrists but persevered. I rolled my butt as far above my head as I could, trying to maintain balance on my upper back while wrestling with my arms.

Blood had started to seep down my arms now. I could feel it and see it on my shirt sleeves. With one almighty push of my butt, pull of my arms and a tremendous amount of pain, which I could only let out the merest of grunts at through the tape, I managed to get my arms underneath my knees. Or, rather, above them considering the position I was in.

Rocking back and forth along my spine, I hoped to get back up to a sitting position through momentum and impetus, however, after four failed attempts, I had to find another solution for as it was, I was a lame duck with less mobility than before I started.

So I tried my side. It took less time and effort to fall onto my left. From here I began the even more awkward task of trying to get my hands around my feet by curling even further into the foetal position.

I've never been the most proportionate of people; long legs

and such. Thankfully my trousers weren't too restrictive. If I'd been wearing jeans, there would have been no chance of me completing this manoeuvre.

As it turned out, it wasn't as difficult as I thought it would be. Though I left the floor smeared with my blood and my shirt cuffs had now turned from a beautiful starched white to very dark pink, my arms were now in front of me.

Had it been worth it?

Well, I could now sit on the chair more comfortably.

Oh and very slowly, I managed to peel the tape off without too much pain.

I could have tried the door handle. I could have done that before my contortionist activities too. That simply wasn't an option. With four cameras and limitless resources, there was no way I could just walk out.

So I chose the chair, except now I sat with my arms up in the air in front of me, hoping the raised position might help stem the bleeding and allow my new cuts to scab over. They weren't deep but they still looked nasty.

It wasn't the blood loss but the late hour in the evening that made my head start to nod. Jerking awake a couple of times, I got the feeling I was most likely being left for the evening. Or perhaps they simply wished to watch me.

Either way, I was tired. My heart was starting to settle down.

It was still very bright so I moved the chair over into one of the corners and crawled underneath. This allowed some shade which would help me sleep a little better. I curled my arms up over my head to try and block out even more light and shut my eyes.

I woke myself up with one of those unnerving body spasms which I read could be caused by falling asleep too quickly. With no idea how long I'd been asleep, I sat up and promptly hit my head against the underside of the chair. That should give whoever was watching a bit of a laugh.

I crawled from under my makeshift tent and squinted against the light.

My small bloodstain was still near the centre of the room.

Same four cameras. Same single door.

I was thirsty, which was okay. If I'd needed the toilet I'd have been more concerned. Then again, unzipping and relieving myself in the corner may actually force them to come down and get me.

So… what could I do?

Rather than leave, I could put the chair under the handle and brace it against the wall somehow. That would stop them from getting in. This being a prison, however, that probably wouldn't upset them as I wouldn't be getting out either.

Using the chair legs, I could possibly destroy the neon lights above me, rendering the room pitch black and perhaps making the cameras useless. Unless, of course, they had infrared or night vision capabilities. Then I'd just be sitting in a dark room, though I'm not sure which would be worse.

I could sit patiently or I could see if the door opened.

Those were my two other options.

Now, if the door opened, it would be a trap, surely. Yet, I couldn't help wondering, to what end? What could they gain from allowing me to walk into a trap?

It could be a means to discredit this version of me in the media: "Famous Actor Absconds From Police Questioning. Guilty?" or some similar stupid headline.

The only footage they would have is of me tied up and bleeding and then walking casually out of the room. If indeed the door opened.

Stupidly, I was working myself up into a mental state about the consequences of opening the door when I didn't even know if the damned door would open.

So I made up my mind.

I would continue to sit.

The chair was still uncomfortable and I sat in it for a few minutes more before standing up, walking to the door and turning the handle.

I was neither surprised nor pleased with myself when it turned easily and I felt the door give when I pulled it. It was like Schrodinger's cat. Neither one nor the other but actually both at the same time.

Letting go of the handle, I went back to the seat and sat

down allowing the door to slide the centimetre or so I'd opened it and back into its jam.

No alarms sounded. Nobody appeared in a hurry.

This wasn't a trap. It was a test. It was the only logical reason for doing all of this.

It now became a question of play along or sit it out. In sitting it out, I could actually be playing along by doing the obvious.

One thing that did occur to me was that the door had an edge. A few in fact, but being it was a sturdy door, maybe those edges could come in handy.

Heading back to the door, I opened it just enough to be able to brace it with a foot on either side. It wasn't particularly sharp but it was worth a try.

I began to saw the cable tie back and forth along the edge.

This reopened the cuts in my wrists, but if it had the desired effect, it would be worth it.

Shavings began to fall off the door itself before I'd made much headway with the tie, though I could see a notch being worn into the black plastic. My arms were beginning to tire by the time I'd gotten halfway through.

When I figured I'd gotten far enough, I stepped away from the door again and pulled my arms apart.

My old body would have had no effect. The strength in this one made light work of the plastic and it fell onto the floor.

Tentatively, I flexed and rolled my wrists and arms to try and get some movement back into the joints.

Great. I was more mobile.

Back to the chair, I went.

Agadoo had become an earworm and after a while, I was battling to think of another song that could possibly drown it out. Every time I'd latch onto something, the chorus would devolve into pushing pineapples and shaking trees. I grudgingly conceded it had been a poor choice of song.

Only six years ago I had a Disney song stuck in my head for a whole year. There hadn't been a day I didn't sing it at least once. Was that indicative of my personality flaws or how brilliant their songwriters were?

A little of both, I'm sure.

My left leg had taken to bouncing incessantly under its own volition.

Three of my previously manicured nails on my right hand had been gnawed down to the quick.

If something didn't happen, or I didn't do something, I may end up cannibalising myself.

The annoying thing is this was probably exactly what they wanted. Now, normally I would gladly do the opposite of what people wanted, but this was different. With what had happened over the last few days, I wasn't in the mental state to simply stay put.

Who was I kidding? I was never anyone to just sit still on my own without something to keep me occupied. This was just a heightened situation which meant I was doing a worse job of being contrary than I normally would.

If something didn't occur, my mind would drive itself batty going over the theories behind my imprisonment, the change of realities and the nature of life itself. Or it would dwindle away on remorse, guilt and self-loathing owing to the fact I had been inept at saving the other reality and abysmal at keeping Andy alive.

I must sound callous putting it like that but if I dwell further on it, I'll never get off it.

Right! Enough!

I jumped to my feet and took hold of the chair. I wrapped the back panel under my right arm and held the base so the legs were in front of me. At worst, a dismal shield. At best, a weapon to hit someone with.

That sorted, I moved back to the door once more.

Being that I'd already opened it twice, I didn't really expect anyone to jump in on me this time.

I also didn't expect the corridor to not be there anymore.

It was still white outside, hence why I hadn't noticed it the previous times. Admittedly I hadn't actually bothered to look outside before.

The décor was the same. White Linoleum, white walls. This was another room rather than the corridor I had watched pass below me however long ago it was.

I could barely conceal my smirk.

This was more my style, what I was used to when dealing with alternate realities. Things being weird, not being where they are meant to be or doing what was generally expected.

Granted, this was most likely a case of motorised walls and rooms. Being that we were several floors below the buildings, it was entirely possible they had designed a mechanised maze to use us like lab rats.

All I had to do now was find that damned cheese.

So, another square room. Larger than the one I'd been sitting in. There were the same black domes in the corners, plus an additional four with one planted halfway along each wall. Two additional doors, on top of the one I'd just come through.

Already a choice.

I could head right, back toward the direction I had been brought earlier or left.

Well, it is always a good idea to weigh up your options.

I moved to the right and opened that door. Of course, I was hoping this would open onto the corridor which would head back to the cross junction.

It didn't.

This was a corridor that ran left to right rather than straight ahead.

The other door offered the exact same, a parallel corridor.

I was about to head toward the right-hand door again when another thought struck me.

The door to my room had closed again due to the swing mechanism. When I opened it again, I nearly fooled myself into thinking it was the same room.

Same size, same room.

The door was about to close again when I stuck my foot back to Prevent it from closing completely.

That had not been the same room. Or if it had been, they had done some cleaning.

My bloodstain was no longer on the floor. Nor was the broken cable tie.

Not only was this a mechanised maze, but they were also keeping it moving.

There would be no definitive way out. Essentially I was

Jennifer Connelly in the Labyrinth. All I needed was a little blue worm to tell me which way to walk, except I'd listen to everything it had to say so I wouldn't miss a trick.

What to do?

I didn't have chalk or a pen. I wasn't going to use my own blood. There was no way to track myself.

If I simply continued, I imagine it wouldn't be long before I go mad with frustration and tiredness. That was their end game. Make me lose it. Break me.

Well, I wasn't empty-handed. The question remained, what could I do with a chair? I'd initially thought of using it as a shield or a weapon. No need so far.

It was steel, so there was no breaking off a leg and blocking doors with bits and pieces to put a spanner in their machine. Though that idea might not be a bad one. If I block the doors, does that prevent rooms from moving?

What I did have were my clothes. A suit, a shirt, socks, shoes and underwear. Hopefully, I wouldn't need to get down further than that, but if I knotted strips around the handles, that might keep the doors ajar. I'd only be able to do it a limited number of times, but better to start somewhere.

I could also make their tracking me a little more difficult, and perhaps I'd be able to trace which rooms I'd been in by breaking the domes in the rooms.

If I encountered a room with broken domes, I'll know it's recycled or I'd been there previously.

Taking my suit jacket off, I blocked the door to my supposed original room. Taking the chair with me, no way I was leaving it behind now, I swung it high and shattered the first of the four domes in the room with the chair back.

The plastic shattered revealing a tangle of wires and broken electrics that dangled from the ceiling.

After doing the same with the other three, I walked back into the larger room and proceeded to destroy the eight in there.

Surely I hadn't been the first to consider doing this so I expected some sort of contingency plan to be in place. Either another means to monitor me or a way to quickly replace them.

With time on my hands, I removed my shirt, sat down on my seat and began to tear long strips of material. Shirt first, jacket later being that it was made of thicker material.

While I was doing this, I kept an eye on the cameras, expecting them to swivel out of sight and be replaced by an identical fixture. Didn't happen.

Once done, I had about twenty rough strips that would hopefully do the trick.

I pulled the handles down on both sides of the first door and tied one end of a strip to it. I then judged the point where the door hit the jam and knotted the strip before tying the other end to the opposite handle.

Picking up my suit jacket, the door swung closed, however, the knot I'd put in the material prevented it from closing properly and it bounced lightly off the jam.

Should do the trick with any luck.

I put my jacket on to look less conspicuous baring my hot body to the new cameras I'd find along the way. Might keep them off the scent of what I was doing a little longer.

Removing one of my shoes, I used it to block the door to the right, I found it was still the same corridor as before. There were cameras planted in the ceiling at even intervals.

This is where it got a little more tricky.

Using the chair back again, I headed one way down the corridor destroying the domes until I reached a door at its end before backtracking and doing the same in the other direction. At this end, however, there were two doors, one on either side of the hall.

Decisions, decisions.

Keep it simple, stupid.

I tied the handle of the door I'd just come through and retrieved my shoe. Again, the door could not close properly.

This would be sufficient to use to backtrack as well, so I would only block the doors I used. That did leave me with only eighteen more doors before I'd have to undress further.

Eighteen doors. Actually sounds like a lot, though I was guessing I was set to encounter a lot more than that.

This could all end up being a pointless exercise, but it was going to keep my mind focused and busy and prevent me from losing it completely. On the other hand, I had to be careful not to get my hopes up too high. If I did, that would make it so much easier for them to break me. Let me think I'm getting somewhere before pulling the carpet from beneath my feet and having me fall flat on my face. And why wouldn't they? I was a walking cliché after all.

Keeping it simple, I chose the single door at the end.

And so it went. Door after door, room after room – or corridor. Leaving a path of dangling ex-domes behind me.

I was being so careful to stay unmotivated, unhopeful, yet when I reached my final three strips of the shirt, I felt my stomach lurch when I opened a door and saw the opposite door had already been tied open with one of my strips.

It was possible I'd simply rounded back on myself. It was a maze after all.

Thankfully three doors led out of this room. Two that had been tied. My initial entry and exit. If there had been only one, then I'd know someone was removing my ties or my system was altogether flawed.

Backtracking to the previous room, which had offered me one other door, I moved on.

It was too late now to consider the old myth of staying to the right in a maze and finding your way out. I'd been wending and winding, going left, right and straight ahead at random times. There had to be a limit to the number of rooms they had.

While I was destroying the last of the domes in the next room, I heard a noise back through the door I'd wedged open with my shoe.

Due to the thickness of the doors, it was hard to say how far away it was or exactly how loud it was, but it started as a dull whirring which ended with a fairly distinct bang before silence fell again.

Should I go back and investigate or keep moving? It had to be relatively close.

With that reasoning, I headed back to the room I'd found I had already visited, picking up my shoe as I went.

The air in the room was different now. Colder and far more humid than it had been.

One of the doors was now missing and a wall stood halfway along the doorway itself. Or rather, the end of a wall.

I'd been correct about the moving rooms after all and I'd found one mid-changeover.

The end of the wall wasn't actually flat. It had indents in it around handle height and around the frame of the door. This would allow smooth travelling of walls without knocking off the handles or obstructing by their frames. This would mean the seams in the walls wouldn't be perfect in the corner. I'd need to check that.

Before I worried about that, I'd have to see what had happened.

Half of the door was now lying on the ground in the section of the room I could see in the left portion of the doorway. The other half hung limply off the top hinge, the lower hinge having been snapped off.

That room must have been on the way out when the wall got stuck on the door and broke it in two. The fact the wall wasn't moving anymore made me think the whirring and bang had been the mechanism giving way as it fought against the door which in turn had been forced against the door frame which had proved unwilling to give. Physics.

I'd been extraordinarily lucky. If I'd made the knot bigger, keeping the door sticking out further, the door would probably have swung open along with the passing wall and snapped off its hinges at the other end, not having anything to push against it and I'd be none the wiser.

On the right half of the doorway was far more interesting.

There was no reflective white room, for one thing – which was a tremendous relief, to say the least.

It wasn't a room at all.

There was no ceiling or floor.

There was a time I would have been absolutely terrified by what I was looking at. You don't just lose your fear of heights, however, my experiences had led me to face up to them and, although my skin was crawling and I could feel a nervous jitter rising in my right knee, I was better able to handle things. Deep breaths and keeping my hand firmly on the door frame kept me anchored in the here and now.

Both above and below me I could see what looked to be roller coaster tracks. Clearly, it was these tracks the rooms ran on.

A few metres above my current ceiling was an identical set of tracks. I could also see the room structures that sat on these rails.

Through the gap below me, I could see the tops of the rooms belonging to the maze one floor down. These had a matching set of tracks, most likely to provide stability.

Was it even a separate maze? Was it possible that they moved the rooms up and down as well?

Either way, I'd found a way out of my tangle of rooms. Either jump onto the top of the rooms below or try to climb on top of my current level.

The fact we had come down in the lift meant I was possibly better going up. I'd be able to find my way to the lift shaft and make my way out that way.

Conversely, I could head down, find the bottom of this establishment and find the lift that way. Then I'd have longer to climb.

I was going to have to climb up the shaft because if I used the elevator itself, they'd surely have cameras inside to see me and either stop the lift, drop it or who knows what else.

Fine. Up.

The problem was I would have to leave my chair behind. There was no way I could get onto the top of this maze without using it as a booster. That didn't mean I'd have to be weaponless.

I grabbed the end of the broken half of the door lying on the floor and pulled it. It was quite a bit heavier than the chair, but manageable, especially with my muscles as they were now.

Standing on the chair allowed me to slide the door board up and onto the roof of the jammed room.

Now to get up there myself. I would have to stand on the back of the chair and still jump a little to reach a handhold. I do this wrong and I could find myself falling.

As luck would have it, the back of the chair wedged neatly into the handle indent of the wall end. This meant the front two legs were an inch or two off the floor.

Testing my weight by stepping on the joint between the seat itself and the back, I found it quite sturdy. Still taking it slowly, I stepped onto the top of the chair back and used the wall end to steady myself. My upper body had to lean out into the dark due to the height of the door frame.

A deep breath and I launched myself up.

It had actually been easier than I thought, managing to grip the side of the roof with both hands and an elbow which helped in levering myself up and over the edge.

It was a tremendously huge cavern that disappeared into darkness in every direction. Large struts were dotted here and there to provide structural support for both the tracks and the buildings above.

I could make out the general pattern of tracks and rooms. It was rather mismatched and hard to discern any architectural structure. I guess this was due to the fact the rooms were of various sizes and shapes. It would have to be a logistical nightmare to coordinate all of this; unless it was all fully automated and worked out by the computer in charge.

Lights were dotted here and there which looked a little like stars. These combined with the odd view into an open-sided room provided some ambient light that allowed me to see the multitudes of rooms above me that made up another mercurial maze one floor up. With that floor in the way, there was no telling how big this establishment was.

The rooms didn't seem to fit snugly together in clean puzzles. This was due to the range of shapes and sizes. Also, some of the rooms had three or even two walls instead of four. This left the odd vertical shaft through which I could look through and see more darkness below or into one of those many white rooms I'd just escaped.

Thankfully, not all that far away, the lift shaft traversed the gap between my floor and the one above. Being that my chair had stayed where it was wedged which would probably let them know what I'd done and the fact I hadn't moved into another room yet would get them curious, I had to keep moving.

Like the level below, the roof was lined with tracks that I

would be able to step over easily. I mainly had to be careful that the rooms wouldn't start moving beneath me. Much like the joins with the walls in the rooms, it was actually difficult to determine where one room ended and the next began. My best bet was to use the tracks to both navigate and as a safety rail of sorts.

I retrieved the broken door piece and took a few tentative steps. I didn't trust the system enough to move too quickly. One wrong step at the wrong time and I could find myself falling down a gap between two rooms that had only moments before been nicely sealed together.

I stepped over three tracks when I heard another whirring sound. This time, without the doors and walls to muffle it, the noise reverberated around the cavern, echoing into the distance.

I looked around and saw where the problem was. A strip of narrow light was flickering out of one of the vertical holes in the rooves. Dancing in its beam was a growing amount of smoke as the mechanism on top of one of the rooms near it worked overtime to complete its move.

The whirring was cut off by a flash of amber light and a deafening crack as the mechanism failed. A cloud of darker smoke wafted through the light and dispersed into the huge chamber.

That's two down that I was aware of. Who knew how many more I'd successfully broken? They had to be on the case already.

Continuing on, I was approximately fifteen metres from the shaft when once more, the same whirring sound.

This time it was coming from behind me. The noise didn't last as long and when it stopped, it was followed by a different, muffled snapping sound before the room continued to move on. Not all of my door blocks worked.

Or perhaps the walls were moving in both directions and rather than facing the thin end of the door, it ran along the length until the handles, straining against the shirt material, gave way instead.

I wasn't going to investigate.

In front of me was one of the vertical holes so I started to make a detour when the room below me started to move.

There was no sound from the mechanism even though it was right beside me. Clearly, someone had worked hard on this setup, that way most people would be completely unaware of what was going on while they wandered the maze within.

The room moved smoothly along one set of rails, gradually filling up the hole I was about to go around.

Due to the fact the network of rails crossed all over the place, I had to step over a perpendicular set of rails while we moved or face losing my knees. I was ready to grab hold of the rail in case we hit an obstacle.

The room slid smoothly to a halt against the room directly in front.

No door blocking the way which meant I must have gotten beyond where I'd been aimlessly wandering.

As I approached what I had thought to be the lift shaft, I realised that it wasn't a shaft at all.

A solid metal backing with more rails running vertically. So the lift, like the rooms, ran on tracks rather than on cables. This would explain why there was no machinery sticking out of the top of the cabin.

The vertical tracks were different, however, in that they were serrated, like cogs. This would prevent the lift from simply sliding back down the smooth edges.

It also allowed for handholds, so I should be able to make my way up to the top.

The lift was nowhere to be seen.

Standing on the edge – or as close as I could comfortably get – of the shaft, I couldn't see it either above or below, merely darkness.

It would take another jump to reach the rail. It wouldn't be difficult, but, again, if I missed it I didn't suppose I'd need to worry about much at all for very much longer.

And I'd definitely need to leave my door behind. I was just glad I hadn't needed to use it for anything.

Another few deep breaths and I hesitated.

There was a noise. Not the same whirring and banging from before.

It was coming from the shaft below me.

The tracks in front of me began to hum slightly as I noticed the light in the shaft was cut out.

The lift was ascending.

I took a few steps back in case it was to go gushing up and drag me into its wake and send me tumbling down the shaft. It didn't go past, however. Instead, it jolted to a halt filling the shaft in front of me.

They had sent someone to investigate and they'd arrived on my floor. That didn't give me much time.

On top of the lift, I could make out small grooves and seams which indicated there was the obligatory escape hatch. If I were to use that, I'd be faced with the obligatory security cameras followed shortly by the obligatory security guards.

But I couldn't just sit here on the roof. They would find the chair, put one and one together and hunt me down.

Looking back over the vista of rails and rooves, I could see several rooms were moving at once now. They were opening up a clear run for the guards to find the problem: me.

Right. I had to move.

I couldn't start climbing up – they'd see me. Or they'd run me over with the lift as they continued searching for me.

First things first, I had to get rid of the door I was carrying.

Walking around the lift, I lay the door flat on the ground below one of the many track pieces. If I were lucky, it might even cause a future jam of its own

Now where?

THE ONLY WAY IS UP

The cavern practically howled with a voluminous silence while I stood contemplating my options.

That didn't last long before a series of screeching howls erupted and echoed throughout the enormous space.

Looking around the lift tracks and back where I had come from, I could see several beams of light coming from below as the trick with my shirt prevented at least three rooms from moving, hopefully hindering the security guard's progress. They would then have to search quite a few rooms in the hopes I wasn't hiding in one of those I'd knocked the camera out.

This was going to give me more time to think; I'd still need to be quick.

I could continue running along the top of this floor. I could continue to do that until I died of starvation or dehydration simply by hiding behind the multitude of rails that would easily block the line of sight of anyone trying to find me.

But what would be the point of that?

I stepped onto the roof of the elevator, took hold of one of the slots used by the elevator's gears to rise and fall and began to climb.

If they were to go up with the lift, well, I'd cross that bridge if it happened.

My biggest problem was going to be my fear of heights. The higher I climb, the worse it would get.

I used to be absolutely terrified of the prospect of being more than a metre above the ground. My last confrontation with The One had done a lot to ease it, but it was far from gone. I could now fly in planes, or else I'd never have made it to London in the first place. Mind you, at this stage of the game, I'd gladly take that back and have remained in Australia.

Gritting my teeth and pushing it out of my mind I pushed on.

Don't look down.

I'd not seen any sign of the visitors to my maze by the time I began my ascent through the maze above me and, though I was keeping my eyes focussed on every hand grip and foot placement I made, I hadn't heard any more noise from below.

I startled myself when I suddenly found myself surrounded by darkness and nearly lost my grip.

It took me a second to realise I had simply entered the lift shaft for the level above me.

Still nothing from below; that did not mean I was out of the woods yet. In fact, it spurred me on even more. If I could get out of sight of the floor below, I'd have a much better chance of escape.

There was an elevator door in the wall I was climbing past. Clearly, not all of the rooms moved then, as the entry hall to each level must be a regular feature. I wasn't going to use this one.

When I managed to get out of the shaft, I stopped, not letting go or getting off, simply resting. I didn't know how many rungs I'd climbed, but my more empowered and muscular frame was still tired. As I rested, my fingers began to numb and tingle, feeling like they were being dematerialised by some Star Trek transporter beam.

Not daring to look down, I looked up instead.

Although I had just climbed past a floor that appeared identical to the one I had been locked in, there was yet another above me. There was no telling how many there were.

I knew I could keep climbing, this new body of mine was a lot sturdier than I was used to. The problem was, it was either keep climbing or hang out on this floor for eternity.

Taking a deep breath to help resolve myself, I shut my eyes and hoped - not preyed, because it seemed the only deity around these days was Grekon – and began to climb again.

By the time I reached the bottom of the next floor, my hands were really starting to ache. My toes, which I had kept tense most of the climb, were also beginning to cramp. I wasn't going to be able to get much higher without a break.

As my head entered the shaft of this level, the rails I was

using to climb began to vibrate. Only slightly at first, but it began to grow in intensity in a matter of seconds.

Only one thing came to mind that could be causing it.

Steeling myself, I knew I had to look down.

There wasn't much to see at first. Just the rails and rooms below me. Then the shaft directly below me that I had climbed through only minutes before disappeared.

Within moments, I could make out the top of the lift as it rose toward me.

Could I have been in a worse possible position? There was absolutely nowhere for me to go except up and there was no way I could climb fast enough to beat the lift.

If I let myself drop onto the top of the cabin as it rose toward me, I knew I wouldn't be hurt, but they would definitely hear me and catch me when we reached the top.

Unless…

Thinking quickly, the lift barely a metre below me, I let go and jumped onto the lift top. I didn't make as much noise as I'd have thought, I guess as it was moving so swiftly, when I'd jumped it was almost like I'd simply stepped down.

Landing in a crouch directly on the hatch, they wouldn't be able to open it with my body weight on it.

A few seconds later and I was well into the shaft of the next floor.

Another few seconds and I jumped off the lift.

This landing was a bit more painful as my calf connected with one of the railings on the roof of this floor. I fell over and rolled, stifling a yell of pain but following it up with a few whispered expletives.

Rubbing my calf which seemed to be merely bruised, I stayed low and tried not to move too much.

If they had heard me on the lift, they would look for me and I'd be gone. If they hadn't, they'll still be searching all over, none the wiser.

Only problem: I was really no better off than I had been a couple of hours ago. I still had no way out, nor anywhere to go.

Then it struck me. If they had people working on these floors and there was some sort of fire or emergency; surely they'd have a way out besides the lift. I certainly couldn't continue climbing now, for if they started back down again, I'd have nowhere to go.

There was a familiar whirring and a shaft of light appeared in the near distance only to disappear again in a few seconds. This floor was active. Someone was on it unless there was just a programmed system in place.

Thinking back on my time on my own floor, I couldn't recall hearing or seeing any of the rooms above my floor move. Nor had any moved while I was climbing.

So I wasn't alone here. However, I wasn't quite sure whether I could go with the argument that an enemy of my enemy is my friend in this instance, as I had no idea what someone would have to do to be sentenced to this sort of punishment.

I knew what I had done. A thorn in Grekon's side in two major attempts at grabbing power. Though, if it had been me, I'd probably have simply had myself killed.

I'm glad he hadn't taken that option.

Another room moved quickly and quietly into a new position.

But why hadn't he killed me?

He knew my heart wasn't the right one despite my numerous interdimensional jaunts, there were still copies of me.

So he was looking for one heart. A heart that was unique to that reality. Well, whatever reality we find ourselves in.

He hasn't got a full-proof system of working it out either, what with the false starts in Kath's reality and the mistake using Andy's. Yet Andy's heart had had some power in it, or else none of us would be in this new reality.

This very facility was an excellent cover to try and find the heart he is looking for without drawing too much attention to himself.

People get arrested and disappear. Some make it out, others don't. Arresting people he suspects to be the key along with some others for good measure.

Well, that's what I'd be doing if I were him.

The lift had disappeared through another floor above me. I

couldn't risk the climb that way with the chance they'd come down again. So I needed another option.

I waited until what felt like five minutes had passed. It was probably only three, but I had to get moving. Keeping low, an eye and ear out for moving rooms, I hurdled the railings and headed directly away from the lift shaft.

There had to be an end to these rooms. There were plenty of structural supports, however, if I climbed these, I would end up hanging onto the railings of the floor above. My hands were not in the state where I could monkey climb from one end of the rails to the other.

So I walked.

Being that the rooms were liable to move without warning, I continued to stay low with my hand ready to steady or catch myself on the rails beside me. As for where I was headed, I didn't have the foggiest. If things got dire, I could simply drop down into the rooms below and be caught again. Dire being I was starving to death or I'd accidentally lost a limb or two. Even then, I wasn't sure the alternative of being caught by these creeps was going to be any better.

I don't know how long I'd been walking. Especially when I combined it with my time wandering the rooms and then climbing the lift shaft. It didn't matter really. They hadn't found me, I hadn't escaped so it was just dead time.

One thing was for sure, I could murder a Coke. Or water. I had an extremely sweet tooth and generally avoided water if I could. Though this new body of mine wasn't so much craving the coke as my mind was. I didn't have the usual sugar low I got from physical exertion without a chocolate bar or the like to back me up. Maybe I could learn from that if I could ever get back into my own body. If I was stuck in this one, I was still going to need to change my ways to maintain this physique. If I survived, of course.

Then, in the gloom, I caught a shadow. Initially, I thought I was hallucinating. Long tendrils crept out of the darkness, taller than a house, thicker than my own body. In shock and fear, I ducked behind the nearest rail and waited, hoping whatever creature it was had not seen me.

There was no sound apart from that odd hollow silence. That didn't mean I had imagined it, only that this monster might have been incredibly stealthy.

I waited a few moments more before lifting my eyes above the rail to see this gigantic newcomer.

It hadn't moved.

In fact, it wasn't moving at all.

It could be asleep, or I could be letting my imagination get the better of me.

Slowly, I continued to rise until I was on my feet again, staying low in case I had to dive for cover.

Not a twitch.

There was no point going back now, not if I could sneak past this dormant thing. It was either that or… I really don't know. Stay safe but waste all that time and get caught.

I moved forward, slower this time.

Another ten metres and I had to stop myself from laughing out loud.

There was no monster. The tendrils were support beams, the very thing I'd been looking for. However, like no other support beams I'd seen before.

They were long and twisted, interconnecting and heading this way and that. A bit further and I could see where the rails of the level above mine were anchored to the supports. It was a veritable spider's web.

Had I reached the end of the maze rooms?

Well, I had a fair bit further to walk before I found that out.

The support beams were themselves made of smaller bars forming multitudes of triangles. I remembered something like it during the 2012 Olympics being built in Stratford. The ArcelorMittal Orbit, that was it. Very similar curves were associated in the structure here too. All that meant was it wasn't going to be a straightforward climb up, I'd have to navigate my way carefully.

The last few minutes before I made it to one of the support tendrils, I was able to map out the general path I was going to have to take, at least to make it to the floor above. Thankfully I'd be able to climb up in the middle of the supports as there was enough space which meant no dangling in mid-air; it also wouldn't be too much of a stretch to reach from one beam to the next.

Squeezing through one of the triangular gaps, I planted my feet firmly on two different beams at odd angles to each other. Looking up the curvy form around me, I could see that it narrowed and expanded at points as it went, which would make it even more awkward to climb.

There was nothing I could do about that though, so I bit my lip and started up.

I passed three other levels of mazes and only stopped once. That was to see if there were any differences between the floor I'd left and the next. There weren't.

I was more impressed by my level of fitness and stamina in this body. I was hungry, sure, I'd already relieved myself before I started the climb, but my body was raring to go. Well, it was starting to feel fatigued by the time I noticed there were no more floors to go. Instead, the support structure, which had previously only been attached to the cavern walls by additional beams, made contact with the hard rock walls and started to angle over the maze floors below creating a ginormous webbed dome.

The question now was to keep climbing to the apex of the dome or to get off and find another way.

No real question there. If I got off, I'd have to find the lift shaft and most likely have to climb that again. By staying on the support beams, it gave me something new to explore and who knew what it would turn up? I'd just have to make sure my grip was firm as I didn't want to be sliding through a gap and falling to my death.

Rather than starting up and over straight away, I rested my arms and legs for a bit, drying off the sweat from my palms on my trousers. They were slightly raw already from the climbing. A manicure and skin treatment would be in order for as much of a muscular build this version of me has, he doesn't appear to really have done any hard work in his life.

When I felt my limbs were ready, I took a deep breath. Like when I was climbing the lift, I was going to be fighting my fear of heights with every move, probably more so in this case what with having to be dangling over a vast height.

The going was slower this time. The incline started softly, however, combining it with the twisting and turning made navigation difficult. I would have to keep an eye out for any adjoining structure that would have me heading back down again. When I reached a gradient of about forty-five degrees, I slowed right down, looking only at the beams and not the darkness beyond, being very sure about every hand and foothold before letting go with my other hand to find the next.

The sweat had spread from my hands and now covered most of my body which was not conducive to climbing metal frames. It was literally running down my forehead, into my eyes. My armpits were soaked, though the other me clearly maintained his body hair as there was a lot less hair under there than I was used to. That meant sweat was trickling from there and around my body as I moved. The jacket was doing little to soak any of it up and being that it was hanging loose, I felt the constant chill of the cavern even more so as the moisture on my working muscles was cooled by it.

This provided an annoying distraction, but I had to admit it kept me from dwelling on the gaping emptiness below me though I could potentially end up getting a cold or something.

With these worries in my head, it didn't seem to take long before I was almost horizontal.

I allowed myself a quick glance down and found I wasn't all that far from the first level of rooms. If I fell, I'd most likely die, but I could still see it in the darkness: the railings like a writhing, mingling layer of snakes

It's amazing how being inside with no windows can completely screw with your body clock. I had absolutely no idea what time it was, or how long I'd been awake. Being that I'd been awake most of the day, then had dinner with a little added entertainment… Andy.

Focus!

I couldn't afford to be climbing like this, pretty sure I'd been awake over 24 hours and I would definitely not be fully focussed on what I was doing.

Every time something other than a thought to do with

where my next handhold was going to be popped into my head, I had to actively divert my attention back.

Conveniently, by keeping my mind so laboriously focussed, time flew by and I barely noticed when my reaching hand connected with something that wasn't the usual rounded beam.

There was a platform - thankfully empty of people - a short metal basket, with which my hand had connected, with a few rungs above it. From my vantage point, I couldn't tell how big it was.

The basket actually blocked my way so I was going to have to manoeuvre my way up through another gap and through or over the railings. This was going to require me to turn over so I could sit on a beam and pull myself up with my arms.

It was a very slow process to start, being overly cautious I was holding on tightly to whichever beam was nearby as I wriggled my body over. Then, to avoid slipping through the gaps below me, I had to keep my body and legs as rigid as possible until I could lever myself up with my forearms and elbows onto the beam above me. As it would happen, below that beam was a gap so my bottom was hanging over dead space.

Now, any other able-bodied person, I'm sure, would be able to complete this operation with minimal fuss, but yours truly… I was ham-fisted when my fears got in the way.

Reaching out behind with my right hand and gripping as tightly as I could with my left, The rungs were just out of reach, though the next beam of the support structure was within my grasp, so I placed my hand on it.

Very uncomfortable now, I noticed I would be able to free my legs from the beam they were resting on if I was to simply push myself up on both beams. In doing so, my feet would then be dangling through a gap below me.

The idea absolutely terrified me.

I had no choice, though, if I wanted to get any further.

I took a deep breath and pushed down on the beams, slowly to avoid snapping my legs off. I felt them inching over the beam until all that was left to go were my heels. When they finally swung free, I felt my hands slip with the momentum and started to panic, creating more sweat, which I certainly didn't need.

As quickly as I could I readjusted my hands only to have the left one slip completely off the support. I felt myself falling as my other hand lost its grip and I felt the emptiness below me reaching out for me.

BREAK

My left hand had slipped off the other side of the beam it had been holding. As I fell, the metal connected hard with my armpit, jarring it and shocking me even more.

As I continued to fall, my brain became a blur of panic. I didn't even notice my left arm hook over the beam and its hand slapping hard against it to find purchase. A completely instinctive movement that managed to halt my fall as the rest of me dangled over the precipice.

The pain from my armpit spread quickly to my shoulder and I felt myself beginning to slip once more.

Heaving my right arm over, I once again found myself in a similar position to the one I had been in moments ago, supported by my forearms, only this time I was hanging free below.

I was shaking so badly that I didn't trust myself to move. Even my legs were twitching with nerves, my palms and toes tingling with pins and needles.

Breathe.

Just breathe. And don't look down.

It was working as I felt the trembling begin to fade. I managed to refocus my mind on how to get into the basket and onto relative solid ground. There was no avoiding the fact I'd have to dangle most of the way because the safest bet would be to simply inch my way around the triangular hole I was clinging to the edge of. It would be slow going, but, hopefully, a lot safer than the last stupid manoeuvre.

It took less time than I thought it would before I was mere inches from the rim of the platform's raised edge. I was going to have to let one arm go to reach for the first rung which was now well within my grasp. If I were quick, I'd minimise my chance of losing balance and slipping.

With what I naively told myself were lightning reflexes, I found purchase with my right arm. I had used the arm as I was mainly right-handed and it would help me with pulling me up, despite my left arm really beginning to throb. There would be a nasty bruise, but I was sure nothing was broken.

From there, with my new upper body strength, it was a matter of moments before I hauled my body over the top railing and landed heavily on the hard metal plating.

Not out of danger, but on much safer ground, I took a moment to smile in relief.

All the injuries I'd accrued tonight then came back with a vengeance. My whole upper arm was pulsing painfully. My leg was fainter, but still making itself known.

I knew I had to move, but despite the pain, it felt better, and easier, to stay right where I was.

Time had begun to lose any impact on me. I knew if I didn't get going, there was a higher chance I'd be found, but, then again, if I just lay huddled on the floor like I was, maybe no one would notice me in the darkness and I could just sleep for a long while.

It was so tempting. I was so tired. Physically and my brain was starting to shut down too.

Then again, I'd made it this far. If I stopped now, I may never get out again.

No. It was time. Time to move.

Taking a deep breath, I hauled myself up, using the rungs to help.

The view was rather spectacular.

A crazy geometric maze of beams arced down in almost every direction, fading into the distant gloom of the cavern. Below me, the railings and runners were barely visible, creating another maze of crisscrossing lines and curves, you could easily forget that below those were rooms to trap and torture people in.

The platform was about eight feet square with two walkways heading at 90-degree angles from each other. These were lit by basic fluorescent bars hanging at even intervals. Because of these lights, though, I couldn't see what was at the end of each walkway as they disappeared into the darkness again.

It was going to have to be potluck. So without another thought, I chose one. So very unlike me to be so decisive, but

I had noticed how I'd been making more progress than if I'd sat back and ummed and ahhed about it all.

I thought I'd become more self-assured having beaten The One all those years ago. I'd taken a big risk then by thinking I was sacrificing myself, essentially giving up the fight, and I had. I really think I had come a long way from who I was before I met Bob and Narelle.

There was still a long way to go. Hell, I was still fighting, but I can see now how many times I'd remained indecisive, less willing to stand up for myself. That must have been one of the big differences between my version of myself and the one I was now inhabiting.

That wasn't to say the new body was the cause of it. Sure I was buff, but so far that had helped me climb. It was more than that. I was encountering situations that pushed me which had nothing to do with my physical strength, but in these events, I haven't really been finding myself lacking as I would have when I wallowed in my apartment back in Perth.

Not only that, though. The fact I had let my good friend Sarah fall out of my life said something about who I was and I have to say, I didn't like it very much.

Did I actually like anything about myself?

Big question.

But I did. I didn't use to. Not before all the crazy began. I whined a lot - I still do - but I wallowed more. If someone had referred to 'Misery Guts' I would have been sure it had been me.

These days I am better than that. More likely to take a risk, stupid ones too it seemed. Proactive.

Still… A long way to go before I could actually say I truly liked who I was.

Meh.

That wasn't going to stop me from trying to survive. Nor prevent me from doing my damnedest to get things back to the way they should be.

As I reached the edge of the light on the walkway, another light lit up ahead of me. Motion sensors, clearly. Handy, but also a good way to let people know where I was.

On a positive note, the motion sensors would also let me

know if someone else was around. From what I could tell, I was the only one making a light trail. There were no other lights around, so I must have triggered the initial ones when I reached the platform. I hadn't noticed, I guess they were blocked by the basket and I had been a bit distracted by the manoeuvring I had had to make.

As I walked, I remained vigilant, my hands running along the rails to keep me steady and on course. The lights furthest behind me began to switch off, clearly on a timer.

A small tremor began under my hands, the railings had begun to vibrate, steadily increasing in intensity until I could hear the slight rumble of the lift. It was either coming up or going down. No idea what it had been doing since I had escaped my maze. The fact it could end up stopping on this walkway level left me tense, palms sweating as I gripped the railing tightly. So tight, in fact, I had stopped myself moving forward, the pain in my armpit and shoulder flared as I pulled against my own hand, seemingly superglued to the cold metal.

I could surmise, from the amount of time it felt I was standing there, that the lift was coming up. There wasn't enough space above me for it to travel that long. Sure enough, my eyes were drawn by a thin vertical strip of light rise from the darkness to my left and streak upward to be swallowed by the motion-triggered light that brought the 'lobby' platform of this level alight and I could watch as the lift cabin disappeared once more into the gloom above.

At least they weren't stopping here.

That gave me the direction I needed, however, and I broke free from my self-imposed shackles, releasing the rail and pushing onward.

I took the next left I could and headed toward the lit platform as quickly as I could. I didn't have much time before the timer elapsed.

One long walkway stood between me and it when the platform went dark; the shadows of the railings and lift shaft were etched as negatives on my eyelids as I blinked. The light flashed back on when I was only a couple of steps away.

This platform was larger, the support beams that led upward were thicker here, part of the main backbone of this level. An electronically controlled sliding double gate was situated to prevent people from falling down the lift shaft. That was considerate. Two other walkways were leading from this point and, for something different, there was a ladder.

Seriously, there was a ladder running upward beside the lift rails.

If they had extended that down to the mazes below, that would have saved a lot of trouble.

I guess they didn't care if the people in the mazes escaped, but the workers, guards or whatever that would be stationed on this level were a little more important in the case of an emergency.

But where were they?

They knew I'd escaped by now. This level should have at least one person stationed here keeping an eye out. They couldn't be so understaffed that they couldn't afford one measly sentry here. I mean, look at the money spent on this place. It must have cost a fortune and not just a small one.

I moved to the base of the ladder and took a deep breath before I started to climb.

This could simply end up with me being recaptured at the top.

As I blew my breath out through my nose, I knew there was no other choice. I couldn't wait here forever. If I got caught, at least I'd have tried and just look how far I'd come.

One thing was for sure, I wouldn't go down easy this time.

Three metres above the platform the ladder entered a hole in the dark rock cavern ceiling.

Beside that dark exit, the lift disappeared into a hole of its own.

There were no lights on, though, from the glare of the platform lights below me, I could see there were light fixtures around me. Probably emergency lighting, red or orange flashing bulbs.

Going a bit slower and making sure each handhold and footfall was secure and supported, I moved into pitch darkness.

I'd forgotten to care how much time passed, but at some point, my hand, as it was reaching for the next rung, connected with a hard metal surface giving a soft dull ring. Giving it a cursory search one-handed, I found a panelled door of some sort. There were all sorts of shapes and curves to it but no apparent way to open it.

Well not until I realised I'd closed my eyes. At some point in the dark, I'd simply shut them and hadn't really noticed.

I blinked them open and saw there was a dull red glow around me, so faint it hadn't registered through my eyelids.

Twisting my neck slightly, I spotted a small red light giving off just enough light to show the shadow of a button. This was located on the wall, not on the door itself. Why it wasn't located behind the ladder so the climber could easily access it, I didn't know. Why should things start being easy now?

To push, or to waste away in the darkness of this literal prison.

I didn't have to think long anymore. I was tired, hungry, in pain and really just wanted to sit down for a moment.

My finger was an inch from making contact when something banged hard against the panel above me.

It surprised me so much that I nearly lost my grip. Instead, I froze. Waited and listened.

Nothing. No follow-up.

My finger edged closer, making contact with a cold plastic and continued to travel, pushing the button.

There was a clunk, followed by a whir and the panel began to rise. I could tell as light sliced into the darkness forcing me to squint and look away momentarily.

Another clunk and I noticed the panel had stopped moving, having created barely four inches for me to crawl through.

The whir continued, sounding strained. Then it was joined by a soft rustling whisper that pulsed momentarily.

Something moved above me, above the panel which ended in a thud and the panel began to move again. I was absolutely sure none of that was supposed to have happened.

The panel opened until it stood vertically behind the shaft and the ladder continued upward with railings now visible to help me out of the hole...

But I didn't move. I felt like a bird in a cage being watched, but I couldn't see what exactly was watching me.

Had this been part of the maze? An experiment of Grekon's? The sadistic monster had taunted me horribly before. Flashes of the mirror maze where I had first been confronted by him when he had first resembled a human came to mind.

I wasn't getting anywhere waiting here, whether this was a test or not.

My hand moved from the button to the next rung and I continued my climb.

It was light in the room above, initially, my view of the room was blocked by the panelled door and the fact I was facing a wall.

When I was halfway out, I paused, somewhat amazed I hadn't been shot or clubbed from behind and looked around as best I could.

"Scott?!"

The voice was familiar, but only vaguely. Not one I had heard particularly recently, nor one I'd known for long. And it was young. A ring of amazement and relief hovered heavily in the tones.

"Thank god!"

That one I knew, having been the last friendly voice I'd heard.

A hand reached out and grabbed my elbow, offering support and Eddie came into view.

He was dressed in black and a beanie, far from the suited debonair fellow I'd seen before.

I almost cried there and then, I could feel a large lump rise in my throat that I swallowed with some difficulty and my eyes welled up.

The arm he had taken hold of released its grip and snared his arm.

Eddie was real, this wasn't a trick.

"Keep climbing! We haven't got long."

I all but sprung from the shaft and onto solid ground and he pulled me into a bear hug.

In the back of my mind, I knew he was hugging the alternate version of me, his feelings becoming very apparent in that short moment. I gave him that and took my own comfort from the friendly body contact.

We were by no means safe, but this was the closest thing to it right now and it felt wonderful.

A hand touched my shoulder, jarring me to attention and I pulled away from Eddie who instantly looked sheepish.

Turning, I finally saw who had initially spoken. Not only that, I think all the pieces started to fall into place.

"Luka?"

He was also wearing all black and grinning like a Cheshire Cat.

"Hello again, Scott. Surprised?"

"Doesn't even come close, in so many ways!"

He turned and moved toward the door at the end of the room. We were in the same room I'd been led through and departed down the lift from.

"We don't have time right now, I'm afraid. We need to get you out of here."

The final piece of the puzzle landed and I realised Luka had it completely wrong, "No! It's you! We need to get you out of here!"

He looked puzzled but hurried on, Eddie pulled me after him, impressive considering my bulk in comparison to his. Though my exhaustion would have been an aid to him.

It was night outside. Whether the same evening as I was brought in or not, I had no idea. Time for that later.

There was a red glow in the night sky that flickered and had the sharp smell of smoke wafting with it on the cool breeze.

The main prison building had been set alight. It wasn't a roaring blaze, but it was obviously considerable enough to liven up the sky above us. A light dusting of ash was falling through the sky like a mock snowfall. Among the ashen flakes ran other people dressed in black, ten maybe fifteen running back toward the cabin we had just exited from the main compound. These weren't guards but appeared to be with Luka and Eddie.

I was surprised by the number of accomplices they had managed to scrape together. When one of the doors on the side of the building slammed open and several more people in black ran out followed in quick succession by scores of people in light green jumpsuits.

"Hurry!" Luka called as he continued to run.

Who was I to argue?

There were four huge buses in the car park with eight different types of four-wheel-drive vehicles surrounding them protectively.

I began to run toward the nearest bus, but Eddie dragged me toward one of the smaller vehicles, black or dark blue, it was hard to tell in this light.

Eddie held the door open for me and I managed to haul myself onto the back seat. Luka jumped in the front passenger side and Eddie ran round the back to get in beside me.

The people in dark clothes were ushering the freshly rescued toward the buses.

Being sat in a comfortable seat in the dark, I felt tiredness drip over me like warm custard smothering my mind but one question nagged at me:

"Where are the guards?"

Eddie cast an odd glance at Luka who didn't turn to see.

"It's over halfway through their evening shift. Intel told us they'd be low on numbers, mostly complacent. Everything planned was non-lethal. They're just doing their jobs, right? We still need to hurry though," Luka tapped anxiously on the dashboard as he spoke.

I got the impression he believed what he had said, but he didn't actually trust it. Were reinforcements imminent? Had he suspicions that some of his own operatives were prone to fatal techniques?

I was too tired to wade through it all, my eyes had been caught by the flickering flames that were now dancing above the black shadow of the building and underneath the spark-riddled sky above.

The fire was almost hypnotic in the way it moved, the heat it exuded and, even though I couldn't feel it, the mental sensation of that warmth, most likely reinforced by the air conditioning in the car, wrapped its arms around me, smothering me and I didn't fight the sleep that swiftly came.

I jerked awake as the car began to move, wheels spinning beneath us before it launched forward. From then on, dreamless dozing toyed with me as we moved, the odd bump pulling me from a deeper sleep I very much wanted to fall into.

Several shouts drew me out once more like a timid mouse from my sleepy hole in search of cheese, but for me, the cheese that was calling to me wasn't all that inviting. I watched blearily as two of the buses headed off in a different direction with four of the other four-wheel drives. My forehead bumped lightly against the glass and I took that to mean it was time to sleep again as the vehicle moved on.

Doors slammed but I didn't even bother opening my eyes as I was yanked once more from a place of worriless bliss.

Strong, warm arms wrapped around me and in a half slumber, I let them guide me out of the vehicles. We were inside somewhere, there was a mild chill from the night outside, but there was a smell and warmth that was taking back ownership of the air around me. I had to help them transport me, I weighed too much in this body for anyone to actually carry me. So I leaned against whoever held me. It smelled like Eddie. The way he held me was so gentle…

He nudged me up one small step and led me into what appeared to be a kitchen. We weren't alone. People followed us in and there were already shadows moving around ahead of us as he brought me further into the building.

Soon there was a bed. A soft bed with a lovely doona to crawl under.

Someone was taking off my shoes.

Duvet. It's called a duvet in the U.K.

A creaking door, whispers.

Was this the U.K.? Was there a U.K. like I knew it in this world?

It didn't matter.

Once I was under the covers, I fell into a beautifully deep slumber.

LET'S GET COOKING

Breakfast woke me up. The smell of frying bacon to be more precise.

My stomach growled indignantly, telling me in no uncertain terms I was not to go back to sleep.

Carefully, in case I'd torn muscles or done some other damage, I stretched under the bedclothes and winced as my shoulder fought back warningly. Maybe I should leave any further climbing or physical exertion out for a few weeks.

Sunlight was streaming through a gap in the curtains above my head allowing me to see the small room I was in.

It felt small due to the double bed taking up the space, a small chest of drawers squashed in the corner staking its own claim on the limited floor.

The bacon was calling if I was going to be allowed to have some.

Pushing the duvet aside, muscles tight from what I would normally associate with post-gym workout fatigue, I unsteadily got to my feet.

Only once I was sure I had my footing, I headed out of the room, following the glorious smell and the faint hissing sound that accompanied it.

There were seven people in the kitchen and another four in the dining room adjoining. All conversation stopped as soon as I stepped from the hallway.

The array of expressions as people looked at me was intriguing.

There was a look of mistrust and veiled almost disgust which I was fairly familiar with. It's the expression I'd regard myself with sometimes when I looked in the mirror.

Concern fluttered across a few faces, which I internally appreciated.

The one expression that took me a moment to identify stood out on three people. They were by no means identical, but they all said the same thing.

It was an expression of awe. More specifically, being star-struck.

This body was a celebrity to them

It didn't take long to get me caught up. Eddie sat beside me on a couch while one of the women, Asalah, explained. She seemed to be one of the people in charge so I listened as best I could. Not that it was difficult to keep focus on her. Her eyes were a bright brown, the brightness coming from within. Her face was fortunate to have the trait completely opposite to 'resting bitch face' in that when she wasn't outwardly showing emotion, she still had a lovely smirk and a twinkle in her eyes. She wore a loose headscarf that covered most of her hair, but wisps of her fringe had escaped and the scarf itself was threatening to fall backward as she spoke.

Everyone else was either poring over paperwork, analysing schematics, on laptops or having a chat in the kitchen or outside. Luka was nowhere to be seen which was unsettling for me, I couldn't stop fidgeting.

Another sign Grekon didn't have complete control over this reality was he had been unable to prevent the forming of a rebellion of sorts. Friends and families of people who disappeared initially held vocal protests until they realised many of those participating would also inevitably disappear. It had required everything to move underground.

This had been a fledgling group still only seven months old and initially only running anti-Grekon in their case as that was what he was known as in this reality - campaigns with flyers, graffiti and hitting social media, whatever that was, some sort of television program maybe. Their tech people used VPNs to hide their online tracks - another acronym I had no idea what it stood for. Things had taken a step up the same day I arrived. The reason for that came in the form of Luka.

He had rallied this group and drawn in several other factions, pulling them together, pushing them to coordinate their efforts, to make an actual change rather than the tokenistic approach they had fallen into like a record player's needle in a rut.

The boy was full of surprises. So little time and he'd pulled together a virtual militia.

They had several hundred participants locally who had officially signed up to the movement with many more connections beyond that.

"That was very brave of all of you to organise and carry out a move like breaking into that place in such a short amount of time," I wasn't sure if it sounded like a compliment. I wasn't sure it was meant to be one. Reckless was more like it, not that I wasn't extremely grateful.

"We already had the location, plans and everything else. Robbie and Selma had been digging up everything they could from even before they joined the group," she looked over at the people on their laptops, "All we needed was some coordination, weapons and vehicles. Turns out, when you have a good leader, it's amazing what you can actually find you have connections to when pushed in the right direction."

"Speaking of," I continued to look around, almost getting up off the couch, but Eddie's hand took hold of mine and held me down, shaking his head.

"Just relax a bit," he said. Eddie had been really worried, the expression on his face when I saw him spoke volumes.

I smiled, trying to reassure him, "I only wanted to know where Luka was. We have to talk."

Asalah checked her watch, "He shouldn't be too long. says he knows you. Well," she blushed a bit, "we all do, really. How often do you get to meet a movie star, I mean."

I shook my head, "That's not really me. I don't know what Luka has told you, but…"

The confused expression on her face told me to stop blabbing, "I just want to be thought of as normal. None of the glitz and glamour. Especially now," I countered which put her at ease.

An hour or so passed and Eddie showed me around the grounds. It was a farmstead of sorts. The house was relatively modern but sat on 14 acres of land. There were a couple of horses, a large barn where, instead of much in the way of machinery or animals, there were vehicles and some boxes of 'guns and things'.

Behind the barn was a small forest, half sat on the property, the other half on the neighbours, though no fence delineated where one side stopped and the other took over. It appeared big enough to get lost in so Eddie and I walked in only a couple of metres and skirted around the edge.

Normally I talked too much, but I couldn't think of anything to say. It was even odder because when I'm unable to talk for a while, I would generally start sprouting any kind of rubbish just to fill the air. Not today. It didn't seem appropriate, nor fair on Eddie.

I'd constantly catch him looking at me as we walked, he was ready to help if I stumbled on a loose branch or rock in the ground. He was clearly still completely in love with the other version of me and I didn't know what to say to help. I'd never been in a proper relationship myself. Work, hobbies and all sorts always got in the way. Or at least that is what I told myself, but it made me the least qualified person to sort this all out.

It would have been romantic in different circumstances.

Hell, it was romantic. But only one half of the couple was here and the longer we walked, the more of an interloper I felt.

"Over here," Eddie headed off ahead a bit faster, I felt a slight relief, but also something else.

Almost begrudgingly, I followed him through the trees.

A sound gave away what he was wanting to show me. Water trickling and bubbling was growing louder as we approached.

Sure enough, when I caught him up, Eddie had managed to find a quaint little stream of water. If he had planned it, I wouldn't have been surprised, as there was a tiny waterfall that refracted the light of the sun as it searched through the canopy above us.

It wasn't large enough to release a spray of any sort, but the shrubbery around it was damp with droplets.

Eddie was focused on the water until I stopped a metre or so behind him. He turned his head slightly, noticing the distance I had put between us, then returned to watching the minuscule water and light show in front of him.

"I know you're not him."

The words hung in the air for a moment and I was still lost for words. I felt I had to say sorry and my brain came up with the lamest three-word response.

"I'm so sorry."

He was talking again as if he hadn't noticed I'd said anything.

"But you're so like him," He turned to look at me properly, "You're better than him. You've done more for the people of this world than he ever did for his friends or his fans."

"That's not fair. He didn't have an apocalypse to worry about."

"And he wouldn't have done anything even if he did. I know I'm a sad case. I fell for his fame, his attractiveness before anything else, just like everyone else. I think that had me blinded for some time. But he had the same qualities as you. Compassion, empathy and a sense of right and wrong. I saw them, he just never let anyone else see. I guess he was too scared of what people would say, how it would be reported. An action hero with a conscience. He kept everything hidden. But those qualities, it was those that I really fell for. And then you came and you're not hiding any of it."

I couldn't hold his gaze anymore and I looked away into the trees, my head ever so slightly shaking 'no'.

"This isn't me, Eddie. It's not him either. I don't look like this and clearly, he doesn't behave like this. I'm some sort of fruit salad concoction of the two of us. I'm grateful he has a body like this. I'd never have made it out if it had been my own scrawny thing."

"And he'd never have survived if it had been him inside there."

He stepped closer and I had to fight the urge to retreat. I didn't want to make this worse.

"I see in you the potential he has. I barely know you, but I see so much of him there too. Only, with you, it's so free. After you disappeared, I knew I didn't want to lose you again."

I took a step back when his hand began to reach toward mine. This was going too far.

"But I don't know you, Eddie. You're not in my life in my

world. And I'm intruding here, masquerading as a hero in this body. Seriously, these people wouldn't have given two hoots about me in my own body. They'd never risk their lives to save me. I'm not a famous movie star. I'm not a charismatic charmer."

"I would."

"What?" I'd forgotten what I was ranting about, I didn't understand what he was saying.

"I'd risk my life for you."

"No!" I could feel something rising in my throat, "You'd risk your life for him."

"But I did. I was there to save you."

"To save this body! His body. This thing dies, most likely he's gone forever too."

Eddie opened his mouth to speak but hesitated. That was enough for me to get my next words out.

"Hold off on all of this until I get him back for you. Then you'll have what you really want. I'll be out of your hair and things will be back to normal."

I turned and walked back toward the tree line.

His response was nearly lost to the undergrowth crunching beneath my feet and the growing distance. Nearly.

"What if I don't want him back to normal?"

I swallowed hard and kept moving, quickening my pace. There was no good outcome to this conversation. I couldn't live in this world, not only because Grekon would be hunting me down, but because it was all too easy. What did I have to work for? This version of me had the perfect career, he had someone who was completely infatuated with him. It was all here on a silver platter, ripe for the taking.

But I really didn't want it.

Sure I complain a lot about my life. My looks, my lack of money and my career. But that's mine. This world shows me how things could have been, but I missed all the avenues and side roads that would have gotten me here. Instead, I want to go back and find them myself. I want to return home and see my family, my friends, Sarah, Morrisey, Andy…

Andy was gone. He wasn't even from my world. I wouldn't be seeing him again. Nor Eddie, if I could get home.

That's what I needed to do before I got sucked into any more of this mess.

I had to find Luka.

Once out of the trees, I headed back to the main house. There were guards stationed here and there in normal civilian clothes but armed.

Luka was standing in the french doors leading into the lounge. Someone was talking to him, but he was watching me as I approached.

When I got close enough, he said something and began to walk toward me.

Somehow, he had come a long way from the street rat I'd met.

"Pretty, isn't it?"

"I'm more of a city boy. I thought you were too."

He smiled, "I'd never had the chance to see what it's like this far out. I could get used to it."

"Me too. But in my own world, thanks very much."

This brought him back on point. He was still a child, but there was something more. I had seen it when I first met him. A sense of responsibility. The way he cared for his grandmother. Speaking of which, "I suppose you've heard about your Grandma?"

He simply nodded. I didn't know what else to say, so I gave him some time. Not that he needed long, "She wasn't really mine. Like that body isn't really yours."

I held my arms out to show it off, wincing slightly at the strain on my aching muscles, "I know, right? Lucky upgrade."

The humour was forced. Neither of us was feeling it. I'd just come from a horrible conversation and both our worlds had been eradicated.

Luka indicated that we should move away from the house and we began a wide circuit.

"So you've been made leader? A teenager changing the world."

He shook his head, "No, not really. I offer suggestions and direction. I found them riled up initially. Now they listen to what I have to say and vote on it. Who'd have thought it? Teachers barely listened to me at school. I could get used to it."

"Don't. We need to find a way to put everything back, if we can, that is."

"Who knows. Grekon's the one with the power."

"But he isn't."

"What do you mean?"

I'd thought about this while I waited for the dinner party. It was all part of how something had gone wrong: "He needed the hearts. That was why he was attacking those people. He used my friend Andy's heart to bring us to this reality. There is an energy there that he taps into, but without it, he is just as stuck as you and I.

"He chose the wrong heart, though. He mentioned something about Andy being from another reality. I don't think that was true. Or if it was, something went wrong. Sure he bought us here, but this isn't his ultimate destination," I took a moment before I laid my biggest theory on him, "He needs you for that."

"Me? What for?"

"Your heart. You're the special one. You don't exist in this reality and I think that's exactly what he needs, someone who is unique to a reality so he can somehow tap that energy, potential, whatever and create his own unique reality. I saw this world's version of my friend Andy, so he wasn't as unique as Grekon had thought. I clearly have another version of me here despite the fact I now inhabit his body. But you. You aren't meant to exist here. Sorry to say but this world's version of your Mum died before she had a chance to have you. So you're the one we need to keep safe. You sure as heck can't be running missions like you did to save me. I also think the fact that you are here is proof. I know I'm here because I was caught in the crossfire when he killed Andy. How did you get here?"

Shaking his head, "I was there. I saw what happened."

"What? What were you doing there?"

"I followed you. Thought I might have been able to help. But I couldn't. He was too powerful. When I saw the world start to fall apart around me, I tried to move into another reality. I found myself here, like you. My Grandma was gone.

My home was gone. Knocked down for a new apartment building. So I put my ear to the ground and found this lot."

"There was already a rebellion? How old is this reality then? How long was Grekon their leader?"

He shrugged, "Could be as old as yours or mine. He just happened to slip into the role that was already there, maybe. Or it could be something he created fresh."

"But he took it out of the oven before it was finished baking."

"Mmm."

We continued walking for a bit. He'd taken everything really well.

It was a lot to lay on a teenager, I should know, I was barely out of my teens when I had to help save reality from Grekon and The One a few years back.

"Of course, it's just a theory, that you're the key to all this," I added, a bit late.

"It's better than anything else we have. But it doesn't help us one bit. Grekon already knows you're missing and has search parties everywhere on the hunt for you."

"But it does help us. He doesn't know about you. For starters, we need to keep it that way."

"Yeah, and what's to stop him from doing it again? Choosing the wrong heart and creating a new reality?"

I hadn't actually thought of that. Even the wrong heart had ruined things once.

"And what if my heart is the only way to change things back?"

That hadn't even been a spark in my previous thoughts, but he was absolutely right. I wasn't going to say that thought, "No, there has to be another way.."

He stopped, "Does there? Why?"

Thankfully my brain had switched back on since I'd been speaking to Eddie, "How did you bring me across to your reality in the first place?"

"That's my power. I travelled to yours and brought you back to mine. It's blocked now. I tried to go home, but it was like the door is shut. Or it doesn't exist."

"We don't know, though, do we? Not for sure. Grekon

may have just locked us in here. I know there were other realities before. I've been to them with my old friends. Grekon's even been there. He's been doing this for a while now, he said. That didn't stop my world from existing then, I have to believe it hasn't stopped it now, not when this whole mess wasn't what he had planned for. Either that or powers from your world don't work here."

"So there's nothing we can do," he was upset. The idea he may have to die to end all of this was clearly still on his mind and my attempts to distract him with hope weren't working. I was very much afraid he was right.

"I've been in worse spots than this, believe me. There is always a way out."

But what was it? I had absolutely no idea. We could run a resistance force for decades trying to destroy his facilities. But Grekon had made himself President of the World. How do we defeat a world superpower?

Grekon had been an arrogant adversary from the get-go, from the way he teased me in the mirror maze when I first encountered him to how he toyed with me and Sarah at our apartment. He liked the game, the chase. Most of all, he loved to show off. The bat look he adopted, the fact he is seeking power over all of reality, no matter what it took or how long.

"We have one advantage."

Luka looked up at me, wiping what could have been a lingering tear from his left eye, "What's that?"

"He is one proud son of a gun."

"So? He is a despot, what do you expect?"

"But he is a despot who is yet to win against me. Well, properly anyway. Every time he has tried to take me on, it never went to plan. He may capture me, but I've bested him in the end. Can you imagine how he feels about me?"

"Likely he wants to take your head off next time he sees you."

I smiled and nodded. I'm not sure that was the correct response to Luka's observation, but he was correct. Grekon wouldn't pass up the opportunity to best me.

"So we need to work out a plan so we can use me as bait, take him down and somehow force him to fix things. It's just that last bit I am having trouble with."

"It needs to be public."

"Why's that?"

I could tell by the look in his eyes that Luka had something, "Same reason you gave. Pride. We use it against him. If this world doesn't have powers and they think he is just a human benevolent dictator, he will do his best not to reveal his true self to keep all his supporters loving him, at least until he figures a way to fix this mess for himself.

"To take you down in public, he will have to keep his facade up, making him more vulnerable."

I was impressed, "Good point."

He was on a roll, "If we can capture him in public, confront him, his powers would be a last resort, so we would need to keep cameras on him, people watching."

"Won't that turn them against us?"

Nodding, he replied, "Some. But you'd be surprised how many don't like him. He doesn't seem to realise that, so it would still be in our favour."

"And then?"

"As you said, it's that last bit I'm having trouble with too."

"Well, we had better get things rolling."

LIGHT THE LIGHTS

There were definitely benefits to fame when you wanted to get publicity.

Asalah rolled out one of the posters, the headline boldly declaring: 'Crossing Swords: Scott Crossman and Grekon in Conversation'. Not President Grekon. And his name went second.

Pride was petty due to the multitudes of ways to poke holes in it.

"Posters won't be enough," Luka huffed.

Eddie jumped in, checking some notes off a tablet computer, "Of course, they won't. Thankfully, I have access to Scott's emergency bank accounts. We have TV spots running internationally starting tonight at prime time, not to mention online, we have social media overloaded with adverts, memes, rumour mongers and influencers," He looked jazzed like he'd found a new life or something. All that cumbersome emotional undertone from our conversation looked to have dissipated. He had jumped to the task as soon as we raised it with him.

I was completely lost, however, with what he was saying. All the words seemed like code. I couldn't have been hiding my feelings very well as he continued, "What, you don't have the internet where you're from?"

Well, we did. It was emails, online encyclopedias and maps. I'd never heard of this social media or memes or whatever he was on about. Luka looked as confused as I did, so I didn't feel too bad.

"The ads are basic, we didn't have a huge budget so I kept them more like political campaign commercials for Prime Minister of The States of America."

"Not so United then?" I joked but clearly, it was lost on Eddie.

"We have the hotel booked, the same as his Gala event the other night. They'll be setting up the street with screens to allow people to watch from outside. No dining tables, just rows of seats. They asked if we wanted them raked, so I figured, sure, we want people to actually be able to see."

Asalah spoke up, "But how can you be sure he is going to bother showing?"

"We can't," I said, "But he would look mighty foolish if he doesn't. The whole world will be expecting it."

"I still think the title is a bit on the nose," Eddie remarked. Luka and I both nodded, "Exactly."

"Tickets have already been sold from word of mouth; I let slip to a few of Scott's friends, colleagues and their own PA teams, not to mention some costume and make-up crew. From there, it just blew up. You're going to have a full house before the end of the day."

It all sounded amazing, Eddie should be in events planning. He certainly has the know-how and tenacity.

"Brilliant, Eddie! We couldn't have done any of this without you. Just one thing, how do we get it broadcast?"

"It'll be streaming live on the internet as well. I've given news channels the heads up and permission to set up cameras if they wish to. Four local channels and six international ones have already made requests and we are expecting more. Floor space, being limited, means the maximum we can manage is twelve. The rest will have to piggyback off the live stream or pay for some rights sharing."

I had sort of given up on paying attention to the details. Eddie seemed to have it all in hand without me knowing all of that.

"Still no word from Grekon or his people, though."

"Give it time," Luka.

I could see by the looks on both Eddie's and Asalah's faces they weren't confident it would pan out the way we wanted. Honestly, I wasn't either. He could opt to not show and make me look the fool. Of course, we would have a backup script in place, putting the onus back on Grekon. Eddie being the PR guru he has turned out to be, I was sure he could battle anything Grekon's minions would throw out.

"We have to have faith," Luka said, "If he doesn't show, then that's just one attempt to bring him out in the open.

Believe me, Scott and I have more running on this than anyone else on the planet. We won't just give up if he's a no-show."

Luka sounded a lot older than he looked. The way he behaved was far from what I had observed back in his world. Then again, the loss of one's reality and only living relative can have that effect.

Eddie took me by the arm, "Well if you're going to be ready for tomorrow night, we need you to be word perfect and ready to pass for this m… This world's Scott Crossman."

Who was I to argue? I noticed his stumble, but let it slip, allowing him to take me into one of the bedrooms to go over everything I was going to have to do.

We had organised to arrive at the venue early, but actually, Asalah, Luka, three other members of the resistance and myself had booked a room under a false name at a hotel just down the street. The idea was some other members would keep an eye out at the venue, mingling with the already growing crowds. If there was a raid of Grekon's minions or the Police, we would be safely out of harm's way. We would arrive amidst the rest of the celebrities in their cars, much like I had done at the previous event.

I must say, I was surprised people would actually go for revisiting the same venue twice in a matter of days. I guess if it appeared worthwhile, people would endure most things.

There was a security team at all the entrances to the hotel, a requirement of course if they are to host the President of the World, yet some additional manpower provided by the resistance was mixed in there too. Better to be safe than sorry. Besides, with them under the guise of security, they would be a lot safer if there was a raid and able to continue the good fight even if things went sour.

Eddie was already at the venue coordinating everything. Having seen how he had managed me and prepped me the first time around, then put up with the hours of grilling of my lines and the plan for this evening, I knew it was all in good hands.

A burgundy striped suit had been laid out on the bed when

we arrived with a freshly pressed shirt, matching tie and socks to go with it all meticulously aligned beside it.

It all fit perfectly and in a way, I never knew possible. Better than the suit from the other night. I'd worn cheap suits for work before, but this was something else like it was tailored exactly to my body… Of course, it was. This Scott surely had a big enough wardrobe that this suit probably got overlooked on a daily basis.

I wasn't complaining, in fact, I promised myself that if I ever got back home, and made enough money, I would be going tailor-made for my next suit.

The mirror told me that this body could definitely wear a suit and wear it well.

Eddie had also provided some basic make-up - foundation and eye-liner suitable for a televised performance. I was no make-up artist, but I knew the basics.

Obviously, that wasn't enough as when I stepped from the bathroom into the small living room of the hotel suite, Asalah jumped to work in fixing up my patches, using a bit of spit and her thumb to thin out the eye-liner and make me more presentable.

"Thank you," I feebly managed.

She shrugged, "Not every day you help a movie star with his make-up. I guess you normally have teams of people helping you out on set."

Only Eddie and Luka knew I wasn't who I seemed to be. We would have lost all support if we had tried to explain the truth. My celebrity was definitely a help in the call to arms and, as awful as it made me feel in taking advantage of these good people, we had to use it.

They essentially knew we were trying to take down the President.

Tonight was meant to be the big takedown of a despot. Once we had him in our hands, the regime would fall.

Luka and I were hoping the same thing but on a much larger scale.

He was to wait in the hotel, be kept up to date on the proceedings and watch everything online as it happened. There could be no risking him. If things turned bad, we couldn't have Grekon get hold of him.

Everything was on track and I already had a huge knot in my stomach. It was hard to say whether I was more scared of facing the evil bastard face to face or to be performing in front of a worldwide audience.

"Time to go," one of the other ladies in the room told Asalah and she nodded and stepped back from me, appraising my appearance.

"Not bad. It will have to do."

We all moved toward the door and as the others exited, I turned to Luka.

"You look after yourself, no matter what happens."

He shook his head and smiled, "It'll go perfectly. It has to."

"Love your optimism. I could use a bottle of that myself right now."

"Go. You were born for this."

That struck me as a little odd, "Taking down a reality-destroying monster?"

A slight chuckle, "No, the performing bit. You're a drama queen through and through, and you don't even need to be on stage."

I wasn't sure if that was an insult or not, but I knew he was right.

I said what could have been my last goodbyes to him and followed the rest down the corridor to the lifts.

Our car was already waiting outside. Odd we were only a five-minute walk away, but we were still taking a limousine.

Everything was happening so quickly; I was getting swept up in it all.

The others were chatting away to each other and over radios and I was trying to focus on my script for the evening. Honestly, I couldn't even remember the first word.

It was a common word but had completely slipped my mind.

If all else failed, I was going to have to improvise. Everyone knew I liked to talk, so that shouldn't be too hard.

The drive took longer than I had figured due to the crowds and the line of cars already arriving at the venue to drop off their VIPs.

To distract my mind, I peered through the heavily tinted windows. Thankfully, I was on the opposite side from the crowd, able to see the hotel.

It was uncanny how alike the old ruined building in Luka's world this one was, just on a much larger scale. Now, large screens had been erected in front of it flashing various adverts for different soft drinks, watches and car brands. Eddie had argued that advertising was essential to making it look realistic and the revenue would help pay this world's Scott back.

Flashes from cameras and screams from fans were rolling over the vehicle from the other side of the limo. It was impossible to hear oneself think even with the thick glass and soundproofing.

Asalah put her hand on my knee, drawing my attention back to the present. Clearly, she could tell I was nervous.

"Ready?" she asked with such gentleness.

I put on my best smile and winked at her. I had to be Eddie's Scott now. Her Scott. This world's Scott.

Maybe I need to change my name; even I was getting sick of the confusion.

"You bet I am. Let's do this!"

The door beside me was opened even as the limousine rolled to a stop outside the stairs leading into the hotel.

Deja vu.

One deep breath and I stepped out.

The volume of the crowd literally double as people cheered and screamed.

The thrill of it ran right through my veins, it was exhilarating.

Taking my moment, I turned to them, flashed a huge grin and waved.

The flashes on cameras and other devices went ballistic, like a firework display on drugs. The roar of the crowd increased once again, which I didn't think was possible.

Asalah and the rest remained in the car as they shut the door. The limousine pulled off as I continued to wave, beginning to make my way inside.

Press had been set up along the carpet leading inside, held back by flimsy-looking bollards and bright red ropes. I didn't recognise any of them as they shouted questions at me.

The first time I endured this, I had been completely overwhelmed.

It was something I could get used to.

Eddie told me I had to approach some of the journalists to answer questions, it was what the stars did. All I had to do was keep my answers short, concise and move on.

"Scott!"

"Scott, over here!"

"Scott, how goes your latest film? There were rumours you refused to turn up on set. Are we seeing more of the Diva Dive?"

I had completely forgotten about the filming. I'm sure Eddie hadn't, but there were much more important things going on. I still had no idea how many days I had missed. Sounded like it wasn't an unusual occurrence for the alternate me. Damn, he needed to get his act together.

Time to try out some improvisation and charm.

Flashing a big smile, I looked the woman who had asked the question straight in the eye and almost instantly wanted to shrivel up. Her glare was not what you would call warm. I battled on, "Not at all, that was a scheduling conflict. Wires crossed somewhere. Those days are far behind me. Working on a film...This film is like building a home. Everyone has their role to play, grips, focus pullers, lighting, make-up, there are too many to mention. Just like in a house.. plumbers, plasterers. You get the idea. But, like with a house, sometimes there's miscommunication. The plasterer turns up a day late and the painter is ready to go, but he had another job to finish first, you see. In the end, however, the house is finished and it's comfortable and warm. Everyone is proud of the work they have put in, and they have all worked extremely hard. We're on schedule for the project to be finished and have a housewarming party when it's all done."

The metaphor was not a good one and the journalist seemed a bit confused by it so I flashed her a big smile and moved on.

That hadn't been too difficult. So I allowed myself to be stopped a couple more times, providing vague but upbeat answers to any questions I really wasn't sure of, though most questions were about who I was wearing, why no one on my arm this evening and what was I hoping to get out of tonight's event.

The last question was from someone who was clearly not there with the entertainment industry or paparazzi. It was a sedately dressed woman, hair tied back and looking a combination of stern and desperate. She had said she was from something called 'The Stately News'. The way other reporters were giving her a wide birth, I had a feeling her paper may be a bit controversial.

"I want the same thing I believe everyone wants, to hear about our future. This country, the people, the world. Where is Grekon planning to take us? What is he doing for the poor, the starving? Are we aiming for space? For true personal equality? And where are all these people disappearing to?"

I threw the last bit in for her. If I was right, it would be right up her alley. The slight smile on her face confirmed as much.

Before I walked through the front doors, I turned and waved at the crowds once more, pitying anyone who wasn't wearing ear protection as the roar of cheers went up.

How was this Scott so loved? Especially with the reputation he had of being a diva.

Inside, it was quieter; the rumble of polite conversation a welcome change to the cacophony outside.

There were familiar faces here, some I'd seen at the party the other night and actual celebrities I knew from my own world. I felt my heart skip a few beats as I let my eyes wander over their faces and that sensation of being star-struck gripped my tongue.

Several very well-dressed people spotted me and began to move my way. Instead, I headed straight to the doors to the ballroom. Security knew to let me straight in so thankfully I was on the other side of closed doors before anyone managed to grab me. I didn't have the skill of small talk enough to bluff my way through all of those people, especially if some of them were meant to know this version of me. How odd would it seem if they reminisced about something we had supposedly done together and I was staring blankly at them, in awe of who they are and completely lost as to what they were talking about?

Besides, if they had leading questions about tonight's event, I had very little to give them.

There were two walls of raked seating in front of me now, a long corridor had been created at the end of which I could see Eddie rushing around two large comfortable-looking chairs. Several other people, techies I assumed, were playing with microphones, cables and lights.

I hurried toward them, already feeling the damp sweat in my armpits and hoping my deodorant and aftershave would hide the abject terror I would be feeling tonight. I still wasn't sure if the cameras were scaring me more than Grekon.

"Thank goodness, you made it," Eddie grabbed my arm and pulled me to the back of the room, near where the secret door was situated, "Everything is set up. As you can see, we have the camera people with some of their techies and producers already set up around the space. We will be opening the doors in about twenty minutes."

He hadn't gotten to the most important part. He could tell I was desperate to hear so he continued, "No word from his people, yet. He may have seen it for what it is."

"But what could he see? Sure he knows there is a group working against him, but he is Mr All-powerful."

Eddie shrugged, "He may be playing it cautious. There's always the chance he's already found his own way out of this."

I shook my head, "No. Even if he had, his ego is too big to just ignore this. He wanted me to suffer, but this wouldn't be the suffering he'd want for me. So I get embarrassed, that's nothing to what I believe he was planning in that cage: to watch me die of starvation slowly and alone."

Eddie looked a little put off by the thought, "Don't worry," I said, "there is plenty of muscle on these bones to keep me going for a while. I'd find a way out in the end. That's what we are counting on here."

This seemed to reassure him a little, but he still wasn't altogether a fan of this plan. Sure, he had worked his but off to put it together. He'd done 90% of the foundation laying, the leg work… everything. Unfortunately, this last 5% was going to be the telling piece and we weren't even sure if it could go ahead.

"You shouldn't be worrying about that right now. You should be warming up."

He was right, "Thanks, Eddie. For everything."

A smile crept to the edge of his mouth, but his eyes spoke even louder. That was why I quickly moved to the back corner, away from the windows and started limbering up both my body and my voice. There was a chance it might get physical, me running or, heaven forbid, fighting, but the voice needed to be ready if I was going to address a large portion of the world.

Would more people be watching this than they would the Oscars? I doubted it. There, they had star upon star. Sure, I may be a bit famous in this realm, but I was not a George Clooney, Brad Pitt, Jennifer Lawrence or Viola Davis.

Honestly, the number of people watching wasn't the important part, just that enough were.

Just before the audience was being let in, Eddie ushered me through the secret door and into one of the rooms off the corridor. It had been set up as a dressing room of sorts. Inside a make-up artist was waiting with all his equipment.

He tried to make small talk, commenting on the make-up I was already wearing – which he had to remove anyway – but soon quietened down when he realised I wasn't in the mood for small talk. Probably put it down to my being arrogant, but I was too nervous to think about how to respond to him. The excess sweat and the fact my right leg wouldn't stop bouncing as I sat in the chair may have told him otherwise. Either way, it was more important I was focused.

A few deep breathing exercises calmed me a bit, though I found I needed a toilet.

As soon as the make-up was complete, I thanked him and headed to the door. A security guard had been placed just outside, I recognised him from the house. I smiled and asked about a toilet. He pointed directly across the hall.

As I left the toilet again, Eddie was waiting for me.

"Still five minutes. Still no sign or word."

"We should have lined up a backup guest," I tried as a joke.

He nodded, seriously considering it, "Easy enough to have added to the publicity."

"I was joking. If he doesn't show, we politicise it, just as we discussed."

"We need you to get into position."

Nodding, I followed Eddie back through the secret door and there was a round of applause. Having had the peace and quiet backstage, I figured it was for the warm-up comedian Eddie had booked to get the crowd pumped and ready. In part it was, but, for the most part, it was aimed in my direction.

I was never going to get used to this.

An Assistant Director approached me, "Mr Crossman if we could get you seated, we can do final checks."

This was hilarious. Everyone was telling me what to do and where to go. I didn't have to make any decisions, right now, I had no responsibilities except to do as I was told. It was a bit of a relief despite the fact everything seemed to be rushing around my head.

It was also the calm before the storm.

People circled me for a few more moments, lights glared in my eyes and, thankfully, blurred the cameras and audience from view for a short time. When I was finally left alone, just me, an empty chair and a small side table with a tall glass of water standing on it – which I was yet to drink any – I found my bladder screaming to be emptied again.

Too late now. This was it.

The same AD that got me in position was standing beside one of the cameras, a big smile on her lips, "And we are live in ten, nine, eight, seven, six…" she went silent, using her fingers to count us down.

The lights dimmed a little, a catchy jingle began to play and a voice echoed from some speakers hidden somewhere in the room.

"Good evening and welcome to tonight's extra special event. One celebrity and our very own President. A man of the people talks with The Man of all People to explore what wonders wait in store for the planet and the billions of residents on it. With no further ado, here is film star Scott Crossman, ready to delve into the mind of President Grekon."

The script was a little naff, but the voice-over artist had hit the right pauses and inflections to add gravitas. It was amazing what a skilled performer could do with a bunch of tripe.

The lights were brought up on the set again and I was alone with the world despite the wash of applause that filled the room once more. It lasted for ten seconds or so as more music played and I found myself standing up.

Silence settled in and I knew I was meant to speak.

Only a moment of hesitation before I forced myself on. There was no going back now.

"G'day," that was not part of the script. Odd how my Australianisms popped up at inopportune times. There was a slight chuckle from somewhere in the seated audience. I gave a wide smile, "You've read the posters, you've seen the adverts, you've just listened to the preamble introduction and I'm sure you still have no idea what this is all about."

More laughs.

"That, ladies and gentlemen; children too, if you're tuned in at home, is the problem."

No laughs, but a definite mumble across the raked seating as I let that sink in.

"We have a President. A President of the World, no less," I scoffed, "How pretentious does that sound? I mean, really? Surely despot or dictator is more appropriate."

A boo and an unintelligible call, but it was isolated.

"Hang on, give me a chance," I put up my hands in a placating stance, "Did you vote for him? I didn't. I know many people who never put pencil to paper to elect Grekon to his all-powerful position."

A used tissue was ineffectually thrown toward the stage, I watched as it seemed to hit an invisible wall as it lost impetus and drifted to the ground just in front of the first row of people. Only three discernible voices were making their disagreement known.

"He is a man of the people. He stands for what is right for

the people of the world. Right? Right? Then why do we still have poverty? Starvation? Deprivation?"

"You hypocritical has been!" one of the dissenters shouted.

Again, I held my hands up, "No, you're right! I'm wealthy, well-fed and dressed. I'm benefiting from the system. And that's why it is up to us to speak out about it. Do you think President Grekon is going to listen to any one of those poor impoverished people? Of course not. But he does need to listen. We all need to stand up and make him take notice!"

There was a burst of applause that drowned out the cries of, 'traitor' and other choice words from several people. Two were already pushing past the legs of people blocking their path as they tried to exit the stands.

Two out of at least one hundred of some of the richest, most elite in town. Those were odds I liked and they were certainly odds Grekon would respond to. If only he were here to see it.

"Just as a side note, all proceeds from tonight are going to charities aimed at assisting drought-stricken communities with water and food supplies. Along with a sizeable donation of my own. Five million pounds."

Another round of applause and cheers. This time, it was audible from outside, all the onlookers outside the hotel adding their voices to those in here. Eddie had said the other Scott could foot that and still be moderately comfortable, besides, some of that was tax-deductible and he was earning more than that on the current feature. That didn't make me feel particularly happy. It made it seem completely disposable which was a huge problem.

I allowed the room to quieten down. One of the people who was leaving was shouting a gabbled insult back at me as he left the hall.

"He claims to be a man of the people. Tonight, I ask him to put his money where his mouth is," now for the biggest gamble and lie, "We sent out a request to President Grekon and his staff. We were upfront about what we wished to discuss this evening from dealing with the problems I've already mentioned to what actually happens during the Reaffirmation Processes. Where do people go, the thousands of missing individuals? His people responded, saying that the President would be more than willing to appear. To tell his people the whole story."

"So, ladies and gentlemen, I would love to introduce to you, the one and only President Grekon!"

I performed it as though I truly expected him to come through any set of doors and join us. Heck, there was a chance he would have.

A big smile still firmly on my face, I waited a few moments before continuing, "But, as you can see, I can't. He hasn't bothered to show. Is he unable to answer these difficult questions? We all know he isn't too busy to attend press events. I was at one just the other night. Or is it…" I paused, playing the crowd; pretending to be almost shy and demure, "No. It couldn't possibly be…"

They were hanging on my every word now the verbal minority had left.

"Is World President Grekon simply," another pause and I looked down the lens of one of the cameras, "Too afraid?"

I pulled a weird questioning face as if it was general knowledge he was a coward – 'how could you not think that?' it asked.

There was a titter of laughter. Small and nervous to start with, but it grew, spreading like an infectious disease.

Letting it ease off, I smiled along with the audience. The crew, I couldn't read for the most part. The cameramen and techies were generally focussing on doing their job. Some were scowling, but that was sometimes normal on sets. Others looked amused or interested, including the AD who had counted the show in stood crossed armed with a smirk on her face nodding slightly to herself.

"The man of the people is scared of his people. Not FOR them, OF them. That is why we have people disappearing regularly. I can't guarantee I won't be one of them after this. But if I do, you'll know. The whole world will know that our very own President Grekon is a cow-"

The doors the audience had used to enter the ballroom burst inward; the bang of the doors sent everything else silent for a moment.

There were gasps from the audience following this and several producers whispered harshly at their cameramen to move to get a better shot.

I had to admit, I felt the blood drain from my face and I only hoped the make-up was thick enough to conceal it.

Grekon stood silhouetted in the double doorway. The shape of his dark shadow was enough to tell me we had hit the exact nerve we had hoped to.

Behind him, in the foyer, people were peering timidly out of hiding spots, obviously terrified by him.

He couldn't keep this moment, I had to take it back.

"Better late than never, they say," I said most jovially.

The nervous laugh was back, but much more subdued.

Grekon wasn't moving. Was he expecting me to come to him?

"May I finally present, President Grekon," I drawled the 'finally', trying to keep a comic atmosphere. That was mainly for my benefit than for any actual audience entertainment.

Not one muscle moved on the man. I could feel his eyes boring into me, however.

I waited, but he held his position.

"Maybe he's shy?" I joked, but then realised I had to continue the same game plan, "Or is he still scared of little old me?"

A wink at the camera and another louder, more confident burst of laughter.

That did the trick.

He took slow steps forward. It was eerie, to say the least.

His head tilted slightly to the side as he eyed me up. I couldn't see his face for all the light and shadow, but I knew he hadn't taken his eyes off of me. The audience may as well not be there anymore for him.

"So clever."

Though he said it so softly, those two words echoed over the audience noise and they went quiet.

Opening my mouth to speak, nothing came out as he maintained that slow stride toward me. Now his head was shaking slightly from side to side and I caught a brief glimpse of his face as he passed through a stray strip of light from one of the Fresnel lamps.

There was anger there, that was obvious, but there was more. His lips were twisted upward in a tight smirk. His eyes glimmered with pure hatred with just a touch of mirth.

"Is this what you wanted?" he asked as his features were consumed by shadow once more. I felt a light relief sweep over me. To look at that face again, I didn't know if I had it in me. He continued talking, "A public confrontation? For everyone to see you show off?"

"That's part of my job," I don't know where it came from, but I wanted to bite my tongue as soon as it left my mouth in a sardonic jibe.

He reached the first row of the audience and stopped. Everyone near him was leaning as far away from him as they could, looking more than a little scared themselves.

"What you fail to understand… Scott," he spat the word, "is it doesn't matter anymore."

One more step and he was in the light.

"This," he indicated to the audience but as he spoke, I realised that sweep of the hand meant far more than simply the people in the room, "it's over. None of them," his glare returned to me and I couldn't help but take a step back, "Not even you matter anymore."

"That's a bit harsh."

He brushed aside my remark and took another step toward me. This time I held my ground.

If my bladder had been fit for bursting before the cameras started rolling, it was about to explode any second now. Grekon had terrified me from the moment I met him. He had been far more sinister than The One had been. His manner was sadistic, hateful and so personal without him actually knowing you. He knew me better now and the sensation I was feeling pouring out of him was beyond hate. I wasn't an easy one to like in the first place, but if he was giving off heat instead of emotion right now, I would be a chargrilled steak.

"I have to thank you, though. Without you, I wouldn't have made it here. To the end."

That surprised me.

The whole thing was surprising me. We had predicted he

would act up for the cameras and offer us an opportunity to sedate and capture him. There was nothing in the plans about him coming in gloating and terrifying.

"We've only been rolling about ten minutes. We've plenty of time."

Grekon reached out a hand toward one of the floor-mounted cameras and squeezed his hand shut. The machine crumpled like a Coke can under an invisible foot.

The surprised cameraman fell to the floor and scrambled backwards over cables and feet.

Multiple screams rose from both the audience and the people outside.

A dull rumble filled the room as finely dressed men and women began to clamber over furniture and each other to get off the raked seating and find their way to the exits.

The crew continued to man their working cameras and equipment, shrugging off the fear and hoping to catch the good stuff.

A laugh escaped his taught lips, "It's over."

Screams rolled back from the doorway to the foyer as a team of eight hefty men dressed in black military gear stormed in. They ignored the celebrities, actively barging into those standing in their way and stepping on those who had fallen over in their path.

It was the ninth person that held my attention, though.

Even though I could only see his silhouette, like I could with Grekon, I could tell who it was. My heart sank and all thoughts of a retort or any other words were swept from my mind.

Grekon was right: it was over.

His grin evolved into a despicable toothy smile. A politician's smile was bad enough, but this self-satisfied gloating was to the fourth power of disgusting. It must have been written on my face and he was lapping it up. My defeat was undeniable now.

The eight men made it to the stage and threw the ninth on the ground in front of us.

Luka.

How?

"You must be wondering how."

Disconcerting, but I nodded in agreement.

"After everything you have put me through. Being a thorn in my side like you are, you honestly thought escaping me would be so simple? This is my world. I made this."

"No, you didn't. Not all of it."

He nodded his head slightly, "I'll give you that. You already know things went wrong. Your friend was flawed, useless. A wasted heart. That's okay. You brought the true one to me in the end."

Grekon was looking at Luka who lay unconscious on the floor.

In a move that made me jump, he spun back to look at me, fire burning in his eyes, quite literally now as his pupils had become little orbs of flame.

"One thing about this reality was definitely not an accident. You're being here."

I thought I had been a mistake, that I had somehow slipped through the cracks because I was at Andy's side when he died.

"Oh, you thought you were here to stop me?" His cackle was loud and animalistic, "You were here to lead me to the one true heart. The only unique heart in this world I made. Every world has one, I just couldn't find it. Yet, I did eventually find a way to isolate one and I brought it here with you and you brought it here to me."

His breath was now hot against my skin and not in a normal way. I felt my eyebrows curl under the heat. The fire in his eyes had kindled and grown, flames were now licking out from under his eyelids.

I couldn't move. Terror and, I was guessing, Grekon's own power were holding me in place.

"It didn't take much to find you again, follow you and your little friend back there," I followed his gaze, managing to turn my head and saw Eddie standing with his back pressed against the wall beside the secret door. Eddie could see the flames too and he was horrified.

"So, before I wipe you out of existence, know this: It was all your fault. I won because of you."

He didn't need powers to hold me in place anymore. I

understood now. All this time I thought I was on the path to defeating him and I was actually his pawn. I was leading him to what he wanted. The destruction of realities as we knew it was on me. Now Grekon could make whatever damnable hell he wanted and I'd been his unwitting right-hand man all along.

That was what he had meant when he spoke about my purpose when he had taken Andy's heart. He knew I would serve him in this reality. That was why he had explained the need for a unique heart. I had found it for him. I'd done all his leg work for him and he had enjoyed watching his most hated foe doing it.

"No," it was barely a whisper but he turned back to me and the hate was gone, it was simply pure gloating now. No pity, just joy and pride.

"Yes," he whispered in my face, "and now you can watch as I wipe all of this away."

With that, he turned and knelt beside Luka's body. The boy was still breathing. I figured Grekon needed the live heart to work his ritual.

"I had expected it to take months, maybe years. But you managed it all within a week. You're efficient if nothing else."

Something banged against one of the large windows that normally looked out over the street. They had large burgundy curtains drawn over them to prevent light spillage for filming. Despite the muffling effect of the thick material, the bang had been considerable and drew Grekon's attention.

It didn't stop there.

Shortly after, shouts were heard from beyond the windows. Not just one or two, but scores. These increased in volume and number as others joined. The windows were being bombarded by something as the banging also increased.

Grekon looked over at his team of eight men. Without a word, six ran to the lobby, two ran to the windows and drew back the curtains.

Through the nicely pruned shrubbery and the scaffold brace of the large screen outside the glass, we could see a surge of people heading toward the building. They had easily pushed down the flimsy waist-high barricade that had held them at bay and were charging the building.

One of the large panes had a crack in it from where it had been hit, but it was clearly heavy-duty glass.

I looked at Grekon and he was simply looking out and smiling.

"They're as bad as you. Think they can truly make a difference," he regarded me with a mock pity in his expression, "you're all worthless. Can be wiped out like…" he raised one hand, ready to snap his fingers, "this."

He let his fingers click and outside the window, the crowd was swallowed by a flash of light.

I raised my hands to block the glare, only briefly aware I was able to move again.

The shouts had turned to screams and when I could see again, the people were writhing on the ground. Some of them, anyway. The rest were motionless. Lifeless, I could only assume. The trees were burning now as were some of the bodies. The beams of the scaffolding outside were blackened.

There hadn't been a sound. Nothing to warn of the attack, nothing to indicate it had happened. Just a flash of light and it was done.

Behind me, I heard people moving. The remaining techies and cameramen were running for the doors, getting as far away as they could.

The monster, now in human form, smiled at me, "Can't you just imagine how glorious it will be when I am finally in charge?"

It didn't bear thinking about.

The deaths of those people hadn't been futile. That I could hold onto. They had been making a stand, showing they would not go down without a fight. Like Andy, they had seen the injustice and decided to take action. Now, like Andy, they had paid the ultimate price. I was the only one who hadn't, yet. I'd been fighting this creep longer than anyone and I was still standing, watching as he dealt out his horrors. He was right. I was useless. I hadn't made a difference in stopping him. It was all my fault we were in this position.

There was another bang against the glass. Softer this time and we both looked over. My vision was blurred by tears that

I could no longer hold back.

A woman was hitting at the glass with her fists. Her face streaked with tears; make-up smudged giving her already desperate eyes a ghoulish appearance.

Others were joining her, stragglers that had survived Grekon's assault.

The two men in black raised assault weapons and pointed them at the glass, but the people continued to lash out in anger, in grief. Soon, the whole lower portion of the glass was covered by the furious faces of the survivors, banging on the thick glass. One lady had taken off her high heel and was using it as a hammer to chip away at the barrier.

Cracks were starting to form under the assault and the weight of the people now several rows deep trying to force their way inside.

They weren't going to give up.

"Enough," Grekon stated simply.

As I cried out a useless, "No!" he raised his left hand and a rippling wall of transparent force slammed against the inside of the glass. The windows hummed for a second before they erupted outward, showering the crowd in tiny shards. The wall of force continued, sweeping the people up and pushing them back at such a considerable speed that they fell, tumbling away.

With the glass gone, a cool breeze filled the room, giving light relief to the warm studio lights still glaring down on us.

Luka moved.

I thought he was waking up, but it was Grekon's doing.

His body began to rise in the air, just as Andy's had done. Not like a rag doll, but supported. When he was several feet above the ground, Luka was rotated until he was upright, his feet now just above the hardwood flooring of the ballroom. Grekon stood up in front of him.

The memory of seeing Andy's heart being ripped out flashed into my mind. Grekon's arm was already raised, his hand open in a grasping claw, ready to violate Luka's chest.

I had been here before. Useless and unable to act when Grekon had first had me believe he was about to take control of all realities. He had been lying then, providing enough exposition that I would help him achieve his ultimate goal. Here I was again, impotent to react to what was going on once more. I was letting him win and I didn't know what to do.

What I did know was what was coming next.

Or I thought I knew what was coming next.

Out of the corner of my eye, I saw light reflecting on something as it rotated through the air. There was no need to turn my head as it soon travelled into view, began its descent and struck Grekon just above his ear. It then fell to the ground and shattered, spraying what little water was left in it on the ground.

Grekon grunted and fell sideways and I turned to see who had thrown the water glass that had originally been standing by my chair.

Eddie stood stock still, eyes wide with fear but a smile of triumph on his face.

"Eddie! Run!"

He heard me and responded quickly, hurrying to the secret door. It wouldn't be long before Grekon had recovered and either taken revenge on Eddie or slammed his hand inside Luka.

I had thoughts whirring through my head. Running after Eddie; but that was pointless, we were about to be wiped from existence anyway. Tackling Grekon, trying to overpower an overpowered foe was pointless. Try and grab Luka and run, but he was suspended in mid-air by Grekon's power and I had a feeling I would have as much luck carrying a tank than moving the poor lad.

That left one option I really didn't want to think about. The sooner I acted, the less I'd have to think about it.

Grekon, who had buckled down in front of Luka's floating body was starting to recover and I didn't have any more time to consider.

I took the two strides to be beside Grekon in mere moments, but he was already up and turning on Eddie. He was startled to see me standing there. If he was surprised by that, he was going to be blown away by what I was about to do next.

I pulled my right arm as far back as I could and, closing my eyes, punched it forward into Luka's chest.

There was no breaking of bones or tearing of flesh as I had expected. Instead, my hand passed through what felt like a thick layer of jelly until it touched something rock hard and vibrating strongly in the cavity.

My fingers wrapped around Luka's still-beating heart and I heard Grekon's breath catch.

Daring to open my eyes, I saw half of my forearm still embedded in Luka.

Grekon wasn't moving, his burning eyes were open wide staring at me in wonder.

With surprising ease and a horrid level of guilt hanging in my own, I pulled Luka's heart from his body. As with Andy, he went limp and his skin took on an unnatural pallor.

The heart itself was now no longer beating, but I could feel it vibrating. Part of that was me as my hand had begun to shake from shock, or whatever that horrid feeling was I could feel growing in the pit of my stomach.

Blood was pouring out of the dangling valves, splashing the floor and my clothes.

I couldn't believe I'd done it.

Actually killed someone. Not just anyone, but a young lad I'd come to know.

Someone more callous would argue it was his fault I was here at all, but I didn't feel that way. Not in the slightest. He was seeking help and I offered my assistance. I took full responsibility for being here. If it hadn't been for me, Grekon wouldn't have been on this rampage in the first place. If I had done my job all those years ago, I'd have stopped him before this mess had even begun.

This was my fault.

Now, so was Luka's death.

"Give it to me."

I couldn't look away from the mass of flesh in my hand, covered in blood and gore. It was quivering as my whole body was wracked with an uncontrollable shake.

Luka's body fell to the floor and I didn't bat an eyelid.

"I said, give it to me!"

Grekon's steaming breath was so close to me; the fetid putrescence would normally make me gag, but all I could focus on was Luka's heart.

He couldn't take it. I could feel that. If he killed me, the connection would be broken. He needed me to hand it to him.

No chance.

There was a tiny flash of light.

It could have been one of the stage lights or some of the flames from outside, but in my soul, I knew where it had come from.

A low, deep rumble was coming from Grekon's throat. A threat? A keening at the loss of everything he worked for?

I was beyond caring.

The flash became a flicker. Underneath the layer of blood, deep in the core of the heart, a pinkish fire had smouldered into life. With it came a calming warmth that emanated out into my fingers, coursing through my veins and filling my whole body.

I say calming. I still felt the revulsion toward myself for having done the unthinkable. I felt the loss of Luka acutely, more so as it had been at my own hand. The calming sensation relaxed the physical tension in my body. The shakes abated and the tension I wasn't even aware I'd been holding in my shoulders eased away.

In my hands was a piece of Luka. I could still feel him inside it and I sensed through that wash of sensation that he was at peace with what I had done.

That didn't make it any better in my eyes. I just had to make sure I didn't waste it.

Brighter and brighter, the light grew and I felt drawn toward it. Along with the light, almost a white noise filled the air around me.

"Scott," it barely made it through, but Grekon was calling me. He was no longer beside me.

He repeated, "Scott. Look what I have."

A ploy, but I let him have it.

Looking up, I saw him standing by the two presenters' chairs. One of his arms was stretched out beside him, fingers splayed in a display of power. Hovering and squirming uncomfortably in the air was Eddie. His eyes and face were red with straining as if he were struggling to breathe. His hands were clawing at an unseen force at his throat.

I shook my head, "No. You really think you're smarter than everyone else."

Eddie's legs were flailing, but I couldn't give into this. I didn't enjoy seeing him suffer, but if I gave in, he would cease to exist altogether.

"Your problem, Grekon, is that you don't know people at all. You don't know what it means to truly depend on people, to care for them. You don't understand what it is to be human. What we are willing to sacrifice, not for ourselves, but for each other. That's why you lose."

"I'll kill him!" He snarled.

"You were going to anyway. We all came into this plan knowing it could go wrong. Eddie risked his life to save me. Luka risked his to save everyone. You know this isn't the first time I've done that. I'm not going to give up this for Eddie."

I looked at Eddie, I could see the pain on his face as he gasped for air, "I love Eddie. I really do. He's truly opened my eyes. In this reality, I was not enough for him. Not the alternate version of me. Not me. He deserved better," I held up Luka's now incandescent heart., "But with this, I can give him everything he deserves. I can undo all the horrors you've created."

The flesh between my fingers was solidifying, still vibrating, but the texture was changing, becoming more crystalline.

Grekon tightened his fingers into a fist and Eddie let out a single gasp, his neck snapped sideways at a horrible angle and his body plunged heavily to the ground.

I wanted to cry out. I wanted to shout and scream and rage. This was it. Eddie was my last true companion on this journey.

I was alone now and I was so tired of being alone. Of losing everyone. Whether it was Sarah when she quite rightly went off to follow her own life. Bob and Narelle had grown distant, their own lives and responsibilities taking their toll. I'd been on my own for years now, just me finding my footing in life.

Then, ever so briefly, I found Andy, Luka and Eddie. And I'd lost each one to the misery I was responsible for.

And right there was my problem. My selfishness, my self-centeredness.

I. I. I. Me. Me. Me.

This wasn't about me.

This had become about billions of lives. Maybe trillions or more.

I hadn't lost them. Sarah, Bob and Narelle had gone to find themselves.

Andy, Luka and Eddie weren't mine to lose. They had been their own people and they had lost their lives. They had never been mine to lose. They weren't my pawns in this terrible game.

But they had all given of themselves to me in the time I was fortunate to be in their lives.

It was time to give back.

Grekon had lost all self-control. He was now flailing wildly, destroying the furniture, the camera equipment. The lights above us were shattering or exploding in his rampage of power.

In my hands, Luka's heart was completely solid and I knew what I had to do. I didn't know how, but it was logical when I thought back to the chinking sound I had heard when Grekon had used Andy's heart to change reality. Like a blacksmith's hammer, I recalled.

I got down on my hands and knees and raised the heart above my head.

"No!" Grekon literally roared. The room went pitch black for a moment, but the luminescence of the heart brought it all back.

He was charging toward me as I brought the heart down hard against the hardwood flooring.

There was that same chink sound and white sparks began to rise slowly from the ground around me.

The heart remained solid.

Grekon was close, I didn't have much time. It looked like he was willing to sacrifice the heart to maintain some control of this reality.

I brought it down again and the whole building shook at the sound. Grekon slipped over mid-step, sprawling toward me.

A crack had formed on the surface of the crystalline heart.

The sparks were coating the ground around me, their white emanations dancing and jostling on the wooden floor, my arms were covered with them. Grekon too was covered in a heavy dusting of the flurry of light.

I managed two more quick hammers with the heart.

The next time I raised my arm, though, I felt Grekon's hot hand wrap around my forearm.

"No! Please!"

He was begging?

The flames under his eyelids had died down and I could see the whites of his eyes again. They were wet with tears. Tears of fear. Fear for himself. No one else. He was worried I would wipe him from existence.

Would I? I was going to have to make that choice.

I couldn't move my arm; he was too strong for me to break free so I sat up on my knees.

"Please?" I asked.

"I..." he looked around helplessly at everything, searching for the words he thought might work.

It was like we were completely alone in the world now. I had no idea where his henchmen had gone. They hadn't interfered at all. The crowd outside apparently chose to run for their lives finally.

Most of the room was now covered in the same white sparks. I remembered trying to dust them off myself and being unable to touch them. Like they were visible to this realm but separate from it. Above us, the last remaining working lights were flickering erratically. I could see several cameras had survived his violent rage and were still recording, the red lights above them indicating we were still on the air. I pitied anyone who had kept watching.

And I pitied Grekon.

Only a little.

"I..."

He still didn't have the words. Did the right words exist? Even I didn't know the answer to that.

I could feel my face was as stoic and as hard as the heart in my hand. I had no more emotion to give this demon.

He gulped back a cry of some sort. The white glow that surrounded him made him appear almost angelic, beatific.

"I'm sorry," he offered finally. He nodded as if he was a good boy in a primary school class who had found the correct answer, "I'm sorry."

Yet his grip didn't loosen on my arm. The fire still lingered in his pupils. All those people were still dead.

And I had the heart.

I reached my left hand up and took it from my right. Grekon had barely registered what I had done when I brought the heart down once more, striking it against the floor as hard as I could.

Another chinking sound, a burst of non-coloured light and the heart began to crumble in my hand.

This time Grekon bellowed in pain. Instinctively his hand let go of my arm as he arched backwards, responding to the same assault I remember hitting me back in Andy's world.

I had to keep going.

Bringing it down, again and again, I heard the cries of people outside as they too felt the effects of this ritual.

Five more strikes and the heart shattered and the world vanished in a wave of rippling rainbow light.

THERE'S NO PLACE LIKE HOME?

This was different to last time. It was different to every time I had crossed realities.

All around me was the twisted churning mess of colour and light I'd grown accustomed to on my travels with Bob and Narelle. Except there were no faces or images. And it wasn't a tunnel. I was in the centre of a large sphere not travelling in any direction, simply hanging there with nowhere to go.

My body was here, that was different too. I could see my hands, my arms.

Actually mine, not those of the body I had inhabited these last few days. My eyes were there too and they weren't coping well with the assault of colour. It seemed when I was a bodiless being, it was easier to cope with.

My skin was awash in that rippled effect when light is reflected off the water. I had to admit, I preferred having a physical presence when travelling in this between state, despite the headache from the visual barrage. It still allowed for so much more focus.

Now I could focus on thoughts like 'What was I meant to do now? Had I solved the problems? Had I destroyed all realities and now I am stuck in the aftermath?'

All I really wanted right now was to be sitting down somewhere quiet, not being blinded by all this mystical mess.

And then I was.

The sphere of colour vanished, replaced by wooden panelled walls like something out of an old English manor house. There were no paintings or decorations. The floor was dark wood as well. Looking up, there was no ceiling to speak of. The walls just continued on upward as far as I could see.

I was sitting on a soft leather, wingback chair. No other furniture to be seen. No doors or windows. Just me sitting somewhere quiet. One second a sphere, the next, what I had thought about.

That was nifty.

What now? A little help would be nice.

"Don't you think it's a little obvious now?"

The voice came from behind me, but I recognised it, though it had been a few years since I had heard it.

Jumping out of the chair, I turned to see Sarah running her hands along the wood panels. She was my age, or what I imagined she looked like now. Her hair had lost a tiny bit of the bright red sheen it had had in her teens, but it was impossible to miss.

She looked at me and raised an eyebrow, "Still getting into trouble, it seems."

Was it really her or just my imagination creating an image of her?

"Does that matter?"

It was a little off-putting that she had read my mind, but that didn't stop her from being right.

"What am I supposed to do now?"

She stopped moving about the room and regarded me, "Again, I'd have thought that was obvious."

"You're not being much help."

She raised her hands, indicating the room, "You need help after you did this?"

"This is a room. Just a room. What more am I supposed to do?"

"Fix it."

I sighed, frustrated, "Fix it. As simple as that?"

A shrug and a smile, "If you want it to be. Grekon did it. Why can't you?"

Good point.

"I know," she bragged.

"So, all I need to do is say I want it fixed?"

Her turn to sigh now, "You'll need to be a bit more specific. Fixed to what? Before you ever travelled across realities? Then you'd never have helped Bob. Before you moved to England? Grekon will still be out there. What do you want? I can't tell you that."

Again, it wasn't what I wanted. It was what everyone

wanted. What they needed. I certainly wasn't qualified to make that decision.

"Nothing too drastic," I said.

She moved to sit in the chair, throwing her legs over one of the armrests, "Okay. That's a start."

"I want all of the realities fixed. All of them that Grekon twisted and murdered people in. Even that last one. I want everyone he is responsible for killing to live again in those realities. A new political system of equality and justice in those worlds though. I want them to remember Grekon and what he did and to learn from it."

"You want to keep all of those different universes?" She was checking her nails like the conversation wasn't all that important.

I thought about it a moment then nodded, "Sure. They existed, who am I to wipe them out?"

"Fine, so every reality back, everyone he killed is back," she looked up at me, "What about the man himself?"

"Grekon?"

She tilted her head to the side saying nothing more.

Interesting question. I can undo all his bad deeds. Do I undo him too?

Am I the same sort of monster as he is?

My mind jumped back only a matter of minutes and the image of my hand jammed inside Luka's chest jumped out at me. I shut my eyes to try and block it out of my head. When I opened them again, Luka was sitting in the chair instead of Sarah.

I was a monster for what I did to him. Did I even deserve to return?

"Good point," he said simply.

"No. I won't become even more like him. He can exist. In his own small reality. No powers, no one to subjugate and no way out. Simple."

"Done," Luka then sat up and leaned forward to regard me. He lacked emotion on his face but what he said next sounded almost accusatory, "What about you?"

I turned away from him. I couldn't bear looking at him anymore.

Why did I have to decide? I didn't much like myself before, but after killing Luka, I really wasn't up for deciding my own future.

"But he's alive now. You did that. You undid Grekon's atrocities."

No need to turn around to know this 'help' had transformed again.

I felt a hand on my shoulder and I was reluctant to turn.

"I'm alive now."

"I let you die, Eddie."

"For the greater good. I knew that then. I know it now."

I realised I could face him now, "But you're not Eddie."

A look of humorous shock swept over his face, "I'm not?"

I honestly didn't know.

"Does it matter? You know I'm right, don't you?"

I leaned against a wall and had to admit, "I guess."

"What is it that you want, Scott? You've given them back their worlds and their lives. What about your life? What does Scott get?"

I actually already knew the answer, "I want to go home. To England of my world. No more Grekon's or other monsters. I want to be happy."

Eddie smiled, "Oh that's easy."

Scoffing, I responded with, "Is it?"

"You'll see," he said very cryptically, then cheerfully he clapped his hands, "Is that everything?"

There were a million ways I could make it more complicated, I knew that, but I knew I wasn't the master of all realities. I had no aspirations to have that role so simply putting it all back together should be enough.

"That should be everything. Before I go though, I want to know Andy, Kath, Luka and Eddie are happy."

"Done. Just look out the window."

I felt the wall behind me move and I knew better than to say anything.

Sure enough, a large window had appeared, four frames with four separate images, though one would have been enough for two of them as they both showed Kath and Luka in their little flat I could see the dust motes dancing in the sun streaming through the window as they drifted over all those little trinkets. Luka was gabbling excitedly to his grandmother, arms flying left right and centre like he was telling a wild fantasy story. I couldn't hear a word. That wasn't how windows worked in my head.

Andy was walking down a corridor, bag over his shoulder, dressed in dance gear. He had a cheerful way about him as he stepped through a door and into a rehearsal room. One wall was completely made of glass and showed a glorious day outside, the sun shining, the street below was alive with people heading about their business. Gone was the gloom that had covered his, Kath and Luka's world. They were back to a happy way of living.

Yet, Andy stopped as he was putting his bag down and lifted his hand to his chest, scratching at it absently. A morose look overshadowed his features for a moment just a moment before he looked up and out of the windows. A smile had taken hold again. He remembered, but it appeared he had hope enough to move on.

That's all anyone could ask for, right?

Eddie's window was flashing erratically. Explosions and smoke filled the pane and I was about to shout at the mock-up of Eddie behind me when I saw the buff version of me step through it all, assault rifle in hand looking like he was about to take on the world. He looked so serious for a few more seconds before letting it all go, standing up straight and smiling at another man who was lying at his feet. Offering his hand, the prone man took it gratefully and got helped to his feet.

I recognised the director as he stepped through the slowly clearing smoke to discuss something with his leading actor.

This was the same film set I had found myself on. Clearly, that Scott who used to be me was doing pick-ups to make up for my atrocious job of it.

The two men walked off the set chatting away until they arrived at a long trestle table laid out with various snack items, a few trays of sandwich quarters covered in a plastic lid, an Esky – icebox – cans of various soft drinks packed inside. Just watching was making me feel hungry.

As they perused and picked at the food, one of the other actors approached and said something. Both Scott and the director burst out laughing and Scott clapped the man on the back appreciatively. That hadn't been the impression of the other Scott I had gotten from everything Eddie had told me and how people had reacted to me on set.

And there he was.

Eddie.

He was walking up behind Scott. As he arrived, he slid a hand casually around the other me's waist. Scott turned and ever so casually kissed his PA on the cheek as he too manoeuvred an arm around Eddie.

The conversation continued as if nothing had happened. Maybe my push for equality in that reality had done more than I thought. I could try it out on every reality, wiping out hate, greed and all those phobic behaviours. Make a peaceful life for everyone under my own personal ethical system but then I wouldn't be restoring them, I'd be becoming a dictator of people's morals. I'll leave this one alone though.

They both looked happy.

It was time to let them be.

I turned back to the Eddie that had been helping me and it was no longer Eddie. Kath now sat in the chair, smiling sweetly at me.

"Have you had enough?"

One last glance at the window, "I think so. It's time to go home."

She simply nodded.

"What do I do? Click my heels together? Say some magic words?"

"Just go home."

Simple as that? Right.

Chuckling she continued, "Or if you really need something more symbolic, go through the door."

I looked around and spotted a tall, plain oak door that hadn't been there before. Its handle was a simple brass knob. No keyhole, nothing remarkable.

Taking hold of the knob I wondered if I should say goodbye to whatever it was that had been with me in the room. The fact the room was empty when I looked back, the word on the tip of my tongue, gave me the answer.

A gentle twist and I began to wonder what I would see on the other side of the door and then it was gone. My hand was empty and I was standing in my bedroom.

I had literally returned to my home in London. It wasn't much. A double bed, built-in wardrobe, chest of draws and a bookcase in a shared flat. I wasn't even near the centre of London, but it was home and such a relief to be back.

Collapsing on the bed, I let my eyes close and all I wanted was to fall asleep for a week or so.

I would have too if my mobile phone that was stuffed in my pocket didn't vibrate.

If it had been just the once, I'd have ignored it for the moment, but again and again, it went. Too quickly to be a call notification. It only just occurred to me; I had gone a number of days without using my mobile phone. Well, I hadn't had it in Eddie's reality and it was useless in Andy's, so cold turkey had been the only option and I hadn't missed it in the least.

Rolling over onto my back, I pulled my phone from my pocket.

Eight missed calls, twelve texts and, most oddly, the date was only three days after I had left. Surely, I had been gone longer than that, or had I simply returned myself earlier?

Only one text from my Mum: 'Just checking in. Haven't heard from you in a bit'.

The rest, as well as the calls, had been from my agent.

I didn't bother with my agent's text messages; I may as well just call them.

It rang five times before being answered.

"Scott! Where have you been? You're supposed to tell me if you're going away! I've been going mad trying to reach you."

Probably more words than Laura, my agent, had said to me since she had signed me up.

"Sorry," I didn't have an excuse and improvised the only logical one, "My phone died on me, only just got a replacement."

"Not to worry, kiddo. They loved you!"

"They did?" Who did? What was she talking about?

"Absolutely. You got the job! I'll email the details later today. But! And it's a big one! The director loved you so much, he's asked if you'd be interested in a small part in an independent film he's doing. I've said yes because I couldn't get through to you. It's not much pay, but the commercial will tide you over for a bit anyway. Great news!"

Lost for a proper response, I muttered, "Umm… Great. Thanks?"

"No worries! Keep it up, we'll have you at the Oscars in no time! Gotta run! Speak soon!"

She hung up.

That was definitely a nice welcome home. I'd completely forgotten about the audition and how awkward it had been. Not to mention the overly energetic and facially hirsute director.

Who was I to look a gift horse in the mouth, though? I had been jealous of the other Scott's career, but I also hadn't been willing to take it without having done the leg work.

If this was going to be my leg work, then bring it on.

I threw my phone onto the bed beside me and my eye was caught by something small and white sitting on the bed.

Two sets of little eyes were staring at me. A sour-looking frog and an ambivalent appearing turtle, the first on the back of the latter. Both were made of ivory.

"Talk to the turtle," I whispered to myself.

Taking the little trinket in my hands, I stood up.

This was Kath's. She had given it to me as a means to communicate with her. I'd not used it in her world and I didn't have it on me in the new one. It was surprising to find it had come back with me.

I couldn't help smiling at the vision of Luka and her at home together again, though I'd not had the chance to say goodbye to either.

Bringing the two conjoined animals to my mouth, I spoke softly, feeling a little stupid. It probably wouldn't even work.

"Hello? Is anyone there?"

I waited, but there was no response and I laughed at myself for being so stupid.

There was a nice spot for the ornament on my bookshelf. I

could at least keep it as a memento of the second time I'd been involved in saving a reality or two.

As I was about to place it on one of the shelves, it spoke.

"Scott? My dear, is that you?"

I recognised her sweet voice.

I brought the turtle back up to my mouth so quickly that I nearly clobbered myself on the lip, "Kath? I didn't think it was working."

"I'm an old lady. It takes me time to get around, you know. How are you?"

It was nice to hear her voice. Confirmation things had gone okay, I guess.

"Great! I'm home," I looked around my cosy little room and laughed, "I can't believe it, but we all made it home."

Her voice was coming directly from the ornament. The turtle wasn't actually moving its mouth, it was simply a sort of receiver, "Thank you for your hard work, Scott. And for bringing my Luka back to me."

A lump caught in my throat which I barely managed to swallow, "Is he there?"

"No."

I wasn't sure if I was relieved to hear that or not. What would I say to the lad? Sorry for ripping your heart out?

"Oh, ok," was all I managed.

"He's there."

A loud knock came from the front door.

"Go let him in, I'll talk to you later."

I was frozen. I'd forgotten he had reality jumping abilities, even though he was the one that had brought me to his world in the first place. Boy did I pick them?

"Again, thank you so very much, Scott. So many people owe you their gratitude and they don't even know it."

"Thanks," it was really sweet to hear it, honestly.

I placed the turtle on the shelf, its new home for now and bolted to the front door. Thankfully my flatmates weren't home, it being the middle of the day and them being at work.

There were two frosted glass panes in the front door and I could see Luka's silhouette. My hand was on the door handle, but I couldn't move it.

"You going to let me in or not?" he called from the other side, "I can see you there, you know."

Did he sound angry?

Taking a deep breath, I turned the handle and opened the door wide.

His expression was hard to read. He had one eyebrow raised and his head was tilted slightly implying he was scrutinising me.

"You didn't bother giving yourself a mansion?"

"I'm sorry?"

He laughed and everything seemed ok, "You could have done whatever you wanted and you didn't give yourself a mansion. Waste of an opportunity if you ask me."

Pushing past me he came inside and wouldn't stop moving. He peaked through every doorway, opening doors even I wouldn't have so he could have a proper nosey around.

"Even a little upgrade would have been nice."

I hadn't moved from the door, instead just watching as he disappeared briefly into the kitchen at the end of the corridor.

"It's enough."

Poking his head around the door frame, he shouted, "Enough? Hardly. You deserve a reward!"

I closed the front door and took a few steps toward the kitchen. He had disappeared inside again. The fridge was opened and I heard the rummaging effects of jars tinkling, tin foil crinkling and plastic bottles crackling.

"You know what I did, though, right?" I asked hesitantly.

The fridge closed and Luka stepped into the doorway. He spoke a little cautiously, "I know. Not sure how, but I do."

"And?"

I hadn't been sure if he would or not. He was unconscious for most of it, dead for the rest. To think he was aware, was horrible.

He shrugged, "It worked, didn't it?"

"I killed you!"

A laugh. I couldn't believe he was laughing, "And you brought me back again. And my Gran! And everyone! If you hadn't done it, Grekon would have. Simple as that."

He could see I was still not happy with his answer. Walking

toward me, he smiled gently.

"Seriously, Scott, don't beat yourself up about it," He grabbed me by my shoulders, "My Gran knows what you did too and she's not holding a grudge in the slightest. Why should I?"

With that, he pulled me into a hug and squeezed me tight.

It was a while before he let go and I didn't mind at all as I returned the hug, grateful he could forgive me like that.

"Right! I've got to get back. I promised my Gran I'd play Rummikub with her."

Moving to the front door, he turned back when he got there, "Don't be a stranger, Scott. No grudge here and we would both like to see you. And I'm sure your friend Andy would be happy to have a word when you get a chance."

He opened the door, gave me a little wave and disappeared.

AAAND... ACTION!

The commercial had been a one-day event, filming on a small studio set a week after I returned to my reality. Sand covered everything and, at the end of the day, everyone. As it was want to do, I kept finding it in my clothes for days after.

The director, Derek was his name, had maintained the same positive energy throughout the day, even when the agency people started changing their minds and trying to tell him how to do his job. He laughed it off and kept the morale of the whole cast and crew on a high.

That was the sort of person I realised I actually enjoyed being around. Nice to not only use but also help cultivate the positive energy, something I was not very used to. So long had I been a sad-sack moaner. This fresh start needed a fresh outlook. Sure, he had scared me during the audition process, but once you understood his upbeat nature, it was really difficult not to like him.

The week directly after that, Derek began filming his independent film. It was a low-budget affair to be shot over a month on various locations in a little town about half an hour past the M25. My agent had confirmed I was needed for a whole week which sounded a little daunting with high-octane Derek.

Then again, after everything I had been through, I was sure I could survive a week of pure positivity.

The film itself was a crime caper with a clown twist. Rival circuses were vying for particular show grounds. It all gets heated between the management that neither notice a set of clowns from both camps come together to rip them off. Initially, it sounded a little simplistic, but Derek had explained he was going for a noirish tone and a little quirk. The quirk was why he wanted me on board for one of the clowns. Even better, I got a death scene. My character, Benny the Buffoon, is meant to be the lookout. He ends up getting spotted himself and chased into a tent full of caged animals. Suffice to say, one of the animals doesn't stay caged for long and Benny meets a gruesome end. Except, he manages to survive long enough to be found by the lead and I die in her arms.

We had had a couple of days of rehearsal at Derek's townhouse in London. Line runs, costume fittings, make-up try-outs. All the necessary stuff so when we got to set, it would only be a matter of quick blocking, running a few takes and hoping for the best. With all that positive energy, it would be a blast.

Once more I was on a train on the way to my first day of work on Derek's film. The first time working with him, I didn't know the man. This time, I was anxiously running my lines for today's scenes the whole journey so as not to let him down. I knew them already, but you can never be too careful.

The announcer called the name of the next stop, my stop and I rammed my script back into my satchel.

It was ridiculous. I was nervous and I hadn't even made it to set. This was manageable though; I'd been in far worse situations only a fortnight ago. Funny how time flies and normality reasserts itself.

Just remember to breathe, I reminded myself as I stepped off the train and, like a real tourist, started searching for the station exit.

My agent told me someone from the crew would pick me up from the station, which was good. I didn't want to be getting lost on the first day.

The large analogue clock by the 'Way Out' sign read 6:47. I was too amped to be tired.

Only one other person had gotten off at the same stop and I followed them through the barrier and out into the car park beyond. It was starting to fill with commuters and cars dropping people off. No one looked to be waiting to pick up yet, so I leaned against the wall by the station exit and pulled out my script again.

No harm in another go-over.

I was halfway through the first page when I heard my name from a distance.

Scrabbling to put my script away, they spoke again and I froze, "Scott?"

I couldn't look up. I wanted to, but I just couldn't.

"Scott? Sorry, I'm a little late, had a problem with breakfast catering. Well, Derek's wife needed help unloading the food she'd made. They ended up asking me to come to get you."

I lowered the flap of my satchel and took another deep breath.

"Are you okay?"

There wasn't any avoiding it. I couldn't keep watching the ground.

Eddie was standing in front of me, a concerned look on his face and looking the scruffiest I had ever seen him. Jeans, a t-shirt with a short sleeve, button-up shirt over the top.

A smile had already crept to my lips and my eyes had begun to well up.

"Woah, hey, are you okay, seriously?"

"No, I'm fine," far from it, really. The last time I saw this man in person, I had seen his neck get broken, even as he struggled to breathe. I'd done nothing to help him. I could never forget that.

Yet, here he was. Not the same one. I knew he was safe and sound now. And happy. That didn't make it any easier. That Eddie had cared for me, supported me over a few days. Risked his life for me many times. He had all but told me he loved me. But it hadn't been me, really.

"Sorry, Eddie, early mornings, just aren't my thing."

He looked taken aback, "How did you know my name? Have we met?"

I wiped my eyes and put out my hand to him, "Maybe in another life. But it is sure great to meet you in this one."

I could have vomited at how cheesy that sounded, but he genuinely smiled as he shook my hand.

"Well, if there is anything you need this week, I'm your guy."

I couldn't stop smiling as I followed him back to his car, "I'll try not to bother you too much while I'm here."

He stopped and looked over the roof of his Ford Fiesta, "Something tells me that won't be true," he winked and got in.

For the third time already that morning, I had to take a

bracing breath. A pleasant little shiver had run from my neck all the way down my back.

This was going to be interesting.

ABOUT THE AUTHOR

Anthony Harwood was born and raised in Perth, Western Australia. He now resides in London where he continues to work as an Actor with a bit of Maths Teaching on the side.

www.ingramcontent.com/pod-product-compliance
Lightning Source LLC
Chambersburg PA
CBHW032049050726
47590CB00001B/188